# fetish

# fetish

anonymous

Entangled Publishing, LLC
644 Shrewsbury Commons Ave., STE 181
Shrewsbury, PA 17361
rights@entangledpublishing.com

Amara is an imprint of Entangled Publishing, LLC.

Visit our website at www.entangledpublishing.com.

Edited by Lydia Sharp
Cover design by Bree Archer
Cover images by Kotin/Depositphotos
Interior design by Toni Kerr

ISBN 978-1-64937-199-7
Ebook ISBN 978-1-64937-219-2

Manufactured in the United States of America

First Edition October 2022

10 9 8 7 6 5 4 3 2 1

an imprint of Entangled Publishing LLC

ALSO DISCOVER:

*Aphrodite in Bloom*

*To my agent for suggesting I write a sample chapter for the first anthology, Aphrodite in Bloom, and to everyone at Entangled Amara and Macmillan for supporting these projects. You're all amazing and have made these two collections a joy and a privilege to write. Finally, as always, to my lover and best friend. I love you.*

# What's Your Foible?

## A Neighboring Hand

*An American heiress rekindles her friendship with a
finishing school chum who coaches her husband
in the fine art of fisting.*

## The Point of No Return

*Pointed pleasure results when an acupuncturist provides an
intimate piercing to an Englishman.*

## Horsing Around

*A horse breeder attends an unusual steeplechase where he
discovers the freedom in playing a pony.*

## How Do You Do Your Do?

*A cheese maid in the Swiss Alps discovers her value when
she encounters an aristocrat who hankers for her hair.*

## How Stimulating

*A nurse in Bohemia delivers her patient a tingling pulse
from an electrical device that neither woman can resist.*

### The Paddle, Pretty Please?

*A widow in Brighton solicits a spanking when she learns her employee is skilled with a strap.*

### Make a Scene

*To his bawdy delight, a footman is publicly humiliated by a widowed duchess.*

### Temptress with a Teapot

*A young wife lures men into erotic trysts—and then spills all the tea to her husband when she gets home.*

### That Tickles

*A burly builder in Auckland can't get enough of the feathery touch delivered by his level-headed bricklayer.*

### The Rubber Match

*A man from Goa meets a seringueiro in Brazil who shares his rapture with rubber balloons.*

# A Neighboring Hand

# CHAPTER ONE

*June 1878, Paris*

"Ma chérie!" a woman's voice called out.

Camellia Zimmerfield suffered a full-bodied jolt of alarm as she recognized Suzette Billaud. She wore *trousers*. Not bloomers but men's striped trousers with a crease. They were topped by a tweed jacket over a shirt and waistcoat. Her red hair was all but hidden beneath a gray driving cap. Her pointed chin and laughing brown eyes were exactly as Camellia remembered, though, and that wide smile provoked a rush of fierce nostalgia.

"Suzette!" They embraced and kissed each other's cheeks. Camellia was thrown back to a more carefree, sensual time as she drank in floral perfume masking cigarette smoke and the salty-wooden scent of ink and damp paper from the printshop Suzette's family owned.

"I was expecting someone in a gown," Camellia said breathily, still recovering from her shock.

"They didn't want to let me in." Suzette glanced back at the gate. "I had to show them my documentation that I'm allowed to wear men's clothes. I ride a bicycle, and these are less dangerous when I work around the press, so the police allow it."

"Mais bien sûr." Camellia felt foolish for agonizing over what to wear.

Ten years ago, Suzette had been her most trusted guide on all fronts—manners, men, fashion, and philosophy. Suzette's family were printers and bookbinders, creating plates for top fashion houses as well as political texts for universities. She'd been well-read even before her parents had scrimped every centime to board her at *Madame Yseult's Académie des Filles pour les Sciences Domestiques et la Grâce Sociale*. Their hope had been that their daughter's social connections would improve their ties to wealthy customers.

Camellia's parents, an industrialist and the daughter of a general, had also sought social elevation through their daughter's education. Their aspiration was achieved when Camellia married Powell, the son of a senator.

Now, Camellia moved effortlessly amongst the highest circles in New York and Washington, but she couldn't come to Paris and not see her amie special, even if she lived an unconventional life.

"You look beautiful," Suzette said, studying her. "Exactly as I remember."

"I was sure whatever gown I had made in New York would be outdated by the time I arrived." Camellia self-consciously brushed at her matching set in prune satin. Bronze roses decorated the jacket, and her skirt was layered in zigzagged flounces of knife-edged pleats. She'd even had her maid add a waterfall of hair to her own curls to mirror the intricacy of her small bustle and train. Her hat was pinned at the latest cock-eyed angle.

Camellia was as well turned-out as any woman at the Exposition Universelle, but next to Suzette's plain, masculine attire she felt like a royal wedding cake.

"Where is your husband, chérie?" Suzette glanced around. "Have you run away from marriage as I have?"

"Oh. I wasn't sure if you were teasing me in your letter. Is it true?" she asked with concern.

"Oui." Suzette spoke with a distinct lack of regret. "He was angry that I wore my cap— No, the other kind," she said as Camellia flicked her attention to the top of Suzette's head. "You know of these?" She blinked enquiringly. "The rubber preventative?"

"You mean—?" Was Suzette really speaking of contraceptives here on the promenade of the exposition?

Camellia glanced uneasily at the visitors streaming toward them from the gate, but as outrageous as Suzette's behavior was, this was precisely why Camellia had always admired her. Suzette said exactly what she thought.

Even so, she urged her toward a quiet path so they were less likely to be overheard.

"To think, I was worried we wouldn't have our old rapport," she said wryly.

"Pah," Suzette dismissed with a wave. "Women should be allowed to speak of useful things. We shouldn't be censured for choosing when or if to have children, either."

Camellia smiled half-heartedly. She hadn't chosen so much as accepted that birthing children was her purpose in marrying Powell. She didn't regret her babies, but if she had known how profoundly she would be changed by motherhood, she might have waited to become one.

"It must have been difficult to leave them at home," Suzette noted politely.

"They're with my mother and several nannies who dote on them. I'm sure they don't miss me." Camellia missed them, though, greatly. But her goal on this trip was to rediscover the woman she had been before she'd lost herself in the role of wife and mother. "I've missed *you*, ma chérie. Tell me more about the life you lead now." She looped her arm through Suzette's as they continued to walk. "You won't divorce, will you?"

She didn't dare tell Suzette there was a voracious appetite at home for booklets describing those court proceedings in lurid detail.

"When France reinstitutes divorce, oui. I'm working with the Women's Rights Society to advocate for it. That is another reason I left him. He didn't like that I contribute articles to their journal. Now I edit and print them." She smirked. "I take the utmost satisfaction in arming women with their own power. What of your marriage. Are you happy?"

"I am. Mostly." A heaviness came into the arm Camellia had linked through Suzette's. It felt terrifying to let her mask slip, but with Suzette she couldn't help it. "My life is so busy I don't have time to question how I feel. Oh, where are we going?"

Camellia paused to get her bearings. Suzette shaded her eyes to take in the grounds.

"Powell is in the Machinery Hall," Camellia said of her husband, "but I wondered if you would accompany me to the head of the Statue of Liberty?" She pointed along the graveled avenue to where the points of the crown were visible above the screen of a leafy tree. "I climbed to the platform on the torch at the Centennial Exposition in Philadelphia two years ago."

"Yes. Let's see whether a woman's head is truly as empty as we're led to believe."

"On the contrary, I'm told we can see how man has constructed her. Try telling me *that* isn't symbolic."

They continued walking, both laughing.

• • •

Powell Zimmerfield had worried his wife would be a distraction if she came with him to Paris, and she was—even when she wasn't with him. *Because* she wasn't with him.

The grounds of the exhibition ought to be free of reprobates who might accost her, and she'd reminded him more than once that she had lived here for four years, but her boarding school had been a sort of convent life in which she had learned to be the charming hostess and doting mother that she was. It was his place to shelter her from the harsh realities of life, and he took that role seriously. He adored her.

She had slipped away to meet her old friend, though. Suzette had been mentioned occasionally through the years, always fondly. A few months ago, she'd written to advise Camellia of the First International Congress of Women's Rights, to be held in conjunction with this World's Fair. Camellia had insisted on coming to Paris with him so she could attend with her friend.

Powell hadn't been sure what to expect from this trip, but, much to his delight, being away from the children seemed to make her more receptive to lovemaking. This morning, she had even wriggled her ass into his lap when they woke and asked if he couldn't stay in bed a *little* longer?

The memory of lazily pumping into the wet furnace of her pussy had kept a smug smile on his face all morning. It also made him a shade possessive. He *missed* her and kept his eye out for her as he demonstrated his screw-cutting lathe.

There she was— Wait... Was she with a man? Who the hell *was* that?

"Powell, darling." Camellia seemed oblivious to the people giving them second looks. "Please meet my dearest intime, Suzette."

Suzette's gaze bounced off the hulking machine behind him and the banner that read Zimmerfield Milling and Lathes, then swept over Powell's dark suit and bowler hat, down to the watch chain that dangled off his pale gray waistcoat, then back up to his black mustache and muttonchop beard. He wore it styled in a curving line from his upper lip down to his jawline and up to his sideburn, leaving his chin bare.

She had the manner of a man in more than her clothing. She studied the machinery and him with equal directness, as if she understood how both worked with one glance.

"You found each other. Excellent." He accepted the kid-gloved hand Suzette offered, thinking her very different from the way she'd been described.

"It's a pleasure to meet you, monsieur."

"The pleasure is mine." He hoped that was true. She seemed charming, but the vaguest prickle of threat dug like iron filings under his skin. He suspected he was jealous of the smile she'd put on his wife's face. He wanted to be the one to make Cami look so vivacious and pleased.

How long had it been since he had? That was a disturbing question.

fetish

"Are you ready to take us to lunch, darling?" Camellia asked.

He grimaced with regret. "I thought you would be tied up at least another hour. I'd like to continue my discussions with these gentlemen from Denmark." The men in question were out of earshot, but he nodded at them to let them know he would only be a moment.

"Of course. Powell is here to make contacts," Camellia explained to Suzette. "We're booked to visit factories in Italy and Belgium, to see what agreements can be negotiated."

"You'll be back in Paris for the congress, though?" Suzette asked.

"Oh, yes." Camellia nodded. "We have an apartment in the Place Vendôme until end of July and will come and go from there. Could we invite Suzette to join us for dinner later in the week, darling? Before we leave for Italy?"

"Of course," Powell said politely. "I'd like to visit properly."

"As would I," Suzette assured him, but he had the vague sense her interest in any man was minimal.

"Why don't you and I go back to our apartment now?" Camellia suggested to Suzette. "We can catch up over a private lunch."

That word "private" and Suzette's warm, "I would love that," conjured an erotic vision of the two women entwined on a bed, clothing in disarray. Their mouths would cling, and a pair of fingers would be buried in a slit. Their duet of moans would fill air laden with the fragrance of juicy cunt.

His cock twitched even as he scolded himself. His straitlaced wife would never conceive of making love with a woman. She was still reserved while making love with her husband of ten years. Not that Powell wanted her to take a lover, female or otherwise. He had no interest in others himself. The vision was an idle entertainment. Nothing more.

But he did wish the promising spark of their earliest days had turned into the bonfire of passion he had once anticipated.

Instead, it was a cozy fire and would have to stay that way. He would never shock her with his prurient inner wants.

It was, after all, his role to protect her. He always would. Because he loved her.

The women departed, and he turned back to his business.

# CHAPTER TWO

"Would you prefer coffee or lemonade with lunch?" Camellia asked as she led Suzette into their suite.

"Dare I suggest wine?" Suzette craned her neck at the high ceilings, the massive mirror over the fireplace, the silk rugs, and the gold-trimmed velvet drapes that framed the double doors onto the balcony.

Suzette continued to have the most terribly wonderful—or wonderfully terrible?—effect upon Camellia. She used her rusty French to request the maid fetch cold chicken, bread, olives, and chilled vin blanc.

"Be honest," Suzette said as the young woman left. "Did you suggest we eat here because of the way I'm dressed?" She removed her cap to reveal her cropped hair.

"No, because of the way *I* am. You look so comfortable, and I feel like a Thanksgiving turkey. Although, I sent the maid away before I asked her to help me change. That's annoying." She paused in removing her hat, wondering if she should call her back.

"I'll help you."

"You wouldn't mind?" That would be a tremendous intimacy and an imposition. They weren't schoolgirls any longer. She didn't wish her friend to feel like hired help.

On the other hand, there had been a time when they had been very comfortable with intimacy. *Very* close. Camellia experienced a pang of yearning for that simpler, naive yet hopeful time. For those uncomplicated pleasures.

"Show me," Suzette urged.

Flustered, Camellia set aside her hat and led her through.

"Mon Dieu, I've always wondered what these rooms looked like inside," Suzette murmured as they entered the elegant bedchamber with the massive bed, fireplace, and the sunlight glowing through the translucent curtains covering more pairs of doors. "Is your home in America like this?"

"It's very showy," Camellia admitted. "My in-laws built it, but they spend their time in Washington and Boston." If that sounded as though she and Powell lived rent-free, she would quickly disabuse Suzette of that notion. Her obligation to her husband's family was incessant.

"I don't dress this formally every day. I wanted you to be impressed," she admitted as she began to release the cloth-covered buttons down the front of her jacket, self-conscious yet not. It had always been easier to reveal herself to Suzette than hide anything.

"Why would you care what I think of you?" Suzette came to tug a closely tailored sleeve down her arm. Her touch was exactly as it had always been—confident but gentle. Innately tender and reassuring while making the slightest brush of a knuckle against Camellia's skin feel as though she caressed her with a downy feather.

"I've always cared what you thought," Camellia said over her shoulder as she turned to offer her other sleeve. "How could you not know that?"

"Shall I be worried what you think of me, then?" Suzette shook out the jacket, then folded it over the arm of the nearby chair. Her gaze sparkled with amusement.

"You've always been too self-possessed to care what anyone thinks," Camellia scoffed. "That's why I adore you and put so much stock in your opinion. I'm too quick to do as I'm told." She opened the buttons on her skirt. "I let myself believe that deciding what *color* to wear is the same as having control over *what* I wear."

"Or how much?" Suzette teased as she kept the skirt from crumpling to the floor while Camellia stepped out of it, still wearing both overskirt and underskirt.

Ten years ago, they had helped each other undress for more than a simple wardrobe change. Memories of their most precocious activities teased Camellia as her gaze flickered over the fit of Suzette's trousers across her backside. Her friend bent to drape the skirt on the foot of the bed, then turned. The swells of her breasts were almost impossible to see beneath the billow of her tucked shirt, but her belted waist was undeniably feminine.

Suzette noticed where her attention had strayed. She lifted a brow. Her amusement turned to something more languid and questioning.

"Do you wear gowns at all anymore?" It was cowardly to pretend her clothing was all she'd been interested in, but Suzette didn't challenge her.

"Only for occasions." She accepted each skirt as Camellia handed them off.

Her cheeks were stinging, but Camellia unbuckled the belt of her wireless bustle and dropped it onto the seat of the chair, finally able to pull her camisole over her head and get to the hidden hook-and-eye closures down the front of her corset.

"That's pretty." Suzette set aside the skirts and made her pause as she splayed her hands on the royal blue silk cinching Camellia's waist. Embroidered silver-green vines embellished it along with ice-blue lace trimmings.

"It cost a fortune." Her insides seemed to feel all those vines reaching and twirling into hidden spaces as Suzette's hands stayed on her waist. Her breasts swelled against the stricture of the cups. "I feel as though I'm being sawn in half when I wear it, but I wanted a second honeymoon. It's distressing to be away from the children, but things between Powell and I…"

"Not good?" Suzette asked with a small frown.

"Not bad, just…fading with age." She tried to make a joke of it.

Except, standing close to Suzette this way, with her friend's lips right there, beckoning, Camellia experienced a surge of youthful risk and excitement for possibility.

What a wayward thought! They were married women of twenty-eight. Suzette might not have children, but Camellia had three. Her amorous needs were met, and she had ceased pining for Suzette years ago.

Disconcerted, she stepped away and began to release the hooks down the front of her corset.

"I haven't felt sexy or even in control of my own body for a long time. Or *not* in control of it," she added with a husky laugh. "I don't suppose that makes sense."

"Of course it does. You want passion. The sort that overtakes you completely."

"Yes." Camellia heard the pang in her own voice, and a sting of emotion arrived in her throat at being so well understood.

She peeled away the corset, sighing in relief. Now she was in her chemise and drawers, both damp with perspiration. She shivered, and her nipples peaked against the muslin.

Suzette took an unabashed and lengthy look at her breasts where they pushed against the filmy cotton. She slithered her gaze lower to where Camellia was very aware of the slit in her drawers.

Camellia quickly stepped into her pale pink morning dress and buttoned up its front.

"Does he fuck you well, your Powell? Or shall I have a talk with him?"

Camellia choked out a laugh, cheeks heating because she knew Suzette was serious.

"He does well enough."

"Well enough is not good enough," Suzette proclaimed firmly. "The only thing I miss about my husband is his ability to fuck me into next week."

"Powell fucked me all the way to Paris," Camellia said smugly, then released an exasperated sigh and began searching for the pins in her hair. "Do you have any idea how much pleasure I derive from saying that word? I don't think I've said it once since leaving this country ten years ago."

"Fuck? Chérie," Suzette chided.

"I have children," she reminded. "And very conservative parents. And in-laws who guard their reputation like the Hope Diamond."

"None of those people are you. Quit living your life by their rules. Sit. I'll do it."

Camellia lowered onto the bench at the vanity table. Suzette passed her the postiche of false ringlets before she searched out the rest of her hairpins.

"I miss this." Suzette reached for the hairbrush, then remained bent, wrapping her arms across Camellia's shoulders and pressing their cheeks together.

As Suzette's breasts pressed into Camellia's upper back and her nose nuzzled into her neck, another rush of want accosted Camellia. It wasn't entirely sexual. It was tenderness and affection and yearning for what they'd had. Maybe yearning for youth.

Camellia turned her head to look at her friend, nose to nose. She cupped Suzette's cheek and pressed the softest of kisses to her lips, wanting to linger, wanting *this*. Intimacy without fear of losing herself.

"I missed you, too," she said sincerely. "But I'm married now and..." She gave a defeated little sigh and looked to all the meaningless bobbles on her dressing table. "I've never wanted another woman, you know. You were the only one, and what you and I had was... I don't know. Adolescent curiosity? Something that was an extension of our partnering as we learned to dance. One more rehearsal for the life we would lead. When I went home, we were both reconciled to marrying and being fulfilled by a man. Weren't we?"

"Oui." Suzette straightened and gave a gentle squeeze on Camellia's shoulder. "I'm not trying to seduce you. I miss you as my bonne amie."

A sting rose behind Camellia's eyes. She dropped her gaze,

embarrassed. "I'm making assumptions."

"Non." Suzette lowered to sit on the bench beside her but facing the other way. Their hips were snugged close. She looped her arm across Camellia's stomach. Their somber gazes held. "I do prefer women. I think I always did, and you are very alluring, Camellia."

She rolled her eyes to the ceiling. "I'm fat."

"Plump. It suits you." Suzette hugged her a little tighter, every kind of love and acceptance in that embrace, then eased her hold to say ruefully, "But I can find a lover without breaking my heart over one who lives so far away and has so much to return to. I've stopped taking lovers, to be honest. They distract me from my work, but I miss this closeness."

"Yes." Camellia hugged her arm across Suzette. "This is what I wish I could have with Powell, talking openly and feeling loved for being myself."

"You don't have petite distractions? My husband and I did." Her hand massaged Camellia's waist and hip.

"I don't think I could have understood such a thing until right this minute." Her heart was thumping in slow, heavy beats of sensuality. She was enjoying Suzette's touch. She always had, but sharp tears came into her eyes. "I would feel so threatened if he showed interest in someone else. I've given all of myself to him. I would feel discarded. Inadequate. I don't want to cause him to feel that way."

"Hmm." Suzette considered that. "Every day I speak to women about what they need. One will say a mother must have the right to stay home to raise her children, that the father must support her so she can love and care for them. Another will say a woman must have the right to work and earn her own money and not be reliant on a man. One says that female education is a priority; another says working conditions must be addressed. *I* say we must have the right to dissolve a marriage that no longer works for us. *You* say we deserve to vote. None of us is wrong. What is true about all of it is that a woman will not get what she needs if she remains silent and accepts the status quo. Decide what you want, ma chérie." Suzette dropped a peck on Camellia's nose. "Then tell him."

• • •

**P**owell entered the apartment with his mind still on increased output and universal screw sizes. It all slipped from his head when he found his wife in the bath behind the screen in their bedchamber.

Camellia was a sensual picture with her head lolled back and her hair spilling off the edge. Her gleaming shoulders reflected the firelight, while the rest of her nude form dissolved in milky, rose-scented water. A half glass of red wine dangled from her fingertips where she rested her wrist on the rim of the tub.

"I hurried back, thinking you must be waiting to go for dinner."

"I thought we'd eat in," she said lazily, bringing a knee up to break the water's surface.

That sounded promising. Powell had spent the afternoon entertaining filthy thoughts and was horny as hell. He went to the bedroom door and called out to the maid, asking her to pour him a glass, adding, "Bring the bottle."

He toed off his shoes, removed his jacket and tie, and moved the comfortable chair from the writing desk to a spot behind the screen where he could put his feet on the edge of the tub and admire his wife. When the maid put the glass in his hand, he said, "Leave dinner on the table and retire for the night."

"What are you planning?" Camellia sent him a sly look as the door closed behind the maid.

"I'm planning to make love with my wife. I thought that was obvious."

Something altered in her expression. Her gaze dropped into her wine as she brought it to her mouth.

He didn't move from his slouch, but discontent invaded his muscles. "No?"

"Can I tell you something I said to Suzette?"

"Of course." He still didn't know what to make of that woman.

"Fuck," Camellia pronounced roundly.

He dropped his feet to the floor and looked around, expecting to find that a knife-wielding robber had walked in on them. "What's wrong?"

"I haven't said that in years. It feels really good," Camellia said conversationally. "Are you appalled with me?"

"Astonished that you know the word," he said drily. She was very conscious of propriety. When their son had said "fart," she had sent him to his room. "Have at it," he invited, settling back in his chair and returning his feet to the edge of the tub. "Say it again if you want to."

"Fuck."

Watching her teeth cut across her bottom lip and hearing that base word from her throat fed all the lewd, indecent thoughts in his head. It made his cock thicken.

"Does Suzette say it? She seems colorful. Why does she dress like a man? Is she..." He hesitated.

"Lesbian? Yes, it would seem so." Her expression remained unbothered.

"You know what that means?"

"Powell." She shot him a look. "How obtuse do you think I am?" She was blushing, though.

"We've never talked about anything like this." It was new territory. He inched into it with suitable care.

"When have we had time to talk about anything but your father's campaign or which investor we must court for the company or *babies*?" Her voice held a throb of helplessness that made his chest tighten. Her head fell back, and she sighed. "I feel like this is the first breath I've taken since you asked me to dance ten years ago."

He didn't move but subtly braced himself. "Do you regret accepting?"

"No." She rolled her head to look at him with the tenderness and affection and, yes, the love that had caused him to catch his breath and forget how to breathe without her. Her expression turned wistful. "But there was a woman I knew here in Paris. I wish you could have met her. She said 'fuck' and drank wine in the middle of the day."

"Is her name Suzette?" he teased. "I don't think I'm her type."

"What if—" She cut herself off and grimaced into her wine.

"What?" he prompted.

She shook her head and reached out of the tub to set the glass on the floor, but she left herself twisted with her arms folded on the edge. She rested her chin on the back of her hand.

"Suzette asked me if you and I have 'petite distractions.'"

His breath gusted out of him.

"How French." He looked into the wine that swayed in the bowl of his glass as he rolled the stem between his finger and thumb. Cami's doctor had asked his permission for her to be fitted with a cap, and Powell had thought it a laughable formality. His wife was *not* sexual enough to step out on him.

Or so he'd believed. But the woman he would swear he knew inside out was becoming more and more like a complete stranger by the minute. His voice sounded as though it came from another part of the room, not his own throat.

"I never have," he said truthfully and lifted his gaze. "You?"

"No." The water sloshed as she sat back and set her head on the pillow, glaring straight ahead.

His heart galloped in belated awareness that this territory was rife with lions and tigers. He suddenly wished for their children to rush in and form the buffer that kept them from acknowledging the small dissatisfactions they ignored so successfully.

He took another swallow of dry wine. "Were you afraid I would have one if I came here alone?"

"It crossed my mind." She lifted her toe from the water and touched it to the sole of his foot where he rested it on the rim of the tub. "Did it cross yours?"

"I love you, Camellia," he said with his whole heart. "I always have. I'm sure I always will."

"I love you, too."

"But?" She hadn't said it, but it rang in his ears and drove a thorny spike into his gut.

"I worry that you couldn't possibly love me, not when you don't really know me." Her gaze was imploring. Vulnerable enough to make his throat hurt. "From the moment we met, I have been trying to be good enough for you, good enough for your parents, good enough to be the mother of their grandchildren. I've been so careful to reveal only my best side that I'm convinced you would leave me if you knew the thoughts and feelings I have deep down."

How tragic. They were in a far sadder state than he'd allowed himself to see.

"I hide things, too, Cami. A man can't show his vulgar side to a woman, especially not one he cares about and respects. But I won't leave you because you've decided to say 'fuck.'"

"I want to say 'fuck' when we're in bed." Her chin came up. She held his gaze, but he could tell she was doing it by sheer force of will. "I want you to fuck me."

# CHAPTER THREE

That punched the air clean out of him. For a moment, his thoughts were as unformed as the murky swirls in the bathwater. His conscious awareness had dropped to how stiff his cock had become and how badly he wanted to free it from his drawers. How badly he wanted to fuck her *right now.*

"Darling." He carefully set his feet on the floor and held himself in such tight control, he expected his glass to crack in his hands. "I can do that. I *want* to fuck you," he assured her. "But I need to know *exactly* how drunk you are." This was a turning point, the kind that could make or break their marriage.

"I had a nap after Suzette left. And coffee. I'm loose, not drunk."

He set his glass beside hers and swooped forward in the same motion, thrusting his arms into the water to capture his little mermaid. He straightened in a great sluice of water that streamed in a trail across the carpet as he headed to the bed.

"Powell! They'll charge us for that." She wriggled, slippery and delightfully warm and nude and shiny, craning to see back toward the screen.

He set her on the bed, and she quickly scrambled to her feet, snatching up the nightdress the maid had left out. She hugged it to her front, dripping and shivering, staring at him with bewilderment.

"Are you wearing your cap?" He raked his gaze over every bit of wet skin he could see as he jerked blindly at the buttons on his soaked waistcoat, wrenching at it to get it off. He heard his watch hit the floor but didn't look for it.

"No."

He opened the night table and found the little box. He

dropped it on the bed. "No, not behind the screen," he said as she picked it up and looked back the way they'd come. "Do it here. I want to watch."

"*Powell.*"

"Why so scandalized, Mrs. Zimmerfield? Would you rather make love? Do you want to put on your nightdress and get under the covers and douse the lights?" He dropped his shirt and peeled his undershirt over his head. He wouldn't force her past any second thoughts she might be having, but fuck did he want this to happen.

"Well, I don't feel very— I'm still fat from…" She swallowed, and her gaze snagged on his naked chest in a way that made him swell with pride.

"Is that why you're always hiding under the covers? You're fucking beautiful, Cami." He tugged the nightdress out of her arms and dropped it, then took the box from her. "Can I help? I've been wondering how this works."

He'd peeked at the thimble-shaped cup a few times, but right now his eyes were fully occupied feasting on ample tits with fat beige circles around tall, stiff nipples. His balls ached, and his cock stung. He rarely got to feel her tits, let alone see them. She almost always kept them tucked beneath the crumpled nightdress that she raised so he could fit between her legs.

He cupped one lush, damp globe in his free hand. What would she do if he told her he wanted to fuck the valley between these glorious swells? He'd wanted that as long as he could remember.

"Are these finally mine again?" He dipped his head to suck her nipple into his mouth, tasting scented soap and rediscovering textures he'd forgotten how much he loved.

She jolted and gasped and set a steadying arm behind his shoulder. "You haven't even kissed me yet."

He was kissing her right now. He was fucking worshipping her. He wanted to trail his tongue over every inch of her. He suckled loud kisses up the slope of her breast and into her throat,

where her pulse throbbed against his lips before he kissed her
the way he did when he was buried inside her, about to come,
protected by the darkness and their riled passion. He cupped her
face in his hand and thrust his tongue into her mouth, wanting
her to know how excited he was. Wanting her streaking to the
same height of arousal that gripped him.

She moaned and slid her clammy arms around his neck and
pressed her damp skin to his hot chest.

She was trembling. He thought it might be chill and closed his
arms around her, trying to warm her, but maybe it was excitement,
because she pushed her mound into the stiffness of his cock,
deliberately inciting him with the grind of her hips.

A groan rattled in his chest. What the fuck had got into her?
She always let him take the lead, only ever whispering a polite
*Could you do that more slowly?* or *That feels nice. Keep doing
that* to guide him into ensuring she came.

He jerked his head up and nodded at the cap. "Show me."
He'd be damned if they would risk pregnancy when this was what
he could have when she wasn't worried about it.

Her arms came down to wedge between them. "It's not a
very graceful process."

He kept one arm firmly around her, offering the box while
letting her know with a steady look that he wasn't put off by a
little crudeness.

She bit the corner of her mouth and took the small rubber
device in the pinch of her finger and thumb, gaze lowered, cheeks
turning bright pink. She pressed him back a step with one hand
on his chest, then placed her knee on the edge of the bed. She
angled her shoulder, trying to hide what she was doing. Her
empty hand went down to part her pussy lips, and the middle
finger of her other hand slid all the way inside her passage.

"Holy fuck, Cami."

He had never seen her touch herself. His knees softened, and
he arrived on the floor beside the bed before he realized what he

was doing. He used an elbow to brace himself on the edge of the mattress, then used his other hand on her hip to urge her to swivel so he could see. He ate her pussy all the time to ensure she was wet enough to take him, but he was always sweating under the covers while he did it, never seeing her like this, swollen inner lips peeking from the pelt of fine hairs on her plump outer folds.

"I wanted to know if I was...slippery enough to put it in or..." Her finger came out glistening. Her hands were trembling, making the little cap quiver where she still pinched it.

Her pussy lips were gleaming and pink, pretty as the inside of an exotic shell, her fragrance intoxicating. "Now this goes in— I can't believe I'm letting you watch this."

He couldn't speak, utterly enthralled. He set his thumb on one plump outer lip, helping her hold herself open while she pressed the cup into a canoe shape and pushed the tip inside her hole. Her finger slid in behind it to guide it mysteriously into place.

The sight of her hand working against her pussy, essentially frigging herself, pushed him right to the edge. He had to clench his cock where it was leaking fluid behind his fly buttons.

When her finger emerged, he steered it into his mouth and sucked her taste from it, gaze still riveted to the pussy folds she released.

He kept his thumb in place, not allowing the hair-sprinkled outer lips to hide her tempting inner lips. With a groan, he let her finger slide out of his mouth and set his mouth on her, sliding his tongue all over those satiny, tantalizing ruffles. Her taste exploded in his head.

"Powell." She grasped at his shoulder.

He lifted his head long enough to say, "Don't close your eyes. Watch me fuck you with my tongue."

She was shaking and unsteady, her gaze shocked, but her eyes were turning glassy with lust.

He could have smiled with gratification, but he was too

captivated by the way her juices were increasing against his lips. He fucked his tongue in and out of her, then licked upward, seeking out the pulsing knot of flesh she liked him to slurp and suckle.

Her stomach quivered with growing tension. Another flood of wetness soaked his chin.

He wanted to bring her off like this, he really did, but his cock and balls were so tight and ready they hurt. He steadied her with a hand on her hip and kept the trace of his tongue very slow as he played it over the little bud that made her squirm. When her hands were clenched in his hair and her breath catching, he rose and dropped his pants.

She stared at his cock as though she'd never seen it, even though she had sucked him off in broad daylight many times. It was one of his favorite things, and he couldn't believe he'd never insisted she watch him do the same to her.

"Turn," he said. "Bend against the mattress. I want to fuck you from behind." They'd never done it like this, but he'd thought about it many times. So many times.

She swallowed, and he wondered if he was going too far, but she slid her knee off the bed and turned to face the mattress and lowered her forearms and face to the coverlet. Her ass came up as she tilted her hips in offering.

If he was dreaming or hallucinating or having some kind of hysterical episode, he hoped he never emerged from it. He shuffled his feet to push hers apart, trousers still cuffing his ankles. He slid the tip of his cock against her slippery folds, squeezing her ass and nudging at her pussy entrance while staring at the arsehole he'd never seen, not in ten solid years.

"Say it," he said in a guttural voice he barely recognized as his own.

"What?" she asked faintly.

"Fuck. You wanted to say it, so ask me to fuck you."

She groaned as though tortured. "Fuck me, Powell," she said

helplessly, turning her face into the mattress so he barely heard her. "Push your cock into my cunt and fuck me."

*Cunt.* His wife had said "cunt." He leaned into his thrust out of sheer instinct. She was so slick, he arrived home in one thrust. Her cunt swallowed him to the root, hot and sleek and exquisite. Her juices were so abundant, his balls were instantly coated. He was scorched everywhere their flesh touched.

"Fuck, Cami," he said on a shaken groan, taking hold of her hips and grinding in a little tighter before he drew back and returned in a firm thrust. All of his skin felt too tight to contain him. "Tell me how hard. Christ, I want to fuck you with everything in me."

"Do it. Fuck me hard. Deep and hard."

He pulled almost all the way out, then drove back in, slapping his hips into her ass with more power than he'd ever allowed himself to use. As the front of his pelvis hit the cushion of her ass, a powerful orgasm gathered across his hips and deep in his gut and down in the well of his ass.

"I'm not going to last," he bit out, pounding into her again. And again. The slaps were loud and earthy and felt incredible.

She cried, "Yes. Like that. Harder. Faster. Oh fuck, oh fuck. Powell. Fuck me harder."

If she hadn't said that, he would have worried he was being too rough, because her fists were clenched in the blankets. Her noises were sobs, but her back was arched, ass up and legs open so she could receive him. She pushed back on his thrusts, increasing the impact.

He was at the end of his rope. "Oh fuck, Cami—"

Her pussy clenched around him. Her high, wild cry was muffled by the blankets, but it was louder and longer than any she'd ever given up to him. Her cunt rippled and contracted and bathed him in a fresh wash of blistering heat.

His come erupted from the base of his spine. He pumped ruthlessly into her, balls practically turned inside out as his pulsing cock spurted molten pools deep inside her.

They must have heard his shout of ecstasy back in New York.

•••

"Suzette, I have to thank you," Camellia confided when they met two days later, intending to board the balloon that would sail them and fifty other passengers into the skies over Paris.

"Pourquoi, ma chérie?" She secured her bicycle near the ticket seller.

"I asked for what I wanted, and I got it."

"Oh, good! Deux, s'il vous plait," she said to the ticket seller.

"I've got them. Powell arranged it." Camellia showed her the tickets. "We're on the next one. Shall we walk in the garden while we wait?"

"If you like. Tell me what you asked for, then."

"Oh, um…" She gulped and looked around to be sure they wouldn't be overheard, then confided in a whisper, "I said I wanted to be fucked. He bent me over the side of the bed." Her voice faded so she was only mouthing the words by the time she got to the end.

"I'm so proud of you!" Suzette hugged her arm. "And you enjoyed it?"

"Yes. But now I'm embarrassed I told you. How unseemly."

"What do you mean?" They veered toward the roses, and Suzette dipped her head closer. "Don't be ashamed you took control of what happens to you. Boast of it. Give me the details so I might do something like it myself. All women can benefit from frank conversations."

"All? Please don't tell anyone I've told you this." But after spilling her soul the other day, Suzette had inspired her to step beyond the status quo. The rewards had been richer than she could have imagined. Plus, she was excited to relive it. To boast.

So she did.

"You see? Now I can tell my married friends that perhaps their husbands would be more receptive of the cap if they inserted it themselves."

"Do you think yours would be if you involved him?" It still shocked her that Suzette wished for a divorce, but she didn't seem to love him the way Camellia loved Powell.

"Jamais. I have always preferred to sit on his face than his cock. Oh! You should ask Powell for that."

"Wha— You don't mean *really*?"

"Ride his handlebars?" Suzette drew a line with her fingertip across her lip and down to her jaw, then up to her ear, indicating the path of Powell's facial hair. "Absolument."

# CHAPTER FOUR

"**W**hat do you mean you *told* her?" Powell was thunder-struck.

He quickly cracked the bedroom door to glance out and be sure the maid had left as instructed. They'd finished dinner with a couple from Austria an hour ago and were readying for bed. He had been looking forward to finally having his wife to himself after a busy few days, but now this?

"Please don't be upset."

"Camellia, I have never told anyone, least of all another man, what we do in our bed. If one asked, I would shoot him dead."

She pressed her lips, gaze lowering guiltily in the mirror.

"Are you upset by what happened the other night? Is that it?" he asked gruffly.

They hadn't talked about it, falling asleep directly after. He'd left her sleeping the next morning, and they'd had engagements every minute since, ones that either took them in their own directions or brought them together in company.

The more time that passed, the more he'd wondered if it had been a dream. He wasn't sure how to bring it up. What was the etiquette after behaving like an animal? A thank-you note? *I enjoyed fucking you like a bull on a heifer. When can I do it again?*

"I'm not upset," she said.

"Then why did you tell her? *What* did you tell her?"

"I told her what happened," she mumbled and continued brushing her hair, still avoiding his eyes in the mirror.

"What did you say? That we made love?"

"I told her I asked you to fuck me and you bent me over the bed," she said in a small burst. "I said I begged you to put your cock in my cunt, and I have never come so hard in our entire marriage."

Powell's ears rang. He had to take a moment to decide if he was shocked, infuriated, insulted, or complimented.

"I said that I hoped we could keep trying new things." She was brushing her hair so hard it was making her eyes gleam. "She said I should ask if I could sit on your face."

Her face was bright red with some mix of embarrassment and pent-up anger. She lifted her chin in the same defiance she had shown the other night, eyes wide with apprehension as she threw out her dare.

All the conflicted emotions in him were coalescing into a bonfire of randy desire.

"I want to fuck your tits," he blurted, unable and unwilling to hold it back, not when they'd come this far. "That's not a condition. Sit on my face. I'd love that. But fucking your tits is something I've wanted for years. I didn't think you'd ever consider it."

She lowered the hairbrush into her lap and turned to face him. "I'm sorry that you thought I wouldn't. To be honest, I might not have. Not until..." She heaved a little sigh, chin tucked with entreaty. "This is new and difficult and embarrassing, but I want us to be able to talk about these things. And try them. We could try that if you want." She looked down as she gathered her breasts in her hands and plumped them together. "How would it work, though?"

"We need oil." He was in front of her in three quick strides, pushing his finger into her cleavage. His blood ran hot from the small act of pushing his digit into that warm, soft space. "I heard a man talk about it once, and I've wanted to try it since. Your tits are beautiful."

"I stopped thinking of them as anything but milk bottles long ago." She released them and looked up at him with anxiety. "Do you really like them?"

He caressed her cheek. "Why don't you wait until I've come all over you before you ask me that?"

●●●

"**D**id he?" Suzette asked, eyes dancing with titillated amusement.

"He did." Camellia looked around. The café tables were full, but the other patrons were leaning to hear their own conversations. "He sent the biggest arrangement of flowers the next morning. His note said, 'I'm happy to reassure you as often as necessary so you will never suffer doubts again.'"

"Scandaleux!" Suzette laughed and tapped Camellia's wrist. "And you? Did you sit on his face?"

"I did. Which I thought would be uncomfortable, or I would be too shy to enjoy, but I was very impassioned by the lewdness of it. I did miss the fullness and friction of his cock, though," she admitted as she reflected on it. "He usually eats me before we fuck, so I came twice and thought, well, where is the rest?" She laughed at her greed. "It was still very satisfying."

"Does he not finger you when he eats you? I had a lover who would put her whole fist inside me. I loved that," Suzette recollected dreamily. "Oh, it takes a little practice," she added when she noticed Camellia's jaw had fallen to the paving stones. "There's a trick— Ah, here is Ursula."

They rose to greet a stocky woman who wore a plain gown, spectacles, and a cheerful smile. Ursula was scheduled to speak at the congress, so the conversation turned to the topics on the agenda and why the organizers were leaving suffrage out of the discussions.

"Too controversial, but I'm sure it will be brought up informally," Ursula said. "In fact, I'll make sure of it."

They were soon comparing acquaintances among the various suffrage committees in America, and Camellia forgot what

Suzette had said until she and Powell were dressing to have dinner with Suzette two nights later.

•••

"You'll never guess what Suzette told me at lunch the other day."

"What's that?" Powell was hurrying to change his shirt, having been delayed at the exposition. They were running late.

Cami was flitting about, searching for his yellow necktie. Half their luggage was packed for their train to Rome tomorrow.

"She said one of her lovers put her whole hand inside her. Ah, here it is. I told you I had it all organized."

"Camellia." Powell stood frozen with his fingers still pushing his collar button through its hole, stunned to his toes.

"What? The maid's not here. I told her we wouldn't be back until late."

He barely hung on to his patience. "Please tell me you did not share details of our evening with that stranger who joined you for lunch."

"Ursula? Of course not. I told Suzette before she arrived."

"You—" He snatched the strip of buttercup silk from her hand, glaring at her. "How am I supposed to look her in the eye?"

"Don't be like that. She won't tease. She wants us to be happy."

"Does she?" he asked, teeth locked with skepticism.

"Yes! That's why she wants us to be honest. I thought you wanted that, too?"

"With *each other*." He moved to the mirror as he popped up his collar and slung the tie behind it, flicking the ends to tie the bow. "You really told her what we did?" He did *not* understand this compulsion she had developed to share so freely.

"I did." She showed no remorse. "She said you should shave so I won't get a friction burn. She meant my chest when you fuck my tits, but it's nicer on my puss when your chin is freshly shaved, too. I've never told you that, but thought I should."

"You—" His hands fell, and the tangled tie flapped around his neck as he moved to pour himself a drink.

"It's good advice," she muttered, adjusting the rings on her hand. "She *knows* things."

"No, she doesn't. Otherwise, she would never suggest a man take a *razor* to his cock and balls. And she wants you to take a fist up your cunt? *Whose?*" He was taking a mocking tone of pleasant conversation, but he was furious. He didn't know Suzette. Did Cami have any idea the damage her friend could do if she chose to be as indiscreet as she was?

"That's not how this is!" Now Cami was offended, but he would be damned if her gaze didn't drop away with defensiveness.

"She is inserting herself into our marriage, Camellia." His chest felt tight, and his arms twitched. The vague uneasiness he'd been feeling about Suzette hardened into a more solid peril. Suzette threatened all he held dear. "I want you to quit seeing her."

"I will not." Her arms shot straight at her sides, hands knotting into fists. "You're angry because she tells me things you never would. You had *ten years*, Powell."

"To tell you that I want to fuck your tits? You said yourself you wouldn't have been open to it until now."

"Exactly. That's not Suzette getting between us. Quite the opposite. She has encouraged me to seek out what makes me happy, rather than wait around like a docile mare for it to find me. I wouldn't even be here in Paris if I wasn't eager to control my life, so don't blame Suzette."

"Who do I blame, then? Myself? Because if I don't make you happy—" His throat locked. He didn't want to contemplate what that might mean.

"For heaven's sake, Powell." The gust in her sails was more exasperation than rile. "I wouldn't have insisted on coming to Paris if you didn't make me happy. I would have stayed home and reveled in the break. I thought what we'd been doing since we arrived here made us happi*er*."

He ran his hand down his face. "Yes, but... Christ, Cami. You're scaring the hell out of me these days."

Her skirts ruffled as she came to stand before him. "I'm scaring myself. But my love for you hasn't changed. If anything, it's grown deeper now that we have more honesty and intimacy between us."

He took her hands and drew her closer, kissed her, needing the softening of her lips and the sigh that told him she was still receptive and willing and his.

In the main room, the clock pinged the hour. He lifted his head.

"I suppose we should go or we'll be late." It was a conciliatory acknowledgment that she would continue to see Suzette.

A touched smile curled her lips. "Thank you, Powell."

He hitched a shoulder. If that other woman would continue to invigorate his sex life for the next few weeks, he supposed he should get to know her.

• • •

Camellia had nearly told Powell a dozen times that she and Suzette had been intimate when they'd been at school. Fear had stopped her—fear that he wouldn't understand or would think there was more to their current relationship. She probably should have confessed it this evening when he'd come close to accusing her of it, but their argument had grown so heated, it would have been fuel on his wrongful assumption.

Now she worried that it would somehow come out, and apprehension caused a discordant tension in her as she watched Powell and Suzette greet each other in the lobby of the hotel where they were dining.

"I've been looking forward to speaking with you again,"

Powell said gallantly. "Thank you for coming."

"Thank you for the carriage."

"Of course."

"That's a lovely color on you," Camellia said of the dark blue gown Suzette wore. It was a quiet statement with a double-breasted jacket and pretty embroidery around the flat collar and the cuffs of her sleeves.

"I told Mother where I was going, and she insisted on having my hair done." She rolled her eyes upward at the auburn braids that had been attached so they fell in loops from a blue ribbon at her crown.

The restaurant had come highly recommended, and Powell had reserved one of their best tables with a view of the Seine. The din of conversation nearly drowned out the string quartet as they were shown to their table. Candlelight sparkled off the diamonds worn at the throats and wrists of guests they passed.

They exchanged small talk as wine was poured, but Camellia was aware that Powell was not as amiable and charismatic as usual. There was a watchfulness about him that kept her from relaxing.

"How are things at the exposition?" Suzette asked him politely.

"Very well, but I'm looking forward to our break in Rome. Cami must be as well?" He glanced at her. "I'm not the only man who has brought his wife. You've had to play hostess several times. You ought to wear a guide hat and earn a wage."

"It's true. Ask me how many miles of pipes are pumping water to power the elevators and cool the Palace of Industry. Twenty-nine." She widened her eyes at what a useless fact that was to have rattling around in her brain. "But I see something new every time I view the fine arts, and I tried the telephone. We had already seen the phonograph in Philadelphia, but we saw the electric lights come on one night on the Avenue de l'Opéra. That was exciting."

"Cami has also indulged her interest in suffrage with you, so

I'm assured this isn't all chores for her," Powell said.

Camellia couldn't tell if he was smoothing over their argument or being facetious.

Perhaps Suzette was equally uncertain. She sat a little straighter and met his gaze unflinchingly. "You don't disapprove of a woman expanding her mind? And speaking openly on things we're not supposed to?"

Camellia nearly swallowed her tongue.

Powell paused as though trying to discern whether Suzette was referring to the vote, sex in general, or the gossip his wife was sharing about their intimate life.

"On the contrary. I believe the discussions she has with you offer benefits to me," he said drily and glanced at Camellia in a way that nearly ate her alive.

Camellia blushed so hard her skin hurt. She rolled her lips inward to bite them.

"You must feel free to be as open with me as she is," Suzette insisted to Powell. "Men and women will never be equal if they continue to treat each other as a foreign species."

"I do have a question." He picked up Camellia's hand and closed it into a fist. "Cami said—"

"Powell!" Camellia hissed and snatched her fist into her lap. "You are not asking her that. Not here, not now. Not ever."

Suzette blinked with incomprehension, then said, "Oh. *Oh.*" She made a noise of mild amusement. "I don't mind, ma chérie. Ah, merci," she added as their first course arrived.

The snails were still simmering in their garlic-infused butter.

"There is a small technique to it." Suzette ignored her plate and leaned forward as they were left alone. "Abundant use of olive oil and all the most effective caresses. Take your time, and one at a time." She held up her hand to show two fingers, three, then four. She fluted her fingers into a cylinder before she tucked her thumb into the tented space between her forefinger and her pinky. "Once arrived—" She tucked her thumb inside her fist.

"Trim your nails prior," she added with a wink.

"Are you punishing me?" Camellia demanded of Powell, ready to crawl under the table. At the same time, she felt...intrigued. Lascivious and sinful and filled with anxious anticipation.

"I was genuinely curious," he insisted. He squeezed her hand, urging her to look at him. "It was just a question, Cami. Not something I expect to happen. You said Suzette knows things. You were right."

She swallowed and gave a tight nod, but her heart was tripping clumsily in her chest.

"Let us go back to talking of the finer arts," Suzette suggested with her laissez-faire attitude. "Has Camellia told you that somewhere here in Paris is a painting of our nude bottoms, along with one of our schoolmates'? We nearly froze to death posing in that artist's garret, didn't we?"

"Ha! Which grace were you?" Powell kept her hand and sent her a wolfish grin. "Beauty," he decided and kissed her fingertips before releasing her so she could eat. "You must have been charm?" he said to Suzette.

"I think we were all 'gullible,'" Camellia interjected. "He paid us with the most terrible wine."

They laughed, and the rest of the meal was convivial and, thankfully, uneventful.

# CHAPTER FIVE

----------------------------------------

Given they would be on the train for over a week, Powell had booked them into a private compartment. It had a comfortable bench seat for day travel and a small table where Camellia could catch up on her letter writing. An adjoining compartment held a pair of bunk beds and a washstand with drawers so they could unpack a few items. They would eat in the dining car, and there was a first-class drawing room where they could stretch their legs or find books or card games if desired. The communal toilet at the end of their car was only shared with two other couples, so that was also convenient.

After a late night with Suzette and an early morning to get to the train station, Camellia was drowsy before the high summer sun was setting.

"You've been quiet. Are you angry?" Powell asked as he found his pajamas and began stripping off his clothes.

"No." She was already in her night dress, sitting on the side of the bed, rubbing coconut oil into her cuticles.

"You thought I was offside asking Suzette what I did," he said.

"No. I mean, I don't know that a public restaurant is the place for that discussion, but no. There's something I've been wanting to talk to you about, and I honestly don't know how."

"Just say it."

She set her hands in her lap. "Suzette and I are not lovers, but we were, in the way of young lovers. Kissing and caressing. That's why it's so easy for me to share my intimate life with her. I already have, before you and I ever met."

"Ah. I wondered." He sat down beside her and gave her a tender look, which eased a little of her nervousness.

"I'm not drawn to women. I prefer men. I prefer *you*." She let the rock of the carriage tap her shoulder against his.

"I prefer women." He made a face of indecision, then winced as he confided, "I know this because I once had a similar encounter. Once."

"With a man? Darling." She drew back, which was hypocritical, she recognized at once, but she had never suspected such a thing.

One of his dark brows shot up. "You think you're the only one with a youthful curiosity that was quenched by our marriage?"

"Touché. Will you tell me what happened?" She looped her arm through his and snuggled her hip closer to his. "Were you in love?"

"No. I barely knew him. I had recently started university. I was very drunk. So was he."

She could feel his tension. "You didn't enjoy it?" she asked apprehensively.

"I didn't *not* enjoy it. He asked if he could suck my cock; I said he could. It felt delightful," he said with a rueful twist of his lips. "Then he asked if I wanted to suck him. I said, 'No, thanks,' but I watched him jerk himself. We laughed it off, but I was embarrassed the next morning, shocked that I'd let myself get so drunk that I wasn't exercising any judgment. You know what my father is like. That's why I'm careful how much I drink and why I asked you that night in the bath if you were drunk. I didn't want you suffering any remorse. He must have had a similar hangover, because I never saw him again." His expression reflected the consternation of wishing he'd handled the whole thing better.

"Thank you for telling me. For trusting me."

"Thank you for telling me about you and Suzette." He slipped his arm around her and nuzzled her cheek. "Would you like to share what you two did?"

"Mr. Zimmerfield," she mock-scolded. "Please do not tell me you are titillated by our very innocent escapades?"

"I'm very fucking titillated."

She reached between his legs, where his thick erection

pressed against the light cotton of his pajama pants.

"So you are. I don't know why. We only ever kissed and hugged and learned how to rub each other until we came. It was hardly anything, really. And it was only during our final year," she added with a blasé shrug.

He groaned and tilted her onto the pillows, saying playfully, "I would like to rub you until you come. Can I put in your cap?"

She nodded, and he reached into the drawer below the small shelf at the head of the bed. Camellia picked up the hem of her nightdress to expose herself to her waist.

"Are you wet?" He brushed a caress down her folds, lightly stimulating the fine hairs, then glanced over his shoulder. "There's no room to slide off this bed and eat you. I'll be in the corridor."

They both laughed.

He licked his fingertip and gently parted her folds, watching as he roamed his touch down to her entrance and up.

A small moan of sheer luxury escaped her. In the past, she had offered timid directions, but now they had learned to speak more freely. They were constantly teaching and learning about each other's bodies. He generously sought to imbue his caress with as much pleasure as possible, lightly teasing her toward arousal, and she knew that his gaze on her spread pussy was a gift of pleasure to him.

"Let me suck your tits," he said. "That always makes you wet."

She wriggled again, peeling her nightdress up and off. The chill of the air made her nipples tighten, but Powell gathered her close, one arm beneath her neck, one thigh between hers. His warm abdomen pressed against her hip as he leaned to suckle at her.

A rush of heat flooded into her loins. He moaned and spread her juices around, circling the swelling bump that made her sigh.

After torturing her other nipple, he lifted his head and watched his finger go inside her.

Before this trip, she couldn't have imagined she would open her legs farther and feel so much love toward him, so much trust in offering herself this way. She hadn't imagined she would ever arch in such a wanton fashion, enjoying the way his eyes became slitted with lust as he dragged his gaze from her pussy, up her stomach to her breasts, hooked on her mouth, then met her gaze.

She cupped the side of his beloved face, liking that fierce tension in his expression as his touch inside her searched out her cervix. He was taking his time, slowly working his finger in and out of her and seeming to revel in doing it.

Her pussy blossomed with spreading warmth, becoming more and more sensitized to his caress. Her inner muscles clenched at his touch, yearning for more.

"Put it in," she prompted, aching for him to fuck her.

He folded the cap and guided it in, then followed with his finger, ensuring it was seated and sealed. "Is that right?"

He'd done this twice now, but this time, he didn't remove his finger. Instead, he continued his very slow and gentle fucking, stoking a very deep, intense fire in her. He held her gaze as she moved her hand to brush against his.

In a flagrant move that would have been impossible two weeks ago, she played her fingertip in her own lubrication, then slid it in alongside his, biting her lip at how snug it felt. How debauched yet intimate, to have them each with a finger tucked inside her.

His nostrils flared, and his lips pulled back to bare his teeth. He dragged his gaze down to her pussy, watching and keeping his finger buried inside her as she worked to reach and feel that the cap was properly placed.

The stimulation caused more heat and wetness to gather, shortening her breath. When she removed her hand, he kept his finger inside her, moving in slow glides.

"Give me that," he murmured. "Do you want two of mine?"

She nodded as she presented her wet finger for him to suck.

Her pussy clamped onto his finger as his suction drew on hers. Below, his touch briefly retreated only to return with its pair, thicker. Somehow stretching deeper. Moving so slowly the sensations grew maddening.

He dropped his head so they could kiss. It was a passionate meeting of open mouths and questing tongues. The air was no longer cool enough on skin that had begun to burn. She ached for him to rub her swollen button, but the way he was lazily fucking her with his fingers was too delicious to give up. The more she tensed to savor the pleasure, the more the friction of his touch excited her, increasing her wetness.

He was scissoring his fingers open, she realized. Stretching her. She moaned at how good it felt.

"Does that hurt?" he asked, lifting his head.

"No. I like it."

"Do you think you can take three?" He nudged with his third.

She bit her lip, nodding, wanting to try.

Three was thicker than his cock. She groaned as he pushed in, but she was so wet it happened with very little resistance from her inner muscles.

"Fuck, you're so hot, Cami. Like the center of a wet fire." He kissed her lips, sucked her bottom lip, sucked her nipple. All the while, he kept up that magnificent rhythm that was echoed by the sway of the carriage.

He typically aroused her by licking her to near orgasm before they fucked. When his cock was inside her, he caressed her to make sure she came before he did. He'd never just penetrated her and left her to grasp at these nascent sensations, ones that were hidden and dark and powerful.

"Do you know what I've been thinking about since that first night, when I had you bent over the bed?" He nibbled at her ear, hot breath a bellows on the glowing embers inside her. "I think about fingering your ass. Would you like to feel your arsehole stretched like this?"

It was as indecent and taboo as anything she'd ever heard, and she could only make a helpless noise, because yes, she thought she might like that very much.

"I think you would," he said. "You're so fucking wet right now, I bet you could take another finger. Should I try?" As he waited for her answer, he gave slow pulses of his three fingers inside her.

She could hardly speak. "I think...if you use some of the coconut oil?"

Yes, she had been thinking of that since she'd put the tub beside the bed earlier. Since Suzette had mentioned needing oil.

Powell's fingers slid free of her pussy, and she shivered, relieved but bereft. She was so aroused, she was sure it would only take a little rubbing of her outer lips and she would find release, but she wanted more of that deeper caress.

She wanted to see how far they could take each other.

He was still braced on his elbow over her, but he held the small tub with the hand that was trapped under her neck and opened it with his free hand. The sweet, tropical fragrance filled the air. He dug his fingers into the jar, then brought a generous gob to her mound.

It melted as soon as he began to work it over her plump outer lips. He grazed her bud as he worked it into her channel. She jerked.

"You want that, don't you? More than this?" He pushed two fingers easily into her.

"No. Yes. I don't know what I want," she admitted on a sob of desire.

"Three?" The fullness was back, so slippery now as he moved in and out of her with barely any friction. All her stimulation came from the stretch. Her flesh was taut and quivering with each thrust of his fingers.

"Try four," she whispered.

"Are you sure?" The stretch increased. His thumb traveled

all over her spread folds as he worked his fluted fingers into her passage.

"Oh God, Powell." She felt stuffed full. It bordered on pain, but it was glorious.

"Hurt?"

"A little. Go slow but don't stop." The sensation was intense. She groaned and dug her heel into the bed, unable to spread herself wide enough. "Push deeper. Oh fuck."

"Stop?"

"No. Give me the rest. Oh my God, Powell." She felt *open*. She spread her legs and offered herself in a way she had never dreamed she could.

His fingers were working in and out of her, slow, slow, slow. It was deliciously maddening and then, "Oh fuck, Cami." He was biting his own lip as his touch shifted, and she knew he had added his thumb.

The stretch kept coming and coming. Her inner walls were vibrating at the sensations. She lifted her hips, inviting more while noises left her that she'd never made in her life.

"Look at me, Cam. Tell me to stop if— Holy fuck."

She took his knuckles. They froze and locked their gazes, neither seeming able to speak. Very carefully, he closed his hand into a hard fist inside her.

Her inner muscles clamped down. Hard.

"Is it too much?" he asked in a strained voice.

She couldn't speak. She was full in a way that defied description. He wasn't moving, but places inside her were being pressed and stimulated by nothing more than the subtle rock of the train.

Time spun out as they remained in this profound moment. Her vision blurred. Her body was fire. She was utterly vulnerable and completely at his mercy, trusting him completely. This was what she had longed for—sharing herself with him in a way that was acutely intimate and thrilling and frighteningly intense. She had never loved him more.

"Tell me you like it," he said in a guttural voice.

She set her hand on his wrist, keeping his fist inside her as orgasm teased. Heat was flaring from her cunt, washing over her in waves. She closed her thighs to hold his fist in place and pulsed her hips in small receptions of barely there thrusts.

That was all it took. She began to come. And come.

Powell leaned down and sucked her tit, causing another orgasm to strike without mercy. Wave after wave of astonishing, nearly unbearable pleasure consumed her. She would never tire of this. Never.

• • •

He could do this to her forever. That's all Powell could think as his wife's jagged moans of pleasure filled the carriage. Her pussy was cinched around his wrist, her muscles contracting on his fist. He had never felt so powerful or so tender, so completely awash in love and lust. Fully in possession of her yet humbled by the gift of her.

He was so aroused he was nearly blind with it, but he held back until she quieted. Then he gently eased his hand out of her pussy, still stunned. He was shaking and wanted to fuck her hard and deep. Now.

It took everything in him not to roll on top of her and do it. She had to be sore. Who the fuck even knew where that cap was after what he'd just done to her.

That had been the most exquisite experience of his life.

Still lost to it, he hitched his pajama pants down and thrust once into the fist that was still coated with the molten honey of her cunt. One stroke of his tight, slippery grip and orgasm crashed onto him and through him. He groaned and bucked as his scorching come spurted across her still-trembling stomach in ferocious, aching bursts. His cock and balls continued to pulse and twitch after he was empty. Helpless cries continued to echo from his throat, and shudders chased down his back as he held on to that sensation of her pussy milking his fist.

Eventually, he was utterly spent. Weak. The sheets were soaked with her juices and stained by the oil and his semen. He didn't give one small damn. He tucked her shivering body close to his in that narrow, too-short bed, pulled the blankets over them, and whispered, "I love you so much."

She curled into him and might have said, "I love you, too."

He wasn't sure he heard it, but he certainly felt it.

●●●

"What lovely flowers." Ursula noted them as she came into Suzette's modest rooms to collect the printed report on the International Congress of Women's Rights last month. "From your husband?"

"Camellia."

"Oh?" Was that a note of piqued possessiveness in her lover's tone?

"Read the card if you like," Suzette invited.

Ursula opened it. "'Suzette, I wish to thank you for the stimulating conversation and handy tips that ensured our visit to Europe remained as pleasurable as possible. I shall write the moment I'm home. We hope you will visit us in America soon. All my love, Camellia.'" Ursula's brow reached for her hairline. "Will you?"

"Someday," Suzette said mildly. "Perhaps you'll come with me."

"Perhaps." Ursula sniffed as she returned the card to the shelf. "Why don't you like her?"

"I think she's lovely." Ursula tugged the fingers of her gloves to loosen them. "Intelligent. Dedicated to suffrage. What's not to like?"

"You tell me."

"You two seemed very close," she said pertly.

"Don't be jealous," Suzette chided, coming to unbutton Ursula's jacket. "I wouldn't have approached you if she and I hadn't shared certain confidences."

"Such as?"

"They're confidences. I won't betray her, but she reminded me that there's a difference between speaking frankly, which I do without any sense of consequence, and speaking openly and honestly about what you desire. That takes courage and a willingness to be vulnerable." Suzette slid her arms around Ursula's sturdy waist and enjoyed the feel of her ample breasts against her own. "Doesn't it?"

"I suppose." Ursula was widowed and hadn't seemed inclined to remarry. It hadn't followed that she preferred women, though, so Suzette had been hesitant to reveal her attraction.

Ursula's tone shifted from mollified to indulgent. "What is it that you desire, then?"

Suzette thought of the graphic escapade Camellia had relayed of her travel to Rome.

"Give me your hand, and I'll show you…"

# EPILOGUE

*Two years later…*

"**I** had a letter from Suzette today," Camellia said as Powell came into the bedroom and kissed her cheek. "She was feeling us out on a visit this summer. Ursula might accompany her."

"They could join us at the beach house." He shrugged out of his suit jacket. "Where are the children? It's like a morgue downstairs."

"With Mother. Most of the servants have the night off. It's our weekend," she reminded with a blink of pending disappointment. "You didn't forget?" They booked one night every month so they would have time together. *Special* time.

"Oh, Christ. I thought that was next weekend."

"You made plans for us?" But she had bought a new tub of coconut oil in anticipation.

"Brunch tomorrow with the Bellincourts. Remind me to send regrets later." They liked to lie in the next morning with some gentle fucking and much snuggling and reconnection. He dragged his tie free, then looped it around her to draw her closer. "I don't know how I confused the dates. I always look forward to this."

His slow smile caused a shiver of excitement to tighten her skin. Her nipples and pussy stung with arousal.

They continued to have sex often, but with their busy lives, it tended to be a quickie bent over her vanity table or she dropped to her knees and swallowed his cock while he kept them from being interrupted by pressing his back to their bedroom door. If they had a little more time, she sat on his face and he fingered her arsehole then fucked her tits until he was spent.

All of that was delightfully thrilling, but the one thing they both craved—the act that had kept her pussy wet all day with expectancy and had him reaching for the front of his tented trousers now—required privacy and patience. They needed to focus on each other completely, and she invariably made so much noise at the culmination, it was best if they had an empty house for it.

"How do you want it? On your elbows?" he asked.

Sometimes she braced her stomach on a pillow and he ate her ass as he fucked her with his fist, making her scream with pleasure into the mattress.

"I want to be naked on my back so I can see how much you like it. I want you to suck at my tits and make me beg for every finger."

"Oh, love," he groaned, catching at the back of her neck and bringing her close for a kiss. He sucked her bottom lip as he released her. "I'm going to make you beg for my mouth, too. When you come, I want you to soak our entire fucking bed."

She always did.

*The End*

# The Point of No Return

*The Point of No Return* will get under your skin and stay with you in the most delicious ways, however it includes detailed descriptions of piercings on various intimate body parts as well as references to drug use and prostitution, so readers who may be sensitive to these, please take note.

# CHAPTER ONE

*January 1890, Hong Kong*

He was here again. And easy to spot, standing head and shoulders above the people waiting outside the shop.

Fitzwilliam Qin Meili gritted her teeth as she continued down the alley, unbothered by the stares she garnered. Her neighbors might be poor and hassled by authorities for being prostitutes, opium addicts, and petty thieves, but they all looked out for one another. They knew Meili wasn't encouraging this Englishman. He was making a nuisance of himself.

Or trying to make her into something she refused to become?

If only he didn't stand out so glaringly. He was not only tall but eye-catching with his gray eyes and hair like burnished brass. He wore a curled mustache, clean-shaven cheeks, and a narrow beard that came to a point on his chin. A wink of gold glimmered in the whiskers under his stern bottom lip.

He also wore an earring, a thick gold ring with two pearl beads and a dangling black stone that held a shattered rainbow within it. He had tried to pay her with that jewel when she had stitched his arm after he was robbed several weeks ago. He had saved the earring but had lost his money.

Meili had waved away the gemstone. She preferred to have a Westerner in her debt than the other way around.

He'd pawned the earring down the alley and settled with her minutes later, but he'd worn it again when he returned to have his stitches removed, so he'd obviously bought it back.

Despite his diligence in paying his debts, she didn't trust him. Not only because he was English. He'd given his name while she stitched him—Vincent. Her brother, Peng, had been about to graduate from Oxford when Headmaster Vincent Harding had written to say Peng had died from a fever. That had been five years ago and was simple bad luck, but in Meili's heart, *all* Vincents were to blame for her loss.

She was intrigued by this one, though. Not that she revealed it. She barely glanced at him as she arrived at her shop door.

Vincent didn't push off from leaning on the side of the building. Everyone else crowded behind her, anxious to get out of the wind.

The bell above the door tinkled as she called out in Cantonese, "Maa-maa. I'm back." She held the door for a hunched, elderly man, a woman with a crying baby, and a weary-looking maid from one of the big houses.

Her grandmother, whom she'd always called Mama, was up from her rest and hobbled out of their shared room with her tea and the money box. Meili slid the screen closed behind her while Mama sat on the stool before the wall of shelves lined with neatly labeled jars.

They dried and ground the preparations themselves. Lower down were tins of ointments and bars of soap they made as ingredients allowed. They also sewed cotton pads meant for bandaging injuries, which were equally popular with women during their flow, especially when tails with buttonholes were added to either end.

The harried mother consulted Mama while Meili tucked her shopping beneath the table and packaged herbs for the arthritic old man. When the maid had left with a physic to purge an unexpected pregnancy, the shop was empty and quiet.

That's when Vincent came in and drank up all the air.

"Welcome," Meili said in the Cantonese used by the elite hongs who did business with taipans like him. "How can we help you?"

"Still no English?" He didn't even try a greeting in her language.

"Tell him to see his own doctors," Mama said. "This is his

third visit in two months."

"He's the reason we're eating meat tonight." Meili padded his bill.

She actually read and spoke English very well, thanks to her English mother. She had practiced by exchanging letters with her brother, and she consulted with missionary doctors when people came to her needing more complex treatment than she could provide.

She and Mama were lucky to have clients. Traditional medicine was only sought by those who were superstitious, distrustful of the West, or too poor to afford the new methods of care. Plus, they were women.

Meili's father had been a doctor, though. He had indulged Meili's fascination with his needles, teaching her to treat her grandmother's foot pain. Her grandmother knew all the remedies for common family ailments, especially female symptoms. Between that and the finer skills Meili had learned from a Hindu woman who had occupied one of the brothels five years ago, they made ends meet.

That latter skill had brought Vincent today. Rather than a swollen joint or a septic cut, he opened a small box to show her a pair of gold shafts stuck through a satin pillow. Each held a horseshoe-shaped loop dangling like a door knocker.

A jolting thrill went through Meili—one that was so telling and inappropriate, she fought revealing it. She knew exactly what those were, and, if he was offering them as a gift, she would be hard-pressed to refuse. Her middle was suddenly inhabited by thousands of silkworms, all spinning and wriggling with excitement.

Struggling to hold an impassive expression, she looked up inquiringly.

"You were piercing someone's nose when I had my stitches out," he said. "Did you do your own eyebrow?" He pointed above his eye, then at her, indicating the silver ring she wore.

Meili tapped her chest with a mixture of anticipation and reluctance. This was why she wore the ring, so people would ask her about it and she could offer her services. Also, she had a small fixation with needles, pins, and piercings, but that was her business, not his.

"Will you put these on me?" He nodded at the box.

*Oh, yes.* A tingling wave went through her as she motioned to the mat behind the screen.

Mama made a disapproving noise at Meili seeing a man's naked chest, but he wasn't her first and wouldn't be her last.

Elation quickened her pulse as she washed her hands then gathered her tools, along with her precious bottle of carbolic acid. Piercing was something she liked to do, and it always gave her a rush of exuberance. When it was something a little more challenging, she relished it even more.

This nervous anticipation went beyond that. She was eager to do it to *him*.

She tried not to dwell on that distinction as she joined him behind the screen. She found him sitting shirtless on the mat, knees up, wrists balanced on them. Her steps faltered, and her heart seemed to stop.

He didn't look threatening or apprehensive or excited or even bored. She didn't know what he was, and that was why she found him so disturbing. Every time he came here, she tried to read him while sensing him do the same with her.

She had an impression he wanted something from her, but what? Sex? Men rarely hid that kind of interest. They either blushed with shyness or pawed her and learned that she carried a knife.

Maybe she was hoping for a glimpse of attraction because she felt glimmers of it herself.

*Glimmers, Meili?*

She pleasured herself in the night, wondering how his lips might feel on her neck, his beard brushing her chin and his thickness driving into her.

She didn't *want* to feel this way about any man, least of all an English Vincent, but he had ropey shoulders and a muscled chest that were an undeniable expression of strength and health. He dressed well and had the means to buy gold nipple rings that were rare and well-made. He wasn't afraid to leave Queen's Road, where the European jeweler who had sold him these rings ought to be able to pierce him.

Should she be flattered he'd come to her for this? She considered that as she removed the horseshoes from the studs and set the studs into a small dish, then splashed carbolic acid over them. He could attach the loops in a few weeks when he'd healed; otherwise, he might catch them on his shirt or a towel and risk a tear.

"My uncle never allowed me to order pieces like that into our London showroom." Vincent spoke as if he knew she could understand him perfectly. "He would shit a brick if he knew I plan to display some here, but they'll do well. If you're good at this, I'll ask you to work for me at the hotel. Our clients will pay in silver, not copper."

And leave her grandmother? For coins that would make them a target for robbery? Not likely.

"One or two days a week. Or by appointment," he said in an abstract tone as he eased onto his back and tucked his hands behind his head.

There were a few fine hairs around his nipples, but his chest pelt was concentrated along his breastbone, fading above his navel, which was visible above the buckle of his belt. His abdomen was so flat she had an urge to lay her hand there to test its warmth and firmness. Maybe allow her touch to slide lower while she teased his navel with her tongue.

"There's a filthy place by the harbor that sailors visit for tattoos and piercings," he continued. "And a jeweler at one of the hotels who will do ears. He refuses to pierce anything else.

Travelers want souvenirs, though. Businessmen like to do things when they're away that they can't do at home. What better way to remember a city than by getting your cock pierced? I did it. Others will, too."

Her gaze flew to the buttons on his trousers before she caught herself.

"I knew you spoke English," he said smugly. "I understand most of what *you* say, as well. Enjoy your meat."

# CHAPTER TWO

Vincent Gainsborough was obsessed with this woman, and he wasn't sure why. She seemingly couldn't stand him, and he was promised to another, but she had begun creeping into his dreams after she'd wordlessly stitched his arm two months ago.

He had been brought here by an old woman who had provided a rag to stem his bleeding. Meili, as she had called her, had sat him behind this screen, where a patient had occupied this mat. The middle-aged man had been face-down with pins standing on his skin. Vincent had been so fascinated with the patterns on either side of the man's spine, he'd made it through the stitching without fainting or screaming.

Meili had worked fast, and the scar was minimal, likely because Vincent was diligent about using the ointment she'd given him. The pungent aroma followed him to bed, where, in the privacy of his mind, he did glorious things to her while stroking his cock.

In the cold light of today, the stained ceiling of her squalid shop reminded him of his childhood. There hadn't been this heavy aroma of opium, but he was all too familiar with that ripe stench of rotting fish and whatever people did in the streets when they didn't have access to a water closet or a bath.

The memory of that penury reinforced his desire to marry Pansy, the daughter of a gentleman. His new venture would put places like this firmly in his past.

Which made Meili a potential business partner. That's all.

Nevertheless, his interest in her sharpened when she spoke in aristocratic English.

"There are three people you never want to antagonize. Your grandmother, your landlord, and the person about to stab you."

"As I learned the day I met you."

She gave a hum of humor as she used a cotton pad to paint carbolic acid across each of his nipples. The wet chill caused them to contract and stand up. The sensation was delightful enough to draw his shoulder blades together.

"What can I call you?" he asked.

"Miss Fitzwilliam."

He didn't miss that using her English name held him at a distance. This was her world, and he was not part of it.

"Not Mrs?" he pried lightly. "How old are you?"

"Twenty-three. I'm not married. A wife lives with her husband's family, but my grandmother needs me." She studied him as she rubbed the damp pad all over her hands. "Where did you get it?" she asked with a nod to indicate his lap.

"Brazil. It was the first place I visited when I began buying goods for my uncle's company. He was disgusted with my earring and threatened to disown me over this." He drew his bottom lip into his mouth so the stud in his chin touched his top teeth. "I had to get something I knew he would never see."

"You hope," she said wryly. "He might see these." She nodded at his chest.

"I know, but I've wanted this for a long time. I kept telling myself it was pointless—" He lifted a brow to acknowledge his inadvertent pun. "I'll have to remove them when I marry, but to hell with it."

"Why would you have to remove them? It's your body."

And that was the source of his fascination with her. It wasn't that she wore a ring in her face with absent confidence. It was the fact she wore one at all. It was a quiet proclamation that she not only owned herself, but also shared a view with him that few others agreed with or understood.

"Our bodies are meant to be returned in the condition our maker provided, or so my aunt has informed me. Do you have more than that?" He flicked his gaze to the small ring she wore at the edge of her eyebrow.

"One needs a body to learn on."

"Oh?" His mind exploded with possibilities.

"Thankfully, my grandmother volunteers."

She kept a straight face, but after his flash of astonishment, he realized she was having him on. He choked on a laugh.

He liked her, damn it. Even before she had revealed that streak of humor, he'd noticed and admired her maturity and unshakable sense of competence. That's what had made him think of her when he embarked on this endeavor. He earned enough hostile glares on his way down the alley to know she was respected and valued by her neighbors. She was pretty, too, with her oval face and shiny black hair and slender figure. Too slender. He was glad she gouged him and ate well off of what he paid her.

"You're ready?" She had finished preparing her instruments and slipped the stud into the piercing needle.

He nodded and drew a deep breath, welcoming the discomfort as she pinched his nipple in a pair of tongs.

"You might find it helpful to count backward from ten. Slowly."

He nodded, but he was only thinking that he was glad he'd waited until now to have his nipples pierced. He liked that Meili was the one pressing the sharp point of the needle against such a sensitive place on his body. That she was using steady pressure to overcome the resistance in his skin, making the pain sharpen to a height that caused him to grind his teeth against a cry of protest.

Tension gave way to a bursting sensation. A fierce burn dried the air in his lungs. The needle seared through his nipple, turning his vision white. The pain was so acute, nausea tightened his stomach. His eyes watered, and the hardened lump in his chest was a condensed scream turned to ash.

He pushed the air from his lungs, overwhelmed by reactive anger and dread that it would happen again along with a sense of accomplishment that the first was done.

She tortured him by wriggling the gold stem inside his fresh injury as she rolled the gold ball onto the free end. Then she covered his bleeding nipple with a pad soaked in salt water. It stung like the center of burning fucking hell, but when she indicated he should hold the pad in place and pressed her hand over his, he closed his eyes and savored the wash of vulnerability that engulfed him.

"Breathe," she reminded.

He did, and she pinched his second nipple with the tongs. "Are you ready? Ten," she prompted softly.

"Nine," he said in agreement.

She impaled him.

Fire seared across his chest. His heart seemed to rock back and forth between the two points of agony. Seconds later, as the tiny shaft was wiggled by her winding the bead onto its end, his whole body trembled in reaction. His muscles didn't know if they wanted to run or curl protectively or fight a foe. His entire chest was stinging and burning and tight with an attempt to throw off this inescapable suffering.

Meili guided his free hand to hold the second pad. He blinked at that infernal ceiling, thinking of all the times he'd stared at a similar one, so hungry his stomach had felt like this—torn and salty and punished. He had often been exhausted but too cold to sleep on his thin mat. His back would be aching from a beating, his lips quivering in self-pity.

He tried to swallow the sob lodged in his throat. This pain wasn't so bad. He was overreacting. He had *asked* her to injure him.

But that old, severe hurt inside him fought to break from his throat the same way blood welled from the punctures in his skin. He wanted to cry. He really did.

"I'll bring you a drink." Her voice was gentle. Her cool knuckle briefly grazed his temple, picking up the wetness that leaked from the corner of his eye.

He popped his eyes open, but she was already rising and

walking away with her basin.

She left him for several minutes while she exchanged a few words with her grandmother and helped a customer who came and left.

Vincent didn't pay much attention. He was searching for remorse over having done this, wondering if Pansy would be repelled or if she would say, *It's your body.*

Meili came back. Her wide cotton skirt and jacket rustled as she knelt to offer him sweetened rice wine, picking up his head to help him sip. His cock twitched, which he knew was only an attempt of his body to prove it still worked after a shock to his system, but his desire for her increased as he gazed on her calm expression.

"Let me see?"

He picked up the pads, and they both stared at his angry, bloodied nipples sandwiched between round, gold beads.

Perhaps it was juvenile for a man of twenty-six to lash out against his uncle in a way that caused himself injury, but there was also something empowering in it. A sense of breaking free. *It* is *my body.*

Meili eased his head back onto the mat and prepared clean, dry pads.

Vincent had wanted to test her work, to see if she was a good fit for something he was determined to offer. There was money to be made. More importantly, quality jewelry and a skilled piercer were things people deserved, rather than clumsy hands that endangered lives with cheap metals and unclean equipment. This was a *service.*

Would he jeopardize his chances with Pansy by offering it? Would his uncle fire him?

Vincent had been sent here for a year. In the four months since he'd arrived, he had assembled the Hong Kong showroom as a mirror to the ones in London and New York. He had gained access to silk and porcelain and tea, along with other items that he exported to the other showrooms, proving he was a levelheaded man capable of sound business decisions. A man who could keep Pansy in the comforts to which she was accustomed.

If all Vincent had wanted to prove was Meili's competence, however, he could have had any part of his body pierced. He hadn't needed it to be a nipple, let alone both. No, this was for him, to mark a moment when he was stepping into himself rather than bowing to the man who kept him in a state of dependence.

*You'd have died in the poorhouse like your father if I hadn't taken you in*, Vincent had been told many times.

"Keep them clean and dry. Rinse them with salt water." Meili had him sit up so she could wrap his chest to hold the bandage pads in place. She offered a small packet of salt wrapped in strips of cotton. "If you're still bleeding after a few days, come see me."

"I want you." His heart swerved as her steady brown gaze flashed to his with shock. "To hire you," he added on a gulp.

*Pansy*, he reminded himself. He wanted the girl who had stolen his heart with a smile, making him believe he could have a woman like her.

He also wanted autonomy and time with this woman who intrigued him. He wanted *her*, but that was something he would reckon with privately.

"You did well," he made himself say. "I like it. Thank you."

A glow of shy pleasure stole into her cheeks. "You're welcome. If you want me to come to Queen's Road, you have to pay for the hours we close the shop along with my fee."

"And buy you new clothes," her grandmother said from beyond the screen. "Wealthy clients will expect you to be well-dressed."

Meili met his gaze with a small lift of her brows.

Vincent nodded. "Agreed."

# CHAPTER THREE

Meili had two reasons for asking the owner of the teahouse to check on her grandmother. One, because she didn't know how long she would be away, and two, because when a young woman left in a new silk cheongsam to meet an Englishman at a hotel, questions would be asked. Best to give the biggest gossip in the neighborhood that particular dandelion of news to blow across the field.

If Meili hadn't been worried about arriving with muddy feet, she would have walked and pocketed the rickshaw fare. It felt pretentious to ride. Plus, it allowed her mind to wander to the deep sincerity in Vincent's voice when he had said, *I want you.*

People said odd things when they were on her mat, mind fogged with pain. She knew better than to take any of it to heart, but she'd been in her own cloud of euphoria from pushing the needle through Vincent's nipples.

She loved the rush of power in piercing, but as she'd seen an involuntary tear squeeze out of his eye, she'd felt a deep privilege, too. A pang had struck in her chest, and she'd wanted to lean down and kiss him.

When he had said, *You did well. I like it. Thank you*, it hadn't been effusive praise, but it had sounded heartfelt. She'd been moved.

Why? They were strangers. Clients often felt a connection to her after piercing. It came from the trust they placed in her. She had never felt such an intense return of that emotion, but she was inexplicably excited to see him today. She leaped from the rickshaw as soon as it stopped. The runner had already been paid, so she brushed the dust from her clothes and entered the Gainsborough Trading Company in the ground level of a hotel.

"Welcome," a middle-aged man greeted her.

She told him her name, and he led her through arrangements of teak and mahogany furniture on silk rugs. Brass bowls, porcelain vases, and crystal glassware were displayed on tabletops. Colorful parasols hung from the ceiling, clocks ticked, and mirrors reflected the green of her new clothes.

They walked past furs and perfumes, rattan baskets and rolled rugs jumbled with cookware, sacks of tobacco, and roasted coffee beans. A cool, pungent aroma hung on the air, teasing her to explore the treasures to be found here.

The man knocked on an open swing door and announced her. Vincent looked up from the papers on his desk. A flash of something transformed his expression. Gladness? He smoothed his face into a polite welcome as he rose and came around to greet her.

"Miss Fitzwilliam. Please come in."

The other man closed the door on his way out.

Meili kept hold of the latch.

"You'll have to trust me if we're entering a partnership," Vincent said of the way she hovered by the door. "I trusted you, didn't I?" He started to fold his arms, then stopped himself, setting his hands on the edge of his desk as he leaned his hips there.

Meili eyed the double-breasted lapels of his suit jacket. "How are you feeling?" It had been three days.

"As though I have salted nails pounded into my chest. It's unrelenting."

She knew. "You must be satisfied, though? Or you wouldn't have called me here."

"I am. A couple is expecting us, but let's discuss terms first. Mr. Kemp is asking for a stud in his tongue. His wife wants something more intimate. Is there any piercing you won't do?"

Meili drew many boundaries for herself, but it felt odd to speak of them. She was exposing her value system. She wasn't embarrassed, but she didn't know him. He was bound to judge.

"Also pricing," he said as he took up a ledger book from his desk. "Do you prefer to charge by the hour or the complexity of the work?"

"The location of the piercing, but every person is different." She took her hand off the door and absently smoothed the strap of her shoulder bag. "Some people have a vein in an inconvenient place or some other restriction. I will refuse piercings that won't work for a particular body. I won't charge if that happens."

"Fair." He searched out his pen.

"They have to be sober," she continued. "A sip of alcohol for courage is fine, but I never pierce anyone who is too drunk to know what they're doing. They must have the sense to keep it clean while it heals. I don't want a death on my conscience."

"I don't want a reputation for causing fevers or infections," he agreed and dipped his pen in the open bottle of ink. "Anyone I deem too careless to manage their healing can find their way to the den at the harbor. So... Start with ears. How much?"

"Don't call me for earlobes. You can do that yourself. The other parts?" She touched the cartilage in her ear, calculating how much wealthy travelers might pay.

Vincent didn't bat an eyelash as she rattled off extravagant fees for nose piercings, in and around the mouth, between fingers, down the spine, and more intimate places.

"That's more experience than I thought you would have."

Had he not noticed the two brothels in her alley? The women had noticed *him*. They also knew a sparkle from an unexpected place drew the eye in a crowded field. Plenty of men were willing to pay for the privilege of watching a woman receive a new and uniquely situated adornment while getting one for themselves. Meili had a *lot* of practice.

"If there's a request for something I've never done, I will quote once I've examined the client," she concluded.

"Good." He finished writing and closed the ledger. "We'll do it like your shop, with a screen for privacy. I'll stay in the room, especially if it's a man. We don't want anyone confused about what sort of service they've paid for."

She had been wondering about that and nodded with relief, only to realize it meant she would be trusting him. Did she? He wasn't wrong. He had entrusted her with his body. He was allowing her to work under his company's name.

"Shall we visit Mr. and Mrs. Kemp?" He glanced at the clock, then tilted a confiding look at her. "She's not really his wife."

"I'm shocked," she said facetiously.

His mouth twitched, and he came to stand at the door. She could have stepped back, could have lowered her gaze, but she stayed where his dynamic aura engulfed her. She fell upward into his silver-gray eyes. Her feet may have left the floor.

This was the push-pull of lust that she had heard about but never experienced. Want warred with ingrained caution. Longing tried to overcome a sense of danger. Something similar was happening to him, because a hungry light came into his eyes while his expression pulled with a grimace as he exerted self-control.

He showed his teeth and sucked a breath through them, nostrils twitching. "I feel them now. All of them."

"All—" Her own nipples were stingingly aware of the small shafts stuck through them. There was a tickle at her navel where her abdomen nervously pulled in, causing the dangling charm to dance. Lower, there was a rush of heat to flesh that plumped, shifting the small rings daintily lining her inner lips. A tickling sensation deep in her folds urged her to rub it away.

Meili was not a bashful person, but her cheeks grew hot as Vincent admitted to reacting to her. She pictured his naked chest and the nipples she'd pierced.

"I have to ask…" He scraped his teeth down to the stud in his bottom lip, then released it, as though it was an absent habit. "What do you like about it?"

"Piercing?" She cocked her head, considering. "I take pride in doing it quickly and cleanly. It's satisfying to see a person happy with the result."

His smile flickered. "I meant what do you like about having it done? Because I had forgotten this part." He waved at his chest. "Waiting for it to heal. I knew the piercing would hurt like the devil. I like that pain. It purges something in me. Once it's healed, I like the sensation of wearing jewelry. Something I choose to wear that others may or may not see. I like what you said the other day, that it's my body. My piercing is evidence I've claimed it. This ache, though? I'd forgotten how much I like it, but I'm not sure why I do."

"Oh, um…" She swallowed. "My pain is self-inflicted, so it's… I guess I enjoy testing myself? I like the effort it takes to concentrate through the pain so I can keep my hands steady and finish. And the elation after it's done. I love that. Then I like the ritual of cleaning it while it heals. I congratulate myself again and again on putting myself through the ordeal." Her throat thickened. She'd never told anyone that and expected him to laugh at her.

He nodded, somber. "That's it. I like the reminder of why I did it, as if my resolve is being tested. The sting of the rinse affirms that I'm the one who decides what happens to me."

"I like the secretiveness," she confided in a near whisper for no reason except that they had both lowered their voices. "My grandmother knows about this one." She pointed at her eyebrow. "And that I pierced my nipples. She doesn't know about the rest. Many of my clients will only show their piercings to their spouse or lovers, but *I* know. I know *your* secret, but no one knows mine." A smile pulled at her mouth. "That pleases me."

*Show me.* He didn't say it, but she saw the excited desire to see her piercings flare in his eyes as he swept his gaze down her body.

The way her heart lurched should have been with alarm. It

wasn't. She had never been tempted to reveal all her rings and rods, but Vincent might genuinely appreciate them. He wouldn't look on them as a novelty or something she did for his titillation. He would understand how deeply personal each one was to her. He would respect and revere them.

Unnerved by how easily she was attributing good qualities to him, allowing him to slide past her defenses, she asked, "Should we go?"

He glanced at the bag she adjusted against her hip.

"If this works out, I'll buy you a set of tools to keep here so you don't have to carry that back and forth. Why don't you pick out a smarter bag in the meantime?"

She stepped away from the door as he started to open it, but hugged her bag tighter. "I like this one. If you change our terms now, you'll think everything is up for renegotiation."

He paused with his hand holding the edge of the door. "You're what we call a stickler, Miss Fitzwilliam. Do you know what that word means?"

He didn't have to sound so patronizing.

"Someone who sticks people?" she asked with an ingenue's blink.

He released a chuckle while waving her to walk ahead of him.

"Yes. Someone who knows how to deliver a sharp jab. It's a very good thing I enjoy that sensation, since we'll be seeing so much of each other."

"I don't intend to show you much of myself at all," she said pertly, but she dipped her head to hide that her cheeks were hot with a desire to do so.

• • •

The green of Meili's skirt and jacket had the effect of giving her skin a golden hue. Her hair was not in one of those rat-nest styles European women insisted on wearing, but was parted in the middle and pulled back, braided and secured at her nape, allowing the gloss in her black hair to gleam.

Yet much of her remained hidden. Vincent wanted to know everything about her—where she was pierced and why she only had her grandmother. How she lived in the poor part of the island but didn't seem fazed by the hotel's extravagant decor or Western architecture.

"Where did you learn English?" he asked as they climbed the wide stairs.

"My mother. Her family were missionaries. My father was a doctor. He was studying Western medicine at the mission hospital. I practiced my reading on his medical books, then we talked about what I'd learned. When I was old enough, he taught me to treat my grandmother's pain with needles. Then he sent me to treat other women with bound feet."

"That was progressive of him, to encourage you to practice medicine."

"Women often refuse to see a doctor because they don't want to speak to a man. He wanted me to become a doctor for women."

"You would make a good one. You're not squeamish, and you have a knack for stitching and remedies. Is that something you're pursuing?" He didn't think he'd ever heard of a woman doctor anywhere, at home or abroad.

Meili choked on a rancorous laugh. "First, I need permission from the government to build a school for girls. Then I need money to build it and salaries for teachers willing to instruct women. Once I graduate from that school, I could request to study medicine at a hospital."

"Not that you've given thought on how to go about it."

"None," she said drily.

"What about England? Could you attend a women's college there? I believe there's one dedicated to nursing. That would be a start, wouldn't it?"

"Who would look after my grandmother?"

"You don't have other family?"

"In England. The Fitzwilliams. My brother met them when he went to Oxford. They don't want anything to do with us. Our grandfather married Mama to gain access to her connections in the hongs, but he already had a wife in England. They had no respect for his concubine and dismissed us as illegitimate. They also dealt in opium, so we don't care for them, either." She flicked her hand to emphasize how inconsequential they were. "After our parents were lost in a storm while traveling to Guangzhou, my grandmother, Mama, said we should sell our house at the Peak so Peng could study in England. She thought a Western education would help him marry into a wealthy family. His wife would care for her, and he would arrange a good marriage for me. Instead, he got sick and died before he could come home."

She spoke stoically, but her anguish speared through his chest like an arrow.

"I'm so sorry."

She nodded. "We are, too. But I'm where I'm needed. If a woman from the brothel is afraid to speak to a doctor, I do it for her. What I earn here today will allow me to help people who otherwise can't afford medicine for themselves or their babies."

For years, Vincent's focus had been on turning a profit to better his own prospects and earn his uncle's good graces. He'd forgotten there were higher priorities. He had forgotten there were women who cared about more than the quality of lace on a gown.

He pondered that as he knocked on the door of an American traveling with a French woman ten years his senior. As far as Vincent could tell, "Mrs. Kemp" was a well-educated widow with limited means and a desire to travel. She had brought Mr. Kemp and his wallet to Vincent's private display case, and that was all Vincent needed to know.

They entered to see the privacy screen—made of silk panels painted with birds and blossoms—had been delivered with a cot and other conveniences like a basin, towels, hot water, and a new bottle of carbolic acid.

Kemp was the type of client Vincent most wished to cater to—adventurous enough to travel far from home and eager to impress others with what he'd picked up along the way. His deep pockets meant he could afford baubles for his tongue and someone to mash his food for him while it healed.

Vincent introduced Meili.

Kemp skipped the niceties to say with bashful curiosity, "I've heard women like a man who has one. Especially when he..." He set the V of his fingers against his lips and waggled his tongue between them.

Meili had every right to be disgusted, but she seemed unbothered. "I've never heard women complain about it. You will have to wait at least a month to test for yourself."

Kemp gave a self-conscious chuckle.

Vincent had a sudden desire to pierce his own tongue to discover if *she* liked it.

"Mrs." Kemp joined them, wearing only a thin bathing robe. She was a sophisticated woman who knew what she wanted and was happy to spend Kemp's money getting it.

Meili asked to see the jewelry they'd chosen. The tongue stud was a simple bead of gold, but the other was a beautiful piece Vincent hadn't imagined selling so quickly. The gold shaft was slightly curved with a small ball on the bottom and a sparkling diamond on the top. It held a chain of three cascading diamonds.

"Where exactly did you want this?" Meili asked.

"My hood. To guide a man toward appreciating what's beneath."

Kemp stopped pacing and brought his straightened arms forward into a single clap. "I know it should be 'ladies first,' but I won't sit still until I've got mine."

"By all means, mon amour." Mrs. Kemp led him to a chair and perched on the arm, then ran her fingers through his hair.

Vincent brought one of the dining chairs from the table so Meili could sit in front of Kemp. He also brought an end table so she could unroll the small mat that held her tools.

She had Kemp lean forward and stick out his tongue. They discussed placement, came to an agreement, and she had him swish his mouth with salt water. He then spit into the cup and made a noise of disgust.

"Get used to the flavor," she said. "I want you to do that every hour for the first few days."

After ensuring everything was freshly cleaned, she asked, "Are you ready?"

"Yes." Kemp took hold of his knees, knuckles white.

Vincent stood behind her chair and watched over her shoulder. There was absolutely no reason he should find another man's tongue clamped in a pair of tongs arousing, but he got a thrill from the way Meili was so damned sure of herself.

"Take a deep breath and count backward from ten..."

*Nine, eight...* Tension gripped Vincent as he silently counted, watching her press the needle into Kemp's tongue. A throaty noise of protest began to emanate from Kemp. His body jolted as the needle sank through his flesh.

Meili was already pulling the stud through. "It's done. Hold still while I secure it."

Seconds later, Kemp sagged back into his chair, face sheened with sweat.

"Fuck me. Oh, fuck, that feels odd." His tongue sounded thick, but he was grinning giddily. "How does it look?"

There was a moment of confusion until Vincent fetched a hand mirror off the dressing table in the bedroom. He made a note to have one delivered with the screen in future.

Kemp was pleased, and Vincent was so proud of Meili he squeezed her shoulder.

She looked up, startled, saw him beaming at her like he was made of electricity, and she grew so shy in his glow, she nearly disappeared into her shrugged shoulders. Why? What she'd done was amazing.

When he glanced back at Kemp, the man had his hand inside Mrs. Kemp's robe. He fondled her tit while she cradled his head and kissed his brow, murmuring in French.

Vincent started to set the screen in front of the cot, but Mrs. Kemp said, "Don't bother. You can both watch if you want to." She rose and walked to the cot.

Vincent glanced at Meili. She shrugged. "I often have an audience."

What sort of twisted person was he that he was more excited to watch her do the piercing than he was to see a woman's sex as it was pierced? The care Meili took with cleaning her instruments filled Vincent with such anticipation, his cock twitched in his trousers. His nipples were stinging with arousal, reminding him of what she had done to him only a few days ago. He wanted her to do it again. Soon.

Kemp had a good view from where he sat and only shifted the angle of his chair. Vincent moved so he was above the French woman's head. He wanted to watch Meili's expression as she worked. She grew more focused as the moment neared, setting everything close to hand before she asked Mrs. Kemp to open her robe and part her legs.

The other woman sat on the end of the cot. She reclined and bent her knees, letting them fall open to expose her trimmed bush.

"You're comfortable? Relaxed? Will you spread your lips for me so we can discuss placement?"

The other woman complied, showing no self-consciousness or nerves. Perhaps she was thinking about the fortune in diamonds about to be attached there.

"This glass tube will receive the needle. I'll slide it under your hood, then pierce into it. The jewelry follows, and you'll be done. Take a few breaths. Tell me when you're ready."

Mrs. Kemp licked her lips and took two measured breaths. "Oui. Proceed."

"Take one more breath and count backward. *Ten. Nine…*"

As the tube invaded beneath her hood, the woman stilled. Her eyes widened as the needle touched her flesh. Her fists tightened on the edges of the cot. Her whole body went taut. Her jaw opened in a silent scream. Her wild eyes stared blindly at the ceiling.

"Fuuuck," Kemp said from across the room.

"*Six, five…*" Vincent reminded calmly.

"The jewelry is in. Keep counting while I secure it," Meili murmured.

"Quatre," Mrs. Kemp said shakily. "Trois. Deux."

"Done."

# CHAPTER FOUR

Meili was trying to think of practical things as she returned to Vincent's office—things like whether she should be charging more. She hadn't realized his clients were buying jewelry that cost as much as a small hospital.

She was too exalted to think properly. People watched her all the time when she pierced, but no one had ever looked at her the way Vincent had when she pressed a pad between Mrs. Kemp's legs and glanced up.

Her stomach was still swirling with butterflies from his undisguised awe.

Once her shock wore off, Mrs. Kemp had been very pleased. Meili had reminded her she should limit how much she touched her new jewels.

"It's very pretty, don't you think?" The French woman had insisted Vincent give her pussy an approving nod before he prepared his invoice for Kemp.

On their way out, Meili had reminded the couple to curtail sex.

"We can amuse ourselves in other ways." Mrs. Kemp had moved to kneel at Mr. Kemp's feet. "I should thank you, cher, for my pretty new bauble."

"That went even better than I expected." Vincent closed the door of his office before he opened his arms. "I could kiss you, I'm so drunk on how exciting that was."

She could have refused, but his exuberance so closely matched her own, she flowed toward him as though pushed by a current in a stream.

He must not have expected her to comply, because he caught his breath and reflexively took hold of her upper arms, holding her off before she crashed into his healing nipples. That made her giggle, but he recovered and erased her grin with the swift, hot press of his mouth.

Meili had few assets, but they were powerful ones—her education, her independence, and her reputation. She knew how much a love affair could damage two of those, so she was careful not to let a man impact her. That's why she had held Vincent at a distance. He was the sort of man who could muddle a woman into imagining a different life only to discover that "different" meant penniless, pregnant, and selling oneself for a place to sleep.

As his lips coaxed hers open, however, and he swept his tongue into her mouth, she thought a kiss like this might be worth ruination. Her senses were piqued by the piercing. She'd had to block out everything except what was before her, staying intensely focused for long seconds until the moment of completion arrived. The act created a need for release that was as potent as a sexual one.

That's all this was, she told herself. They were burning up the kindled tension of sharing something intimate.

He acknowledged as much, nuzzling across her cheek and grazing his lips against her eyebrow. "I didn't mean to do this. Stop me."

She didn't. She pressed his back to the door and opened his jacket, watching him as she slipped free the buttons of his waistcoat. By the time she was working on his shirt buttons, his nostrils were quivering. His heavy hands ran from her shoulders to her waist and hips.

She spread his shirt and lifted his undershirt. The redness was fading, and the tiny beads caught the light as he took uneven breaths.

"I want to lick them." She couldn't. Not until they were fully healed, but she framed his nipples in the notches of her thumbs and forefingers while she pressed her mouth to his breastbone.

"You don't want to know the things I want to do to you." His chest rose when she branded him with her lips and scraped her teeth on his muscles and licked at his collarbone. "I want to kiss every hole in your body. Take that however you want."

He shifted his feet open and slid down the door until he was eye level with her, then dragged her into the space and kissed her again.

This time, when his tongue swept into her mouth, she let him find the shaft and beads in the webbing beneath her tongue. He groaned with delight.

She was between his legs, arms framing his head on the door, carefully holding herself back from pressing on his nipples, but her stomach brushed his. His steely erection pressed through their clothing, the ridge of it hard against her mound.

He splayed his hand on one cheek of her bottom and pulled her tighter against it.

A flash of pleasure-pain speared through her as her nether piercings caught in silk and were pulled a little too roughly.

"Let me." She slid a hand down to make a small adjustment, ensuring the rings all lay in the same direction, then pressed her vulva against the line of his cock.

He watched her through his lashes, voice rasped with lust as he asked, "How many?"

"Enough to keep your lips busy. Does this hurt you?" She thrust against him. The small tugs of her piercings added to the stimulation on the stud over her clitoris. Her breath shortened.

He slid down another half inch and released a moan. "It feels perfect. Come here."

He cupped her cheek, and they kissed while she moved in the slow rhythm that sat on the edge between pleasure and pain. If he had tried to take control, he might have hurt her, but he held still and let her take the lead while he whispered encouragement between his kisses.

"Christ. Right there. Can you do it harder? Fuck that feels good."

She clenched her hand in his bunched undershirt, bracing her fist in the hollow of his shoulder while she kissed him flagrantly and ground herself harder, reaching for the pinnacle that danced teasingly out of reach. Almost there. Almost…

"Ahhhh." Climax arrived in a sweet burst of joy, showering her in lovely, throbbing waves of tingling pleasure.

"Fuck," he said in a guttural voice, liable to leave fingerprints on her buttock. His body shuddered, and he hissed with anguish. "I'm coming. Ah, fuck."

She was glad, so glad, and kept rubbing into him, drawing out the pleasure for both of them, losing herself in bliss until his head clapped back against the door with a dull thud.

"What the hell did you just do to me, Miss Fitzwilliam?"

• • •

Days later, Vincent was still embarrassed at popping off like a first-year browsing descriptions of ladies' corsets. And contrite. He should have told Meili about Pansy before letting things go that far.

He hadn't expected her to be all over him like jam on biscuits, though. His brain had fallen into the flesh she'd been grinding against so exquisitely. He had only come back to his senses when she had said ruefully, "I'll give you privacy," adding as she slipped around the door, "You may call me Meili."

He should bloody well hope so, but, *What am I to do with you, Meili?*

What was he to do about Pansy? They weren't formally engaged, but he'd spoken to her father. Having that marriage prospect had persuaded Vincent's uncle to entrust Vincent with this showroom in Hong Kong. Vincent was here to prove his worth, not fuck around with local women while embarking on a questionable business enterprise.

"Miss Fitzwilliam is here to see you," his showroom manager announced.

Vincent's heart soared as Meili entered. The soft look on her face tugged him between tenderness and loss, the reaction so visceral and agonizing, he cleared his throat as he stood. He instinctively set his hand on the letter that had only gotten as far as *Dear P.*

"Meili," he said gruffly, swiping his damp palms on his trousers. "You left before we settled up. Let's attend to that first." He opened a drawer and offered the purse of coins he'd counted out.

She tested the weight and glanced to see they were silver. Her expression rearranged itself into something more aloof as she set it back on his desk.

"That's too much." Shadows of resentment came into her eyes.

Oh, fuck. "That's not what this is. I didn't add for—" *Shut up, Vincent.* "Kemp offered a gratuity. You did the work, so it should be yours."

"Kemp did?" Her mouth twisted with repugnance. "This won't work after all."

Vincent caught the glimmer of hurt in her eyes before she turned away.

"Meili."

"Miss Fitzwilliam," she corrected sharply, already at the door.

"I told you I didn't mean for that to happen." He dropped into his chair so hard it squeaked with protest. "This doesn't have anything to do with that." He nudged the purse closer to the front of the desk. "I saw Kemp this morning before he left. He thanked me again and said he would recommend us. Don't walk away before we have a chance to see how successful we can be."

Her fist was clenched around the strap of her bag, her conflict obvious as she flickered her gaze between the purse and his face, trying to read him.

"A pair of young men upstairs want their lips done. There's a woman who wants a very expensive stone in her navel. You'll make that again." He nodded at the coins, thinking he should write her a draft so she would be less likely to be robbed. "Do you really want to walk away because we *both* exercised poor judgment?"

Her chin set belligerently as he called her out as an equal participant in their tryst.

"It won't happen again," he swore.

"No, it won't," she assured him, cheeks flushed.

He believed her. She might as well have driven a stake into his chest, but he knew it was for the best, so he nodded at her to take the money. When she did, he asked her to sign the ledger that she had done so. They left to make their appointments.

# CHAPTER FIVE

Two months passed with nothing between them but professional conversations. Meili went to the hotel once or twice a week and earned more in an hour than she made in three months at the shop. She began accepting drafts and had to open a bank account.

That made her nervous, as did this whole arrangement. When she had the opportunity, she spoke to Vincent's comprador. He was Vincent's go-between with the hongs, and she asked him for advice on how she might invest her money. She had considered offering to buy out her landlord, but she didn't want to count on this piecework income from Vincent lasting forever.

The comprador found her a building close to their shop. It was in good repair and had a comfortable living area for her grandmother, an alcove for treating clients, and two rooms that could be rented to help pay their mortgage.

Meili told herself she was being sensible, securing a future for herself and Mama, but she felt hollow inside. When she looked back on her argument with Vincent, it seemed childish. Why had she presumed he wanted to pay her for their embrace? Why was she so crushed by his *It won't happen again*?

She was freezing him out because she was hurt, but would she rather he had pressed her into an affair?

"My comprador tells me you're moving," Vincent said beside her, pulling her from her ruminations to the hotel stairs they were climbing.

She frowned, wondering why he was speaking to his comprador about her.

"In two weeks," she replied. "I won't be able to see clients for a few days."

"Can I help?"

"With the move? Why?"

"Because we're friends."

"We're business partners."

He left a heavy pause, then said, "You have all those jars and shelves. I don't want you to injure yourself and be unable to work. I could hire men and a wagon. Your grandmother would be more comfortable in a rickshaw than walking."

"I've spoken to some men in our neighborhood."

"What kind of men?"

"The kind who take odd jobs to feed their families."

"Not the kind trying to court you?"

"Is that why you spoke to your comprador about me?" she asked with affront. "Did you think he and I were forming an attachment?"

"No." That was a lie, she suspected, but he stopped at a door and gave a firm rap. "Before we go in here, I should apologize for—"

"Vinny!" The door swung open, and a cheery man with red-brown hair urged, "Come in, come in." He waved them to the sitting area and closed the door. "This must be your special friend?"

"That's not what I called you." Vincent set down the box he often brought to potential clients. He self-consciously squeezed the back of his neck. "Miss Fitzwilliam is my business partner."

Was that resentment in his tone that she had affirmed that's all they were?

"Andrew is an old friend from London. We were catching up last night. I told him about our side venture. He asked for a consult."

"I wanted to get a look at you," Andrew said with a boyish grin. "When a man talks of throwing away his future, you get curious about the woman inspiring it."

"That's not what I said." Vincent swore under his breath.

"We were drunk. I said I like it here and wouldn't mind staying. London is cold and damp, especially this time of year."

The humidity here would be appalling soon; then they would be into typhoon season. It wasn't paradise.

"He also thinks the women in London are terrible. I'm paraphrasing." Andrew winked at her, letting her know he was deliberately winding up his friend. "He thinks you're smart, running your own business and investing your additional income in a building."

"Miss Fitzwilliam's time is as valuable as mine," Vincent declared firmly. "If you brought us here to waste it, we'll leave."

On the contrary, Meili had all day for this. She pressed her lips together, trying not to be flattered, but embers of warmth in her belly glowed. Vincent thought she was smart!

"I *am* curious." Andrew waved at Vincent. "Show me what you have."

They all sat. Vincent removed the stacked trays from the box and set each on the coffee table. The first held modest gold bars and studs. The intimate jewelry was in the middle, and extravagant pieces with precious jewels were kept in the bottom tray.

"Where do all these go, then?" Andrew asked Meili.

It was common that she speak with clients who simply wanted to know more. Sometimes they called her back after thinking about it. Other times she never saw them again.

When they got to nipple bars, Andrew lifted his chin at Vincent. "Show me yours."

Vincent made an impatient noise. "You've seen them."

"I was drunk last night. Miss Fitzwilliam put them in, didn't she? Don't be modest."

With a muttered curse, Vincent stood to unbutton his jacket and waistcoat, then his shirt. He picked up his undershirt to show one nipple. His attitude was very churlish, gaze pinned to the window while Andrew examined her work.

"You've put jade on them." Meili almost reached out to touch the polished bead on the gold horseshoe he had attached to the studs. She tucked her hands in her lap but couldn't drag her gaze off how lovely it looked. "It's not too heavy?"

"I felt it for a few days. I'm used to it now." He pinched the flesh of his flat breast to lift his nipple and allow the bead to roll on its ring.

"It's beautiful," she said with heartfelt sincerity.

"Thank you." He dropped his hand and pulled his undershirt back down, avoiding her gaze as he straightened his clothing, but there was a pink tinge across his cheekbones.

"Wait. Do you really have one downstairs?" Andrew nodded at Vincent's trousers.

"Yes." Vincent continued tucking the tails of his shirt.

"Show me."

"I know you think this is something to be laughed at, but Miss Fitzwilliam and I take this very seriously. Quit being a lobcock."

"Pun intended?"

Vincent shot him a glower before he said to Meili, "I'm sorry about this. There's a couple upstairs who have already purchased the jewelry they want. Your trip isn't wasted."

"Come on," Andrew cajoled. "You have to admit your claim sounds outrageous. Show me, and I promise I'll buy something even if I don't wear it home. I'll pay you for your time," he added to Meili.

Vincent's mouth tightened. "Would you prefer to wait in the hall?"

"I've inserted similar pieces. I'll stay if you don't mind." She'd been curious since he'd told her he wore one.

Expression twisting with annoyance, Vincent opened his trouser buttons. He shifted aside his underwear and grasped his cock at the base. His handling caused it to firm, especially when he stretched the skin back from the tip, revealing the thick gold ring with a bead that plunged into his hole and emerged from the bottom of his shaft.

If Andrew hadn't been here, Meili would have taken that tip in her mouth. She would have run her tongue everywhere she could reach and would have sucked hard, making him grow thick and pulse until he spilled down her throat.

Andrew was agog. "I'm sorry for the language, Miss Fitzwilliam, but do women really want to fuck that?"

She did. She really did.

"Some enjoy it." She fought to retain an impassive expression and a steady voice. "I heard of a chipped tooth once from a woman pleasuring a man with her mouth. Once it heals, the man can remove it if his partner doesn't like it."

"How much does it hurt?" Andrew looked to Vincent.

"Like a motherfucker." He tucked his stiff cock back into his clothing and buttoned up.

"What about when you..." He shook his loose fist.

"It adds a little something." Vincent shrugged. "I like it."

"Hmph." Andrew sat back in contemplation.

"I would recommend this." Meili picked out a simple curved bar and handed it to Andrew.

He turned it over in his fingers. "Is there a thinner one so it wouldn't hurt as much?"

"You don't want it too thin or it may cut your skin as it heals. This is a good gauge." She explained the process, including how to keep it clean and how long he would have to avoid sexual contact.

They left a short time later and went along to the other couple, where Meili pierced the woman's navel and the man's scrotum.

Vincent hadn't said much by the time they returned to his office. They typically made a few notes on the clients they'd seen, agreeing on charges and discussing which days she might be free to come next. It was always a tense few minutes during which they pretended they weren't reacting to whatever piercing she had performed, but she always left wishing he would kiss her again. She wanted him to fuck her. That was the truth.

Today, the air was laden with even more undercurrents. She was sorry they'd been reduced to this antagonistic relationship. If he was complimenting her behind her back and embarrassed to be caught doing it, he wasn't holding a grudge against her. She was the one making things uncomfortable, calling them business partners when he considered her a friend.

"I hope you don't mind I saw your pierce?" She peered up from where she was tucking her bank draft into the secure pocket of her bag on her lap.

"Are you asking if I'm feeling exposed? I am," he muttered, closing the ledger and pushing it aside as he sat back in his chair. "Not because you saw my todger or because of Andrew's prickish meddling, either."

"Mr. Gainsborough—"

"You just saw my cock, Meili. Call me Vincent."

"Vincent." His name felt lovely on her tongue. "I know I've been cool. I want us to be friends. You've given me a tremendous opportunity and treat me fairly. I appreciate it."

"I haven't been fair, though. The things Andrew hinted at…" He blew out a frustrated breath. "Don't walk out until I've told you everything. Promise?"

"Why? What are you going to say?" She closed her hands on her bag and pressed into her chair, sensing she wouldn't like it.

"Promise me."

She jerked a shoulder, acquiescing.

"You have to understand where I come from." His chair squeaked as he shifted with discomfort. "Gainsborough isn't my name. It was my mother's. Her brother, my uncle, told me to use it when he took me from my brute of a father after my mother died. As much as I resent my uncle's control over me, I'm indebted to him for my education and the standard of living I enjoy."

She nodded, unsurprised to hear he'd come from a difficult background. People often pierced a private part of themselves to exorcise deeply private pain.

"I hated being poor. One of the reasons I urged my uncle to carry the jewelry we offer is the potential for profit. He only sees the lewdness, not the beauty or reward. I haven't told him I'm doing this. I invested my own money, and it *is* lucrative. We're doing well, yes?"

She couldn't deny it. She nodded hesitantly.

"It doesn't take away from my work in the showroom, and those profits are healthy enough my uncle shouldn't have any complaints about what I do on the side. If he learned about it, however..." He drummed his fingers on his chair arm. "It's especially sticky because I'm only meant to be here a year."

*Oh.* This was why he had secured her promise to stay and hear him out. She clenched her hands tighter on her bag. "How much longer do you have?"

"My assignment ends in September."

Five months. Her heart squeezed. Her mind raced. At least her financial choices had been sound. She had suspected there could be an abrupt end to this. She couldn't afford the fancy jewelry that the fancy people wanted. She and Vincent depended on each other to make this work. If he left, his clientele were out of her reach. This income would be gone.

"Andrew is here on business for his father. My uncle asked him to check on me and report back on my activities."

"And you told him what we're doing?" That would force him to stop, wouldn't it? Loss slid into her like a hot blade. "You shouldn't have."

"I was drunk," he said with a twist of his lips. "We're old friends, and he's acquainted with a woman to whom I'm..." He pinched the bridge of his nose. "Somewhat attached."

"Some— *What?*" The word gusted out of her.

"You promised," he said quickly, noting how she had thrust her weight to the front of her chair. He held up a hand and pinned her in place with his intense stare. "Pansy and I are not engaged. Her father wouldn't allow it until I demonstrated my ability to provide her a good life." He waved at the showroom beyond the door. "My intention was to go back and take over the London showroom, where I would assist my uncle with running the company as a whole. I don't love her, Meili. I loved the *idea* of her. She's a fashionable young woman with a powerful father. Marrying her would prove I was no longer the starved, desperate rat my uncle rescued."

Meili heard the words, but she was too scorned to absorb them. Her heart wasn't ready to be moved by the agony that tightened his expression.

"No one here knows that I was a downtrodden wretch. I have nothing to prove here except that I'm an honest businessman. I am. I like it here. I like working with you. I like *you*."

"What?" Confusion scrambled her head, making his words impossible to comprehend. Her heart rate picked up as she waited for him to say more.

His palm opened in entreaty. "But if I throw over Pansy and tell my uncle I'd rather stay here to pierce cocks, he will take all of this away." He waved at the showroom. "Which wouldn't make me much of a prospect, would it? Not for you."

He wanted her to see him as one? Her heart flitted inside her chest like a trapped bird.

"That doesn't matter," she blurted, but it did. They both knew it. "What will you do?"

He shook his head. "I don't know."

• • •

As Meili rearranged pillows in an armchair and draped towels over them, Vincent said, "We should have a specialized chair built—something that would be comfortable for the client, but also allow you the access you need."

"That would be a big expense," she murmured. "Too heavy

to carry to the rooms."

True, but Vincent also wished they could build a dedicated parlor in the showroom. It would be more convenient than carrying everything to different rooms. He understood clients liked to be discreet, but time and effort would be saved if customers came to them.

He heard what Meili was really saying, though. *You won't be here.*

She could put the chair in her shop, though. He wanted her to be comfortable, too.

He wanted to give her a lot of things, he acknowledged moodily.

"What's too heavy?" Andrew asked, emerging from the bedroom in a quilted dressing gown. "Me? Am I liable to faint and need carrying to the bed?"

"Are you the fainting type?" Meili asked.

"I'll probably swear." Andrew had gone to the mainland for a week and returned with the blunt news that he wished to have his cock pierced.

Would it make Andrew more or less liable to tell Vincent's uncle what his nephew was doing between dickering over the cost of porcelain plates and teacups?

"Do you prefer privacy, or are you comfortable with me watching?" Vincent asked.

"Do you *like* to watch?" Andrew asked with surprise.

"I do." He didn't prevaricate. What was the point? As Andrew had noted last week, Vincent was on the verge of throwing away a very sound future, and for what?

This. Watching Meili perch on a footstool and unroll her mat of instruments on a small table, then begin cleaning them. He listened to her explain what each would be used for so Andrew knew what to expect.

"I'll pierce from beneath the head and come out your eye. Then the end of this bar..." She took the bead off the curved gold stud. "Goes into the hole in the needle." The needle was hollow, the tip cut at an angle to form the necessary point. "The bar will push the needle out the way it came in. It stays embedded in your tip. It's very quick."

"Fuck." Andrew was white. "Okay." He nodded. "Do it."

She read people so well, too. If they needed time, she slowed down and answered their questions, reassuring them. If they were like Andrew, agitated and wanting it over, she deftly got down to business.

"Most of my clients like to place their hands over their scrotum. Yes, like that. I'll paint you with carbolic acid…" She did.

Andrew's cock twitched, swelling slightly at the stimulation. Then he caught sight of the needle and swore. His hands clenched protectively over his balls.

"I'll ask you to take a few breaths, then count backward from ten. Start when you're ready."

Andrew took a gulp of air, held it for a long moment, then whispered, "Ten."

No tongs today. Meili gripped the head of his cock as though grasping a turtle behind its ears. The needle pushed in, and Andrew's head pressed into the back of the armchair. A garbled "Nine" left his unmoving lips.

"Eight, seven," Vincent murmured calmly, but fuck he loved watching how Meili moved. She was like a dancer, graceful and not wasting a single motion. "Six, five…" She pressed the gold stud into the needle and guided the needle back and out. "Four… You're almost done. She only needs to secure it." Vincent patted Andrew's shoulder. "Three, two…"

"Done," she said.

Andrew sputtered a choked sob while Meili finished screwing the second bead into place.

She smiled. "In mid-June, you can replace it with something a little bigger, or a ring like Vincent's."

"That's really it?" Andrew clenched his eyes a couple of times, working the dampness from his lashes. "It hurts like the fucking devil, but I thought it would be worse. Well, hello, handsome," he said to his own cock.

Meili bit her lips and glanced at Vincent. Her look held everything—amusement at Andrew's reaction, pride in her accomplishment, appreciation for how well they worked together, and gratitude at his bringing her into this. It was a wonderous look that encompassed all they shared. She filled Vincent's heart with a far greater emotion than anything he'd ever experienced.

*Fuck it.* He knew what he needed to do.

# CHAPTER SIX

A s Meili hurried from the market toward her new shop, she noted her neighbors were still curious about her two days after they'd moved in.

No. They were wondering about the man who was peeling himself from the shade cast on the side of her new building. Vincent lifted his hand in greeting.

Her stomach fluttered in wary pleasure. She hadn't seen him since Andrew's pierce and had been worried about what that meant. As she and her grandmother had packed their belongings from the old shop, Meili had told her grandmother that her income from Queen's Road might dry up and explained about Vincent's dilemma.

"Have you been with him?" Mama had asked.

"Not like that," she mumbled. Only in her dreams.

"You like him, though? You want to marry him?"

"I won't leave you, Mama."

"That's not what I asked. Who will look after you when you're my age if you don't have a son?"

"I'll look after myself."

Her grandmother made a disparaging noise.

"I know you think the work I do is immodest," Meili said. "But Vincent respects my skill. We complement each other. I would marry him if it was possible, but it isn't."

Her grandmother had fallen silent, then, and the lack of word from Vincent seemed to have underscored the bleak truth in her statement that a future with him wasn't possible.

As she came close enough, she said, "I sent you a note that I could begin seeing clients Friday. Did you not receive it?"

"I'm not here to see you," he said blandly.

"Who, then?" Not someone from the brothel. She would rip out his nipple rings.

"Your grandmother asked my comprador to come. I decided to accompany him."

"She's resting." Wasn't she? Meili hurried to unlock the door. "Mama—" She cut herself off as she found her grandmother serving tea to the middle-aged man seated at the table by the window.

Meili greeted him with a respectful bow and glanced between them, then at Vincent as he came in behind her. This shop was twice the size of their old one. It had a south-facing window and a screened alcove for private treatments, but Vincent still seemed to take up all the space simply by arriving in it.

"Is everything in order with the building?" Meili asked the comprador. If something had gone wrong with the purchase, she didn't know what she would do.

"This isn't something I've ever arranged," the comprador said, glancing at her grandmother with humor. "But I think we've made a good start."

"We're very close to an agreement," Mama agreed.

"On what?" Meili asked.

"Your marriage to Mr. Gainsborough," Mama said.

• • •

Vincent had made his decision. He had handed off his letters to Andrew, who had promised to deliver them to his uncle and Pansy.

For better or worse, Vincent was staying in Hong Kong. His uncle might fire him, but Vincent had realized after ten years of working in import and export, he could do it for anyone, including himself. In fact, he would prefer to. Then he could have a parlor in the back for piercing. He might even find a tattoo artist to join them.

He had thought he would have to work harder to convince Meili to take a chance on him, so he was stunned to receive a message from her grandmother through his comprador.

"She asks if you would like to engage a marriage broker to negotiate your union with Miss Fitzwilliam," the man had said.

Since his comprador had already done business with them, it seemed simplest to keep him as their go-between. Vincent promised to support both women and renounce any claim to the building they had purchased or any of the money they made from their medicines and other care. If Meili decided to further her studies toward becoming a physician, he promised to support her in that, too.

Her grandmother was not without a few tricks up her sleeve. One of her conditions was that Vincent's comprador was to send a letter to Vincent's uncle, warning that the hongs who currently dealt with Vincent would not be as welcoming to a newcomer. It was in the best interest of Gainsborough and Company to keep Vincent running their showroom.

Vincent was comfortable with these arrangements, as was Meili. They married and went to the hotel for their wedding night. Vincent's comprador was looking for a home suitable for the three of them. In the short term, a young mother had moved into one of the rooms at the shop to help when Meili was out and to assist Meili's grandmother as needed.

"I don't think I should wear my ring. Not for the first time." Vincent rolled the bead to unscrew it. "I'm surprised you haven't done this. Have you never been tempted?"

His bride was a sensual woman who might have strict standards for herself, but she wasn't a prude, and she flouted conventions in other ways. If she had wanted a lover, she would have taken one.

"I never wanted to show anyone…what I've done," she said from behind the screen.

"How many piercings do you have?" He withdrew his ring

and set it aside, then reclosed his robe. "*Show me.*" He was as eager to see her piercings as he was for the things any groom was excited for.

Meili emerged in a loose, muslin nightgown with the neckline unbuttoned. She clutched it closed with her fist.

"You've seen my ears and my eyebrow. And this one." She lifted her tongue, then opened her neckline an inch. "I also have these," she said of three perfectly spaced bars down her breastbone.

He came across and brushed her neckline open farther.

She let it gape and fall off her shoulders, revealing the two bars that sat on the inner swells of her breasts, forming a V.

"That's pretty." He set his fingertip where the two bottom beads nearly touched.

She let the nightgown drop to her elbows, exposing her pert, brownish-pink areolas and the crossed double piercings in each, as well as the delicate chain that ran between.

"I put this on for you today." She shimmied so the chain swayed.

"I appreciate it." His cock was straining with arousal, anticipating the feel of those vertical shafts or the horizontal loops through her nipples against his tongue. "I love you more than you can possibly imagine."

She straightened her arms so the nightgown fell to her wrists and showed her hips. Five shafts in a starburst pattern surrounded her navel. The end of the longest vertical one held a dangling charm in the shape of a dragonfly.

"That's pretty." He touched it. "We can turn most of this to gold. Add gems. Would you consider letting an artist paint them for a catalogue?"

"Such romantic talk for our wedding night."

"You know I'm enthralled with you." He caught her chin and set a lingering kiss on her lips. "I would peruse that catalogue all day every day."

"When you could see the real thing? Make better use of your time, Mr. Gainsborough." She turned and revealed her lower back. A stud sat above each cheek like a dimple and three studs sat in a line from her tailbone into her crack. "I wanted to see if I could pierce blindly. You're the only one who has seen it. Not even myself. How is it?"

"Perfect. Level and evenly spaced." He set his hands on her warm waist and stroked her hips, dying to bend her against the edge of the dressing table and look at those as he fucked her. He wanted to run his tongue across them while fingering her pussy. "Are there more?" He nudged the bunched nightgown, urging it to fall.

"Yes, but…" She stepped out of it, then turned very slowly. Her hands flexed in front of her before she let them fall away.

He covered his mouth and backed up to the bed, sitting down abruptly.

"I don't know what that means." Her hands shielded the thin red ribbons laced through the loops that framed her bush and tied in a bow at the bottom.

"It means I thought I loved you when I decided to stay here. Now I'm in awe. Come here. Let me see properly."

She shyly stepped over her nightgown and set her hand in his, pussy mostly shielded by the crisscrossed ribbons, but he glimpsed fine black hairs and a hint of her pink slit.

"You did all of these yourself?" He traced his finger next to the four rings in the crease of her thigh.

"Yes, and…" She bit her lip. "There's more."

"Hood?"

"And my inner lips." Her voice faded shyly.

"May I?" He touched the tail of the ribbon.

She nodded. He carefully drew on the ribbon to release it. He took his time unlacing her, making no effort to keep from brushing her intimately, discovering to his delight that she was already wet. By the time he dropped the ribbon to the floor, they were both breathing unevenly.

He swallowed and reverently traced the four small rings that decorated her inner lips. They were offset so they lay in a pretty ladder pattern down her slit. He used his finger and thumb to spread her so he could see the simple curved bar pierced through her hood. A groan of craving left him.

"We will definitely find something special for here," he promised. His light tap caused her to catch her breath.

Oh, he liked that.

"I will have to be very, very careful, won't I?" He was glad he'd removed his own jewelry. Things could go very wrong, very fast, but he was deeply excited by the look and feel of her adornments. "I like how warm this is." He rubbed the bar that sat against her clitoris.

She shook, and he liked that, too.

He carefully drew the loops apart, spreading her inner lips and watching his finger slide between them as he searched out the source of her wetness. He delicately spread her juices around, coming back to polish that bar again and again, making her shiver with each contact.

"Come closer. Let me lick it."

Her feet shuffled forward. He dipped his head, using his tongue to learn the shape of hard metal beads and thin, smooth skin, hot round loops, and the pulsing knot of her clitoris. He learned how to make her clutch her fists in his hair and rise on her toes and grow wetter against his lips, her taste so sweet and heady he went into a fog of blind, carnal need.

"Do you want to come like this?" he asked, voice hoarse with lust.

"I want you to kiss me."

He drew her to the mattress, and they kissed, moaning at the ecstasy of finally being like this, alone and naked, skin brushing skin as his robe fell open. Unabashed in their want for each other.

"Any fresh ones?" he asked.

She shook her head.

"Good. I have a promise to keep." He started with the one at her eyebrow and kissed his way to her ears, the tip of her nose, her mouth—he kept returning to her mouth. He couldn't get enough of her taste and the way she arched beneath him when their tongues brushed.

Her breasts were so pretty with their chain. He opened his mouth on one nipple, suckling lightly, growing harder and harder as he tongued her pliant nipple trapped within its textures of metal and links and beads.

"I'm afraid I'll hurt you if we leave this here." He found the hook catches and removed the chain. While he did, she lifted her head, and her mouth closed on his nipple. Her tongue worked under the loop and jade bead, tugging at the shaft, sending a hard bolt of feverish need straight to the tip of his cock.

"Oh, fuck." It felt so *good*.

Like him, she seemed tantalized by his piercings. Her tongue found the one beneath his lip, and her fingers played against the hole beneath the head of his cock. Then her hand closed firmly around his shaft.

"Pierce me with this."

$$\bullet\bullet\bullet$$

Vincent's cock leaped in her hand, but he sobered. "The first time hurts."

She knew, but she didn't care. Her skin was so sensitized, she felt the air as downy feathers. Her mouth was swollen, and a joyous emotion expanded her chest. Her loins ached with need after the way he'd licked and tantalized her. She craved the shape of him inside her.

He cupped her face in his hands. "I really do love you."

"I love you, too."

If she had had any lingering doubts in her feelings for him, her love was reaffirmed as steadfast and right when he asked, "Do you want me to wear a condom? I bought some in case you don't want to get pregnant. Or I can pull out."

"Pull out. I want to feel you."

They kissed again, and he rose over her, sliding between her legs. He used his knees to push her legs wider. They both watched as he rubbed his weeping tip between the folds of her sex. He groaned as her tiny loops tantalized his swollen crown.

"Smooth those out of the way," he urged. "Do you want to take them out?"

"I want to try with them in."

He swallowed. "Stop me if they catch. I'll go slow."

Her hands trembled as she used two fingers to spread her inner lips, exposing her molten core for the silken arrowhead of his cock.

"Do you want to count backward from ten?"

How could he tease at a time like this? Her body trembled with anticipation. The candlelight turned her vision to gold. All her focus was on what he was about to do to her.

"I forget how," she said truthfully.

He gave a small grunt that might have been agreement. She wasn't sure, but his broad head pressed against the tight resistance of her entrance.

It hurt. It burned ferociously as she was stretched by the wide dome, by the implacable forging of his shape into the most sensitive place on her body. Tears rose to her eyes, but she set her hand on his buttock, insisting he continue.

When her pussy swallowed his tip, he paused. The sting was unrelenting, but she was wholly caught up in the sensation of his thick heat lodged within her. The burn of her flesh accepting his.

"There's more," he warned on a groan.

She nodded. He slowly settled the weight of his pelvis on hers, forcing the length of his cock deep into her, pushing the searing burn deeper, pressing pain-fueled tears onto her eyes.

"Love," he murmured, cupping her face and kissing her softly. He pressed his lips to the wetness leaking from her eyes. "My beautiful love."

The fiery sensation grew and grew as he penetrated deeper and deeper, until he was buried to his root. The blunt shape of his pelvic bone dug against the small piercings on sensitive lips stretched thin. Her clitoris stung and danced in a confusion of pleasure-pain. Her entire body trembled in reaction.

It was the most intensely intimate moment of her life, and she was so glad he was doing this to her. That he was in this moment with her. That it was his mouth pressed to the pierce on her eyebrow. That it was his smoky gaze that looked on her with that mixture of tenderness and wonder and earthy desire.

"Should I apologize?" His thumb rubbed a tear into her temple.

"No. I like it." She slid her hand between them, feeling where he was buried between her taut lips. "Can you feel these?" She touched all her piercings, soothing her stinging flesh, lingering at the bar in her hood.

"I can." He gently rocked his hips, withdrawing a little before he pressed back into her.

The movement pulled at the small loops and nudged the bar against her clitoris. She made a noise of agonized bliss. It hurt. It hurt so much, but the friction inside her and the tremor in the piercings filled her with waves of euphoric pleasure. Her eyes fluttered closed.

"Keep doing that," she whispered, then brought her hands up to cup his head and draw his mouth to hers.

He did, gradually lengthening his strokes until pain and pleasure blended into one sensation. Until she was consumed by fire and the return of his thrusts shot lightning from her shoulders to her pelvis and out to her limbs. Until her tension condensed and shattered with climax. Her sheath clenched on the unfamiliar hardness lodged within her, amplifying the contractions of pleasure that gripped her.

He rocked within her for a few final moments, then, with a tortured groan, he slipped free of her completely. Relief from the worst of the pain washed through while he thrust against the piercings in her navel. As he shuddered and released jagged moans, wet heat spurted across her stomach.

For long minutes they trembled, hearts hammering and lips clinging until their breaths slowly evened out. Finally, he rolled away and reached to the nightstand for a towel he must have left there for this purpose. As he dried her belly, he noted the pink.

"I made you bleed." He frowned with concern. "Does it hurt?"

"I don't mind." She traced his eyebrow and his mustache and his bottom lip. "If I'm sore for days, it will only remind me how much I wanted this."

He leaned down to press his smile to hers.

*The End*

# Horsing Around

*Horsing Around* is a fun frolic where people are consensually placed in horse tack and other costumes that restrict their movements while they are treated as animals and controlled by others, so readers who may be sensitive to this, please take note.

Also, readers should be aware that oil breaks down rubber-based condoms, diaphragms, and cervical caps, but oil was the most commonly used lubricant at the time, and so for historical accuracy, that is what is used here.

# CHAPTER ONE

*May 1882, Norfolk, UK*

Qahhar Al-Zahrani adjusted the angle of his theodolite, lining it up with the tree across the channel, and glanced through the telescope again. A movement flashed within the lens.

He lifted his head, unable to see much through the thin copse, but a rider wearing a brown coat and trousers tucked into tall boots sat atop a piebald mount. The horse was being coaxed through high-step training. Dressage?

With a small kick, they shot out of sight.

Qahhar waited for his estate agent to catch up with the chain they were using to survey his property.

"I have ten outs and forty-two, sir," Franklin said.

"Same." Qahhar put a checkmark beside the figure he'd already written in his notebook, then chucked his chin toward the far shore. "My neighbors keep a stable?"

"Yes sir." Franklin removed his cap and gave his head a scratch. "They, uh…"

"I've heard the gossip," Qahhar cut in. He'd never seen the sort of pantomimes that had been alluded to, but in his extensive travels, he'd learned that every place had its conventions and its people who flouted them. "I didn't know they keep *real* horses."

"Yes, sir." Franklin brightened. "Since the first Oliviers came from France. Huguenots, if folklore serves. A widow occupied Auburn Hall when I was a child. Her stable was full of Trotters. Her nephew, Mr. Warren Olivier, took up residence after she passed. He's been keeping Roadsters the last fifteen years or so. They're well regarded as breeders, but they're fussy about parting with their stock. Private sales, not auctions."

"And their staff? I saw a rider taking a horse through its

paces."

"Mr. Olivier's nurse. She came back with them from Ibadan. That's in Western Africa." He seemed to realize he was schooling Qahhar on the continent of his birth and cleared his throat. "You'll see her in the village. The men stay closer to home."

They held elaborate parties, though. Lady Meddleton, the wife of the couple who'd been in residence here when Qahhar's father purchased this estate a decade ago, had informed Qahhar that *They bring stage performers from London yet neglect to invite local gentry or hire from the peasantry.* Her ladyship had been most slighted by her exclusion.

Qahhar was not so desperate for entertainment. In his opinion, drinking lemonade on the lawn, making small talk with strangers, was the greatest waste of time ever created.

However, he had just arrived with twenty Barbs and needed to build a fortune on horseflesh. For all the lectures Qahhar had attended on steam-powered carriages that would soon be invented, horses were in more demand than ever. They drew barges up canals, dragged machinery in farmers' fields, pulled omnibuses, and were still the favored mode of transport after the train stopped at the station.

Barbs were hardy riding mounts with excellent stamina. Roadsters were reliable working animals with good speed. He would be a fool to overlook an opportunity to improve his stock and stablemen.

"I'll ride over tomorrow," Qahhar decided, ignoring Franklin's wince of concern. "I'll introduce myself, see how we get on."

• • •

The diagonal of Kikiola Adeleke's half pass on Bluebell moved her into a view up the lane, allowing her to spot an unexpected guest approaching from the road.

Warren and Chaucer were out of sight behind Auburn Hall,

but she gave a short, sharp whistle of warning—not that they would care. They took an attitude that this was their home and they could live as they wished, but she liked to give them a choice.

Warren drew Chaucer and the sulky to a stop.

"Guest," she called. "I'll go meet him." She kicked Bluebell toward the break in the hedge and cantered out toward the front of Auburn Hall.

She was immediately taken by the stranger's stallion. A curl of admiration in her belly became so visceral she nearly groaned with it.

The stallion had to be seventeen hands. His coat was sleek silver, his legs obsidian black. His swishing tail was a charcoal streak of mostly black with silver threads. His luxurious mane on his powerful neck held more distinct streaks of silver.

The animal broke his trot to toss his head as he scented Bluebell.

Kiki felt a shiver chase through Bluebell beneath her and heard the brief piddle of urination. Her bottom dropped slightly, and Kiki sucked her teeth. *Not now.*

The other rider's body bunched with readiness as he kept a firm control of his mount, forcing the stallion to maintain his gait. The man wore English clothing and a black felt derby that kept the spring drizzle off his face. His complexion suggested ancestry similar to her own African roots. He was so powerful and eye-catching she felt another tendril unfurl in her middle, one that was akin to want and hunger and covetous desire.

It wasn't his looks so much that captured her attention, even though he possessed a tall bearing and wide shoulders and well-muscled thighs. As they drew closer, she placed his age near her own thirty years and noted he was very handsome with strong, winged brows and a neatly trimmed beard that defined his square jaw and framed his wide, full lips. He had an air of command and an ability to dominate a spirited animal that she immediately admired.

What drew her most, however, was the virility he exuded. He was looking on her with the same consideration she was giving him. With the same elemental response his stallion was demonstrating toward Bluebell, nostrils flared as though he searched for her scent.

Like Bluebell, Kiki was reacting with heightened awareness, all of her wanting to twitch and draw closer and nuzzle and touch. Her blood was quickening, responding in an instinctual way— which wasn't like her. She didn't find men particularly attractive. Or women. Not anyone, really. She felt a sibling-like love for Warren and Hamish and had warm friendships with many of their staff and guests. She enjoyed sex when it suited her, but her eyes and heart were drawn to horses, not people.

Which wasn't to say she didn't consider herself a person. She wasn't like Hamish or some of their guests, who felt such a strong, inexplicable affinity with certain animals they wished to be treated as one. No, she was definitely a woman, but she'd never *felt* like one. Not in this way.

"Good morning." She halted Bluebell in a not-so-subtle insistence that he halt as well.

"Good morning." He tipped his hat and spoke with an accent similar to Warren's crisp Cambridge intonations but with a warmth in his deep voice that reminded her of home. "I'm from Sheringham Manor. Qahhar Al-Zahrani."

"Ah, yes. We heard the owner had taken up residence. Welcome to Auburn Hall. I'm Kikiola Adeleke." She used the excuse of steering Bluebell out of the stallion's attempts to sniff the mare's hindquarters to force Qahhar to turn and face back the way he'd come. "Please call me Kiki. Most do."

"Thank you, Kiki. You may call me Qahhar." He took a moment to settle his horse but turned the stallion like a compass back toward Auburn Hall. "I'm told you have an enviable stable. Show me."

*Show me.* An involuntary shiver chased across her skin at

his exercise of dominance, but she commanded creatures ten times her weight every day. Right now, she was trying to keep a mare—who had seemingly burst into season—from backing her hindquarters into the stallion's extended cock.

"Today is not a good day." She glanced back to the hedge. "Mr. Olivier has health concerns." Which were greatly exaggerated when convenient. "Let me check with him and send word when—"

"No need to disturb him. It's you I came to see. Your reputation for animal husbandry precedes you." His mouth stretched into a smile that had become rueful, as if he knew the state of his stallion's readiness.

Her cheeks stung as she wondered exactly how much of her reputation had preceded her, but his stallion was now trying to circle her mare, wanting to edge behind her.

Bluebell was skittish. She didn't know this new male, but she was receptive enough that she was continuing with her teasing signals.

"I think another day—"

"Kiki," Warren called out, forcing both of them to look to the corner of the hall where he had brought Hamish, who was still dressed as Chaucer and hitched to the sulky.

Chaucer preferred to be harnessed upright and wore hoof gloves, leather ears, and a bridle. He gave a soft lip flap of greeting around his bit.

She glanced at Qahhar to see his reaction.

His brows went up in surprise, then pulled together with curiosity. Perhaps he'd been warned. All the staff here were paid very well for their discretion, but when a few dozen like-minded people spent a week at Auburn Hall, cavorting in full tack, racing sulkies and chariots, running obstacle courses, and performing dressage, rumors slipped out.

"Come meet the owner of Auburn Hall." She kicked Bluebell into a swift canter, trying to put some distance between the animals and give herself a small breathing space from this compelling man.

Qahhar's stallion leaped to keep pace, pressing his nose against Bluebell's flank, trying to steer her so Bluebell zigzagged, still not sure if she wanted to invite him or shy.

As they approached the hedge, Kiki gave a sharp whistle and let Bluebell stretch into a gallop. Chaucer whinnied as Bluebell cleared the obstacle with ease right in front of him.

So did the stallion, throwing up clumps of dirt and blowing out a snort as he landed and caught up to where Kiki was wheeling Bluebell around.

Qahhar kept his seat and grunted out an imprecation, wrestling the stallion's reins as he kicked him into a flat run, taking him around the pavilion to remind him who was in charge.

Warren tapped Chaucer's bare, tailed haunch. Chaucer obediently pulled the sulky over to where Kiki was trying to bring Bluebell to a stand, but the mare was picking up her hooves, still restless.

"Mr. Al-Zahrani is our new neighbor," Kiki told Warren as Qahhar trotted back toward them, still being challenged by his head-tossing mount.

"Qahhar, please," he reminded her.

She nodded and said, "Mr. Warren Olivier."

"And you must call me Warren. It's a pleasure to meet you." Warren smiled with admiration as he took in the stallion. "We were told your Barbs were very handsome. Do they all have that remarkable coat? Hamish will go mad for those streaks in his mane. He was very taken with the zebras while we were in Africa."

Qahhar flicked his gaze to Chaucer but took his cue from her and Warren. He didn't address him, only patted his stallion's neck where the mane in question draped so attractively.

"I have his sister. She bears similar markings. Then I have three solid black, a dappled gray, and the rest are chestnut. This is Honor. He's struggling to live up to his name today." Qahhar's lips formed a flat line as Honor danced his hooves.

"Chaucer has his feisty moments," Warren said with a nod. "Kiki says I should geld him if I want him to behave more consistently, but I haven't ruled out using him for stud if the right opportunity comes along."

*Yes, Qahhar, you are being tested.* Warren was the kindest, most open-hearted person until it came to close-minded people. He'd been particularly dispassionate toward Lady Meddleton, who had made very uncharitable remarks about them in the village.

Qahhar's reaction was only to warn, "If he swims the channel and harasses my mares, we'll have words, but if you'd like a more formal breeding exchange, that's why I'm here."

Kiki bit her lip. *This is what falling in love feels like*, she suspected. She was instantly suffused with warmth and wanted to hug this perfect stranger—emphasis on perfect—for his simple act of accepting her dearest friends exactly as they were.

"Breeding and training are Kiki's expertise." Warren gave her a deferential nod.

"I have no schooling in animal science," Kiki dismissed with a shake of her head. "But I'm passionate and dedicated and would be honored to view your stock."

"Passion and dedication go a long way with me." Qahhar met her gaze in a way that caused the trickles of heat in her middle to intensify and reach into her erogenous areas. Pulsating sensations hit the tips of her breasts and lodged between her thighs. Her ears felt as though they were filled with water. "I shall be completely honest and declare my intention is to poach you," Qahhar continued. "If the rest of your skills are consistent with the horsemanship I've seen thus far." He nodded at the hedge.

"I couldn't leave my position here. I'm Warren's nurse." Not formally trained in that, either, but they had their roles and were all comfortable in them.

"We would never hold you back from what you love, Kiki,"

Warren chided. "Please show Qahhar around and visit his stables. Allow him to make you an offer if he wants to."

Chaucer gave a whinny and a toss of his head, causing his bridle to jangle. That startled Honor into a side step.

Like all the horses, Chaucer had great affection for her. If she were trapped in a burning building, she had no doubt he would kick down the door and drag her out. Hamish would do the same.

As Chaucer pawed the ground with his right hoof-boot, Warren took a firm grip on his reins and ensured the brake on the sulky was set.

"Let him make you an offer," Warren repeated patiently, voice mild but eyes laughing. "Then come back and tell me what it is so I can make you a better one."

# CHAPTER TWO

Qahhar left Honor in the small paddock next to the stable, where the men stood by to admire him.

They were an interesting pair. Warren was a well-dressed gentleman in a white shirt and yellow waistcoat beneath a frock coat the color of a robin's egg. His brown mustache was curlicued at the ends, and his boots were polished to a mirror finish.

The other was a husky fellow with chestnut hair and a small apron over his loins. Mud spattered his harnessed chest and thick, naked thighs. He wore gloves and boots shaped like hooves, leather ears atop his head, and a bridle with a bit in his mouth. A long horsetail that matched his hair protruded from between the cheeks of his pale, hair-sprinkled ass.

Qahhar couldn't help but wonder what Kiki's duties as a "nurse" were.

He accompanied her into the stables. It had the typical atmosphere of dusty light and cool air laden with musty, woody aromas and the baser scents of leather oil and manure.

Qahhar took it in with an absent glance before returning his attention to the intriguing Kikiola Adeleke. She was tall and slender and graceful. Her oval face and heavy eyelids gave her such a serene expression, she almost seemed haughty with it. He might have thought her aloof to the point of arrogance, but there was a gentleness to her voice that made him want to stand still so he could listen with his whole body.

He resisted that temptation, clinging to the urgency of his greater goals. He needed to keep his edges sharp. One couldn't match ruthless swordplay with a dull blade. Faster horses meant faster money meant swifter revenge. The only reason he was speaking to her was to explore breeding potential.

Definitely not to wet his cock.

Sexual hunger was digging its claws into him, though, pulling his eyes to her modest curves outlined so fetchingly in her masculine riding clothes. She rode astride. He found that enthralling in the extreme. Qahhar wasn't so delicate he grew embarrassed when his stallion's cock hung out, but his own was twitching and pulling, heavy with readiness, refusing to ignore the attributes of the woman at his side.

Kiki seemed oblivious to his struggle. She introduced Qahhar to a groom named Perry, asking the young man, "Will you unsaddle Bluebell for me, please?"

"Happy to, mistress." He took Bluebell's reins.

Above them, a questioning "Meow?" sounded with the tinkle of a bell.

Qahhar glanced up to see the round-cheeked face of a young woman. She wore black satin cat ears with fine white hairs on their tips. They were attached to a band that sat over her sleek black hair so the ears looked very much as though they grew from her head. The shapes of her eyes were emphasized to make them even more catlike. The tip of her nose was blackened, and she had a sprinkle of long, stiff whiskers stuck to the skin between her nose and upper lip. The bell on the ribbon around her neck gave another tinkle as she walked her paw-shaped gloves against the edge of the loft, searching for a means to come down.

"Sorry, mistress," Perry said with a slide of his gaze toward Qahhar. "I put Mittens in the loft and took the ladder, thinking she'd stay out of sight."

"Cats insist on being curious, don't they?" Qahhar said. Bloody hell, *he* was curious and growing more so by the second. "Decent mouser?"

"Terrible," Kiki said wryly. "But very affectionate. Perry looks after her. She sleeps on his bed."

The groom blushed as he drew Bluebell into a stall.

"There isn't much to see in here," Kiki said in a colossal

understatement, escorting Qahhar between the rows of empty stalls. "Our mares are grazing in the lower pasture. We're confident three will foal next spring. We've loaned our stallion to friends. We have another arriving soon who gives us beautiful foals with Bluebell."

"From which estate? Could you make an introduction when he arrives?"

"Their reason for visiting is actually, hmm." She pursed her mouth, then wrinkled her nose as she looked up at him. "You may have heard we host pageants?"

"I have." He glanced through the open door to the harness room as they passed it. Narrow stairs led to what was likely the living quarters for the groom and his kitten. "I was told locals aren't invited."

"Warren makes the guest list and protects the privacy of those who attend. If you're interested in meeting anyone, you should discuss it with him."

"I see." He squinted against the brightness as they came outside from the coach house.

Across the paddock, Warren had unhitched Chaucer and held his reins as Chaucer poked his nose over the rail of the fence. Chaucer whinnied softly to Honor.

Honor lifted his head from the water trough and ambled across. It wasn't like him to take to strangers so quickly.

"How did you come to be a nurse here?" Qahhar paced alongside Kiki as she took him toward a stone wall.

"My father ran cavalry stables in Ibadan. Warren and Hamish were staying in rooms nearby when Warren took to his bed with malaria."

"No quinine?"

"He ran out. Hamish spoke to my father, who procured more, but it took time. My mother nursed Warren, and I met Hamish in the stables. I was mucking stalls and grooming since before I can remember. Hamish was very agitated. I did what I could to reassure him. Once Warren had his tablets again, he improved, but Hamish knew he had to bring Warren home to continue his treatment. He wasn't in a fit state to look after him."

"So he asked you? How old were you?"

"Fourteen."

"Your parents let you come all this way with a pair of men who must have been twice your age at the time?" He glanced back, judging them well into their forties.

"I was their youngest of five daughters and two sons. My siblings all lived in Ibadan with their families. A man had offered for me, but he already had three wives. They seemed happy with their situation, but..." She paused as they reached a stile over a stone wall.

"But?" he prompted, holding out a hand to steady her as she climbed the steps.

It wasn't necessary. She was sure-footed as a goat, but the strength in her grip squeezed more than his fingers. His chest grew compressed. His cock swelled anew. His throat tightened, and his balls ached as if clenched in a hot, tender hand.

She released him as she reached the other side and descended to look across the wall at him. Her cheeks wore a blush of pink beneath her dark brown complexion. Her eyes were bright, her breasts rising unevenly. It couldn't be exertion. It had to be a mirror of the want that gripped him—from the mere act of their holding hands.

The fire of sexual heat in him roared higher. A groan of need tried to fight its way free of his burning lungs.

"I wanted other things." She pressed her lips and glanced at the hand he had held, as though searching for the scorch marks he'd left there.

His own felt the sting of heat from hers. He closed his fist to hold on to the sensation.

"My grandmother visited a fortune-teller when I was born." Her lashes came up to watch his reaction. "The woman said I had a talent for calming restless spirits but that I possessed one of my own—one that would compel me to travel far from home. She said I would live among Englishmen and never marry."

Qahhar didn't believe in fortune-tellers so much as he believed they reinforced for people what they already wished to believe, but who was he to scoff at what might have brought her to meet him here today?

He went up one step, set his palm on the moss that grew atop the stone wall, used his free hand to keep his hat on his head, and vaulted over, landing before her.

"So you are not married." He straightened and brushed his palms.

Her brows lifted in amusement that he had latched on to the most innocuous detail, though a woman of her age who wasn't married *was* remarkable.

"I grew up aware of the prophecy and have chosen to make it come true."

"Have you." He pondered that. Surely, she took lovers, though? She was reacting to him on a physical level but expressing little confusion or coyness. Her air of self-possession was as intriguing as the rest of her. "I'm also unmarried," he volunteered. "I came close, but my cousin persuaded her to marry him instead."

"Oh?" They fell into step as they walked across a hillock that provided a view of the bottom of his estate across the channel and the sparkling water of the broad in the distance.

"I gave them my blessing." Begrudgingly. He had been enamored with the young woman's beauty. She had been enamored with the ill-gotten power and riches that his cousin had been grasping after. It all left a sour taste in Qahhar's mouth.

"Where is your family?" Kiki asked.

"Casablanca. While my father was alive, he worked as an official with the makhzen. He represented the sultan in London for a time. That's how I came to study at Cambridge."

"It was a surprise to all of Coltingfield that the Meddletons had sold Sheringham. And so long ago!"

"To clear their debts, yes. My father bought it with the anticipation my mother would breed horses here. She passed from consumption, so he left it on lease to the Meddletons."

"I'm so sorry you lost her," she murmured.

"Both of them," he acknowledged with a festering ache. "I left to travel shortly after she passed, trying to escape my grief. A few years later, my father returned to Morocco and died soon after." Killed by his brother-in-law, if Qahhar's suspicions were correct.

"That's a great deal of loss for you." She touched his arm, sending feathery ripples through him that were sensual yet painful, like kissing a bruise.

"It is," he agreed. "Made worse by my uncle taking control of our family lands, declaring his son his successor. He exiled me."

"No! Could you not fight him?"

"The knife at my throat persuaded me to leave quietly."

He heard her gasp of shocked outrage, but his mind had slipped back to the alleys he had stolen down, taking what belonged to him, though he'd had to do it under cover of night.

"I took my father's herd." He nodded toward his estate. "I had to sell four to bring them here. The Meddletons were unhappy to be evicted, but I had nowhere else to go. I have no income except to breed them. When this estate is turning a profit, I'll sell it and return to Morocco, balance the slate."

She didn't ask how. He wasn't sure himself yet. There was a bloodthirsty part of him that would only be satisfied with the grimmest of outcomes, but he had time to decide exactly what form his revenge would take.

"So you don't want to be here," she noted with consternation. "You won't stay?"

"Not any longer than necessary, no." He turned his face up to the cloudy sky, tasting the soft rain that landed on his lips, wondering how he could be homesick for the grit of sand in his teeth, but he was. There was a hollowness inside him he didn't know how else to fill.

"Don't *you* miss home?" he asked her.

She scanned the soggy field, the waterlogged branches of the distant trees, the weak sunlight that left the greenery gleaming.

"I miss my family, but this is my home now. And I have a family here who are equally important to me." She nickered and held out a hand.

A mare trotted toward them and pressed her muzzle into Kiki's hand, no doubt searching for a lump of sugar or a bite of apple. Kiki scratched between the mare's ears and hugged her neck and stroked her hand across the mare's withers.

Qahhar was jealous of a mare, he realized. And was bemused she could be content here, leading a life that was... Well, a mystery.

"Do you..." How did one ask? He couldn't envision her pretending to be a horse when she had looked so elegant seated upon one. He wasn't sure it mattered to him if she did.

Kiki looked up at him, expression patient. She knew what he was trying to ask. Without any words passing between them, she heard the questions churning in his mind.

"I calm restless spirits," she said simply. "It doesn't matter to me what physical form that spirit takes." There was that voice again, the one that inexplicably eased the places inside him where thorns had dug their barbs, growing septic and angry. Her dark eyes beckoned the way a shadow next to a wall offered shelter from the intense Moroccan sun, inviting him to step into its relief. "Does your spirit need soothing, Qahhar?"

Could she not hear his heart galloping back and forth inside his chest, trying to break through the fence of his rib cage to get to her?

"It does."

# CHAPTER THREE

"Will you soothe me, Kiki?" His big hands cupped her face. Kiki caught her breath. She hadn't expected him to do this, step close and block out the sky. She hadn't expected she would react so strongly to such gentle strength. Such command. Such tenderness that she found herself encased in shivery ripples as her senses came alive. She had an impression of heat and muscle and a scent in her nostrils that was horse and man, masculine and sharp. Strange yet familiar. She was overwhelmed by a force within herself, compelled to stand receptive as his mouth came down on hers.

On contact, a storm rose up within her, unsettling in its burst of energy but welcome. She had been wondering how his lips might feel against her own. *Divine.* That's how. He tasted as spicy and powerful as he looked. Hot and knowledgeable and thorough.

She grasped his strong, flat wrists for balance and kissed him back, opening her lips wider for the brush of his tongue against hers, moaning as lightning shot straight to her belly. She moved one hand to the back of his head, dislodging his hat as she pressed her fingers into his tight, shorn curls, urging him to kiss her harder.

With a gruff noise, he slipped his arm behind her back and pulled her against the wall of his chest, crushing her breasts and imprinting her stomach with the thick shape of his erection. She could hardly breathe, but after one gasp for air, they switched their heads to angle the other way and dove back for another long, impassioned kiss, lips sealed, tongues dueling. She wrapped her arm across his shoulder and let him hold her up. He arched her to his will as he bent over her.

*This is heat*, she understood for the first time. She was in season, hot all over, completely immersed in physical sensations, barely able to form a thought. It was different from the times she had shared caresses with someone until arousal peaked in climax. This was elemental. A compulsion to submit. Her knees weakened, and her body urged her to let him take her to the ground and penetrate her, to scratch an itch she had never experienced before, one she couldn't even describe.

He yanked up his head, still crushing her with his tight arms as he scanned the field.

"Let's go into those trees." His voice was guttural and urgent.

She blinked, so dizzy with desire she let him take her hand and stumbled behind him.

He found a bed of grass and dried leaves at the root of an elm and dropped to his back, releasing the front of his trousers. "Ride me."

"Take my boot." She set one foot near his hip.

He gripped behind the heel, and she dragged her foot free, unbuttoning the front of her riding breeches so she could skim one leg free. She wore muslin drawers with a slit that opened as she lowered to settle astride him.

His one hand steadied her hip. The other dove into his trousers to free his cock.

The sight of it, dark and turgid with that white droplet seeping from his eye, caused a rush of fresh heat to dampen her folds. Her breath was already uneven. Now she forgot how to breathe altogether.

"You'll have to pull out. I don't have my—"

"*You'll* have to pull away," he said with a fierce flash of his teeth. His fist clenched the base of his shaft. "I'll wait until you do."

With a sob of helplessness, she knelt straddled over him and closed her eyes, stroking her touch against her wet folds, parting her lips, then guiding the velvety tip of him along the same path, lining him up to her entrance.

He was smooth and hot, slippery there at the tip, seeking her entrance and imposingly thick as he sought admittance. The breadth of him forced a stretch that needed a caress of her clitoris to encourage more wetness, more silky give and wanton opening. There. His hard shape began to fill her.

"Ahh." She let her weight carry her down so his hot, hard cock impaled her and his pubis took the grinding circle of her own.

He grunted and set his hands on her hips. "Run me hard."

"I will." A faint smile might have touched her lips. She couldn't be sure because she was losing herself to the sensation of his hips lifting beneath her, coaxing her to a testing pace that awakened all the most lovely places inside her. Her inner muscles squeezed and caressed him as he shifted inside her with every lift and return.

As they moved, wetness continued to rain from her. The friction became a sweet glide as she rose off him, then returned to impale herself upon him.

Birdsong and the fragrance of crushed grass surrounded them. His hands slid upward, stopped by the fit of her coat. Growing hot, she unbuttoned it and leaned into the palms that cupped her breasts. Now his hips undulated beneath her in a more purposeful rhythm, meeting her each time she let her weight drop.

In a move that was not unlike when she pushed into her stirrups, she rose higher. Her thighs burned. His shaft was cooled by the morning air each time he left her, stimulating her further when he plunged back into her.

He huffed a noise that was frustration at being held to this steady trot, but she forced it so they could fully enjoy this moment.

As his hips lifted to meet her next return, a sharp thrust of need spiked through her belly and loins. A sense of urgency she couldn't ignore. She set her hands on his hard chest, leaning into the faster pace he sought. Now he bucked her up, and she gloried in the slap of her buttocks and thighs and intimate flesh against his pelvis when she returned. The impact nearly bounced her out of her seat, only to be secured by his hands on her hips, meeting the power of his loins against her own once again.

They were both breathing raggedly. Her saddle was wet, the friction between her thighs delicious. The stimulation on her clitoris was driving her toward climax, and the feel of him inside her was so satisfying, she couldn't take him deep enough.

She clenched her hands in his shirt, urging him with the roll of her hips to carry her faster. To take her over that wall—

He arched, holding her fully off the ground as she climaxed. She gripped his shirt and hugged his tense body with her thighs. Joyous convulsions struck her abdomen and sent heat scorching through her extremities. She moaned with abandon, fully gripped in ecstasy.

When her contractions began to fade, her knees touched the earth again. She collapsed atop him, and he rolled her to his side.

He pulled free of her still-quivering sheath and clenched his cock in his fist. Angling his hips away, he pumped three or four times, then released a long groan as his come spurted across the ground.

• • •

For several moments, Kiki was too befuddled to move. Qahhar seemed equally overcome, catching his breath beside her while they both stared into the canopy of trees above them.

As her mind began to form thoughts, she realized she ought to have been more careful. Pregnancy wasn't something she worried about too much. She took precautions for convenience, but Warren and Hamish had told her they would welcome her baby into their family if she were to have one. So that wasn't the reason she felt self-conscious and clumsy as she sought to put her free leg back into her breeches.

Qahhar had seemed accepting when he had met Chaucer, but Kiki had heard enough stories of heartbreak from guests to know the way she lived wasn't always welcomed by a lover.

Not that she and Qahhar were lovers. Not really. They had shared a moment. It might feel profound to her, but it could be insignificant to him. She didn't know him.

Yet she knew it would hurt her deeply if he rejected her over something that felt so intrinsic to her soul, especially now that they had shared their bodies.

Usually she cared very little what people thought of her. She had walked her own path from the time she had realized women were meant to clean homes, not stalls, and feed husbands, not horses. When it came to lovers, she enjoyed affection and caresses and mutual orgasms, but she was rarely affected on an emotional level by those interactions. Not deeply. She would cry for days over the sale of a colt, but sex was a pleasant afternoon diversion, her partner blithely sent off with a promise to correspond in future.

She and Qahhar had only just met. There was no reason she should be so sensitive to what he might think of her, but judging by how heatedly they had thrown themselves together, there was something powerful between them. It would break her to lose that before she'd fully explored it, but she did not want to open herself and her life to him only to watch him close her out and leave.

"Kiki?" His wide hand settled on her bowed spine through the weight of her coat. He was still flat on the ground beside her while she had sat up. "Did I misunderstand—"

"No," she hurried to reassure him. "I wanted that. Very much. Thank you." She searched for a smile. It faltered, and she looked ahead again. "But I should have explained more fully what I do here. Before..." Before she wanted more from him, but she already did.

Qahhar finished closing his trousers and stacked his hands beneath his head, staying on his back. His voice grew alert with caution. "I presume it has to do with Chaucer? And Mittens?

Restless spirits?"

"Yes." Kiki gave a dry chuckle at herself for asking him if his spirit was restless. It was. She could see and hear it, but not in the same way that Hamish's was.

Not that there was a "typical" person who was drawn to taking other forms. Some were burly men like Hamish; others, slight and effeminate. Some were women like Xian and preferred to be a cat—or a wolf or a lizard. These spirits came in all different sizes and colors and classes. Some were well-educated; others, less so. Some used the role to break free of a restrained life; others sought it specifically for its constraints. Some enjoyed it as a lark; others went to extravagant lengths when committing to their role.

There were no rules except that she, Kiki, must let them set their own rules and go along with them.

"I said Hamish was agitated while Warren was sick…" She absently shredded a blade of grass. "When Hamish is upset, he finds solace in removing to a different form of himself. It allows him to empty his mind of heavy thoughts."

She glanced to see Qahhar's reaction, but he was only listening intently.

"He was starving himself into listlessness. I found him in an empty stall. He wouldn't speak, so I treated him like one of the horses when they're off their feed. I petted him and crooned to him and hand-fed him. After a while, he started to cry and said Warren was the only one who understood him this way. He didn't know how he could live without him. When they were ready to leave, they begged me to come with them. Warren was worried he wouldn't survive the journey. He wanted to be sure Chaucer would have a groom."

She knew how far-fetched that sounded, and there was some incredulity in Qahhar's face, but also compassion in his voice as he asked, "And you had a prophecy to fulfill?"

"I felt deep empathy for both of them. The way they live is so different. Everyone I knew fell in line with what was expected of them. Some thrive on that, but I knew I would suffocate if I tried to push myself into a mold that didn't fit. I looked at these men who had seen more of my country than I had. *I've* never seen a zebra." She touched between her breasts. "I thought, 'Why shouldn't I see where they are from?'"

Which sounded naive. She had been. She hadn't been prepared for the culture and customs and weather or the side-eye from the Lady Meddletons of the world. From those who believed themselves above and better because they wore convention so well.

"It was still an enormous chance," Qahhar noted. "What if you had been unhappy? How would you get home?"

"I knew I wouldn't be." She flashed her cheekiest grin at him. "Warren promised me a stable."

Qahhar chuckled, which made her chest swell with joy. He sat up and looked in the direction of his estate, amusement fading into consideration.

She held her breath, wondering if he would distance himself after all.

"*I'm* offering you a stable." He swung his weighty gaze to hers, catching her mooning at him. "One twice the size of your own. Will you come see it?"

●●●

Kiki arrived on horseback the next day. Warren and Hamish accompanied her, all of them dressed for riding. Hamish had his face washed, his beard combed, and wore a gray suit. He had a completely different air about him—much more engaged with his surroundings. He smiled as he dismounted and shook Qahhar's hand.

"I apologize for missing you when you visited yesterday," he said with a Scottish burr in his voice. "Hamish Taggert."

"It's a pleasure to meet you. Please call me Qahhar." With a glance at his butler, Qahhar instructed, "Four for lunch. Move it to the terrace." So much for the intimate meal in the rose garden he had planned with Kiki, adjacent to a comfortable parlor with a day bed.

Judging by the amusement in Warren's face, he knew what he had gotten in the way of.

"I hope you don't mind our tagging along. Hamish would have expired from envy if Kiki saw your stable without him."

"True," Hamish said with a nod, moving so his elbow brushed hers. Kiki was so slight and Hamish so bulky, she nearly disappeared when Hamish stood close to her like that. "Kiki couldn't stop talking about Honor last night."

"I didn't want Honor bothering her mare if she wanted to ride." Qahhar shifted so he could see her. "I kept his sister in the pasture behind the stable for saddling, but let me introduce you to our newest addition first. She arrived last evening."

Qahhar waved over two of his grooms to lead the Auburn Hall mounts into the paddock for watering. As he turned back to his guests, intent on offering his arm to Kiki, he found Hamish had switched to her other side. He was between them again and already offering his own arm.

Warren was on her other side, so Qahhar led them into the stable to the mare whose foaling had interrupted his dinner. The day-old filly was solid black with a pair of white stockings on her forelegs.

Kiki and Hamish went into quiet raptures, congratulating the dam and putting their heads together as they discussed the filly's attributes.

When they all started through to the pasture, Hamish again managed to insert his wide shoulders between Qahhar and Kiki, much to Qahhar's annoyance. Did Kiki notice? Was this what she wanted? Because Qahhar had an urge to cut himself between them in a very rude but indisputable way.

They came out to the field, and Hamish set a wide hand on her lower back, steering her toward a better view of the silver mare grazing nearby. They were so keen in their interest, Qahhar couldn't be churlish about being overlooked, but he was privately annoyed.

Warren seemed content to hang back. Qahhar glanced at him and caught Warren scratching into his mustache, possibly laughing behind his hand.

"I have the sense the world's a stage to you," Qahhar said, surprised by his rush of possessiveness. A wife was something he had presumed he would acquire at some point, but Kiki had said she didn't wish to marry. They had made no promises after their tryst.

He had made presumptions, however, he realized. Ones that included her moving into his home and sharing his bed and overseeing his stables. He was aggravated that Warren was witnessing him trying to grapple with her seeming preference for Hamish.

"Forgive him," Warren chided, making no effort to pretend he didn't know that Qahhar was irritated or why. "Hamish is very protective of her. We both are. Which isn't to say she needs it. Our Kiki is very capable and headstrong, but she's precious to us."

"How precious?" Qahhar asked, still prickly.

"It's difficult to quantify. Hamish and I are lovers, but we love Kiki exactly as much. As a sister or niece, perhaps. She owns all the purest parts of my heart, and Hamish adores her with every twisted corner of his. I daresay he would kick a man to death before I could stop him, if he thought she had been hurt by one." Warren's tone was blithe and pleasant, but Qahhar didn't mistake his words for a joke.

"Based on how she came to live with you, it sounds as though she makes up her own mind when it comes to risks."

"She does. You should take that as a warning." Warren grinned with unmistakable affection, then grew more serious. "Kiki said you were interested in our parties. She wasn't sure if I should invite you because she's worried you might not fully accept her as she is, particularly as she is there. As *we* are. I told her that if you cannot accept that part of her, you don't deserve any part of her. I'm unforgiving that way." Warren spared no apologies.

"How *are* you?" Qahhar prodded lightly. "How did you and Hamish come to meet and…live how you live?"

"A performance of *A Midsummer Night's Dream* while we were at Cambridge. Hamish played Bottom; I was Puck. He took to the role with tremendous enthusiasm, and I…" Warren's cheeks hollowed. "I should mention that our parties may sound frivolous, but some of our guests are extremely well-placed. There is a reason the Meddletons' debts were called and your father was able to capitalize on that. Rumors were started in London that were not appreciated by some of our acquaintances."

"Is that a threat to keep my lips sealed?"

"It's information you should have before I share things that are very personal to me. Shall I continue?"

At least he knew where he stood. Qahhar had to respect Warren for that. He folded his arms and nodded curtly.

"I took very well to the role of supporting Hamish in his, which I might have questioned within myself if not for…" He ran his tongue over his teeth before smiling with wicked enjoyment. "Knowing it was a family trait. I struggled more with my desire for men than I did with my desire to treat my lover as a horse."

Qahhar lifted a brow. "It's a family peccadillo?"

"Not openly. I discovered it as a teen. Between school years, I was cloistered here with my aunt. I had nothing to amuse me except dusty chests in the attic, where I came across a trove of debauched art. Prints and playing cards that I've since had reproduced. You'll see them for sale at the party. They're filthy."

Qahhar tried not to betray the way his cock tugged with sinful curiosity. "That's quite a find for a young man."

"I about wore my todger down to a nub," Warren confided, shaking his head in self-deprecation.

"No doubt." Qahhar chuckled.

"There was also a very provocative gown with matching cat ears and a man-sized dog collar with a leash. My great-great-grandmother's diary detailed her husband's predilection for barking and sleeping at the foot of the bed, along with accounts of sexual acts witnessed and enjoyed by the pair of them. He was a banker and kept a ledger for orgy parties that make my pageant look like a wholesome outing to the seashore. His salary for his discreet bookkeeping allowed my family to purchase my estate."

Qahhar whistled under his breath, impressed.

"When I met Hamish, we discovered quickly that our needs and desires meshed," Warren continued. "It was a perfect arrangement until I contracted malaria. I was so sick I feared I would abandon him. Fortunately, Kiki joined us. To be honest, we would struggle if she left us. She makes her own decisions, though. We will always respect that."

Nevertheless, Qahhar had the sense he was being asked about his intentions.

His intention was to leave England. Not tomorrow but eventually.

He shifted his gaze to her and found her watching him. She wasn't nearly so oblivious to him as he'd feared. In fact, the flick of her gaze told him she was trying to read the mood between him and Warren, concerned whether they were playing nice.

As her gaze met his own, she smiled in a way that expanded a bubble of lightheartedness in Qahhar's chest while provoking a more sensual expansion in his groin.

He knew what the honorable thing to say was, but his instinct was far more simplistic.

"There is no barrier that could keep me from knowing Kiki better. Invite me to your party or not," he told Warren. "I'll be there regardless."

"Come Thursday, then," Warren said drily. "You can help with preparations."

# CHAPTER FOUR

I t was Saturday, and Qahhar still wasn't here.

Which was entirely his right, Kiki reminded herself. She only wished Warren hadn't invited him and told her that he was coming. She had begun to look forward to his presence. Now she took his absence as rejection. Qahhar had sent a note to say he was delayed, but she still feared Warren had revealed too much.

She did her best to throw herself into what was a celebration of being oneself. Guests had begun arriving Wednesday night. It made for a slow start Thursday morning as everyone battled a hangover, but by Thursday afternoon, the rest of the guests were arriving and they were all pitching in.

Warren greeted carriages, assigned rooms, and handed out schedules. Hamish supervised construction of the obstacle course and the temporary stables for pets, while Kiki ensured visiting horses were pampered and sent to pasture with old friends.

There were two dozen guests in all. Each brought two or three trusted servants who helped prepare and serve food, assisted with costume mending and laundry, minded market tents of specialized items, and even participated. One, a tiny housemaid with bright red hair, was about to become the main attraction in one of their most popular events. Since there was a steeplechase portion, several mounts would be run by footmen in place of less agile owners.

"Are you expecting someone, cara?" One of her sometime lovers, Lorenzo, noticed her looking around. "You know you can come to my room if you're lonely. Just to talk or…" Lorenzo left the invitation open with a shrug as he gave her arm a comforting squeeze.

She wasn't even tempted, which gave her a pang of melancholy.

Lorenzo was very generous and attentive whenever they spent time together, but she wasn't interested. She wanted—

*He was here.* The sudden sense that Qahhar had arrived gripped her. She *felt* him.

She turned her head, and there, across the stretch of lawn, she glimpsed Qahhar between the milling bodies. If he had ridden, his horse was already in the stable. Sunlight glanced off the flecks of silver in his waistcoat beneath his dark blue jacket. His jaw was set to a stern angle, the rest of his expression hidden in the shadow of his hat brim.

She swallowed, not sure if the ball in her throat was the joy of seeing him or premonition of impending disappointment.

At that moment, Warren sounded the hunting horn, forcing everyone to quiet and give him their attention. He wore a red jacket, riding breeches, and tall boots, even though he would be running behind the galloping Chaucer.

"Welcome to the tenth annual Auburn Hall Fox Hunt. In a moment, I'll take the hounds to the southeast pasture. We'll flush the fox across the lower field along the channel so those of you staying behind can watch from the ridge." Warren pointed. "You'll hear the hounds once they've caught the scent. Lorenzo will lead the first flight through the steeplechase. Perry will lead the second. Kiki is our whipper-in. Ah, Qahhar, welcome. Perhaps you can help Kiki? We'll overlook your lack of proper attire."

Kiki sent Warren an admonishing look.

He pursed his lips in what might have been a blown kiss, but he raised the horn to his lips at the same time and gave another signal that had the hounds barking wildly. When he snapped Chaucer's reins, Chaucer burst into a gallop. Warren ran behind him, and the hounds fanned out after them. A few hounds soon sprinted ahead into the copse of trees.

"Whipper-in?" Qahhar fell into step beside her as Kiki briskly followed the pack.

"We keep the strays from straying." She veered aside to clap her hands and whistle at a bitch that had stopped to pick up a stick. Her coat was a mottled black, brown, and white, her one eye painted black. She had a tendency to stay on all fours rather than run on two legs like the rest, which was why she was lagging behind.

Wrestling the twig from her teeth, Kiki teased her with it, holding it high to excite her up onto her back feet. Kiki hurried her step and threw the stick in the direction of the pack, hoping the bitch would grow curious enough to catch up to the hounds.

As the bitch took off ahead of them, it struck Kiki that she had been silently urging Qahhar to arrive, yet now he was here, she was tongue-tied. The longer she'd had to wait, the more she had begun to worry that he couldn't countenance this eccentric life she led.

"I was concerned when you were delayed," she settled on saying. "Are you well?"

"No. I have discovered that my uncle has maligned me at home. He's ensuring I have no supporters if I return. I'm furious. I wrote letters to everyone I could think of, offering my side of things. I had to be frank and call him out on his crimes, which leaves me facing a death sentence if I return. So that bridge has been burned to a cinder."

"Oh, Qahhar. I'm so sorry." She touched his arm. It felt forged in iron. "You didn't have to come. I would have understood."

"I shouldn't have come. I'm filthy company, but I wanted to see you. *Had* to."

Her heart lifted at that remark, but the smile forming on her lips fell away as he spoke again, voice grim.

"Who were you talking to when I arrived?"

Her mind blanked. Everyone else had become insignificant once she'd spotted Qahhar.

"Lorenzo," she recalled. "An old friend."

"He invited you to his room."

He heard that? "If I hadn't met you and been waiting for you, I might have been tempted," she said calmly. "But I wasn't."

"Hmph." His mouth twisted in self-disgust. "I told you I'm filthy company." He took on an impatient expression and moved away from her.

She almost called him back, but she heard him speak in Arabic as he tapped the naked side of a hound who had his head buried in a clump of long grass. The hound lifted his head and sniffed Qahhar's leg, then nuzzled his hand with his nose.

A brief head scratch and a handful of Arabic, then a light swat on the hound's back end urged him to rejoin the pack.

Kiki bit her lips, wanting to hug him. As he came back toward her, she said, "When you didn't turn up, I thought it meant you were put off."

"By this? No. But I didn't know how to dress for an orgy, as Warren pointed out."

"He meant riding costume. And that's not what this is."

"No?" Qahhar nodded to where one of the hounds had mounted a bitch. She was hunched down on her forelegs, tail up. The dog was braced over her, pumping his cock into her with fast, steady thrusts. They were both vocalizing with whimper-yowls.

"Well, yes, that happens." Kiki had to drag her gaze off them because they were very sexy to watch and she was already prickling with sexual awareness of the man at her side. Her breasts felt full, her bones a thick liquid that wanted to slide toward him. "They belong to a lovely older couple and do that all the time."

"But it's not an orgy? Perhaps my English needs work."

"When animals are responding to their basic urges, they don't think about sex the way humans do. It's not something that should only happen indoors with the drapes closed and the lights off. Our guests come here so they can be free to express however they feel in the moment. Yes, some play these roles *because* it arouses them, but there are many other reasons they adopt a role."

"Such as?" he challenged laconically.

"They want to be admired," Kiki said promptly. "Our dairy maid, Xian, is very shy, but when she is Mittens, she thrives on attention and adores being praised for how pretty she is. Our fox loves the challenge of outrunning the hounds and outsmarting the hunters. Some like to feel insignificant so they can stand on the sidelines and not have to interact in human ways. Others are daunted by any loss of control and challenge that fear by giving control to someone else."

"Still." He waved at the pair as they howled out their culmination, the male's hips giving a final buck. "That's arousing as hell. Isn't it? Don't you find it whets your appetite?"

"Of course." She looked up at him, recognizing he was searching for a win. He was frustrated with more than sexual arousal. He was angry, and it was all bottled inside him.

She instinctually stepped close and cupped his jaw, lifting her mouth in invitation.

He swept his mouth down to hers, crushing her lips with his own while his wide hands crashed her hips into the erection straining in his trousers. A gruff noise sounded in his throat as he plundered her. It was rough and elemental, exactly how he was feeling in the moment.

Kiki had known she was stepping into a maelstrom, but she wasn't prepared for how quickly he overwhelmed her. How her blood flashed through her veins and desire tightened into such a knot in her center, pulsing urgent signals into her loins.

She lifted her hips into the ridge of his erection, panting and eager to feel him inside her. He thrust his hand inside her jacket and growled as her breast filled his palm. His thumb scraped her nipple, and he sucked sharply against her neck.

He yanked his head up and said, "I want to fuck you."

"We're in the trees," she noted with a shaky smile. Her whole body was trembling with arousal. "The hounds have moved on."

"I don't want it to be like this, when I'm angry." His hands set her away but remained firmly around her upper arms, as though he couldn't make himself let her go. "I'm going to stay angry, which is fucking frustrating." He yanked her close to kiss her once more, hard and urgent, then made himself let her go.

She touched her tender lips, aroused and disappointed to be denied but consumed by a need to ease that turmoil inside him.

Just then, there was a burst of snapping twigs. She turned to catch a flash of red hair. The hounds began to yelp and howl.

Warren signaled on the horn that the fox had been flushed. The pursuit was on.

●●●

Kiki was the tether holding Qahhar this side of madness. It wasn't fair of him to put that on her. She was in the middle of a celebration. She didn't need his foul mood dragging her down. He had to manage this rage himself, but his fury had only flared into a greater conflagration as he'd written his letters, spelling out all that he had lost—his father, most importantly, but also the rest of his family as they had been persuaded to align behind his uncle. Then his home. The land that should have been his upon his marriage had been taken, and now, even his ability to visit the country of his birth was denied him.

As he had brooded on all of that, facing a bleak future where his path to regaining any of those pieces had become narrower and rockier, Kiki had kept flashing in his periphery like a glimmer of water in the distance. He was in no fit state to socialize, but he had been drawn here like a camel to an oasis. When she had let him kiss her... Ah, he could have taken her right there against a tree.

There was an animal inside him, one that wanted to claim her indelibly, but he didn't have control over that beast right now. He shadowed her for the next hours, but that was as much as he would allow himself until he could find a more rational mindset.

She must have sensed the chaos inside him. She grew wary and watchful, but she didn't push him away. On the contrary, she seemed determined to distract him by pulling him into her world, introducing him to guests once the fox was captured and victuals were served.

The fox's tail had been awarded to the hound who had run her to ground. The hound was strutting proudly with the tail dangling from its jaws.

Qahhar noted the rubber device on the end. "I've been wondering about the tails. Are they...?"

"Plugged into arseholes? Most are, yes. One of our guests makes a variety of them. I'll show you." Kiki drew him toward tables set in the shade of Auburn Hall.

They perused the variety of tails, some very lifelike and made with natural hair. Others were made of colorful silk ribbons or leather tassels.

"Have you ever worn one?" Fuck, just imagining it made him want to see these bright ribbons protruding from between her firm, round cheeks.

"I was the fox one year. I was terrible at it. It's not my nature to run away from the hounds," she said with a rueful laugh. The way she traced her fingertip on an oversize glass plug made his cock throb with urgency. "I've always wanted to try it with sex. I understand it can be very pleasurable."

Was she trying to make him faint? Qahhar took her elbow and squeezed it, silently promising both of them that, soon, they would find out if she did find that enjoyable.

Was this who *he* was? He enjoyed sex, but he'd only been with women and, aside from his tryst in the forest with Kiki, always in a private setting with the drapes closed. He liked to think he had some skill and few inhibitions, but his mind was exploding with possibilities as he looked over the leather hoods he'd seen some horses and dogs wear, complete with muzzles and ears. There were harnesses and bits, coats of fur and faux-hoof gloves and boots.

"Why are these ones so long?" He examined a stilt-like device that started as gloves and turned into the foreleg of a horse, very different and much longer than the gloves Chaucer wore.

"They extend the length of your arm." Kiki demonstrated by leaning forward onto it. "Most ponies like to run upright on their hind legs. Some go down on their hands and knees if they want to carry a rider. This lets you stay on your feet and bend forward to do it."

"If you put your hand in, sir," the woman minding the stall prompted, "you'll find a grip. You're tall. Try this one."

He was too curious not to. The leather climbed past his elbow. As his hand slid in, he found a wooden structure within. It felt like two saplings that formed a Y. Between them, a wooden brace was sanded smooth. He gripped that cross-piece and bent forward so the hoof-shaped tip touched the lawn. He was still on his feet, but his upper body was parallel with the ground, his weight braced on his arm through the crutch.

"I see the comfort, but it would take time to build enough strength to carry a rider, wouldn't it?"

"We encourage bucking to develop your strength," the woman said.

"Hmph." He straightened and started to remove it.

Kiki touched his hand to stop him. "Do you trust me?"

He opened his mouth to say *Of course*, but something in him hesitated. He'd just spent days—years, in fact—dealing with treachery that had struck from someone close to him. Someone he had trusted. It was impossible to say that he would fully trust anyone ever again.

"You're carrying a heavy load that you need to shake off, Qahhar." Kiki picked up the matching stilt and smiled at the woman. "Will you put these on my account, please, Mary?"

Mary dutifully wrote it in her ledger while Qahhar warned darkly, "I won't carry on in front of people, Kiki."

"I don't expect you to."

"Or in front of people pretending to be horses," he clarified through his teeth.

"Everyone is still on the green. See over there? We've set up stalls for those who prefer to stay in a stable while they're here."

Despite his dour mood, he was drawn to inspect the pressed and twined bricks of hay that made up the walls. They were stacked as high as his shoulders across the back and up the ends. They were one layer shorter between the stalls to allow the ponies to see each other, much like a typical stable.

"How do you make these? We have a mower, but the loft is full of hand-wrapped bundles."

"Warren purchased one of the new baling machines last year. Honestly, I think he was more pleased that it allows us to build these temporary stalls than any ease of moving the actual hay. Here. This one is empty." She opened the gate attached to a pair of heavy posts braced against the walls of bales. "Let's put on this other foreleg. I'll close you in, and you may let yourself go."

"I came here to see you, Kiki. Not to play your games."

Hurt flashed across her features, giving him a pinch of guilt. He hadn't meant to disparage the way she lived.

"These games *are* me, Qahhar. You and I are revealing ourselves to each other. You needn't do it if you don't want to. This is not a test or any demonstration for my sake. I'm offering it because I believe it will help you. If you don't want my help, that's fine."

"Help *how*?" he growled with exasperation, staring into the empty stall. The sweet, musty scent of the dried grass filled his senses.

"Are you not feeling trapped and oppressed and hobbled in some way?" She held up the second foreleg, reminding him that his angry fist was still clenched inside the first one. "Find your strength within your constraints. Break free of the walls that *can't* hold you."

He shook his head in conflict, but refusing outright felt too much like a refusal of her. Of who she was. He couldn't turn away from her right now. He needed her too much.

With a curt nod, he held out his free arm.

These odd little stilts did make him feel hobbled. They were snug enough they couldn't be removed without help. He supposed he could step on a hoof to pull it off, but he would have to break the sapling bone inside it.

As he leaned forward to rest his weight on them, Kiki's hand settled on his neck. Her touch sent a juddering feeling down to his spine and into his heart, keeping him bent over even as something else in him told him to straighten, to not let her dominate him with something so light as her fingertips on his nape.

"There you are now," she crooned, shifting the pressure of her touch to walk him into the stall. "I won't tie you, but I'll leave you while I fetch some water. You stay here and get used to where you are. If you don't like it, find a way to express that."

Such as stand up and shout *I hate this*? That's what he wanted to do as she left and closed the gate.

He could hear the voices carrying on in the distance, but the silence that closed around him told him he was alone here. Utterly alone. So alone that a disturbingly cold emptiness washed over him.

He could have stood and called her back, but there was something broken within him, a tiredness in his soul, that kept him bent with his arms aching as the crutches supported him. With all four of his "hooves" on the ground, he couldn't see much beyond the strewn straw and yellowed walls of hay that surrounded him.

What was he supposed to do? Wait for her to fetch him? He *wanted* to fight his way free of his situation. The more he thought of it, the more his anger roared back to life inside him. With his weight balanced on the stilts, he lashed out with a foot and discovered the walls were solid but possessed a satisfying give, absorbing the impact of his heel.

He did it again. And again.

If Kiki had stood at the gate and watched him, he couldn't have allowed his emotions to bubble up this way, but he was alone and *furious*. He balanced on the wobbly crutches and kicked out with both feet, using all his strength.

Some of that power rippled back into him, shuddering up his spine, but he sensed the fragility in the walls around him. He could topple them if he kept at it, and he *wanted* to.

A hoarse cry left his throat as he bucked again and again, pressing his weight onto his arms and crashing his heels into the walls of straw, intent on knocking them apart.

A bale fell, and he kicked it to pieces before he moved to a different wall and bucked afresh, unsatisfied with the small hole he punched through. He wanted to destroy the whole damned thing.

"There, there, fella. You're safe here," a male voice crooned.

*You don't know that*, Qahhar thought with helpless fury. He kept bucking and kicking. It struck him that he didn't even care someone was witnessing his performance. It wasn't a performance. It was him. He was exorcising the angry beast inside himself. Freeing him.

"He'll settle when he's ready, Perry. Thank you," Kiki murmured. "I'll look after him."

*Would she, though? Would she?*

Qahhar continued to buck and kick. His muscles were aching and shaking with exertion. Sweat was running into his eyes.

When he feared his arms wouldn't hold him any longer, he leaned sideways on the battered, unsteady wall of prickly hay, still precariously bent forward on his stilts.

"There you are." Kiki's soothing voice washed over him. "You're safe here. I'm coming in now. Is that all right?"

The gate squeaked, and she held it open, leaving him a space to run, but he didn't. He closed his eyes against the sting of perspiration in his eyes. He hoped it was perspiration.

"You must be thirsty." The gate swung shut, and he heard the handle of a pail fall against its tin wall. Her cupped hand came to his lips, cooling and wetting them with a splash of water.

He had panted his mouth dry. He opened his eyes to see the bucket at her feet. He would have thrust his face into it, but these wretched forelegs made bending that far impossible.

Kiki leaned down and scooped water with her two hands and offered it to him.

He took it, drawing it in and swallowing a gulp, then again, unable to imagine what she thought of him acting so helpless like this.

"There you are," she said again, smoothing her wet hands over his hair and neck and ears, drawing his face against her chest.

He could feel the hardness of her breastbone against his brow and drank in the smell of her linen shirt and the spicy scent that was uniquely her own. That particular fragrance went into him the way a branding iron went into a hide.

"I'm going to groom you. Would you like that?" she murmured. She reached down, and this time, when she came up from the bucket, she held a sponge that she wrung over his head.

As the cool trickles ran down his temples and cheeks, behind his ears and into his collar, he sighed with relief.

"I think you would." Her voice held him in a spell, still braced on his trembling arms, back aching.

When she smoothed a cloth over his brow and face and neck, wiping away the water and sting of sweat, he couldn't help the small noise that left him.

She did it again before she said, "Let's remove your tack."

He finally straightened, muscles still trembling, and swayed on his feet.

She guided him to a pair of bales he hadn't noticed had tumbled. She sat him down and removed his forelegs, then washed his arms and hands, taking great care as she worked the sponge between each of his fingers and across his palms and wrists. Afterward, she set it aside and dug her touch into his muscles, massaging from the heels of his palms up to his elbows.

"Now your shirt and jacket?" She opened his tie and his collar button while he sat in a state of numbness. When he didn't protest, she bared his upper half. "I should have brought liniment. You'll be sore tomorrow."

He didn't care. Not about that or the fact his trousers grew damp when she poured the water over his shoulders and chest. She ran both sponge and hands over his skin, soothing his aching, twitching muscles, turning them to soft, warm wax.

"Shall I do the rest? Would you like to stand?"

He did. She stripped him down to his bare feet and washed him, sliding the cold sponge between his ass cheeks and under his balls and bathing his straining erection with tender care.

As she closed her wet fist around his cock and stroked it, slow and loose, she swept her thumb across his weeping tip and murmured, "I could take you in my mouth? Or you could cover me? Would you like that?"

"Yes." It was a single, ragged word with its origin somewhere deep in his chest.

A whisper of a seductive smile touched her lips as she removed her clothing. He had a vague thought that anyone could happen by to gawk at them, but it was an inconsequential concern when Kiki was naked and turning like a candle flame that beckoned a moth.

She braced her hands on the straw bale, offering her ass to him. The pink of her pussy winked at him. It was all the encouragement he needed.

Some distant part of him needed to know she was ready and receptive, though. He dropped to his knees and pushed his face into where her scent was most intoxicating. He licked at her plump folds, parting them with his tongue as he searched for her entrance, tasting salt and sweet nectar. As the flavor of her juices swept into him like potent liquor, she shivered and shifted, arching her back for more and stepping her legs farther apart.

He could have kept his face buried there all day, licking along her slit, searching out her clitoris and growing drunk on her juices, but he stood and positioned himself. He took hold of her hips and slid all the way into her slick heat, making a guttural noise as he arrived.

She pushed back on him, wriggling to draw him a fraction deeper, moaning encouragement.

"I'm wearing my—ugh." She grunted and braced one hand on the wall, accepting a harder stroke. "You can come inside me if you w—" Another gasping moan left her as his thrust landed.

He barely heard her. He was enthralled, watching his shining cock reappear and plunge back into her hot cunt. His fingers unconsciously dug into her hips as he kept himself to a steady pace, wanting her to come first but not sure he could last. Each time her pussy locked tight around him, he nearly died with the exquisite pleasure of it.

Fuck, her ass was beautiful. He ran his palms all over it, making noises he'd never made that were pure joy at the shivering ecstasy of fucking her. When he slid his touch to search out her swollen clitoris, he felt the tension that immediately overtook her.

"Good?"

Her answer was a nonsense word of helpless pleasure and a lean of her weight back into his hips.

He kept rocking his fingers in her soaked folds, brushing the tense little bump that made her whimper while he fucked her harder. Faster.

Her back swayed deeper, lifting her hips higher, encouraging his rough thrusts. As her jagged sounds turned to desperation, he grasped her shoulder and fucked her with all his strength.

Her sheath clamped over his cock and rippled. Her cries shredded into musical notes of joy. He held back his own release for long, pulsing moments, pumping into her, exalted by the knowledge he was delivering her such intense pleasure.

Then he couldn't hold back. His balls contracted with a delicious ache. Scorching heat shot through his cock, burning his crown as thick bursts of come left him, pooling in her depths to bathe him in the sweetest satisfaction imaginable.

# CHAPTER FIVE

"Thank you," Kiki murmured as she picked up her jacket. She was still shaking and glowing from her incredible orgasm. With the whole experience of watching Qahhar lose himself, then letting her touch every inch of his body as if she had the right to. He'd released every part of himself, and she felt privileged to have witnessed it.

She would have gone into his arms, but Qahhar bent to plunge his hand into the last of the water in the bucket, then splashed his face in a half-hearted wash.

"I didn't expect that." He flicked the water off his hand.

She had never felt so close to anyone, but she could see he was turning inward, shutting her out. Had she gone too far? Her chest tightened.

Before she could ask, they both heard Perry a short distance away. "Mistress is indisposed. I'm sure she'll be along shortly."

Kiki poked her nose over the gate, and Qahhar said, "You should get back."

"You're not coming with me?"

"I need a minute." He pinched his cuff and glanced for his links. They'd fallen into the straw strewn across the ground. He sighed with a lifetime's worth of resignation.

Perhaps he'd released his anger, but he was still off-balance. She wanted to touch him, but more for herself. She wanted to reestablish and reinforce the link that had felt so strong and true when he'd been thrusting into her, their bodies so finely attuned, she hadn't been sure where hers stopped and his began.

She had to respect his desire to be alone, though. "I shouldn't be long. I'll get some food. We could go into the orchard," she suggested.

He gave an absent nod, and she slipped away.

When she got back, Perry said he'd saddled Honor and gone home.

• • •

"I'm ready to lie around in a field and do sweet fuck all for days," Hamish said when he came down to breakfast after the last of their guests were gone. They finally had the hall to themselves. "Will you take me down, lass? Warren said he would, but he's still abed, and I'd rather sleep in the clover."

"I will, but can we talk a minute first?" Kiki touched one of the hands he had set on her shoulders in an affectionate squeeze.

"'Course. Let me fill my plate. I'm starving."

He ate only greens when he was Chaucer and had had an active few days. He'd won the sulky race and had come second in the obstacle course, not to mention running Warren through the fox hunt and allowing Kiki to put him in dressage.

"What did Qahhar think? I saw him at one point, but I never spoke to him." He joined her at the table and noted her plate was mostly untouched. "Off your feed, lass?"

"A little. Qahhar only came for a few hours. I..." She heaved a sigh of despair. "I think I put him in a position that made him uncomfortable."

"You?" He frowned as he shoved an entire sausage into his mouth. "How?"

"I encouraged him to play, to express his emotions. Perhaps he thought it was the only way I was willing to be with him." She set her glum chin on her hand and spun the handle of her teacup. "How was it for you and Warren in the beginning? I know Chaucer was part of your relationship from the early days, but did you have any moments when you felt you might have to choose? That he would only love you if you were Chaucer or the other way round?"

"No, but there were times when our circumstance demanded Chaucer take a long rest. That was hard. When I thought I would lose Warren, I thought Chaucer would die, too. You saw how wrecked I was. Is Qahhar making you feel as though you have to make such a choice?"

"No," she said with a pang. "I fear he's made his own choice, and I'm not it."

"Ah, lass. I'm not a man for finding the right words in a time like this. You know that." He rose and brought his chair and plate around the table so they were close enough his shoulder brushed hers. "We'll eat, then go down and watch the horses graze. That always cheers you."

Usually, it did. Today, she wasn't so sure.

●●●

Qahhar caught his letters before they were posted. He opened and rewrote every one.

He owed Kiki an explanation for leaving without saying goodbye, but he wanted this off his mind first. He was no longer enraged. She had helped him with that, but in discharging his anger, he'd been faced with guilt. So much guilt. Guilt that he'd been traveling when his father had passed. Guilt that he hadn't been his father's emissary in Morocco to prevent his uncle taking a foothold in the first place. Guilt that he was not there now, fighting for what rightfully belonged to him.

Guilt that he wanted to stay here and explore the life he might have with Kiki.

As his fog of resentment had cleared and he'd been awash in the joy Kiki promised him, he'd seen the excuses he had tried to feed himself. The promises that he would go back and fix things *after* he put his house in order. Would he, though? Was it worth carrying a grudge for some years before he could act on it? Was that how he wanted to live?

Was that something he wanted Kiki to live *with*?

In forcing him to break down the walls he had placed around himself, she had forced him to see who he was and look to who he wanted to be. He didn't want to be the man who was so angry he kicked at straw walls. One who planned to fight the past into the future.

He wanted to be a man who recognized when his circumstance had changed. One who accepted this new life and saw the value in it. In fact, if he looked toward building a life here instead of focusing his energy on revenge, he believed he could have a very fulfilling life, so long as Kiki was willing to be part of it.

So he rewrote his letters with a much more dispassionate tone. His accusations against his uncle were still true, but he made no efforts at persuasion. *It is not in my power to change your mind*, he wrote several times. *That is something you must decide for yourself, based on what you see and know in your heart.*

When he let those letters go with his footman, he breathed a sigh of relief.

Then, as he was climbing the stairs, intent on changing to ride over to Auburn Hall, his butler caught his attention.

"Beg your pardon, sir. One of the grooms says a lady has returned your stallion?"

He halted. "Returned?"

• • •

Kiki rode Honor bareback. She'd caught a handful of his glorious mane when he'd dismounted Bluebell, and he'd allowed her to leap atop him. It had felt so natural, she hadn't bothered to take him to the stable for drying or saddling despite the fact his coat was soaked.

He knew his way home—by land this time. He ambled with such smugness, he ought to be whistling as he took her along the edge of the channel, through the clay yard, and across the stone bridge.

They were very good friends by the time they arrived at Sheringham Manor.

"Kiki." Qahhar appeared in the stable yard in half dress. "I was about to change and come see you. How did Honor get to Auburn Hall?"

"Swam the channel. Bluebell was down in the lower pasture—"

"Ah, shit. Is she hurt?"

Kiki snorted. "Not at all. I'm surprised Honor didn't *jump* the channel, given how she was calling him. She was waiting for him as he came out of the water. I saw it all from our east field. It was over before I could get there to prevent it."

"You're not upset?"

"If it was anyone else, I might be." She leaned forward to hug the stallion's neck. "But he's too beautiful. I *will* keep his foal if she drops one."

She slid off Honor to stand before Qahhar, uncertainty returning as she faced him.

He grunted with mild disgust and scratched under his chin. The way he eyed her suggested he was hesitating in some way as well.

"Will you come have a cup of coffee or tea? I want to talk with you."

"Do you?" she asked warily as they fell into step toward the manor.

"I've neglected you; I know." His profile held consternation. "I needed to put my head right."

"Because of what I coaxed you to do at the party? I—"

"Kiki." He grasped her wrist, stopping her in the middle of the path. "What you encouraged me to do helped me. I loved how you behaved at the party. I'm falling *in* love with you. That's not something I imagined myself capable of until I met you."

"Oh?" Her eyes and throat began to swell with pressure.

He shifted his grip so their fingers intertwined and drew her into a fragrant rose garden.

"I came here filled with plans. Destructive ones. I intended to play out a prophecy of revenge that I had foretold to myself. But why should I go to all the trouble of falling in love with you, then go back to Morocco to fight for...what? A life there without you? The life I want is here. I can have it. Can't I?" He stopped walking. His hand tightened on hers.

Her heart soared, but she couldn't help the quaver of uncertainty as she said, "Yes?"

His brows came together. "You don't sound convinced."

"Are *you* certain? After everything you saw?"

"What did I see? People making lives for themselves that fit their needs. Other people respecting that. All of them coming together in companionship. I'm not delighted by the idea of people watching us in our intimate moments, but I'm not entirely put off by it, am I?" he noted drily. He released her hand and drew her into his arms. "I love making love with you. I want to do that again. Daily, if you have time for it."

"I have time right now," she assured him, leaning into the wall of his chest.

"How convenient. So do I." He drew her into the house and up to his bedchamber.

# EPILOGUE

*Eleven months later…*

"Shall we marry so he might be legitimized?" Qahhar's gentle voice penetrated Kiki's euphoria. It had been a long night of labor with a healthy delivery. Now she was in a blissfully happy place of utter contentment.

"If you wish him to be your heir, I think we must," she murmured.

"At the pageant next month, then."

She lifted her gaze to send him a look of amused admonishment. He was dressed impeccably, freshly shaved, and looking on her with such a light of love, she caught her breath.

"Are you really proposing to me as I sit here in this dirty straw, covered in afterbirth?"

"It's where you are happiest and therefore most beautiful. Is he well?"

"He's so well, Qahhar. Look at him." She was completely enamored with the colt Bluebell had dropped. He wore a coat of dappled silver-gray. His tuft of mane was black, as were his ears and feet. He was the sweetest, most eye-catching thing she'd ever seen.

"Come," Qahhar coaxed. "I've ordered a bath. You need to eat and rest."

She did. And they were in safe hands. Hamish had arrived last night, the minute she had sent a note to Auburn Hall. He had stayed with them the whole time but had become Chaucer a short while ago. He was dozing in the stable opposite so he could keep watch over foal and dam. The colt had stood to nurse and was now folded to the floor, enjoying Kiki's adoring pets and nuzzles while sleepily dropping his head.

Kiki experienced a visceral tug and ache as she made herself stand. With a parting hug and some praise for Bluebell, she slipped out of the stall and accompanied Qahhar through the dawn birdsong to the rooms they shared in Sheringham Manor.

"Do you really think we should marry?" she asked as he followed her into the bathing room, where a steaming tub sat ready.

"I would marry you ten times over, I love you so much. You know that." He dispatched her soiled, masculine attire and held her hand as she stepped into the tub. He began to wash her, soaping a cloth and picking up her arm to gently scrub the length of it. "But Sheringham is already bequeathed to you. We can find our own Kiki to adopt and love and provide for them to inherit the way Warren and Hamish have set up for you to receive Auburn Hall. We don't have to make our own children unless you want to."

The cloth went into her underarm and down to her breast, where the light friction on the underside awakened her nipple. Sexual hunger sparked to a glow within her.

"If I fell pregnant, I wouldn't be upset, but I like the freedom of riding every day, doing as I wish. I like that you and I can do as we wish." She let her head loll on the back of the tub, voice growing languid as she asked, "Will you fetch the tails?"

"You're tired," he protested, but glints of desire arrived in his dark brown irises.

"I'm tired but awake. I need something to help me relax."

He left, and she continued bathing herself. Thankfully, her hair had been plaited and wrapped before she went to the stables last night. It probably still smelled of horses, but she didn't have to wash it.

When Qahhar returned, he was naked, cock already hard and bobbing as he moved. His black horsehair tail hung from between his ass cheeks, swishing behind his powerful thighs. He liked to insert his own and *loved* to insert hers. They had discovered they both very much enjoyed wearing one while they fucked.

He had brought her preventative cap along with the oil and her tail. He left everything on the linen chest and shook out one of the loomed cotton towels, holding it for her.

She stepped from the water into his waiting arms, lifting her mouth for his hungry kiss. He trapped her in the towel and shifted his hands across her shape, further awakening her senses.

"Turn," he said gruffly, dropping the towel to allow it.

"Here?" She breathlessly bent to take hold of the furled edge of the cast-iron tub.

His answer was a growled noise of approval. He went to his knees behind her and gripped her ass cheeks to part them. His tongue began to rasp along her crease, licking from the dampness of her entrance to her tailbone, returning to reach and tantalize her clitoris, encouraging her to bow her back for more. Then his tongue rimmed and prodded her arsehole, teasing her to part her legs and wiggle in helpless arousal.

With a groan of lust, he rose and brought her cap. He was well-versed in slipping it into her pussy and seating it to prevent pregnancy. She gripped his fingers as his touch left her, but he was fetching her tail. Seconds later, he rubbed the oiled tip of the plug against her arsehole before pressing for entry.

Kiki bit her lip, liking that pinch of pressure and stretch, the insistence and the widening sensation. The implacable feel of it inside her, then the tickle of hair as he fanned it across her ass. She knew he was admiring what he saw and gave another wiggle, enjoying the silky brush against her skin as the hair fell to caress her inner thighs.

Now the part she loved most, when he grew too aroused to wait any longer. He gathered her tail and lifted it, shifting the pressure of the plug inside her while he guided his hard cock to her cunt. They were both groaning and growling, rarely needing words at this point, always perfectly attuned.

His cock sought and prodded, then slid deep. The press of

his hips landed against the plug, giving her a zing of pleasure-pain that made her tighten her grip on the edge of the tub. She pushed back on his thrust, encouraging him to do it again. To let loose his power and thrill her with that sensation again and again.

He swept her tail fully onto her back so it tickled her spine and shoulder blades, then took a firm grip on her hips. His next withdrawal and thrust forced a cry of ecstasy from her. And another.

For long minutes, she took his steady pumps while they both crashed into each other, chasing climax, voices combined in noisy ecstasy. Soon tension had her in its grip. Her inner muscles clamped down before expanding with an explosive pleasure that shattered through her whole body.

His hips slapped once more against her ass. He held himself deep, arching into her with a grip on her hips that was liable to leave bruises, but she didn't care. It was a perfectly timed culmination that held them both in a stasis of soaring bliss. Nothing else existed but this.

Slowly, the pulses faded. They were both shaking.

"You took me well after such a long night." His voice was unsteady. He gently withdrew and helped her stand, embracing her with tender arms and setting a loving kiss on her mouth.

He had served her well, but she was too foggy-minded to say so. She let him steer her to their bed, where he pressed her onto her stomach and reclined beside her.

His hand caressed her back, squeezing the last of the tension in her shoulders and rubbing the ache from her lower back. He took a firm hold of her tail, murmuring a soothing noise as he worked it free with a fresh pinch, causing a small noise of discomfort to sound in her throat.

"Shh. There, there, love. I'll look after you," he murmured in a voice like warm butter. His long fingers explored between her thighs, gathering up oil and semen and the remains of her juices to work them against her stinging arsehole and the tender folds of her pussy. "Does that feel nice?"

She sighed, wanting to tell him it felt very nice, but her eyes grew heavy. With a final stir of consciousness, she fought to murmur, "Will you…" She couldn't remember what she wanted to say.

"I'll look in on the foal," he promised. "And Chaucer. I'll send word to Warren and wake you when he arrives." His mouth touched her shoulder in a soft kiss before he shifted off the bed.

She smiled. It was nice to be so well understood.

*The End*

# How Do You Do Your Do?

*How Do You Do Your Do?* features a young man who finds his perfect match, however the story contains a minor character who briefly engages in verbal and physical abuse, along with references to classism and indentured servitude, so readers who may be sensitive to these, please take note.

# PROLOGUE

*June 1870, Paris*

Lord Ingram Uxton, second son of the Duke of Havershire and recent recipient of a postgraduate certificate in law from the University of Oxford, came upon a wig shop before he could avoid it. His heart lurched, and his feet rooted to the walkway.

*Don't*, he ordered himself, even as he turned his head to the window, allowing his gaze to eat up the brunette braids and blond coils, the chestnut rosettes and black cluster puffs. An erection began to chub in his trousers. His stomach twisted with longing and helplessness.

"What use is a tour for him?" his father had blustered. A trip to the continent had rounded out his elder son's social sophistication, but as a younger son, Ingram was destined to make his own way. Enough had been spent on his education as it was.

Ingram's brother had advocated for him, persuading their father to underwrite it. "He may go into politics one day. That would be a useful connection. He'll need a broader outlook for that sort of career."

To Ingram, his brother had advised sternly, "We can't have rumors that reflect badly on the title. Get any nonsense out of your system while you're away, then come back and settle down."

This was the "nonsense" to which his brother had been referring. They had never spoken openly about it, but Ingram knew his brother suspected he had this inconvenient and inexplicable fascination with hair.

Perhaps if he had stayed in London, where he had exhausted the shops, he wouldn't be so tempted to enter. Perhaps if things had proceeded as planned and his two friends had joined him,

Ingram would have other commitments, but one had fallen ill, and the other had chosen to join an uncle headed to America.

Ingram had come away with only his brother's copy of *The Handbook for Travelers in Southern Italy* as a companion. It was the most current edition and the one his brother had used when he'd spent a summer traveling Europe with their cousin five years ago. They had marked up the best sights and places to stay and eat, but Ingram had yet to remove it from his haversack, preferring to let the novelty of freedom from expectations guide him.

Which had brought him here. Damn it.

He shifted the haversack on his shoulder, using the strap to press against his hardened nipple.

"Monsieur?" A woman of late middle age opened the door to poke her head out. "May I be of assistance? Our selection of toupees is limited, but they're very nice."

"Non, merci." His voice came out strangled. He cleared his throat and tried to find a normal tone as he responded in French. "I'm actually..." *Don't do it.* "Soon embarking on my career as a solicitor. I've yet to have a peruke made." It was a lie. He had several stored in their cases at home, hidden under the bed, but it was a convenient excuse to enter her shop.

"Ah. I have one I can show you." She held the door open and invited him in with a wave.

His whole body trembled with near ecstasy as he entered. His nostrils drank in the musty aromas of wool and burned hair and the flour baked onto curls to hold them, along with the softer fragrances of lavender powder and rose oil used between boiling to ensure an owner's wig always smelled fresh.

She led him to the back of the shop, where an elegantly lacquered round case stood on a table. A brass buckle held it closed, and a brass carrying handle was affixed to the top. "We use horsehair. Excellent quality. This is not our only style. We have many illustrations to choose from."

Ingram used all his effort to keep his focus on her as she opened the case and used the two wire handles to lift out the silvery white wig. She set it next to the case for his inspection. The thickly loomed top was surrounded by abundant curls. Two thin queues fell off the back.

He swallowed, already imagining snipping those off.

"My brother-in-law makes them and would measure you for a precise fit. When it's complete, your name would be sewn here." She showed him the warp and weft of silk and hair inside, with its overlay of cotton netting and silk mounting ribbon. "His son will paint your name on the case."

One of the reasons Ingram had chosen law as his vocation was the excuse to buy and wear and caress a wig. Wigs had long fallen from favor with men, especially among the aristocracy. They were too affordable for the lower classes. Women, however, demanded elaborate additions for their fashionable styles, which meant the trade in hair was brisk.

His gaze drifted inexorably to the loose switches of hair hanging from hooks on the back wall.

"Were you thinking to have something made to your specifications?" The woman followed his gaze and moved to lift a switch of dark brown from its hook. "If you remove your hat, I can help you select something that will match your natural color. This is similar to your mustache."

"No. Uh—" He didn't need to hide a bald patch. He needed to hide his arousal. He ensured his coat was closed across his trouser buttons and searched for something intelligent to say.

"There's no embarrassment, monsieur. Many young gentlemen wear our enhancements. They're so well blended, you may not notice."

"I was thinking of something for my sister," he blurted. He had no sister. "Her color is similar to mine." He snatched off his hat.

For a man soon to practice law, he lied very brazenly. This

was not "getting it out of his system."

"I see." Her pleasant smile faltered with surprise, but she returned the dark brunette to the hook and selected something more auburn, holding it up to the side of his face.

"Not quite," she murmured.

*Yes*, he silently groaned. The hair hadn't even touched his skin, but his cock was fully engorged and his balls pulled tight. He shifted his weight, trying to hide his reaction, but only felt the dampness of leaked dew that had begun to stain his underdrawers.

"My husband is in Provence right now, collecting hair." She absently made conversation as she shifted the switches around. "Our daughter is assisting him, but I often go. Have you ever seen the traders doing their work? What do you think of that one?" She lay a wavy switch of hair across his palm.

He shook his head, unable to speak. He'd only heard of the markets and had once seen a heavyset man striding down a cobbled street, haircutting shears swaying from his belt like a mesmerist's watch. The memory aroused him to this day.

"That one doesn't suit?" She continued searching her inventory. "We pay well, so we always have a good turnout of maids and thus a good selection. Most have never cut it in their life. This one?" She withdrew the switch he held.

The tresses slithered across his palm only to be replaced with a thicker hank of dark chestnut.

"I remember this girl very clearly. She was paying her father's debt. We had to dicker a long time, but look how long it is. It fell well past her backside. So fine and soft, but so much."

He closed his fist on the girth of it. His cock was quivering in his pants, throbbing with his stumbling heartbeat.

"Usually, once I've tied it, my husband only needs two or three clips to take it off." She worked her fingers like the blades on a pair of shears. "This was seven or eight."

*Oh fuck me. Fuck me.*

"She was very pretty, voluptuous, and sweet. When it was

done, she touched her nape and blushed." She demonstrated. "So shy! I could tell she felt naked."

Ingram shoved his free hand into his pocket, desperate to reach his fingers to caress the tip of his cock. There was a rushing in his ears, and a euphoric urge to laugh swelled his chest.

In his mind, the sound of the shears was right behind his ears. The scrape and snap of the hair strands and the clip as the blades closed. He *loved* that sound of hair being cut through. It made his scalp tighten and his chest itch and his cock pulse even harder.

"Come to the mirror and hold it to your face."

He couldn't. He already tasted blood, he was biting the inside of his lip so hard. His feet were trying to curl in his boots, and the tightness in his balls was a cruel threat of impending orgasm.

"I'll take it." He thrust it at her.

"Mais bien sûr." She was startled but moved to the desk, where she coiled the switch into a small round box.

He had to rearrange things in his haversack to fit it in. As she made his change, he hurried to stow it, then took his leave so abruptly, he bordered on rude.

"Les cabinets?" he asked.

"Behind the fishmonger—" She started to give him directions, but he was already striding from the shop.

He followed the smell of fish and hurried into the wooden stall erected around a privy.

Urgently unbuttoning himself, he took his engorged cock in his hand. He could barely touch himself, he was so aroused. In his mind, he was watching the tail of hair slowly tearing away from its owner.

With only one squeeze of his fist, his climax struck without mercy.

# CHAPTER ONE

*August 1870, Swiss Alps*

Flora Kohler had few pleasures in her life, but a stolen hour in a meadow of wildflowers was one of them. Vater Werner would berate her when she got back, but he wouldn't leave his cheese-making to come find her.

She sank to the ground next to a stream and bared her feet, setting them in the icy water. It was so cold it made her ears ring, but she kept them there as she removed her straw hat and eased onto her back.

The height of the wildflowers gave her the sense she'd fallen into a lacy crevasse of green stalks and blades. Petals of yellow and pink and blue competed with the small puffs of white clouds floating in the summer sky. The bells of the cows clinked softly in the distance. The stream trickled, and the insects buzzed back and forth across her, lazily collecting nectar. The sun warmed her through the layers of her apron and gown, so she picked up her skirt to cool her legs and set her foot deeper into the water.

The sensuality of the moment overtook her. She let her eyes drift shut while her fingers found the slit in her drawers. As she tickled her touch over the fine hairs protecting her folds, she let her thoughts drift to the interlude she'd witnessed between a pair of young lovers some weeks ago. Johann, a boy from the village, had been kissing her foster sister, Hendrika. Mutter Gertrud would faint dead if she knew her daughter had allowed a goatherd to touch her daughter like this, but Hendrika had seemed happy for Johann to do it.

Flora had felt a libidinous stir between her own legs when she'd been sent to take lunch to Vater Werner and happened upon the pair kissing and fondling behind a boulder. Johann's hand had been high beneath Hendrika's skirts.

Flora almost never had time to herself. At night, she was usually too tired to bother exploring this particular mystery, but she was a curious person, and today she was feeling soft and lovely. Her nether lips seemed to bloom like the flowers around her as she caressed herself. The more she firmed her touch, the more the sweet sensations gathered and doubled on themselves. There was even a strange, slippery honey that made the passage of her fingertip more smooth, somehow making the friction more acute yet more enticing.

She spread her legs a little more and explored deeper, finding the source of the wetness and spreading it around, returning again and again to a spot that seemed to swell under her rolling fingertip. The more she played with it, the more tumescent the small bump became, standing up so tall, she barely had to touch it and the sensations were moving through her like a song.

She had never imagined anything could feel this frustratingly delicious, as though a force was building inside her, becoming more and more gripping, until she was nearly out of her mind with the tension of anticipation...

A release happened that was so shocking and acute, she cried out with surprise and pleasure even as she cupped her mound, afraid she had broken herself. The pressure both soothed and exaggerated the pulsing sensations. For a few breaths, she was in a type of ecstasy she had never known. Nothing in the world mattered but this lovely sensation that bloomed repeatedly inside her.

Just as she began to fear it would never end, the sensations faded. She was able to catch her breath. Her heart steadied, and she felt both relieved and saddened to come down from such a great height.

She blinked open her eyes, surprised to find herself still in the meadow with the intense blue sky and blinding white clouds above her.

A pang of discontent intruded as she realized she must return to work now, before she was found and punished for neglecting her duties. She felt so lovely and lazy, she wished she could stay here all day.

She sighed and stood, bare feet numb to the prickle of trampled grass as she straightened and let her skirts fall.

As she spared a moment for the view of the peaks across the valley, she spotted a man a little ways down the hill. Her heart lurched. Had he seen her? *Heard* her?

His back was to her, and he held his hat in his hand as he scratched his head. When he glanced back at her, his expression was guilt-ridden.

Oh *no*.

• • •

Apparently Greek nymphs were found in the Swiss Alps. As Ingram quietly hurried away from his inadvertent discovery, he had a hysterical thought to write to John Murray, publisher and vigilant editor of *The Handbook for Travelers in Switzerland and the Alps of Savoy and Piedmont*, to advise him that such creatures should be added to the list of "Native Fauna."

In his haste to leave the Paris wig shop, Ingram had inadvertently left his brother's guidebook behind. He'd discovered the loss the next day, when he'd been preparing to leave for Rome. He'd been too mortified to go back for it and tried to replace it at the bookshop near the train station. They had only had this one in stock.

He had reasoned it would get him halfway to his destination, but once he'd begun following its recommendations, hiking glaciers and soaking in mineral baths, he couldn't seem to find any interest in visiting hot, dusty Italian ruins. The grandeur of the mountain peaks was something he would be hard-pressed to describe when he returned home, but he anticipated becoming one of those tedious people who tried.

He surely wouldn't know how to describe what he'd just seen, though.

After climbing all morning, he'd heard the trickle of water and approached the stream, anticipating an icy cold drink. What he'd found was a young woman with her skirts up and her drawers open. She was frigging herself.

It had taken him two or three shocked heartbeats to realize what she was about, and another to retreat. He hadn't known women did that!

Everything in him wanted to go back and watch. He paused, clenching his eyes against the mountains across the valley and saw *her* valley, pink and shiny and plump with arousal. Her intimate hairs were blond, which had been as spellbinding as the way her finger had worked against her pussy like a bow on violin strings. Her back had held an arch of tension. Her brow had been pulled with concentration. The edge of her lip had been caught in her teeth.

He would hold that exquisite vision in his mind forever.

Along with the faint moan of her climax. There was no mistaking that noise as it struck his ears. He damned near fell into a paroxysm of ecstasy himself as the sound echoed sweetly behind him.

He wished he could have watched her. He had the sharpest urge to go back and hold her and kiss her as she blinked herself back to this fine day. Wouldn't it be lovely to share such a thing in such a beautiful place?

He glanced back and saw she was on her feet. The grass and wildflowers were a sea around her aproned skirt. Her expression turned to horror as she realized he might have heard her. *Seen* her.

She didn't even pick up her boots or hat before she was racing down the hill away from him, sure-footed as a chamois.

Fuck that was a lot of rolled plait on her head. How long was it?

*Fuck.* He was being a complete asshole.

"I won't hurt you!" Shit. He struggled to find the word for "safe" in German, brain still in his swollen cock. "Du bist sicher," he yelled at her back.

It didn't matter. She was down the next hillock and out of sight.

What a fucking toad he was. He called himself a few other choice names as he retrieved her boots and hat and ambled down to the collection of sheds called "alps," if Mr. Murray was correct in his interpretations.

As Ingram neared the alp, he saw the young woman standing with her arms folded and her shoulders hunched, head hanging low. She had one bare foot over the other while a grizzled older man berated her in guttural German. He took the rag from over his shoulder and smacked it against her skirt, demanding, "Where are your boots?"

"I startled her by the stream, sir." Ingram set her boots and hat beside the axe, where it was driven into the chopping block.

"Why were you not *in* them? Put them on." The man slapped her skirt again.

It wasn't a blow that would physically hurt her, but it irritated the hell out of Ingram to see her treated that way.

She gave him a malevolent look as she approached him, eyes blue as the summer sky, hair a burned gold.

*Don't look at her hair.*

He made himself step back while she plucked her socks from her boots. She perched on the chopping block with her back turned to him as she reshod her feet.

"Who are you?" the man demanded.

"I wonder if you need any help here?" Ingram said, exactly as he had at other alps. "I can turn hay." Any fool could. "And milk the cows."

"That's what Flora is for. When she's not sleeping in the pasture." The man sent her another glower.

"I could chop wood?" He glanced to where Flora was re-pinning her hat over her— *Don't think about it.* "It's a long walk up from the village, so I bring enough food for myself to stay overnight." He showed the small bag on his shoulder. "I don't mind sleeping with the cows. I would only stay one night."

"I have to get back to my cheese. You show him," he grumbled to Flora on his way back into the shed. "And bring me my lunch."

The man disappeared with a clap of the door.

Ingram supposed he was lucky the man hadn't used the axe on him.

"Hello, Flora. May I call you that? I'm Ingram. I'd like to apologize—"

"It needs to be this size. No bigger, no smaller. Understand?" She held out a stick of wood. "So he can control the heat. Think about what you want to be hit with if you get it wrong." She stalked away.

# CHAPTER TWO

Flora usually liked milking, especially in the evening. It was a quiet time when she finally had an excuse to sit. She found it relaxing to set her face against the warmth of the cow's side, breathing the scent of animal and hay as she pulled the warm teats.

This evening when she looked across, there *he* was.

He was English, but his German was very good. He was handsome and well kempt, even with a day's shadow coming in below his dark mustache. The sculpted band of bristles across his top lip curled up at the ends in a friendly way, like a smile. The quality of his clothes told her he was only playing at being a peasant, but he wasn't afraid of work. After chopping for several hours, he had rolled up his sleeves and was getting his bearings beside the cow.

His claim that he could milk was an exaggeration. He understood what had to happen, but he was awkward about starting, and the cow sensed it. She shifted her weight, which forced him to adjust his bucket and stool.

*Dummkopf.*

As the milk finally began to hit the bottom of his bucket with small hisses, he checked over his shoulder to ensure Vater Werner hadn't followed them in.

"I'm sorry about this afternoon. I walked away as soon as I realized—" His face was staining red. "I thought only men did that."

Her face stung with embarrassment. She had resolved to hate him until the day she died, but suddenly she was wondering, *Did he?* She was curious to hear *how* men did it, but she turned her face away, punishing him.

For several minutes, there was only the liquid sound of the milk hitting what was in the bucket. A cow huffed, and her stool creaked as she leaned to reach the far teats.

"What if I tell you something that is equally private? Would that calm your anger?"

She turned her face back to him. "Why do you care if I'm angry with you? You'll leave in the morning, and we'll never see each other again."

"True, but it still bothers me." He was copying her, leaning his face on the cow's side, wearing a look she couldn't interpret—not discomfort, exactly, but pained. "Forget it."

The loss of a chance to learn more about him struck surprisingly deep, causing her to blurt, "Tell me, then."

"I like hair," he said in a near whisper.

She snorted, not sure what she had expected, but that was such a plainly *not* private confession, she couldn't help but dismiss it by turning her face away again.

"A lot. Too much," he insisted in a voice that also held traces of frustration and anger. "I'm aroused by it. The feel of this cow hide against my cheek is filling me with lust. When I look at your plait, I want to…" He cleared his throat. "I embarrassed myself in a wig shop in Paris. The woman was showing me switches of hair they'd bought off peasant girls. It was humiliating, the way I became so aroused, but I bought it and hold it while I…do what you were doing." He sounded miserable.

That struck her as odd. When she had caressed herself, it had made her feel lovely.

"Do women do that?" She rose and poured her milk into the canister.

"Play with themselves while fondling hair? I have no idea, but now you've put *that* thought into my head…" He made a strangled noise and sent an exasperated look down to his thighs.

A tiny smile tugged at her lips. Her antagonism turned to wry amusement.

"I meant, do women sell their hair? How much do they get for it?"

"Are you teasing me?" His eyes widened with horror. "Please stop." He turned on his stool so he faced the same wall as the cow, his back to her. He braced his elbows on his knees and held his head in his hands. "Please don't talk about doing that."

"Cutting my hair?"

He whimpered, making her feel cruel when she only wanted to understand.

She moved to the other side of his cow to finish milking her, trying to explain why she was being so persistent.

"I can sew and cook. I learned to read while my parents were alive." Her father had been a teacher. She read very well and practiced on any printed words she could see. She was usually put to work before she could get through more than a page or two, though. "I thought I would grow up to marry a boy from my town, but my parents got sick and died. I was sent here to help Mutter Gertrud with her twins while her older boy and girl go to school."

Flora had helped all of the children with their reading and numbers, but she was still only seen as a minder. A servant who required food and clothing, so she had to pull her weight to earn it.

"In summer, their son apprentices with the blacksmith. Their daughter is home to help with the little ones, so I'm sent up here to help Vater Werner. They keep me because they need help, but they think I'm arrogant and ungrateful. I don't want to live with them, so I suppose I am. I have nowhere else I can go. I would marry, but the boys in the village aren't interested in me because I'm not from here. If I had value to bring to a marriage, though..."

"I understand." He still sounded unsteady. "I'm a second son. I only have value if my brother dies, which would devastate me if it happened, so I hope it never does, but our father treats us very differently. I'm held to higher standards and allowed less room for mistakes. I must be serious and consider how I will contribute to the family fortune. I mustn't outshine my brother or draw the wrong sort of attention to the title. My father wanted me to start my articles straight away and arranged a position for me in the law office he uses, but my brother persuaded him to fund my trip to Italy, same as he'd been given. He thinks I need to…grow out of my inconvenient desire."

"You're going to Italy?"

"I'm expected to, yes. My mother gave me a list of goods I'm to have shipped back to her." He tried to take up milking again, but his cow was done.

Flora carried the pail to the canister and brought the next animals in.

They didn't speak again until all the cows were milked. Then she prepared Vater Werner's dinner. He called Ingram to eat with him, eager to tell him about the art of cheese-making. Vater Werner was well regarded in the village for the quality of his milk and cheese and the sausage he made from the pigs that ate the slop. Flora washed her face in the whey before she fed it to them, but she had never been described as a beauty, so she didn't know why she bothered.

This idea of selling her hair stayed on her mind. It could only be done once, at least only once in a very long while. That was the problem. She would need a plan beyond the sale of it, and she didn't have any idea how much she could get for it. Worse, if Werner or Gertrud found out, they would surely expect her to give them the money. She hoped Ingram wouldn't mention it to the old man.

She was still perplexed that Ingram found hair so beguiling. It was an oddly endearing secret to share, and, try as she might, she couldn't continue to resent him when he'd given her a ray of hope, if only she could unravel how to use this knowledge.

"Why didn't you join us for dinner?" Ingram asked, interrupting her meal of buttered bread and milk under the stars.

"I told you; he doesn't care for me."

"How long have you been living with them?"

"Since I was thirteen. This is my fourth summer here." It was a mixed blessing to be in the hills. It was beautiful, and she was glad to have so much time alone, but the work was hard, and the days were long.

Ingram's silhouette was eye-catching as he stood with his hands in his pockets, gaze on the stark glow of snow on the moon-shadowed peaks across the valley.

"You must be terribly rich for your father to send you to Italy." She hadn't stopped thinking about that.

"The riches are my father's. They'll go to my brother."

"But you have a little money," she prodded.

He seemed to know where her mind was headed. "Flora." Her name was a garbled sound in his throat.

"I only thought a little," she said in a near whisper. "So it wouldn't be noticed. But never mind. I'm sorry I brought it up."

"No. Yes. I mean, I want that. Yes." With the darkness, it was hard to tell if he was excited or on the verge of tears. "Please."

• • •

Ingram barely slept, he was in such a sweat of anticipation. His bed of hay had been reasonably comfortable, if poky, but he couldn't stop fantasizing about what was to come. His hand spent so much time on his cock, he was chafed when he finally passed out from sexual exhaustion.

He was abruptly awakened at first light. Flora was bringing the cows in for their morning milking.

Werner came in to help and offered Ingram some heavy cream for breakfast, saying to Flora, "After you help me wash the cheese, you'll bring down the hay you were supposed to fetch yesterday."

She barely nodded an acknowledgment, but Ingram frowned.

"That's heavy work." He'd seen grown men bent under the weight of the giant nets of hay on their back as they carried it down from the meadows where it had been cut and dried. "I can help."

"You said one night. You'll move on." Werner flicked a hard look between Ingram and Flora. Whether he sensed they were forming a closeness or merely expected that a young man would have designs on a young woman didn't matter. He was putting a stop to it.

The slam of frustration that chopped into Ingram's chest was more than a fear of being denied her hair—although that was such a sharp sense of loss, his throat went dry. More than that, he felt for her. He knew what it was like to be underestimated and undervalued. To be stuck in a box that limited you, never to deviate from what was expected. To know that what you needed was disregarded, maybe even considered wrong.

Flora wanted more from life than she was being afforded, and Werner was deliberately holding her back for his own gain.

Ingram glanced at her, but she wasn't looking at him.

He gave Werner a jerky nod. "Thank you for your hospitality."

As he stepped outside, the stars were fading, the sky purple, the air crisp and fresh. It was the perfect morning to find a ledge where he could watch the sun rise.

He headed back the way he'd come yesterday and hoped Flora would know to look for him by the stream.

• • •

Flora couldn't help her smile of pleasure when she saw Ingram waiting for her by the stream.

"I was certain you would have moved on by now." After the milking, it had taken two hours to wash all the cheese wheels in the cellar. The sun was high and growing warm, the day a fine one for hiking, so she had been convinced he would take advantage of it.

"I gathered the hay onto the net." He waved self-consciously to where she had abandoned her tools yesterday. "I tried making more. It's harder than it looks."

The ground was chewed up near some freshly cut grass, proving he'd never swung a scythe before. The blade was bent and would need hammering and sharpening before she could cut more, but she was touched that he'd tried.

"Will Werner come looking for you?" he asked with a glance down the hill.

"No. He's tied to his cheese pot, making today's wheels, but we should move into the trees, in case one of the other cowherds sees us."

# CHAPTER THREE

They fell silent as they made the hard climb up the steep slope into the trees. Flora led him to a shady, private spot at the foot of a rocky escarpment that would hide them well.

"I made sure Vater Werner had plenty of linen cut and brought these." Flora drew the scissors from her apron pocket.

"Oh, fuck." Ingram was still trying to catch his breath and fell forward, bracing his hands on his knees. "I'm sorry," he said after a moment. He straightened and clutched his fist in his own hair. "I know there's something wrong with me, but *fuck*…"

He looked so tortured as he stared at the scissors, she was compelled to squeeze his arm with reassurance.

"Don't be upset. It is odd, I suppose, but it's not bad. You don't run around stealing women's hair against their will, do you?"

"No." He ran his hand down to his stubbled chin, wiping across his grimaced expression. "I tried watching at one of the markets and couldn't do it. There was a young woman whose parents were making her sell her hair. She cried the whole time. It upset me to see her shorn when she didn't want it to happen. I would never force you…" He looked at her hair piled beneath her straw hat. He swallowed, and his hand moved into the air as though he was tempted to touch it. "I won't ask you to do anything sexual. I just… How long is it?" His voice cracked with helpless turmoil.

She started to unpin her hat, and he sagged into the wall of rock behind him, looking the way a puppy might when it wagged itself into rolling onto its back.

"Have you always felt this way?" She lowered onto a mossy boulder and set her hat upside down in her lap to hold her hairpins.

"As long as I can remember." His voice was distracted, his gaze eating up her movements as she drew pins from her hair. "When my mother had the hairdresser come, her friends would gather in her boudoir. I was very cute as a child. They treated me like a pet. They would let me sit and watch all of them trying on dresses. They would have their hair curled and styled, all half naked and half drunk, laughing and happy— Can I?" He straightened onto his feet and took a half step forward. "Please?"

"If you like." She let her hands fall to hold her hat while he came across and stood behind her, removing the last of the pins before he began to unwind her hair and unravel the plaiting. She could hear his uneven breaths catching with excitement.

She was midway between soothed and tantalized. It felt nice to be touched and petted, and it was flattering to know he was so pleased with her. She didn't seem to please anyone, and he was being very gentle. Reverent, almost. It brought tears to her eyes as they shared this quiet moment of intimacy.

"Oh, Flora." He swallowed loudly and ran his hands through her hair, splaying the ends across her back and wide rump. His face pressed into the crook of her neck. He breathed deeply, whispering, "Thank you."

"I haven't done anything," she protested with a bemused smile, reaching up to cup his cheek. Perhaps he was on to something, because the feel of his stubble was strangely stimulating against her palm.

"You're being kind. I've never had the courage to talk about it with anyone. You're making me so happy, you don't even know."

She smiled into her lap, tempted to sit and let him play with her hair all day because it felt so nice, but awareness of time slipping away crept in.

"Ingram—"

"I know." He swept her hair forward on her shoulders and came to crouch in front of her. "I wish I had my brother's camera. You're so beautiful."

For the first time in her life, Flora *felt* beautiful. She smiled, not worrying that her teeth were crooked or her nose was too round and tilted up.

"I thought this much?" She dug beneath the fall of her hair, drawing forth a hank of hair that was about the width of heavy yarn. She kept it in one hand while brushing the rest behind her shoulders again. "And leave this much so I can still pin it up and hide that it's been snipped?" She held the spot that would keep it long enough to reach her shoulder. "You would still have all of this." The remainder was nearly as long as her arm.

"Yes." His eyes were pinned to her selection of hair. "Anything."

"Shall I plait it?"

"Yes." He tipped forward onto his knees before her.

She dug out the length of twine she'd brought in her apron pocket. She left it on her knee as she began to work.

It was such a small, fine length, it took a long time. Ingram didn't seem to mind. He knelt before her, patient and quiet as though worshiping at an altar.

She was only a third of the way when he sheepishly pushed his hand into his pocket and shifted uncomfortably.

Flora realized there was a firm shape behind the slouch at the front of his trousers.

"You can take it out if you want to."

"Flora." He sounded deeply embarrassed.

"You saw me," she reminded pointedly. "I've never seen a man do that. I'm curious."

Blushing, he said, "This is the best and worst thing I've ever done." He glanced around, then opened his trousers, shifted aside his underdrawers, and sighed as he released a thick cock with a bulbous, red tip. He bit his bottom lip and groaned, fingertips dancing up and down his shaft.

"Can I feel it?" he asked.

"My hair? Yes." She leaned forward.

He inched closer, cock still in his hand, squeezing himself.
His other hand shook as he stroked the ribbonlike plait she was
forming. He made a helpless noise and lowered his head to kiss
it. His hand was moving more firmly on his cock, and his breath
was broken as though he'd had to sprint all the way up here from
the village.

He was leaned close enough she could have kissed him on
the lips. She wanted to. All the sensual feelings that had gathered
between her legs yesterday returned without any of her tickling or
caressing. She shifted and pressed her thighs closed and clenched
internally, trying to ease the longing there.

His pinched fingers slid down the plait to her busy hands
where they continued to weave the strands together. The backs
of his knuckles grazed her nipple. For some reason, that sent a
jabbing rush of pleasure into her loins, making her jolt.

He looked into her eyes. "Do you like that?" He moved
his hand on the plait with more deliberation, ensuring that he
brushed against her nipple again.

"I do." Her lashes fluttered as he sent more of those lovely
feelings through her. "Do you want to kiss me?"

His answer was a helpless groan. His arm went around her
shoulders, and he covered her lips with his own. She didn't even
know how to kiss, but as he rubbed his lips on hers and pulled
away a little to make an anguished noise, she pinched the hair
end with one hand and cupped his face with the other, inviting
him back.

They kissed the way Johann and Hendrika had done, as if
they wanted to consume each other. It was strange, and Flora
feared she was being very awkward or forward or wrong. She
couldn't imagine what he thought of her, opening her mouth and
letting him push his tongue in to brush against hers, but it felt
divine. She sucked on it.

He groaned and stopped kissing her but tilted his forehead against hers. He released his cock and lifted his hand to where she was still pinching her hair. He rubbed against the upper portion that she'd managed to plait. His hand made a small twist, and that plait encircled his wrist. He shuffled even closer and massaged her breast and rubbed her nipple through her clothes. They kissed again, sucking at each other's lips and stabbing tongues and leaning ever closer.

"I'm going to come," he said into her mouth.

"Where?" she asked, uncertain what he meant.

"On your gown?" He swore as he shakily sat back on his heels and carefully took his hands off her, squeezing his cock as though suffering deep pain. "Are you… Do you want me to…touch you? While you finish?" He nodded at the half plait.

The dazed lust in his eyes was impossible to resist.

She looked around, then used her free hand to gather her skirts. She opened her thighs, and his hand went to the slit of her drawers, unhesitating.

"Hot." His eyes flared with excitement that matched her own as his touch explored, searching the boundary of her patch and playing briefly against the nap of her curls. "I love this hair. *Love* it. I want to lick it."

The suggestion, coupled with the way he rubbed the fine hairs of her mons against her most sensitive place, caused such reverberations of pleasure, she nearly fell off her rock.

"Careful." His laugh scraped, and he caught her with his free arm. "Fuck, this is exciting. Can you keep plaiting?"

Not really. He was pushing his finger inside her as he spoke. It was the most startling sensation! Snug and intimate.

She sagged to let her head rest on his shoulder, trying to assimilate this new sensation of his finger moving in and out of her. Her inner muscles were clenching, and even though she desperately wanted him to move his touch back to the little nodule that had so pleased her yesterday, she liked this, too.

"Oh, Flora." The hand behind her played with her loose hair, picking it up and letting it fall against her back. He kissed her temple, and his finger dug deep, pressing all the way in so the heel of his palm was flush against her spread folds.

She clamped her hand over his, silently telling him to stay pressed firm as she adjusted her position on the rock. Instinct compelled her to rock her loins against his hand while she made herself finish the plait. She could hardly see it. Her eyes were damp and trying to close as if she could somehow contain all this pleasure by doing so. The hunger and need from yesterday were crossing into themselves inside her, weaving and tightening like this plait, nearing the end of her ability to withstand the tension of it.

Ingram was swearing and combing his fingers through her loose hair while moving his hand in time with her light humping rhythm, fixated on the plait as she brought the finished end up to where she had said he could cut it. Her hands were shaking. She couldn't work out how to hold the hair and tie it off, not when her mind was brimming with desire, body on the brink of cataclysm.

Panting, Ingram gently removed his hand from her pussy and sat back.

She sobbed a protest.

"I know. I'm sorry," he murmured.

Her hat had long fallen off her lap, but he found the length of twine and tied off the loop of hair. His hands were shaking as he lifted the scissors. His eyes were all pupil.

"Thank you for this, Flora. *Thank you*."

She couldn't help it. Her loins ached so much, she had to slip her hand between her thighs and find the nodule that ached so. She tried to soothe it, but there was no such thing, only further incitement, especially as she looked at Ingram's bobbing cock and sensed the same swollen urgency throbbing within him.

He stood on his knees as he took hold of the plaited tress

and set the scissors against it. She reached out to hold his cock while she frantically rubbed herself with her other hand.

There was an excruciatingly slow crunch of hair strands breaking and a loud snip of blades coming together. He groaned loudly, and his cock began to pulse in her hand. Joy flowered in her loins, burying her in an avalanche of glorious sensations while hot fondue coated her fist.

# CHAPTER FOUR

I t had been a week since his tryst with Flora in the forest—longer than Ingram had stayed in any one place so far.

He couldn't leave. Each time he thought about continuing on to Italy, he touched the hair looped around his neck beneath his collar. It tickled his skin, and the bow of twine itched his breastbone, urging him to stay another night. Every morning, he followed yet another goat trail in hopes of glimpsing Flora across the valley.

At night he relived their remarkable experience. He hadn't imagined he could experience anything so wonderful. The ecstasy on her face while she plaited her hair and the wet heat of her pussy clutching his finger had sent him into a mindless, wondrous place where nothing existed beyond the sensations they were sharing.

He hadn't had enough hands. He'd wanted to be naked with his cock buried inside her when he severed her lock of hair. When she'd closed her warm hand on his tumescent cock and rubbed herself with vigorous friction, then cried out with pleasure, his hand had clenched involuntarily. The scissors had snipped, and his orgasm had been so powerful and rapturous, he'd nearly passed out from the force of it.

Since then, fantasy and memory had braided together with her sweet, sweet acceptance of his strange desire until he was sure he was falling in love with her.

He had no idea how she might feel. She had looked hurt when he had given her the few coins in his pocket. It hadn't been much, only what he thought might buy him a night on the alps if needed. He'd felt embarrassed by his miserly offering. His guilt at having this strange foible had nipped at him, and their leave-taking had become awkward.

The whole thing ought to have been embarrassing enough to make him leave this village forever, but he couldn't make himself do it. He wanted to see her again.

Why? What purpose could it serve? He didn't run around seducing peasant women, but marriage wasn't a serious consideration. They were strangers. He hadn't properly started his law career. In five years, he might have enough of a living to support a wife and children, but when that time came, his parents would choose someone they thought appropriate. His mother was already culling the herd for the right fashionable young woman who would be an asset for him professionally and for the family socially.

A Swiss orphan with no English or advantageous connections would appall them.

He felt melancholic just thinking of going home to the struggle for their approval. This summer was the first time in his life he hadn't had to constantly suppress his peculiar interest. When he returned to London and settled into the life that was planned for him, there would be no clandestine visits to a wig seller, no frigging a woman while she plaited her hair for him.

He would have to fight against his desire for the rest of his life. Either that, or tell his future wife he had this peccadillo. Both options filled him with sick dread.

Keeping his desires private was one thing, but he didn't know how he would go back to lying and secrecy and shame. He couldn't. Not without seeing the sunny acceptance of his sweet, soft-hearted Flora one more time.

"More tea, sir?" The voice of the widowed innkeeper forced him to make a broader decision.

"Nein, danke. But I'll take two of your travel meals, if you could prepare them?"

"You're catching the train to Italy today?"

"Not yet. I'll remove my things from my room in case you need it, but I plan to stay on the mountain overnight."

• • •

The mist had clung stubbornly to the slopes all day; otherwise, Flora would have seen Ingram before he was upon her in the meadow.

"Flora." He smiled with what looked like genuine pleasure. "I heard you singing."

She'd been thinking about him, and here he was, even more handsome than she recalled. He was shaved, with his hair flopping across his brow and a light flush of exertion on his cheeks. That smile of his had refused to fade from her heart.

She grew weak with joy even as she said, "I told Vater Werner you wouldn't come back."

*No. He won't*, Vater Werner had agreed forcefully.

Ingram's face fell. "Did you tell him that we…?"

"No!" She widened her eyes in horror at the thought, then felt a guilty blush creep into her cheeks. "He accused me of having an infatuation."

*Whatever dreams you are spinning, forget them. Men like that do not want a future with girls like you. They only say they do to get what they want, then leave you forever.*

Much as she wanted to believe Vater Werner was being cruel, in this case she had feared he was only being honest. Ingram had left after getting the plait of hair he had wanted.

Even so, she had wanted to protest to Vater Werner that Ingram hadn't left her empty-handed. She was keeping her coins a secret, though, along with what she had done to earn them.

She knew many would look down on this sort of transaction. They'd clearly never been in a position of needing to resort to such things, had they? She had no regrets. Half the dreams she was spinning for herself were about how she would spend her few coins and how she might earn more if she sold the rest of her hair.

"What made you come up this trail today?" she asked.

"I can't stop thinking about you. About what you let me do." Ingram took a step forward and lifted a helpless hand.

Flora dipped her head and self-consciously touched the fine hairs at the nape of her neck, reminding herself his interest wasn't *her*. It was this.

A pang of inadequacy struck in her heart. She knew she wasn't much, but she would like to be wanted for more than what grew out of her head.

At the same time, she was practical enough to see the opportunity that had climbed up an entire mountain to present itself before her. She would be a fool to ignore what he was offering.

"Did you bring more money?" She glanced up to see his smile fade as quickly as it had formed.

"I— Yes." His conflicted gaze was tracking over her face, lingering at her nape when she dropped her hand away.

"It's only, I'm worried he might notice if I let you cut more here." She waved at the back of her head. "I have other hair," she pointed out.

"You would let me *do* that?" His hand went out and wavered as though he sought a support and nearly lost his balance. He stumbled a step, face so pale it was as though she'd punched the breath from his body.

"If you want to." She hurried forward, embarrassed that she was so venal, especially because there was a part of her that simply longed to be touched by him again. Yearned to be touched *there*.

Ingram didn't seem to think poorly of her. He had fallen to his knees and was bracing his hands on his thighs, drawing in wheezing breaths.

"Are you dizzy from the climb?" she asked with concern, touching his cheek.

"No. Yes." He grasped her hand and held it against his throat, where his pulse was galloping like an unbroken horse. "Yes, please. Can we do that? Now? Please?"

"You're shaking."

"I'll be very careful. I brought my own scissors." He pulled the knapsack off his back. "I bought them this morning. They're silver. So pretty. I wanted to use them with you if you let me take another... I really am going to faint." He braced a hand on the ground, head hanging as though it was too heavy for his neck to support.

"It's the air. People who aren't used to it grow light-headed when they climb so high so fast." She stole a few pets of his hair and smoothed his cheek, finding him so endearing with his excitement over a pair of scissors. Silver ones, no less.

They really were from different worlds, she noted with quiet despair.

"I'll go to the stream and wash, then meet you in the trees?" She pointed.

"Yes," he agreed in a small choke. "But, Flora..." He tugged her hand until she crouched before him. "I think you should know. I'm falling in love with you."

She smiled, elated and sad at the same time. She let him kiss her because it felt nice to have his lips move across hers so sweetly. When she drew back and saw the tenderness in his gaze, she almost believed him.

An invisible thunk hit her chest, though. *Be sensible, Flora.*

"You don't have to say that to persuade me," she told him gently. "I like it when you touch me. I want to do it." She rose and walked to the stream.

• • •

Ingram was fighting very hard to think through his haze of lust.

As he'd climbed, it had begun to impact him that London was much farther from these alpine meadows than the village.

If a few hours of walking felt too far to reach Flora, how would he survive being a month of expensive travel away from her?

His thoughts had been a jumble of yearning and anxiety when he'd finally spotted her, but when he did, his heart had nearly expanded beyond the limits of his rib cage.

She assumed he'd merely come for more hair, and that pinched his conscience because, yes, he had hoped she would let him take another snippet of hair.

More importantly, he'd simply wished to *see* her. To assure himself they were still friends and she didn't look down on him for what they'd done. He wanted to know she was well. He wanted to do something more than offer a few coins to help her improve her life and be happy, but what?

Here she came, smiling shyly as she caught up to him and lowered to sit on the wool blanket he'd spread on the ground for her. He'd found a flat spot out of the wind where the needles from the surrounding trees formed a soft bed.

In his wildest, most prurient fantasies, he had dreamed of trimming a woman's bush, but what *lady* would ever consent to such a thing? Requesting it was liable to have him consigned to a hospital for sexual deviants. That's what he'd always believed.

"Do you think me disgusting?" he was compelled to ask as he knelt beside her. The narrow blades of his new scissors were clutched in his fist.

"No." She quirked her brows as though perplexed and hugged her upraised knees. "I thought you must think me terrible for…" She swallowed. "Doing things for money."

"Don't be ashamed." He squeezed her shoulder, trying not to be offended that she saw him as a means to an end. They were both getting something they needed. That's how he looked at it. "If you're ashamed, then I must be ashamed."

They shared wobbling smiles of sheepishness.

"I took off my drawers so they wouldn't get wet while I

washed." She waved at the bundle of muslin he hadn't noticed. "Do you want me to take down my hair?"

"Would you? God, Flora. It's like you were made for me." He kissed her again, unable to express how much he adored her.

She giggled, and they bumped hands and mouths, and his elbow tapped her knee as he tried to get his hands into her hair and touch her breasts and put his lips on her throat and ear and chin.

"I wish I could see you naked," he told her. "I wish I could fuck you while I cut your hair."

She paused, sobering. "I would get pregnant."

"It's just a wish. I won't do it." He ran his hand down her freed hair. "But it feels good to be able to say it. I wish I could sit you in a chair naked and watch you frig yourself while I cut your hair. I wish you'd suck my cock while I cut it. I have a lot of wishes," he admitted ruefully. "This is enough, though." He drew her hair forward to the front of her shoulder, astonished that this was even happening. "It's more than I thought I would ever have."

She smiled very sweetly and lay back.

Ingram set his hand on the mountain of her knee and rested his forehead on the back of his hand a moment. All the blood had rushed from his head to his cock again.

"Ingram?"

"You are making me so happy, Flora. So happy I could cry."

• • •

She could sense how high his expectations were, and it made her nervous that she would disappoint him. That anxiety caused her to press her thighs tight as he began to lift her skirts. It took pure willpower to open her knees and let him see her thatch, even though he'd seen it before.

"You're so pretty." He reached out and ever so lightly grazed his fingertips across her freshly washed curls.

A lovely tingle followed his touch. It increased as he took a few hairs in a light pinch to rub them together before he traced his touch into the crease of her thigh.

"Can I…?" His eyes clenched shut, and his jaw hardened as though he was trying to keep the request inside, but it burst out in an exhale of yearning. "Can I keep it?"

"The hair?" She had thought she was done being surprised. "If you want to."

"It's bad; I know it is."

"Ingram. If you're ashamed, then I must be," she reminded.

"Right." He gave her a crooked smile as he withdrew his linen handkerchief and touched her thigh. "Can you lift your bottom?"

She did and bit her thumbnail as he tucked the edge of the linen beneath her cheeks, then arranged her with her legs spread wide.

He was swearing softly again, lightly exploring with his fingertips down to the place between her cheeks, touching every single stray hair while a delicious heaviness collected in her flesh as he caressed her.

"I didn't know women could be blond here. You're a lovely golden treasure, Flora. So beautiful." His fingertip was playing lightly at her folds, spreading the petals, skimming the little nodule that made a noise throb in her throat. "I wish I had my shaving blade. Sometimes when I shave after I've worn a beard for a few weeks, my skin is very sensitive. I wonder if that's how you would feel if you were naked here." His trembling fingers grazed her mound.

Flora couldn't imagine feeling more sensitive than she did with his touch growing more sure and intimate. Then the hard, cool tip of the scissors pressed against her skin near her arsehole. Her stomach tensed. She heard a snip, and he groaned.

She opened her eyes and saw how enthralled he was. She would have sworn he was taking it one hair at a time, he was working so painstakingly slowly. It was torture when her sex felt as though it was pounding with her pulse, but the curve of his mouth beneath his mustache and the avid light in his eyes made her happy to be able to give him this. She touched his arm in a small expression of her pleasure.

He glanced at her and smiled before adjusting his position so he was on his stomach between her legs, propped on his elbows as he carefully nipped off her hairs at their roots.

"How does this feel?" he asked, giving her outer lip a brushing caress.

She jolted. Her skin was more sensitive.

"Good?" he asked with gratification and gently blew across her flesh.

"Oh." Her thighs quivered, wanting to close and protect what was suddenly more vulnerable than it had ever been.

"Do you like the feel of the scissors? Tell me everything about how it feels for you."

"It's a tease." She let him hear her frustration. "The blades are hard and cold, and the touch of them doesn't satisfy me. I want your finger rubbing me and pushing inside me."

He made a noise of pity and dipped his head to run his tongue along her channel. The sensation was so hot and slippery and intense, she cried out. Her knees folded instinctually, trying to close.

He set his hand on her inner thigh and lifted his head. "Did I hurt you?"

"No, it felt really good. Too good."

"No such thing." He hitched himself closer and pushed her thighs farther apart. "But I couldn't resist a taste. I might need another." He looked up at her while he stretched his tongue down to dandle at her nub.

As need gathered like a storm in her loins, she groaned at

the tree boughs above her.

"Oh, my beautiful, beautiful Flora." His thumb pushed inside her, and he used his finger to press her plump lip open. The nip of the scissors danced along her most sensitive tissues.

She clamped down with her inner muscles against his thumb and started to roll her hips, but he said, "Hold still, my darling. I don't want to hurt you. Christ, you're wet." His thumb worked in and out a moment. "This is the most exciting thing I've ever done in my life."

Holding still was excruciatingly thrilling. Every few seconds, he rewarded her with a small withdrawal and return of his fat thumb, shifting his touch this way and that. Each spot he bared was anointed with a sweep of his tongue, soothing and inciting. At one point, he lingered to lick slow circles around her nub, making her stomach quiver.

"Oh, fuck," he groaned, licking again at her outer lip, sucking on the plump flesh. "I can feel those rough little stubbles on my tongue." He did it again and again, causing a fresh gush of hot fluid to slick her channel and make the glide of his thumb even easier.

She ran her hands mindlessly in his hair, muscles clamping tightly around his intrusion, all of her yearning toward that pinnacle that felt so close and so elusive.

When he ceased trimming and removed his thumb, she made a noise of protest. Her loins felt so swollen and needy, she started to rub away the ache.

He caught her hand. "Shh. Wait, love." He lightly brushed her flesh, blowing softly, making her inner thighs shake.

Then he carefully folded his handkerchief and set it aside beneath the scissors. A groan escaped him—the kind someone might release when faced with a wedding banquet. He gathered his arms under her thighs and began to lick and suckle at her shorn flesh. His tongue slithered and poked and claimed every inch.

"I can feel your mustache," she groaned, catching a fist into his hair as she instinctively lifted her pussy to grind against his open mouth and clever tongue. "Oh, Ingram. I'm going to..."

She was struck by lightning. There was no other explanation for the fiery, blinding sensation that opened her mouth in a silent scream. Ecstasy held her in its suffocating grip before releasing her into the clouds. She shook, and her pussy convulsed while he made animalistic noises, lapping at her until it was all over.

# CHAPTER FIVE

"I came in my drawers," he groaned against her thigh. "I need to wash." He didn't want to, though. Flora's juices were all over his face, and he had absolutely never in his life been so happy. Never. "Will you marry me?"

"Don't be silly," she dismissed shyly, sitting up to touch her shorn puss before she disentangled her leg from the loose embrace of his arms and pushed her skirt down to hide her sex.

"Why is it silly?" He made himself sit up. The wet spot in his drawers shifted tackily. Her taste was on his lips when he licked them. There was probably at least one stray hair stuck to his chin or cheek.

"I'm not a proper lady." Her curt tone and the way she struggled to get the leg of her drawers over her boot emphasized how far she was from being any such thing.

He knew she was saying what was sensible. His family would say the same thing, but he could only see the hollow emptiness of his life if he couldn't share this part of himself with someone who accepted it.

"I don't care about that," he insisted, using his hand to wipe at his jaw.

"You will. Others will." She wiggled to get the drawers up over her hips and angled away to lift her skirts and tie her drawers into place. "That's just another wish that can't come true."

"I didn't think *this* wish could ever come true, but it did."

"Well, my wish is to sell my hair for money." She crawled around, feeling for hairpins that she stuck in her mouth before efficiently putting her hair back up. She wasn't looking at him. "Did you bring any?"

Stung, he reached into his knapsack and said, "I brought

notes this time." A lot of them.

She stared at them a long moment, expression conflicted. Ashamed?

"Just go," she said crossly.

She rose and hurried away with a snap of twigs beneath her feet.

•••

Flora was trying not to cry, but she was still sensitized and tender, both blissfully satisfied and filled with remorse. The faintly cooler sensations creeping through her clothing and the way the muslin of her drawers grazed her bare mound was an incessant reminder of what she'd allowed to happen.

A reminder that she had taken incredible pleasure in allowing something very shocking and probably sinful to happen. Part of her was thinking that if she could live the rest of her life with Ingram's face between her legs, she could possibly do without food and water.

But as much as she might dream of falling in love and leaving the village, she couldn't say definitively that Ingram was the man who could make that dream come true. She barely knew him. Aside from his intense interest in hair—*anyone's* hair—all she knew of him was that he was English and had a brother who would be a duke. When he reached into his pocket, money came out.

That was certainly a seductive prospect, but he and his family would have expectations of her that she would never be able to meet. Did he not realize that? She knew how to stack wood and churn butter and, judging by the width of her hips and the ampleness of her breasts, could produce a few healthy babies. Other than having more education than most people thought useful for a woman of her station, she had nothing to offer him.

As she realized how long she'd been lingering with him, she

hurried to gather hay onto the net, unsurprised when Vater Werner came stalking up the hill in long strides toward her.

"I've finished the cheese, and you're not back yet," he berated. "What are you doing up here?"

"Nothing," she mumbled.

His head turned sharply toward the trees, and she followed his glare to see Ingram had come up from the stream. He paused to watch them.

"Nothing?" Vater Werner spat. "Slut." His hand came up. "Flora!"

She threw her arm up, catching the blow mostly on her wrist, but it was still hard enough to make her stagger across the uneven ground. Then Ingram was beside her, grabbing her elbow to keep her on her feet while shoving himself forward, placing himself between her and Vater Werner.

"I'm marrying her. She's coming with me." He took up a stance of raised fists and bunched muscles. "Get my bag, Flora."

"Ingram, don't." She touched his upper arm, trying to step around him, but he blocked her, keeping himself between her and Vater Werner.

"I will never hit you. *Ever*," Ingram said while keeping his fists up and his eyes fixed on her foster father. "Get my bag and come with me."

"He will leave you in the next village," Vater Werner warned her with a sneer. "We won't have you back. You'll be ruined."

"I won't come back," she said, absorbing that heartening prospect. Perhaps Ingram would abandon her. Perhaps he would take her home and his family would shun her. She had already endured worse. At least she would know she had tried to make a better life for herself.

She turned and ran for the knapsack that Ingram had dropped in his haste to assist her.

"Are you sure you wish to marry me?" she asked him some hours later, when the moon was rising and they were still descending the mountain. "Perhaps you're only infatuated because of what I let you do."

"I'm very sure." He held her hand and lifted it to kiss her knuckles. "To prove it, I won't make love to you until we're properly married."

"No? Because I was going to suggest we stay in one of the alps here. They're empty right now while the cows are farther up."

"Really? Fuck." His mouth tightened with temptation.

She chuckled. "Perhaps I could suck your cock while you cut my hair."

"Fuck, Flora." He stumbled and caught himself, then braced his hands on his knees. "Don't tease."

"I'm not." Perhaps she had been a little. She set her hand on his back and discovered his heart was crashing against his spine. "I won't do it again," she promised.

He straightened and pulled her close, tucking her head under his chin while he held her as though she was made of something delicate that had to be protected, even though she was a very sturdy woman.

"Maybe this *is* only infatuation, but I believe it will become love." He drew back to look into her eyes. "I don't want anyone or anything to hurt you. I want you to feel as happy as you make me feel. That's something, isn't it?"

"I can honestly say my most pleasurable memories have all occurred when you've been near me. *That's* something."

His laughter echoed across the hills.

# EPILOGUE

After a wonderful honeymoon that took them briefly to Italy before they returned to England, Flora spent two years homesick for the Alps, mostly because London was sooty and soggy and Ingram was unhappy in his job. Also because his family was unhappy with him for marrying her. Their only bright spot was their shared secret and their passion for each other, which bound them closer as they endured those first, difficult years.

Slowly, his mother convinced society that Flora was a lady and her different manners were cultural, not due to being lowborn. She had always wanted a daughter, so she warmed to her first and, by the summer of their third anniversary, invited them to the family's lake district estate. They never left.

Ingram, having now been admitted to the Law Society, partnered with a local solicitor. Flora oversaw improvements with the dairy cows and soon had the estate turning a profit off its unique cheese, its apple orchards, and its specialty sausages.

That earned Ingram's brother's respect, and his father grew a little more mollified with each child Flora bore, three of them boys and two girls. They were energetic and earnest, clever and polite, and all were regarded to have excellent singing voices.

Once the youngest was old enough to travel, Ingram had promised Flora they would take a family trip to revisit the Alps. Flora missed the magnificence of her homeland, but as time wore on, that was all she missed of her life there. She had a husband who provided her everything she needed, offering her loving regard, sensuality, and deep affection.

And she gave him what he needed, she supposed, though it seemed a very little thing to strip naked and allow him to shave her mound clean. Then she would sit on his cock and tease him while she braided a small section of hair. He would stroke his hands over her back and buttocks, lift her breasts and pinch her nipples and twitch inside her, groaning as if tortured beyond bearing.

When she tied off the end of her plait, she would tickle him with the end, playing it over his throat and chest and, because it was long enough to reach, down to the root of his cock where it was buried inside her. He would buck in reaction, taking her to the edge of her own endurance of pleasure.

When they were both ready to climax, he would shakily reach for his silver scissors and...

*Snip.*

*The End*

# How Stimulating

*How Stimulating* will leave you tingling all over, however the story includes mention of forced marriage, sexually transmitted infection, and financial dependence, so readers who may be sensitive to these, please take note.

Also, while a full-body treatment with electric current (faradization) was a legitimate therapy in the late 1800s, readers should be aware that it is generally regarded as unsafe to apply electrostimulation above the waist and should never be used by those with heart problems or a pacemaker. Readers interested in exploring this fetish should thoroughly research safety precautions and purchase a device made by a reputable manufacturer.

# CHAPTER ONE

*June 1872, Marienbad (West Bohemia)*

"My dear sister-in-law is infertile," Dame Thomasina Trowbridge volunteered to a pair of perfect strangers in the middle of the Hidden Spring Pavilion. She waved at Maura so they would know exactly to whom she was referring.

Maura Norcross spat her gargled water into the spittoon and prayed for the earth to crack open and gulp her down. How could it, though? She was already in the ninth circle of hell. There was no farther depth to which she could plummet.

"From hysteria," Thomasina continued, voice echoing off the domed roof above them. "She and my brother have been married three years, yet there is no sign of an heir."

*To what?* Maura wanted to cry. She had brought her own fortune to the marriage, though calling it a "fortune" was an overstatement. Now it was mostly gone, thanks to her husband using it to pay off his creditors.

"On my physician's advice, I have brought Maura to the healing waters to cure her."

The pair of middle-aged women sent Maura weak smiles of pity.

They had only the barest idea of the agony to which she had been consigned. Thomasina's physician had prescribed six weeks at a health spa, and it was no accident that the man had recommended the resort farthest from London. He was as weary of Thomasina as Maura was.

Maura managed to keep a polite expression on her face as Thomasina failed to detect how uncomfortable she was making these women.

"My brother, Alford, is a colonel. Very busy with his official duties. Virile."

*Which he demonstrated by picking up hidden afflictions from
all corners of the world.* That's also what Maura wanted to say.
Stridently. If his disease had been from some accident, she would
not have such a grim opinion of him, but he made himself a vessel
and a weapon, openly disparaging sheaths and visiting prostitutes
or any unsuspecting woman who would have him.

*I wouldn't touch him with a barge pole, let alone invite him
into my private parlor.*

Every time Maura thought about the life she was obliged to
live, she wanted to scream so long and loud, she had to wonder
if she *was* suffering hysteria.

"Perhaps you'll take my recommendation?" one of the women
offered, sending another sympathetic look to Maura. "I arrived
with a concern of a female nature. It's this time of life," she added
in an aside to Thomasina. "I'm sure you understand. I found Dr.
Winternitz at the Clinic for Women's Ailments very helpful."

"Oh?" Maura feigned interest, despite having no disease
beyond disgust and even less of a desire to cure it.

Privately, she relished the way Thomasina stiffened at the
reference to her age. Thomasina was Alford's eldest sister. She
had nearly grown children and was approaching forty. Did she
really expect to be viewed as Maura's dewy, twenty-year-old
contemporary?

Thomasina stiffly listened to the directions from the women
and dismissed the pair with a cool, "Thank you."

•••

"That was very kind of them, wasn't it?" Maura said with
spiteful cheer after the women were gone. "I must
commend you on always being willing to ask for advice when
you need it."

Maura fully expected Thomasina to send her a glower and

pooh-pooh the women's suggestion. Instead, Thomasina lifted her chin.

"One does experience certain symptoms as a result of childbirth. Since the clinic is on our way back to our hotel, we'll stop in and inquire." She started out of the pavilion.

Maura held back a few steps, glaring up to the painted god in the dome, the one who kept subjecting her to such unremitting pressure to fit a role she had never wanted.

"Are you coming?" Thomasina's skirts swished as she turned to look back at Maura.

Did she have a choice?

Never. Not once.

She grudgingly followed.

•••

Zhara Yatim was familiarizing herself with Dr. Winternitz's notes when Mrs. Maura Norcross was shown in by one of the maids.

Mrs. Norcross wore one of the clinic's shapeless robes and a pair of leather-soled slippers. She was pretty, with brown hair, fair skin, and a mutinously set pink mouth. She barely glanced at Zhara, holding her arms folded across her front as she scowled around the small room, taking in the electricity apparatus mounted on the wall, the two chairs, and the papers Zhara held.

"Thank you, Sally," Zhara dismissed the maid. "Good morning, Mrs. Norcross. I'm Zhara, and I will be your nurse today. Would you like to take a seat?" She indicated the wooden chair used for treatments.

Mrs. Norcross's sullen frown deepened as she sank into it and glared resentfully at the far wall, seeming to rebuff Zhara's friendliness.

The married woman of twenty years had presented with a diagnosis by a London physician of infertility and low libido caused by hysteria. After an interview and examination, Dr. Winternitz had determined there did not seem to be any physical or traumatic cause for her symptoms, but he was always on the lookout for a more specific diagnosis than the overarching "hysteria."

*Nervous tension resulting from the pressure to conceive* was his postulation. He had lengthy instructions on diet, gentle exercise, bathing, massage, and general faradization.

Zhara kept her welcoming smile pinned to her face, but the rest of her tightened at the hostility she sensed from her patient.

"Are you comfortable discussing your treatment with me? Would you prefer I ask one of the other nurses to speak with you?"

"Pardon?" Mrs. Norcross lifted her head and properly looked at Zhara, frown deepening. "I'm trying to decide if I want treatment at all. It won't work," she stated firmly.

"Oh?" Zhara had found that when a patient began to open up, it was best to encourage them with as few words as possible. She lowered into the other chair so they were eye to eye, practically knee to knee. Two women sharing a confidence. That's how these quiet moments of insight usually worked.

With Mrs. Norcross, though, something different happened. Zhara became arrested by Mrs. Norcross's dark amber eyes. Not so much the color but the troubled light in them that shifted into a more startled focus on Zhara. Mrs. Norcross's mood seemed to flicker between conflicted polarities, defeat and defiance. Refusal and reception. Disinterest and sudden curiosity. The deep indecision within her tipped toward confusion as she held Zhara's gaze.

A strange lifting sensation happened within Zhara as she felt that shift within the other woman. Zhara felt as though her heart fell out of its natural rhythm for a few uneven beats before settling into a new space that was offset within her chest. In the length of their held glance, something within her filled with light in a way she hadn't experienced in a long while. Warmth and hope and—caution.

This excitement suffusing her was disconcerting and inappropriate enough to halt the smile that had begun to fill her cheeks and pull at her mouth. Zhara dropped her gaze to the notes before her. Maybe she *should* ask one of her colleagues to treat Mrs. Norcross.

As she lifted her lashes to suggest it, she found Mrs. Norcross was still staring at her with a soft, bemused expression.

"Your eyes are very blue." Mrs. Norcross dragged her brows together in a fret of self-recrimination and looked at the fingers she was pinching together. "That was rude of me. I apologize."

"No need." Zhara had heard many times how remarkable she looked with her dark brown skin and sea blue eyes and hints of red in her otherwise dark, curly hair.

She was out of the ordinary in many ways—secretly agnostic, traveling far from her birthplace, and devoting herself to her vocation rather than seeking a husband and starting a family.

"I'm not myself." Mrs. Norcross sighed, and her eyes might have grown shiny with frustration or some other emotion, but it was difficult to tell, since she dropped her head again. "My sister-in-law has brought me here. She expects me to accept help, but..."

Zhara was feeling something she hadn't felt in a long while, and it was not the sort of feeling that should exist in a professional situation like this, but such a pang of compassion hit her as she witnessed Mrs. Norcross's misery, she couldn't make herself rise and ask another nurse to treat her. Not yet.

"My job is to ensure your comfort in every way," Zhara said gently. "If you don't wish to accept treatment, I cannot force it upon you. Dr. Winternitz is very adamant on that."

Mrs. Norcross lifted her face, almost brightening toward hope. "That's refreshing."

Zhara knew. She'd worked with many doctors in the twelve years since she'd presented herself at the mission house in Cairo and asked to be trained as a caregiver. Some physicians were overbearing and dismissive. Others were earnest and genuinely wished to learn and help. She had landed here because Dr. Winternitz was one of the good ones.

"The type of electrotherapy that Dr. Winternitz has recommended is a soothing pulse meant to relax you, but it won't ease your tension if you have fears about it. In that respect, you're exactly right that it won't work."

"No. My fears are..." She tilted her head toward the ceiling and blew out a breath. "Oh, I don't suppose it matters. Go ahead and do what you have to."

"Your feelings do matter, Mrs. Norcross." Zhara reached over in what was meant to be a reassuring pat on the other woman's hand. Mrs. Norcross was threatening to twist her fingers right off, but the second Zhara's palm touched the other woman's knuckles, a jolt went up Zhara's arm and into her heart.

Mrs. Norcross sucked in a breath and sat up straighter.

They blinked at each other.

Zhara jerked her hand back and looked absently to her notes. "I was only wishing to offer comfort." But it had flashed into something else, and she was embarrassed that she'd allowed it. "I apologize if I made you uncomfortable."

"You didn't," Mrs. Norcross said, quick and strong. She hugged herself and averted her gaze. Her cheeks were bright red. "Is that what it feels like?"

Zhara's heart stopped. "What *what* feels like?" Love? It had, when she'd experienced it before.

"The electricity." Mrs. Norcross nodded at the apparatus in her line of sight. "Like the shock you get on a dry winter's day?"

Was that how it had been on her side? For Zhara, it had been more of a lightning strike of recognition. A burst of yearning.

"It can," she said, trying to regain her composure and sound professional. "For the treatment you've been prescribed, it should feel like a strong tingle. If you feel discomfort, I will turn the level down. Your energy has been depleted over time. The electricity is meant to restore it, not demand exertion from nerves that are already overwrought."

"That makes me sound weak." Her shoulders sloped.

"Weak*ened*, perhaps, but we all wax and wane, don't we? There's no shame in going through a spell of feeling low."

"How long is a 'spell'?" Mrs. Norcross grumbled, not waiting for an answer before wrinkling her nose to ask, "Have you had it?"

"Electrotherapy? Only as part of my training." Zhara leaned forward a little as she confided, "We were instructed to deliver a sharp shock to each other so we would understand why we should avoid doing it to our patients."

"Really?" Mrs. Norcross perked up. She had a very pretty face when she wasn't sulking. "What did *that* feel like?"

"A burn. But only for a moment. There's no scar." Zhara pulled back the cuff of her sleeve and pointed to the back of her wrist. "It startled me, but the sensation faded quickly."

"Hmm." Mrs. Norcross slowly dragged her gaze from Zhara's wrist to her chest, then up to her eyes. Her lashes swept down, and her cheeks suffused with pink again.

The hop-skip happened in Zhara's chest again, accompanied by a yearning that ground against her conscience.

"I wonder if you would prefer I bring in one of my colleagues to administer it?" Zhara made herself ask again, then held her breath, bracing for rejection.

"I trust *you*." Mrs. Norcross's anxious gaze came up, glimmering with injury. "Do you not want to treat me?"

Zhara couldn't help the smile of compassion and shy pleasure that touched her lips. This was a dangerous compulsion, but she couldn't resist it.

"Of course." She stood, then teased, "It would be my pleasure to shock you."

# CHAPTER TWO

Nurse Zhara had no idea how much she was shocking her. Maura only half listened to the explanation of how the different wands would be used.

All this time, Maura had thought she had no desire for her husband because he was a dissolute man ridden with disease. He repulsed her. And even though she had found other men attractive at different times, it was usually in an objective way, not with any strong desire to be physically close with them. She had agreed with her diagnosis that she lacked a healthy libido.

Now, old feelings she had fought when she'd been at boarding school were rushing back with a vengeance. She was thinking fleshly things that the sisters at the school had taught her not to think. *How would Zhara's lips feel against my own?*

Zhara's mouth wasn't wide, but her lips were full, turning her mouth into almost a perfect circle. It made her look very pensive and serious, but also as though she was about to bestow the most innocent of kisses. Soft, tender kisses that made Maura's heart flutter with longing.

Zhara was slender, with an elegant oval face, and her hair was covered by a simple pleated cap. The rest of her was in a plain gown with a long apron that did her no favors, yet she was so graceful and expressive, Maura was spellbound by her every word and movement.

Then there was that confidence in her gaze that melted Maura's insides when their stares happened to lock.

"Are you feeling more comfortable with accepting treatment?" Zhara asked, hands brushing down her apron in a way that was her first sign of being self-conscious.

"Of course." Maura still wasn't sure what she was in for, but she trusted Zhara. *Your feelings do matter, Mrs. Norcross.*

Zhara would have no idea how much that statement meant to her, but the antipathy that had filled her since leaving school was draining away, edged out by a sense of optimism.

"May I ask you to remove the pins and ribbon from your hair?" Zhara said.

Maura did and absently ran her fingers through her waves. Her scalp tightened when Zhara indicated she should sit sideways on the chair, then briefly combed her fingers through Maura's hair herself. A pleasant shiver raced down her spine.

"No tangles? Good. I'll start with this wand." She showed Maura something that looked like an oversize comb with teeth made of glass. "Do not be alarmed if you detect a scent of burned hair. That is within the machine. Your hair is perfectly safe, but tell me to stop at any time if you have concerns."

Maura's throat locked with nerves, and she nodded understanding.

Zhara turned away to fiddle with the machine mounted on the wall, adjusting dials. There was a *click*, and a low, steady hum rose to fill the high-ceilinged room.

Maura sat very still as anticipation built with anxiety and uncertainty. She had to fight to keep her shoulders from climbing up to her ears. Her stomach began to knot, and she ground her teeth as Zhara moved behind her again.

Maura clenched her eyes shut, almost hoping to be electrocuted on the spot and finally escape the strictures of the life she led, but that wasn't what happened.

The blunt ends of the hard glass tubes touched her hairline with a sensation like small, fine claws grabbing into her skin. The tubes filtered through her tresses, dragging the prickling sensation in its wake. It felt almost like a sharpened quill or freshly filed nails lightly scratching along her scalp. Dozens of them. It was odd but not unpleasant.

"Comfortable?"

"Yes. Keep going," Maura said, growing curious.

The dull-sharp sensations skittered across her scalp again, sending out prickling, crackling tendrils. She didn't hate it. It was acute enough to provoke tension in her but soothing once the sensation passed to another area.

Maura let her eyes close and ignored the metallic taste in her mouth, focusing instead on the way the electricity seemed to shimmer down the rest of her body like water trickling down her skin. She *did* feel as though her vitality was being restored.

"Good?" Zhara asked as she removed the wand, and silence filled the room.

"Yes." Maura was bereft. *Please don't stop.*

"Would you open your robe and drop it off your shoulders? Only as far as you're comfortable," Zhara said. "I'll use this damp sponge across your shoulders and spine now."

Maura dropped the robe, so it was a puddle around her hips, and only kept her arms in the sleeves so she could bring the loose cuffs up to cover her naked breasts.

She bit her lip as the hum started, warning her that the next prickle of electricity was about to arrive. It was a cool sponge that warmed as it passed across her skin. The electrical tingle was more concentrated, giving off the same scratching sensation but more firmly and deeply, as though a ball of pins was being rolled across her skin. There was an attempt by her muscles to resist, but tension was futile, and, once the sponge moved on, the relaxation that followed was an enormous relief.

Maura's shoulders melted. Her spine grew soft as she exhaled. Her arms were too heavy to hold across her chest. She let them drop into her lap and slouched in submission.

Zhara painted the sharp, dancing sensations all the way down to her tailbone and across the tops of her buttocks. Why that sent a small zing into her loins, Maura couldn't say, but her eyes popped open, and she stared at the floor, waiting to see if it would come again.

Zhara lifted the sponge away, however, and gently drew Maura's arm out of her sleeve. Holding her arm extended, Zhara began running the sponge down to her elbow, then back to her shoulder.

Now the muscles in her upper arm jumped in reaction. Sensations chased into her fingertips, making her fingers wiggle of their own accord. Another internal tickling trailed up into her chest and blossomed as a hot weight behind her breasts. Within them. The soft globes felt amplified. Swollen.

Maura couldn't seem to catch a full breath. She pressed one arm across her chest, but the pressure didn't alleviate the fiery hardness that contracted her nipples. Heated sensations swirled down her torso, into her loins, teasing her with a sensual awareness between her thighs.

She swallowed, embarrassed to be reacting in such a carnal way, but the stimulation was also very beguiling. As the places that had been touched by electricity felt almost numb, the rest of her was awakening with an expectation of touch. Calling out for it.

Zhara gently set Maura's hand back into her lap, and Maura offered her other arm without prompting, practically in a trance of growing need. Her heartbeat seemed to have dropped into the flesh between her legs and was hammering there with dull thuds that echoed in her throat.

Her stomach knotted, though. This treatment was supposed to relax her, not cause lascivious thoughts to form behind her closed eyes. She kept peeking at Zhara's breasts. They looked small and firm, and now Maura was wondering if Zhara's nipples were brown like her lips or pink like her tongue? Did her skin feel as smooth as it looked? How would it feel to hold her and have her naked body brush against her own?

So many thoughts she knew she wasn't supposed to have! Was the electricity causing them to rise to the forefront of her mind like this? Would it purge her of them next?

Her hand was replaced in her lap, and the hum abruptly silenced.

Maura could have cried at the loss.

"Would you like to place your arms in your sleeves and close your robe? I'll open it from the bottom to do your legs." Zhara didn't meet her eyes. Her hands didn't seem quite steady as she moved the other chair out of the way and set a footstool in its place.

Maura adjusted the robe and shifted so she could lean on the slatted back of her chair and set her feet on the stool. Zhara opened the bottom of her robe, and cool air crept up to make Maura starkly aware of the libidinous dampness that was welling like a spring between her thighs.

Zhara started the machine and held a Y-shaped wand now. The nodules on the ends were about three finger widths apart. She started on the soles of Maura's feet, making Maura's toes curl. The current had become a razor-sharp wire that seemed to cut through her flesh, but in a way that was so finely balanced between pleasure and pain, Maura didn't know how to fight it. She wanted to resist, but her tension melted as quickly as she mustered it. When the softness of relief arrived, it was as heady as what she imagined smoking opium would feel like.

Zhara stroked the implement along her ankle, and the current ran up her leg and caused the pooled heat in Maura's loins to intensify. It was even stronger as the electricity arrived in her calves.

Unconsciously, Maura gripped the edges of her chair and made a noise that even she wasn't sure was pleasure or pain.

"Do you wish me to stop?"

"*No.*" Maura had never felt anything like this. It was exquisite.

When Zhara rubbed the nodules on the muscles above her knee, the top of Maura's thigh contracted and released. Sensations shimmered down into the soles of her feet while the heat in her loins intensified. Her inner muscles clenched with urgency.

Zhara moved to the other knee, and a fluttery sensation

arrived in Maura's intimate flesh, a crazed, heightened sense of *almost* that she had only experienced during prurient dreams.

Before it could fully manifest, the wand disappeared, and Zhara rose. The hum stopped.

Maura's head swam. She wasn't sure she was breathing. She tried to open her eyes and escape from the foggy miasma of pleasure-pain she'd been submerged in, but it was as if she was trying to swim upward from the bottom of an endless lake.

"If you'd like to return to your bathing room, the mineral water will still be warm in the tub there. Afterward, you can rest on one of the couches in the lounge and enjoy a tisane. Aside from Dr. Winternitz, we're all women here, so your robe is perfectly acceptable attire."

"It's over?" A crackling, snapping fire roared inside her.

"Yes. The rest of your treatment plan will be available at the front desk when you leave. You can make the rest of your appointments for electrotherapy then." Zhara kept her back to her and picked up a pencil. She hovered it over the papers as if Maura was nothing more than a curious insect she was reporting on for a scientific periodical.

Maura had never felt so rejected. She hurried to close her robe and subtly sniffed with hurt.

"I will add some recommendations for bathing pools to your plan," Zhara said, voice conciliatory. Her brief glance at Maura was equal parts conflict and remorse. "There's one with a floor made of sand. Bubbles emerge in a very soothing sensation."

*I don't want to be soothed*, Maura wanted to shout.

The feeling gripping her needed an explosion, not yet another smothering bath.

As she saw Zhara chew the corner of her mouth, however, Maura couldn't be angry at this perfect stranger who was only trying to help her.

Without another word, she left and walked across the hall to the private room where she'd left her things. As she moved, she was disconcerted by a sensation of slippery friction between her thighs. She locked the door and investigated, discovering an abundance of fluid that—

"Ohhh." She gasped aloud as her fingertip skated and slid, practically plunging into the valley between her plump, sensitive folds. An approximation of the electrical sensations immediately concentrated beneath her fingertips.

This was bad, so bad. She knew that, but a need akin to intense hunger gripped her. She couldn't deny herself. Her free hand reached to clasp the back of a chair, and her foot rose to the seat. She bit her bottom lip as she continued to explore. *There.*

She stopped thinking and lost all sense of where she was. There was only the circling friction that sent runnels of pleasure emanating through her lower spine and buttocks and the memory of Zhara's electric touch. The flutters that had so teased her returned, and an incredible tension took hold of her, clenching her inner muscles and locking her breath.

She was undoing all of the relaxation she had found, but the pleasure hidden in this straining bliss was profound. She had never felt anything like it! She hadn't known her loins could feel so swollen and hot and—

A sharp contraction caught her by surprise. An equally sudden sense of expansion brought a giant wave of euphoria that had her gasping—*groaning*—aloud.

She swayed where she stood, afraid she might faint, but she kept rubbing, too enamored with the joyous feelings saturating her. The waves of pleasure kept rolling over her, eventually slowing and easing and leaving her so calm and tension-free, she could have fallen asleep right where she stood.

She sank into the tub and dozed briefly, then rose, still feeling as though a spell had been cast over her.

•••

When she caught up to Thomasina later, she smiled without any of her usual guardedness.

"Did you enjoy your treatment?" Maura asked her.

"It was disturbing." Thomasina's mouth pursed. "I won't come back. You?"

"I'll come every day."

# CHAPTER THREE

Zhara was tied up with another patient the next day, but Mrs. Norcross remained on her mind. After she ate her dinner, she took advantage of a bright summer's evening to stroll off her lingering conflict.

Everyone reacted differently to the administration of electricity, and mild arousal was not uncommon. Mrs. Norcross seemed to have found the treatment more sexually stimulating than most, which wouldn't be an issue if Zhara had managed to remain objective. Much to her chagrin, however, Zhara had enjoyed the knowledge that Mrs. Norcross was reacting sexually. It had aroused her to arouse Mrs. Norcross, and that was *completely* inappropriate.

Since she was liable to be assigned to her again tomorrow, Zhara needed to quash her—oh, she would have to call it what it was—her *attraction* toward Mrs. Norcross, or she would have to distance herself from Mrs. Norcross altogether.

How was she supposed to do that when, like some bee to the center of a flower, she had made directly to the likeliest place she would run into the woman? *Think, Zhara.*

She often ran into patients when she walked the nature paths between the ponds and pavilions. Dr. Winternitz had recommended a morning and evening constitutional for Mrs. Norcross, something that Zhara had read in her treatment plan. Therefore, Zhara had no right to reflect Mrs. Norcross's surprise when they met in a gazebo overlooking a pond.

"Nurse Zhara! I missed you at the clinic today." Mrs. Norcross flushed a hard red and offered an uncertain smile while searching Zhara's gaze.

"Good evening, Mrs. Norcross." Zhara couldn't help smiling

with pleasure at hearing she'd been missed. "I was attending a birth. It filled my whole day."

"Oh. Um…" She seemed to take heart from that, and some of her wariness receded. "Please call me Maura. You're a midwife? I assumed…" She shrugged and shook her head. "I don't know what I assumed. That you only administered the electricity, I suppose. How did you come to work here with Dr. Winternitz? I'm given to understand the town is new and few people are *from* here."

"That's true." Zhara saw an opening to circle around to a delicate topic, but one that was necessary to her decision-making where Maura was concerned. "My arrival is a little by chance, a little by design. I was born in Cairo and was left at the mission there as a baby."

"You're an orphan? I'm so sorry. Both of my parents are gone, too."

Was that the only thing they had in common?

Another couple arrived in the gazebo. Zhara and Maura sent them vague smiles and moved by silent agreement onto the path, where their conversation would not be so easily overheard.

"I was raised by a foster mother," Zhara continued. "She was very loving and allowed me to attend school until my menstruation started, but then she began looking for a husband for me. I didn't wish to marry, so I went back to the mission and asked to be trained as a caregiver instead."

"Goodness. How old were you?"

"Thirteen."

"You've been working as a nurse ten, fifteen years?"

"Thirteen. At first it was very simple duties. Cleaning. Some bandaging. Soon I learned to stitch a wound, and I attended many women as they labored. I caught my first baby at fifteen, and I still wasn't entirely sure how they were made."

"I imagine there are many women pushing out babies with the same vague sense of it. We were lucky enough to have a sister at school who gave us a thorough explanation of how it all happened. If she hadn't, I wouldn't have known—" Maura clammed up and waved an inviting hand at Zhara. "I'm sorry. Please continue."

She sensed Maura had thought better about what she had been about to say.

It gave Zhara a moment of pause, and she had second thoughts about what she was confiding. She rolled her lips together, choosing her words carefully.

"One of my colleagues was German. We were very close, but she was homesick and wished to come back to the motherhouse in Kaiserswerth. I wanted to accompany her, so I applied to be transferred there." She watched Maura, wondering if she read between the lines. "Her family was adamant that she marry, though. She soon left, and, with nothing to keep me there, I decided to apply to the midwife program at the teaching hospital in Vienna."

Maura's eyes had been fixed on her as she spoke. Now she glanced away, brow furrowed. It wasn't possible for Zhara to be sure what had held her interest or what caused her frown.

"I was accepted and met Dr. Winternitz while I was training there," Zhara continued. "He was well known in the maternity ward for being a stickler about handwashing and treating overwrought women with patience and respect. He was looking for nurses to accompany him here, to open a clinic where he could study female ailments and test and study modern, holistic treatments. It seemed too good an opportunity to refuse. It would be hard to ask for a more beautiful place to live and work." Zhara indicated the sparkles of evening sunshine coming off the water in the pond they were circling.

"I'm envious," Maura said as they arrived at a bridge. She paused in the middle of it to look into the water. "Not just that you live in such an idyllic place, but that you've made your own way in the world."

"Please don't think my life has been easy. My foster mother

was very poor. She took me in because she knew the mission would ensure *all* of her children had food. I was angry when I was taken from school simply because I had become a woman. I saw the mission as my only alternative. Caregiving has become a calling, but it's very challenging work." Messy and frustrating and oftentimes heartbreaking. "Dr. Winternitz is fair, but my wage requires I lead a very frugal life."

"Yes, but they're *your* wages. You may decide how to spend them. I had money from my parents, but I wasn't allowed to touch it until I married. I was pressured into marrying a man who was a friend of my guardian—a favor between them, I think. Alford freed my guardian of the burden I presented. In exchange, Alford used my inheritance to mop up his debts. We subsist on his income as a colonel, and I have a small allowance, but this trip has been paid for by his sister. She's determined to cure me of my infertility and provide her brother an heir, but I keep wondering, *For what?* He has no title or holding that requires one. If he were to die, I'd be left at her mercy, rearing a child I couldn't afford to house or feed."

"I'm so sorry." Zhara reached out in a way that she often did with a patient, offering a bolstering pat of Maura's upper arm. She had a near overwhelming urge to draw the other woman into a warm hug of comfort.

Maura stiffened, and Zhara dropped her hand away. She clenched her teeth at herself.

"I didn't mean—"

"It wasn't the same." Maura spoke in such a low voice, Zhara stopped speaking and turned to face her, listening closely.

"What wasn't?"

Maura was looking into the water again, profile conflicted. "The treatment. Today. With the other nurse." She lifted her face and bit her lip, expression tortured.

Zhara drew a breath but didn't know what to say.

More people were coming along the path toward them.

Maura glanced at the approaching strangers, then back at Zhara.

"Will you come to my room so we can speak in private?" Maura invited.

Zhara knew she shouldn't, but her heart began to race with excitement. "Yes."

•••

Maura's hotel room was smaller than her sister-in-law's suite, but it was very comfortable, with a canopied four-poster bed, a wardrobe, a table with two dining chairs, and a tall window that caught the fading gold of evening light.

"I should have asked if you preferred to go home and change from your uniform."

"Oh. No." Zhara brushed at the front of her apron. "I wear it when I walk because it keeps men from bothering me. They think I'm working."

"It must be nice to walk wherever you like." Maura had to sneak away from Thomasina and the hotel porter in order to have one minute of thought to herself. "Would you like a glass of— Oh. Dr. Winternitz said I shouldn't have alcohol." She looked at the bottle of herbal bitters made by local merchants left in the room as a welcome gift. "This is supposed to be medicinal," she noted and looked to Zhara for guidance.

Zhara lifted a brow. "I won't tell."

They shared conspiratorial smiles, and Maura poured a little into the thimble-like stemmed glasses provided for sipping the potent concoction. She sat, nervous but excited to have Zhara here. They touched the rims of their small glasses, and the sharp burn and thick bitterness of the liquor swept across her tongue.

"My husband has syphilis," Maura stated, practically throwing it at Zhara the way she had her husband on their wedding day. "I found his mercury pills as we were preparing to consummate our marriage."

"Oh?" Zhara barely blinked, but her expression remained interested without giving away her thoughts.

"You don't seem shocked. Or skeptical. Every doctor I've told has pretended a gentleman couldn't possibly have contracted such a thing. They're more upset that I, a lady, know of such things."

"Is this what you almost told me earlier? When you said a sister at school had explained such things?"

"Yes! And she was dismissed without a reference for it," Maura hissed, still outraged years later. "For giving me knowledge that has kept me safe. Thank goodness she did, because the doctors keep telling me that only prostitutes get syphilis. Never well-traveled army colonels, never their unsuspecting wives. Never their *children*."

"Is that what Dr. Winternitz said when you told him?" Zhara's eyes widened with concern.

"I didn't tell him," Maura admitted glumly. "I'm tired of being told I'm frightened over nothing. But I *am* frightened, so… This is something only my husband knows." Maura drained her teaspoon of bitters and held the delicate glass between the fingertips of her two hands. "We've never had relations."

"Oh." Zhara sat back. "That explains the lack of success with conception, doesn't it?"

"Indeed. I find him utterly repellant." She refilled her glass and topped up Zhara's. "Thankfully, he hasn't tried to force me. Access to my money was his goal in marrying me, and I don't think he wishes to have children, either. We have a truce of sorts."

"I'm so sorry, Maura." Zhara offered her hand, so quick and generous with affection.

Maura set her hand in Zhara's palm, nearly moved to tears. She hadn't been touched with more than a patronizing pat on her shoulder since her parents had died.

"This is why you said the electricity treatment wouldn't work," Zhara said with a small smile of understanding.

"Yes." Maura felt enveloped by Zhara's warmth as Zhara

kept her fingers closed so firmly over Maura's hand. She clung to that sense of acceptance as she admitted, "But the treatment did seem to restore my..." She cleared her throat and tried to delve into Zhara's deep blue eyes for a confirmation of the notion that kept catching in her mind. "*Libido.*"

Zhara's hand trembled as she gently extricated it to lift her glass and sip.

Maura felt as though she was edging onto an unsteady plank over a raging waterfall.

"When you mentioned being close with your former colleague..." Her throat constricted, making her voice thin to a near whisper. "What exactly did you mean?"

Zhara's bee-stung mouth remained pursed in circumspection. "I meant that we were..." She swallowed. "Lovers."

Cupid's arrow. That was what this piercing sensation was, Maura realized with befuddled happiness. Zhara's unflinching gaze sent a sharp burn jolting into Maura's chest. It stuck and quivered there.

Zhara's lashes swept down. "I don't wish to make you uncomfortable—"

"You don't." Maura reached out to cup Zhara's warm hand in both of her own, trapping Zhara's fingers around the crystal glass she still held. "I haven't felt this way since boarding school. I was so confused by it then, but this feels like *clarity.*"

Zhara's smile was unsteady, touched, but her brow pleated in concern.

"I'm glad to help you understand yourself better, Maura, but this isn't a clear sort of road. This I know from my experience. You have pressures from home. A life there. I respect that, but I also know it means this sort of attachment ends in heartache. How long are you here?"

"Six weeks."

Zhara nodded fatalistically.

The barbed head of the invisible arrow was yanked from

Maura's chest.

"You're saying you don't want"—*me?*—"to continue seeing each other?"

"I'm saying we should keep our expectations realistic," Zhara said gently, but she brought her free hand up to fold it over Maura's. "But yes, I would like to know you better."

Such a light dawned in her, Maura couldn't speak for a moment. The backs of her eyes stung, and a massive lump filled her throat.

She choked a small laugh from her dry throat, admitting, "I feel so gauche."

"Don't. There's no expectation," Zhara murmured with a small smile. "This is enough—talking, sharing. Being honest about what we think and feel." Her hand shifted so she could caress Maura's hand in reassurance.

That small touch created the most lovely waves of sensations that rolled up her arms and blossomed in her chest.

"I want to kiss you," Maura confessed with a cringe of clenched eyes. "It's all I think about." She turned her hand to cling to Zhara's.

"I want that, too." Zhara sounded as though she was smiling.

Maura opened her eyes and saw it was happiness, not laughter, that was putting that beautiful smile on Zhara's face.

Zhara stood and tugged at Maura's hand in gentle invitation to join her. They were close to the same height, with Zhara only a fraction shorter. She cupped Maura's face, and it made Maura feel so valued, she could have wept.

Then she learned how Zhara's mouth would feel on hers, and it was every bit as powerful as the electric pulses. *More.* There was a sweetness to it that became sharp enough to cause a pang deep in her heart, but it was a good hurt. She couldn't help but slip her arm around Zhara and try to draw her closer.

Zhara opened her mouth, and the damp tip of her tongue swept along Maura's lips. Maura didn't know how to kiss her back, but she wanted to. So badly. She let her lips part, and now the fullness of Zhara's warm lips seemed to encompass her own. She followed Zhara's lead and rocked her mouth, drawn into a sensual world where she could only cling to her budding lover in fear that she would drown in this deepening pool of pleasure.

Fresh, carnal hunger came alive in her as an incessant craving. She didn't know how to appease it or express it and could only kiss Zhara with all the passion taking her over, trying to convey how grateful and excited and needy she was.

"Goodness," Zhara said breathlessly, breaking away to press her cheek to Maura's and pant against her ear. "You're making my heart feel as though it will burst. Feel how hard it's beating." She drew Maura's hand to the spot over her breast.

"Mine, too." Maura's heart was galloping like a wild horse. She brought Zhara's hand to her chest, then let hers slide lower, glancing to Zhara for permission.

As Zhara's breast filled her palm, Zhara sighed and let her head fall against Maura's shoulder. Her lips touched the side of Maura's neck, and Maura nearly died at how lovely and right this felt.

"Please come into my bed with me," Maura whispered. "I want to feel all of you."

# CHAPTER FOUR

Zhara was unspeakably happy, yet a shadow of impending anguish hovered over her as she undressed. She didn't want to think of her first love, of the heartbreak of losing her, but she couldn't escape the similarity of circumstance. Maura was far from home, stepping into something new and exciting, but as perfect as it might feel in this moment, taking a woman as her lover wasn't the life Maura had been raised to expect.

It wasn't the one Zhara had been taught to expect, either, but it was the one she had realized from an early age was what she wished for herself. Finding someone who felt the same had been such a precious gift, she couldn't regret that it had ended painfully.

And she couldn't deny that gift to Maura—not when it was something she wanted so badly herself.

Maura was radiant as they revealed themselves to each other, smiling with dazzled joy as she took in Zhara's modest breasts and slender hips and thick, reddish-brown bush. Maura was more well-endowed in the chest, had round hips, and a plump bottom and meaty thighs. Her vulva was demure with fine, flat hairs that offered a hidden peek of pink lips blooming from her arousal-swollen labia.

The erotic sight sent an invisible clench of need into Zhara's middle. Of carnal hunger and celebration of the wonders before them.

When Maura held up the sheets and invited her to follow her into the bed, it was easy for Zhara to convince herself their affinity would last forever.

Maura let out a nervous, husky giggle that turned into a shaken sigh as they slid their naked bodies together beneath the fall of the sheet. Zhara was stunned by the sensation, as though she'd been enveloped in a field of electric static that made her body cling naturally to Maura's.

"I knew you would feel soft and smooth, but I didn't know you would feel so hot," Maura whispered, running her hands over Zhara's back and bottom, then up to her shoulders and returning to her hips and upper thighs.

Zhara was doing the same, weaving her legs with Maura's, trying to wriggle closer, as if they could interlock forever even as they rubbed, enjoying the divine friction of skin on skin.

They kissed, and the heat of desire built, damp and fiery, filling Zhara with urgency while dulling her brain to any thought beyond how Maura felt in her arms. How she smelled faintly of lavender and roses, how her breath hissed in when Zhara cupped her breast and rolled her thumb across her nipple, how the artery in her throat throbbed against Zhara's lips.

"I did something the other day," Maura confessed in a broken whisper. "After you treated me. I felt as though I would burst. Can I show you?"

Zhara lifted her head, and Maura stroked her hand down Zhara's belly to her vulva. She lightly worked her fingers against wet curls, making Zhara gasp as her touch slid into the swollen petals of her inner lips.

"I won't hurt you," Maura whispered. "I think you'll like it."

"I know I'll like it," Zhara said throatily. She ran her own touch between Maura's legs and covered her mouth in a passionate kiss.

Maura groaned and stiffened as Zhara found her clitoris. It flowered dewy and swollen, so responsive to Zhara's caress, Maura sobbed and broke away to pant as she worked to find words.

Zhara smiled and moved her mouth to suck at Maura's nipple while she continued playing with her clitoris. Maura arched in shock, and her wetness increased, bathing Zhara's fingers.

Maura's hand had fallen limp between Zhara's thighs,

seemingly overcome and enraptured by the pleasure Zhara was delivering. Zhara didn't mind. The way Maura squirmed under her touch excited her, especially when she began to buck her hips up to Zhara's firming caress.

"I want you to feel it with me," Maura gasped, suddenly pressing her open palm over Zhara's mound. "The crisis. Help me make it happen for you."

"Push your fingers inside me."

Maura stiffened with surprise. "*All* of them?"

"Two." Zhara demonstrated by lightly probing Maura with one fingertip, working her touch into her slippery, welcoming heat.

Then she closed her eyes as Maura did the same, tenderly working two fingers into her soaked vagina. Zhara's inner muscles clung with delicious tension as she coached Maura on how to move her touch in and out of her while stimulating her clitoris with the heel of her palm.

She offered a similar caress to Maura, and they began to writhe in a rhythm of increasing tempo, perfectly attuned as they kissed and sighed, catching at an earlobe or a lower lip with their teeth, muffling their moans.

"Maura, I can't wait," Zhara gasped as her vision hazed. "I'm going to climax."

"Don't stop. Please." Maura bucked uncontrollably against her hand. "Oh…!"

They convulsed in perfect harmony, capturing each other's groans with their deep kiss while the waves of orgasm washed over them.

Zhara fell onto her back after, damp and gratified, forcing away the cloud of knowledge that this heavenly paradise was only hers for a limited time.

• • •

"May I show you something?" Zhara asked in the dark of night.

"Of course," Maura said, still feeling innocent against Zhara's greater experience, but learning fast. Eagerly. Everything her lover was teaching her was salacious but delivered so tenderly she knew it couldn't be wrong.

They had made love and whispered secrets and dozed and made love again. This time Zhara had woken and said, "I should leave soon."

Maura didn't want to let her go. She never wanted to sleep in an empty bed again when she could have Zhara beside her.

They kissed and caressed, and now Zhara was working her way down Maura's belly in a trail of damp kisses that made Maura's loins ache with scandalous anticipation.

"Are you going to—"

Zhara's damp tongue darted out to flick at delicate lips that were sensitized by all of their urgent rubbing.

Maura had thought she understood how much pleasure they could deliver to each other, but Zhara was showing her there was a new level—one that made her abdomen shake and her legs spread with abandon.

Zhara licked and suckled at the nub of pleasure she called a "clitoris" and pressed a finger inside Maura. At the same time, she reached her hand up to caress Maura's breast and pinched her nipple and filled Maura with such sharp and passionate need, she could hardly bear it. She had no inhibition left. She gave herself over to her lover, confident Zhara would catch her if she fell.

Oh, Zhara knew well how to make this dangerous edge a place of wonder, though! Maura lifted her hips and pulled a pillow across her face, groaning without reserve as the tension within her coiled to unbearable levels. She was going to explode if she didn't find release soon. The flutters began, and she bore down, eager for the contractions to hit.

When the first struck, a burst of wetness left her. Her body was completely not her own, shaking and convulsing, doing things that made her smother the pillow across her face to muffle her scream of shocked rapture.

And even though it was so dark she couldn't see the canopy of the bed, she read the smugness of Zhara's smile when her lover pulled the pillow off her face and pressed her weight upon her and pressed kisses to the racing pulse in her neck and her panting lips.

"Unfair," Maura accused when she found enough breath to speak. She rolled them so she was on top. "Show me how to make that happen for you."

●●●

Delirium. That's what this was. Zhara managed to keep a professional smile on her face when she greeted Maura at the clinic the next day, but the moment they were behind the closed door of the treatment room, they kissed wildly.

It had only been a few hours since she'd slipped from Maura's room. How could she be this insatiable for her?

"I missed you." Maura slid her hand between Zhara's apron and gown to fondle Zhara's breast.

"Did you sleep late?" Zhara had lingered as long as she dared. They had invented an excuse of "female cramping" for Maura if Zhara's overnight presence in her room was questioned, but it wasn't something they could repeat without raising suspicions.

"Thomasina insisted I join her for breakfast. She said how well-rested I looked, and I wanted to say, 'Really? Because I barely slept!'" They muffled their snickers against each other's shoulders.

As voices passed beyond the door, Zhara reluctantly straightened and asked, "What do you want to do about this?" She waved at the apparatus on the wall. "I could speak to Dr. Winternitz.

His treatments are superfluous if you're not even trying to conceive."

"I still want the treatment." Maura narrowed her lashes in a coy look. "It definitely stimulates my libido. Especially when *you* administer it."

"It's not meant to entertain, Maura," Zhara scolded, but she couldn't deny that titillation had been chasing her since their first time. "When you said it wasn't the same with my colleague, what did you mean? Who was it?" She went to look at Maura's file.

"She wasn't as warmhearted and pretty as you are." Maura came up behind Zhara and embraced her. Her hot breath tickled Zhara's ear. "She didn't make me think, 'Please press that thing into my slit.'"

"Good thing. No one should," Zhara protested over her shoulder.

"No?" Maura wore a pout. "Is there not some scientific value in trying it?"

Zhara wavered but was compelled to be honest. "There is a specific wand and treatment that may be done internally, but it's not something I could try on *you*. What if something happened? How would I explain it?"

"Oooh. Does that mean I can do it to *you*?"

"*No.*" But Zhara was so enraptured by the sparking lights of possibility in Maura's eyes, she had to admit, "I *am* curious how you found it so arousing. I wasn't sexually stimulated when I had it done. Although, there were six of us in the room, including Dr. Winternitz. Not one of them attracted me a fraction of the way you do." Zhara touched beneath Maura's chin, holding her mouth where she wanted it while she kissed her soft lips.

"Could we play a little bit?" Maura coaxed, still behind Zhara and now circling her palms over Zhara's hips so her skirts shifted enticingly against her drawers.

"A very little bit," Zhara whispered, trying to be sensible, but impish excitement was climbing in her, heightened by a sense of risk as she began to prepare the wands.

"Don't bother with that one." Maura dismissed the comb. "I want you to use that one." She pointed to the Y-shaped wand, then made a V of her fingers over her mound. "*Here.*"

"Maura." Zhara double-checked the door and glanced at the small window set high on the wall. It was well above ground level, placed to allow in light while maintaining privacy.

"Please?" Maura begged.

Zhara bit her lip with indecision. "I'll try it on myself first."

Maura softly clapped her hands, then got in her way as Zhara slipped off her slippers and drawers.

"You're not helping," Zhara said ruefully.

"Am I not?" She gave Zhara's bottom a stroke and pat, as though checking the firmness of a melon at the market.

They kissed, then Zhara glanced at the clock, aware they didn't have much time. Anyone could knock and interrupt them. It added a clandestine scent of danger that tantalized Zhara as much as the presence of her new lover and the sensual memories they had begun amassing between them.

"I'm already so wet," Zhara confessed as she set the dials on the lowest setting and prepared the wand. "Let me show you how to turn it off."

She did, and Maura nodded, then watched avidly as Zhara lifted her skirts and held them away by setting her foot on the chair. The position forced her thighs apart. She glanced nervously at Maura as she brought the double-headed wand to her inner thigh.

As she brought the device near her skin, anticipation warred with fear. She held her breath, nervous. Then the cool glass made contact, and the pulsing prickle caused her inner thigh to shiver. It quickly went numb, but a feeling like fingers running over piano keys went down the inside of her calf to her ankle. A second sensation came up to pulse near her vagina. Heat and lubrication gathered there, tightening in her labia, telling her she was swelling with arousal.

Maura absently stroked her own throat and licked her lips. "Do you like it?"

"I do." Zhara hadn't expected to. It was prickly and sharp and shouldn't be pleasant, but it was undeniably stimulating.

With a nervous swallow, she carefully lifted the wand away and hovered it over her pubic bone. Her mat of hair seemed to stand up with static, sensitizing the skin beneath. She held her breath with apprehension as she slowly set the nodes closer to her mound.

As they touched her skin, a spark of heat went straight through her clitoris.

She gasped and jerked the wand away, head swimming.

"Did it hurt?" Maura asked with concern, grasping at her wrist to steady her and hold the live wand well away from contacting her body.

"Not exactly." Zhara set the split wand back in place. The flickering heat permeated her labia and clitoris and pulsated *everything*. If pleasure were a color, it would be the white gold that arrived behind her eyes. If it were a scent, it would be the fragrance of her abundant lubrication, welling and dripping into the crack of her buttocks like nectar from a flower. If it were a taste, it would be Maura's tongue as she leaned forward and sealed her lips over Zhara's.

Zhara flagrantly sucked Maura's tongue into her mouth, but Maura broke away with a tender laugh and cupped her face.

"Shh, love, shh," she urged and kissed her again, smothering the moans that Zhara realized were rising from the depths of her chest without her conscious awareness of them.

She tried to silence herself, but the searing pleasure was so intense, she could hardly control anything about herself beyond holding very still and applying the pressure of the wand. She was burning alive in the glorious, thrilling, throbbing energy that fucked her into a powerful climax before she recognized how close she was to arriving at one.

Orgasm struck forcefully, and she bucked hard, fluid spurting from her in excited, glorious gushes.

Thankfully Maura took the wand before she dropped it. Maura hit the "off" switch while Zhara gripped the edges of the chair and fought to keep her cries inside her throat. Her whole body continued to shiver and quake in stunned ecstasy. She could hardly catch her breath.

"Oh, darling," Maura whispered, sidling close to slip her arms around her, keeping her upright in the chair. Her lips nuzzled into Zhara's neck and the hollow beneath her ear. "Look at the puddle you made. Did that feel good?"

"So good," Zhara said shakily, holding on to Maura with what strength was left in her. She was utterly dazed. Drained and euphoric.

"There's no injury? You've established it's perfectly safe?" Maura dipped her chin in a cheeky look.

Zhara *tsk*ed, then had to laugh into Maura's breast. "Yes, you vixen. You may have a turn."

● ● ●

Maura continued to book the electricity treatments. They didn't always use it, but they did both try the internal nodules, placing one in the vagina, one in the rectum. Zhara's climax had had her biting the heel of her hand to keep from screaming, it had been so strong. Maura had declared the Y-wand that sent a current through her clitoris remained her favorite.

When they weren't "shocking" each other, they met up in other ways. Zhara made "house calls" at the hotel, or Maura slipped into Zhara's tiny, one-room flat, where they shared lunch and a few stolen caresses. They often met to walk early in the morning or, if Maura could get away from Thomasina, in the evening before the sun went down.

The sun was going down on *them*, Zhara knew. They avoided speaking of it, but Maura had told her she was only here for six weeks, and yesterday had marked the end of that. The way Maura was so quiet as they walked around the pond this evening told Zhara the end of their affair was very close.

"Do you want to tell me what has you sighing so heavily?" she prompted when they reached the gazebo. She braced herself.

"Hmm? Oh." Maura's shoulders sank, and she glanced around to be sure they were alone. "Thomasina accused me of adultery while we were eating dinner."

Zhara quirked a brow, surprised it had taken this long.

"That's not what this is," Maura hissed but crossed her arms defensively. "Alford still sees prostitutes. Thomasina knows it as well as I do." Maura set her hands on the rail and scowled at the water. "I don't think she cares about whether I'm engaged in infidelity. If anything, she wants to hurry me home if I'm pregnant so she can take credit for curing me."

Zhara gave a small huff of dark amusement. Thomasina seemed very overbearing and unpleasant, but she held the purse strings. There wasn't much Maura could do except fall in with whatever she decreed.

"Does she wish to leave?" Zhara asked.

"Yes, but I tried to talk her out of it."

"Hmph."

"Zhara." Maura straightened and clenched her fists into her skirts. "It's really hurtful when you act like you don't believe me. I want to stay with you. *I love you.*" She glanced around again, but there was no one close enough to hear her vehement words.

"I believe you. I love you, too." Zhara was somber and no less sincere. Her heart had been expanded and reshaped and enriched by this woman. Zhara brimmed with happiness when Maura was near. "But there are forces greater than our love. Things we can't control. I know that. I always have."

"And you're not angry?" Maura asked with ire. "You just accept it?"

"What choice do we have?" If she could turn a dial and stop this current that flowed between them, she would. It would be so much less painful than sustaining this pull and stretch over distance and time.

"You could come with me," Maura suggested with a pang of desperation in her voice.

Zhara had already considered that, but... "I followed someone once before. In some ways, being an orphan is an advantage. I have nothing to tie me down and no one to please but myself. But it leaves me orphaned again when the person I count on abandons me."

Maura's mouth fell open, and her brow wrinkled with hurt. "I wouldn't!"

"Perhaps not deliberately, but what sort of relationship would we have? How often would we see each other? I can't live with you in your home. I would have to find a position that pays well enough to support myself. Who knows if that would be near enough to you to see you often? You would have to hide our attachment from your husband. It would be a lot of clandestine trysts, which I realize has provided you some satisfaction while you're here, but there are consequences if such things are found out. I have to be more clearheaded."

"You think I've been seeing you as a rebellion?" Bright tears stood in Maura's eyes. "That is the most hurtful thing you could have said to me."

Perhaps that's why she'd said it. Zhara had known this parting wouldn't be easy. She was trying to sever it as quickly and dispassionately as possible. Maybe there was some anger inside her at the injustice, though. Anger that she aimed at her lover because she had no one else at whom to direct it.

"You said you were envious that I make my own way in the world. I told you that it's hard. It is, Maura. You want to keep the life you have as well as get the one you want. That's not possible. *You* have to decide what sort of life you wish to live, then find a way to make it happen."

Maura's mouth trembled. Zhara wanted to cradle her and kiss her and apologize for being so blunt. She didn't want to hurt her. She wanted to make promises and bend her life to fit Maura's and be with her always.

Into their charged silence, the voices of children intruded. They both glanced to where a family was walking toward them.

Maura sucked in a shattered breath and hurried away.

# CHAPTER FIVE

M aura kept her tears to herself, preferring to use her hurt and anger as a wall against Thomasina and her endless chatter about absolute nonsense. Was this all *Thomasina* wanted from her life? Interfering in someone else's life, bossing them about so she could feel important and useful?

Maura was tired of feeling pushed around by other forces, told where to go to school, whom she was allowed to want or love or marry. Left to rattle around a drafty house, awaiting the return of a man who meant nothing to her. Allowed only the barest autonomy, always relying on someone else.

But what was her alternative? Married women couldn't walk into the nearest mission house and request to be trained as a nurse, not unless they abandoned their husband, worldly possessions, and the secular world to take up orders. She wasn't sure she had the temperament for that sort of work anyway.

What other potential did she possess, though? She had enough education to become a governess, but that was a notoriously penurious and dependent existence. Even if she did secure some sort of employment, she would be tied to it. She would work in England, and her wages would belong to Alford.

As she explored these discouraging possibilities, she couldn't fault Zhara for turning her back on trying to make a future with her. Maura had so little she could claim for herself and nothing to offer the woman she loved. Zhara was right to hold on to the life she had managed to fashion for herself.

Maura suffered anguished loneliness nonetheless. She felt every mile as the train pulled her farther and farther from the heart she'd left in Marienbad.

They arrived in Frankfurt, and Maura was once again

relegated to being Thomasina's pet. Gone was the freedom of wandering paths and pavilions and having fulfilling liaisons with the woman she loved. Now she was on Thomasina's leash as they rode the new tram and visited the botanical garden and wandered the shops in the fashion district.

Maura was standing at a shop window, awaiting the tram and trying to ignore that Thomasina was telling strangers her personal business, when her eye was caught by a strange contraption inside the shop. It looked like a pincushion with lettered keys arranged in a half sphere over a plate of some kind.

It caused a kernel of an idea to pop in her mind. She went inside to inquire.

"Maura!" The door jangled a moment later as Thomasina entered behind her. "You can't disappear like that. We missed the tram."

Maura ignored her and accepted the wooden box from the man, agreeing that it was surprisingly lightweight for such a complex little machine. "Will you accept a direction to send the bill to my husband?" She was prepared to trade her earrings and her wedding ring if necessary.

"What is it?" Thomasina demanded, hurrying forward.

The shopkeeper explained, and Thomasina's expression changed to curiosity.

"A typing machine? How novel. I suppose Alford would find that an amusing souvenir for your parlor."

"Could you perhaps pay for it and have him reimburse you?" Maura suggested.

"How much? Oh, goodness. It's expensive, isn't it?" Thomasina hesitated, and Maura bit her lip. "But I don't know anyone else who has one. Yes. I'll cover it for now." Thomasina nodded.

An hour later, they arrived back at their hotel. Maura was forced to allow Thomasina to play with her new purchase before she was allowed to try it herself. Then Thomasina insisted they attend the first dinner seating.

"We'll have an early night, since we're catching the train first thing," Thomasina said. "It will be good to get home, won't it?"

Maura made a noncommittal noise.

At eight o'clock, Maura was finally alone in her room. She slipped a fresh sheet of paper onto the plate and began to type the message she had spent all afternoon and evening composing in her head.

Thomasina,

As you surmised, I was unfaithful to Alford. I cannot in good conscience continue our marriage. Please encourage him to divorce me for adultery when you return home.

Thank you for all you have given me on this journey. Though I doubt I shall ever conceive, I have been cured of hysteria. I am calm and optimistic for the future.

Yours sincerely,
Maura (formerly Norcross) Walsh

• • •

"Maura!" Zhara was shocked to see her lover waiting in the patient lounge less than a week after they had parted so painfully. She had been trying to draft a letter ever since.

*Tell me where you are. Tell me you still want me. I will come to you.*

She had asked all the hotel porters to save the English-language newspapers for her in hopes of seeing ads searching for nurse-companions in London.

Before Maura could properly greet Zhara, one of Zhara's colleagues said, "Dr. Winternitz will see you now, Miss Walsh."

Walsh?

"May I speak to you after?" Maura asked Zhara anxiously as she rose. "Do you want to walk after you've finished work for the day?"

"I was about to leave for lunch. Come to the electricity room after your meeting. We can speak there."

Zhara kicked herself for suggesting it as soon as she entered that particular room. There were too many memories imbued in these walls. She tried to sit and felt as though she perched on pins. She tried to read the notes for her afternoon patient, but her mind wouldn't absorb the words. She was in a fever of curiosity over how Maura came to be back here. Was she continuing her treatment? Was that why she was seeing Dr. Winternitz?

When Maura finally joined her, she brought a wooden box and wore the most elated smile Zhara had ever seen.

"What...?"

"I am a typist," Maura pronounced as she set the box on one of the chairs. "I have two clients. One is a novelist I met on the train. He likes to pace and dictate. He advanced me the cost of paper and will pay me five pounds a week for four hours of typing a day. He plans to stay here in Marienbad as long as it takes for him to complete his manuscript. I have also just secured Dr. Winternitz. He has a paper he wishes to write and publish next spring on electrotherapy as a treatment for hysteria."

Zhara groped the other wooden chair for support and dropped onto it. "I don't know what to say."

"Say you wish to keep seeing me. Say that you see a future for us. Say—"

"I love you," Zhara interjected. Sharp tears came into her eyes. "I'm so proud of you I could burst."

Maura's smile of shy pride was everything. "I love you, too."

"Will you show it to me?" Zhara asked with a nod at the box.

"It's not nearly as stimulating as your tools of trade," Maura said with a sly look as she bent to unlatch the box and reveal the strange little machine. "But I hope it will be equally valuable to our long-term sense of well-being."

"Shall we take it home?" Zhara rose.

Maura's expression grew tentative. "You don't have to take

me in. I sold my jewelry and found a room I can afford for a few weeks, until I become proficient. Soon I'll be able to take on more clients and—"

"Maura. I want you with me." Zhara held out her arms.

"Then yes!" Maura threw herself into Zhara's arms with a laugh. They kissed and squeezed each other tight with happiness. Maura abruptly pulled her head back. "Wait. Has everyone left for lunch?" Her gaze slid to the dials and gauges on the wall.

There was a quiet stillness through the building.

"Lock the door," Zhara whispered. "We'll move you in later."

*The End*

# The Paddle, Pretty Please?

*The Paddle, Pretty Please?* is a tender tale that features a widow who desires discipline, however it contains mention of nursing a spouse with protracted illness and there is corporal punishment—physical striking with either a hand or an object—on the page, so readers who may be sensitive to this, please take note.

# CHAPTER ONE

---

*March 1883, Brighton, UK*

Mrs. Eleanor Tudley felt the presence of Mr. Lucas Warden the moment he entered the kitchen of the tearoom, even though she was in the empty dining area. There wasn't so much as a flicker of the curtains to indicate he'd brought the gusting sea breeze in with him, nor a slam of a door, but she *knew*.

For the last three days, she'd been more aware of him than ever, and that was saying something. From the time her late husband had hired him to manage the tearoom in her stead, she'd been very aware of Mr. Warden—which left a pall of guilt in the pit of her stomach.

A married woman should not find any man but her husband interesting. A widow still in mourning gray shouldn't either, but as the dismal days of winter were giving way to spring blossoms, she was feeling...*everything*. Young in all the wrong ways. Uncertain in who she was and plagued by sinful desires. Filled with an inappropriate longing to shout at the top of her lungs.

She couldn't shake the sense that Mr. Warden knew it.

Which put a heavy feeling in the bottom of her abdomen, a swirling mixture of guilt and something else. Yearning?

Oh, she wished she were more in control of herself!

"Good morning, Mrs. Tudley." His deep voice caused her to drop the spoon she was polishing. It clattered against the china plate she'd just set.

"G-good morning, Mr. Warden." She was stammering worse than Opal, the girl who came in to help with serving. She was twenty years younger than Eleanor's thirty-seven but always seemed to hold on to her composure. "You startled me," she lied.

In an effort to avoid his cool gaze, she picked up the plate to examine it for damage. Her mother had brought these dishes from Canton as a keepsake of a country she had grown to love when she worked there as a missionary. It had been Eleanor's idea to use them in this tiny tearoom, which Cornelius had quickly taken over from her, appropriating it for his temperance club and other works.

She could hardly see the blue border or the pretty etchings of willows and bridges and birds. Her mind's eye was filled with her brief glimpse of Mr. Warden's tall, military bearing, his dark suit and neatly trimmed beard. She liked that he shaved his cheeks bare and wore his iron gray whiskers in a tidy frame around his mouth. It spoke of self-respect and attention to detail, whereas Cornelius had worn his in the same neglected, disarrayed fashion as he had done everything else.

"Is it chipped?" Mr. Warden appeared beside her, holding out his gloved hand so he could accept the plate and turn it over, searching for fractures.

"Mr. Warden, I feel we should have a conversation," she blurted, taking a step back and feeling her foot bump the leg of a nearby chair. She nearly stumbled.

"Oh?" He carefully replaced the plate in its setting on the table.

"About w-what happened Tuesday." She twisted the polishing cloth in her hands. "When I spoke to you about my intention to..." She cleared her throat. "Release you."

"We did discuss it. I considered the matter closed." He set his hand on the back of a different chair and regarded her with patience. "Was there something else?"

"I fear you took offense."

"Not at all."

"No?"

"I'm not in the habit of lying, Mrs. Tudley." A hint of affront arrived in his tone. "You own the building and the business. You wish to learn how I've been running things so you can manage it yourself. I completely understand."

"Yes, but I don't wish you to think I mistrust you or your judgment. That wasn't my intention. The business has done tremendously well under your authority. That's why I wish to learn from you."

"So you said on Wednesday. We really need not discuss it further."

"But you've been very circumspect since. I've effectively given you notice of a job loss. That must make you feel usurped or disregarded? If there are hard feelings, I'd like to address them."

"I don't carry hard feelings, Mrs. Tudley. If I have a difference of opinion with someone, I express it. Any reticence on my part has been ruminations on my options. Rest assured I have many. Don't trouble yourself about my prospects."

She searched his inscrutable expression. "You would tell me if you were angry with me?"

"I would."

She didn't believe him.

"You don't believe me." His brows drew together a fraction.

She looked to the floor in compunction.

He sighed. "It seems we *have* arrived at something which deserves further discussion. If you think me a liar, Mrs. Tudley, why maintain my employment at all?"

"I don't!" She swung her alarmed gaze up to his challenging one. "I promise you I think you completely honest and honorable. I would not have a living if not for you taking such care with the business while Cornelius was in his decline. But I sense an atmosphere of unresolved conflict. I find it very uncomfortable."

"I see. May I ask, when you and your husband had an argument, how did you dispel this sort of atmosphere?"

"Well, I deferred to him, of course. He was my husband."

"Always?"

She tried to curl her toes in her short, tight boots. "Usually."

"And if you didn't defer to him? Or transgressed in some way that he didn't approve? Bought a bit of lace that he thought was too extravagant? Something like that?"

"I'm not one of *those* wives." She was a member of the Rational Dress Society. Her clothing was quite practical and comfortable. "But if he was unhappy with me, he would let me know by being very quiet and aloof." Which was how Mr. Warden had seemed these last days—not that he'd ever been effusive or overly friendly, but she'd felt a certain accord with him that was absent now.

"How long would Cornelius treat you that way?" Mr. Warden asked it very casually, as though it wasn't the worst sort of drawn-out, painful punishment.

"Weeks," she admitted dourly, circling her hand so the towel became wrapped around her fist. "I had to wait for him to simply not be angry anymore." It had been impossible to tell when that would happen or even that it had.

Mr. Warden looked at her hands. "I see. And you fear that is happening between us."

"Yes." Her whole body wanted to sag. "And I wouldn't wish to have that sort of cloud hanging over us."

"I fully understand, Mrs. Tudley. But what you fail to understand is that I was completely honest with you when I said I was not angry. So the cloud that hangs over us is your lack of faith in my word. I am insulted by that, but I don't wish it to color the rest of our day. Let's settle this as efficiently as possible." He withdrew his pocket watch and clicked it open. "Go stand in that corner for ten minutes as punishment."

"Wha—" The floor seemed to go soft beneath her feet. She had never in her *life*… "You cannot be serious."

"Since you are still doubting my word, we'll make it fifteen."

"But…"

"We open in twenty-five minutes, Mrs. Tudley. You may stand there for thirty if you continue this argument, but I thought we were attempting to curtail drawing these things out." He held out his hand for the polishing cloth. "Go stand in the corner, put your hands on the wall where I can see them, and think about why I have sent you there. Go now or you really will be standing there when customers arrive. I will ensure it."

That last command, delivered with such quiet force, had her stomach turning over with nervous anxiety. She shuffled in a state of shock into the corner. It was thankfully off to the side of the front window, and the shades were still drawn. She always left them closed until it was time to open.

She took up her position beside the window, her back to the dining room. No one but Mr. Warden could see her, but she still felt hideously exposed as she set her hands on the two walls and stared at the seam of the striped wallpaper in the depth of the corner.

"Higher," he said from some distance behind her. His voice sent a shiver down her spine.

She slid her palms higher on the walls, now excruciatingly aware he was watching her even as he moved about, adjusting chairs and softly clinking silver.

She had never been punished this way. Her father had been one to lecture and shame. Her mother had drilled her to be quiet and obedient, but she had known other children who were given swats or a switch. For as long as she could remember, she'd had a morbid fascination with how such punishments might feel.

A little like this, she supposed. Embarrassed and remorseful. Humiliated but also wishing to be seen as obeying. Tears were standing in her eyes even though she could turn at any moment and fire that wretched man for even suggesting she do something so debasing.

She didn't. She listened to him go through the swinging door into the kitchen and take the bakery delivery. Her breathing was uneven as she fought inexplicable tears and curled her hands into fists against the wall. What if the baker came in and saw her being punished like a recalcitrant child? What if Mr. Warden came back and caught her turning to look for him? Disobeying?

She felt so helpless this way. Her heart was in her throat, pounding so hard her entire chest ached. Her skin burned, and her muscles trembled. She wanted to turn and run away to hide. This was ridiculous! Wrong.

Just as she considered giving up this silly charade, the door swished again. His dynamic presence returned to the silent dining room. She couldn't tell what he was doing. Was it even him? She *knew* it was. She felt him, but it took all her self-discipline to keep from looking.

She was doing exactly as he'd commanded, standing here waiting for him to release her. Did he notice? Approve? What was he doing? He didn't sound as though he was going about his business, ignoring her, so he must be looking at her.

Her stomach sucked in as she felt his gaze in hot licks across her back and bottom and thighs. Trickles of heat began flowing into her loins, and that was the greatest mortification of all. This should not be stimulating. It should *not*.

"That's fifteen minutes." There was a muted click of his watch closing. "Come here, Mrs. Tudley."

For a moment, his words didn't penetrate. She was dizzy as she brought her hands down from the wall and rubbed her arms. She turned but didn't want to go over to him. He would see how thoroughly he had peeled away any sort of dignity she possessed.

"Come." His voice was coaxing and gentle. "Let's properly make up now."

Some of the tension in her stomach eased. Fresh tears pressed into her eyes as she wove between the tables to stand before him. She realized she was shaking.

He held out his gloved hands, waiting patiently for her to put hers in them.

"You see?" he said as he warmly closed his hands over hers, pressing heat into her cold fingers. "I said it would be fifteen minutes, and it was. You have accepted my correction, so I can't be angry anymore. We've learned we can trust each other. Do you have anything you want to say?"

"I'm sorry." It was the most sincere apology she'd ever spoken in her life. Her heart was heavy with remorse, but it lightened as she acknowledged, "I won't question your word again."

"Thank you." He gave her hands another warm squeeze. "I predict we'll be much closer friends as a result of this. You may call me Lucas if you like."

"I'd like that. Thank you, Lucas." She swallowed, but a small glow of pride remained as a lump in her throat. "Please call me Eleanor."

"I will. Thank you, Eleanor. But if something like this happens again"—he pressed her hands into a firm sandwich between his, and his voice changed to that implacable tone that seeped to the marrow of her bones—"you'll call me Lieutenant or Sir."

The dizziness came back, and her lips went numb. Her voice was a thin rasp from her dry throat. "Yes, Sir."

# CHAPTER TWO

Lucas Warden heard the bell and quickly finished tucking in his shirt and buttoning his trousers. He glanced in the mirror to see his cheeks were wearing a slight flush, eyelids puffy.

Bloody hell, this wasn't like him to be so self-indulgent, but he'd been unable to stop himself. He'd spent the day in a state of heat after his encounter with Eleanor this morning and had just appeased himself for the second time.

*Eleanor.* It's what he had been calling her in his head, and now he could say it aloud.

He hurried down the stairs to let Horace in.

"Good evening, Lieutenant," Horace greeted, removing his cap.

"Do you mind if we talk first?" Lucas asked him, holding open the door of the cottage he rented a short distance from the barracks.

"Of course." Horace immediately lost his formal demeanor. "Is something wrong? Good God, someone hasn't made a complaint?"

"No, no. It's me. Something I should tell you before we start. Do you want tea?"

"Later is fine." That's how they usually did it. "Unless you want it?"

"I don't know what I want," Lucas said with mild exasperation. He waved at the sofa for Horace to sit while he could. Lucas paced a few steps, still questioning his own behavior today. "That's not true. I do know what I want. I just don't want to say it aloud. But I must."

"You want to quit?" Horace rubbed his hands on his thighs and swore under his breath. "I understand, Luke. It's fine."

"No. Horace." Lucas choked on the very idea. "I've been looking forward to this since this morning. I need it. But my mind's scattered. That's why I thought it best to talk it out with you."

"Oh. Of course." Horace sat up straighter, alert. "That's not like you. Your head is always screwed on right. What's happened?"

Lucas pushed his hands into his pockets. "This doesn't leave this room. That's not to protect me but the person I'm about to talk about."

"Nothing of what goes on in this cottage leaves these walls," Horace stressed with eyes widened in *Can you imagine*?

Lucas quirked his mouth in agreement, then admitted starkly, "I put Mrs. Tudley in a corner today."

"Oh, shit." Horace sat back. "And she let you?"

"Took to it like a duck to water." Lucas had hardly been able to function, watching how she stood unmoving with her hands splayed on the walls over her head. She was still in semi-mourning clothes, wearing a long, drab gray-blue coat over a darker gray skirt and dove-gray blouse. Despite not wearing a bustle, she had an ample behind that filled out the drape of the light wool most enticingly.

"For some reason that shocks me," Horace mused. "That she accepted it. Maybe because Cornelius was such a whiny sort. I thought she must be the one in charge. A harridan, perhaps."

Lucas instinctually recoiled at that description.

"She's laced very tight, but I've always found her pleasant." Considerate and earnest, tentative at times, but wishing to please.

She was also the wife of a childhood friend, so he'd done his best to ignore that she was bosomy and had a clear complexion and flecks of gold in her eyes. Lately he'd begun noting how sensual she was, as she took a moment to enjoy a sip of tea or smell fresh scones or admire a fine day.

She was the furthest thing from a harridan. Their conversation on Tuesday, then again today, had taken all her courage. He respected that she'd done it regardless of her fearfulness. He would have rather kept his job, but he'd tried to be as accepting and nonthreatening as possible, until she mentioned Cornelius and his sulks.

"Cornelius may have been the problem," he mused, always frustrated himself by those who would rather pout and manipulate than deal with an issue head-on. "I doubt he gave her the structure and clear expectations she seems to desire."

"You want to thrash her?"

"*No.* Don't say it like that. I thrash you because that's what you ask for. I just want to *guide* her." He wanted to set limits and watch her toe them. He couldn't stop thinking of the way she had beamed when she'd realized he was pleased with how she behaved. "I think she'd enjoy it."

He thought they both would.

"I thought this wasn't a sex thing for you?" Horace shifted with a hint of discomfort.

"It's not." Lucas sent him a hard look that told him he'd pay for that accusation later. "It isn't with men, anyway. Even with women it's not." Usually.

He ran his hand through his hair, keeping to himself that he'd had to hammer his cock twice since arriving home, both times imagining Eleanor standing in the corner with her skirts lifted and her ass cherry red.

"You've paddled women?" Horace asked curiously.

Lucas kept his activities very private, but this was Horace. They'd grown up here, had gone into the militia and regular army together, and had had this other side of their relationship almost as long. Thanks to Horace, Lucas understood and accepted how necessary this felt to some people, including himself.

"There was an officer's wife who liked a proper tanning. Her husband liked to watch, and I taught him how to do it. There were many women in the flagellation brothels. More than one was paid to take the caning she wanted anyway, whereas men always paid to receive *or* issue a strapping. I had an arrangement like ours with one of them." He motioned between him and Horace. "We never had sex. It was just this."

"Have you *ever* done it with a lover?"

"Not properly. Only a playful spank here and there in the heat of the moment. It's a difficult conversation—one that invariably ends an association." It was the reason he was still a bachelor. He loved sex, but he couldn't imagine a wife accepting his special room or the visitors he welcomed there.

He couldn't imagine giving it up for anyone, either. It was a difficult balance: one that allowed him occasional fulfilments but also forced him into solitude for most of his life.

Horace was nodding. "Suzy wanted to leave me after I asked her to do it." He self-consciously rubbed his thighs. "It was a difficult few years until you returned. She sees the benefits now, though. We might have a niggle about something and she'll say, 'You haven't seen Lucas lately, have you?' I act up, and this settles me down. It's not a sex thing for me, either, but I'll tell you what. In three days, when I can bear to lie on my back, she'll ride me and I'll come so hard our neighbors will ask if I spilled the cookpot on myself."

Lucas snorted, not mentioning how often he'd been invited to fuck a man's ass after he'd finished paddling it raw. He'd never taken anyone up on the offer, but if Eleanor were to ask…

"Do you really think Mrs. Tudley is one of us?" Horace asked.

*One of us.* Lucas absently rubbed where his breastbone seemed to be cracking like fine china.

"I don't know," he admitted. "I fear trying to find out would sever our friendship. That would bother me. I'm fond of her."

It was a disturbing admission to make. He hadn't really known her until she had screwed up her nerve to ask him more about the day-to-day running of the business, admitting it had always been her intention to run it herself. She hadn't said as much, but he'd immediately realized that Cornelius had snatched the reins from what had been an attempt on her part to find some autonomy.

That was when he'd begun to find her intriguing. He liked that spark of independence in her and couldn't help wondering what other fires in her spirit were being smothered by dull clothes and leftover loyalty to an even duller man.

"Do you want me to ask my wife about her?" Horace offered. "They're acquainted."

"No," Lucas said promptly. "I'll get to know her in my own time, but now I've got that off my chest, you'll know to stop me if I show any signs of distraction. Remind me of your words."

They both repeated the French they used for more, faster, harder, softer, wait, and stop.

"You're going to thrash the living shit out of me, aren't you, Lieutenant?" Horace's shoulders lifted nervously, tense fingers digging in above his knees.

"That depends, doesn't it? Have you prepared your list?"

"Yes, Sir." Horace stood to remove the folded sheet from his pocket and offered it. He stayed on his feet.

This was a leftover practice from their militia days, when a new recruit who stepped out of line was given a chit he had to present at the appropriate time. Lucas couldn't be expected to remember each transgression and what punishment had been decided. The young men soon learned that a lost or forgotten chit was immediately replaced with a double round of the big cane.

"You've been a scoundrel, haven't you?" Lucas also liked the list because it allowed Horace to tailor his punishment to his own needs as he cleared his conscience. "You called your wife a cunt?" That was new.

"Not to her face. In my head, but not in a nice way. She likes it when I use that word when we're fucking, but we argued. I had uncharitable thoughts after. Best to atone for them." He nodded nervously.

"Did you have anything else you want to add before we begin?"

Lucas moved to the writing desk and dipped his pen.

Horace cleared his throat and stood a little taller. "Yes, Sir. The, uh, remark I made earlier, questioning statements you'd made in the past about whether this was something more carnal for you. That was uncalled for on my part. I think a—" His bottom lip pulled wide in a grimace of dread. "A third round when you get to the cane might be in order? I have to trust you, or this doesn't work."

"Indeed. I was going to say six, but twelve it is." Lucas made the note, then took out his key from his waistcoat pocket and handed it to Horace. "Open the cabinet and set everything out. We'll start at the footstool."

"Yes, Sir. Thank you, Sir." Horace's hand was trembling as he took the key.

Lucas hung back to review the list again, forcing himself to push everything and every*one* except for Horace from his mind. This was what drew him to this activity, the demands it put on him to focus and perform with precision. He would be as tired mentally as he was physically after this, but it exorcised his emotions and cleared his mind.

It was a service Horace offered him as much as the other way around, and he was grateful for it.

A few minutes later, he walked into the parlor. It was arranged conveniently for these activities but could be quickly rearranged to disguise them. The curtains were drawn, the fire unlit.

There was a backless divan in the middle of the room where there was ample room for swinging an arm from many convenient angles. A wooden stool sat in one corner for scolding. The armchair stood in another, facing outward so it could be knelt upon and the back gripped while facing a corner and presenting a behind.

Horace was touching his toes, limbering up. As Lucas entered, he straightened, rocked his shoulders, and flexed his elbows back. He moved to set his flat hands on the footstool before the armchair and shifted his weight from foot to foot before settling still.

On the mantel, he had laid out the coiled leather strap that would be a ten-minute warm-up over his trousers, the paddle that would be used on his drawers, and the tawse that resembled the strap they'd received at school from a headmaster who'd brought it from Scotland. Lucas would finish him with the cane.

"Ready?" Lucas asked.

"When you are, Sir."

Lucas rubbed his palms together to warm them and ensure they weren't slippery with sweat. He picked up the strap and folded it, giving each of his palms a good thwack to ground himself and remind himself of the pain he was about to deliver.

He had been utterly truthful in telling Horace he had been looking forward to this. Even earlier in the week he'd begun thinking about it, glad that it was coming. He'd been irritated by his first conversation with Mrs. Tudley and angry with himself for letting it get to him. It wasn't the fact she was pushing him out so much as the deprivation in not seeing her every day. He needed the tearoom as his excuse; otherwise, he'd have to court her—and how likely was she to accept *this*?

The fact she'd let him punish her today, however, had offered him a sliver of hope. A tension of a different kind was growing in him, and that, too, needed a release.

He glanced at the list again.

"So, Horace. You've been to the pub three times this week, even though your parents are teetotalers and you've pledged to them that you would be as well. Let's see if we can get you back in line."

Lucas allowed the smallest pause for Horace to speak, then let the strap fly. Despite the layers of cotton and wool, Horace jolted and grunted. *One, two, three.* He switched hands and sides, delivering another three in quick succession. That was his own warm-up. The small pause would give Horace a moment to adjust, but now all the pressure in Lucas would begin to transfer into Horace and release in Horace's reaction.

Each time Lucas drew back his arm, he felt the power build within him. Horace tensed to brace for it, jolted under the impact, then shuddered in reaction. Build and release. *Swack, swack, swack.* Like the waves coming in on the beach.

Lucas kept up that steady pace, not too fast, not too slow, smiling with satisfaction when he finally heard Horace's groan of real suffering.

"One more minute," he informed him without pausing. He was starting to perspire and was glad of the small break when they arrived at the ten-minute mark. "All right?"

"Yes, Sir." Horace swiped his face inside his elbow and sniffled, taking a deep, shaken breath.

"Trousers down. I'll have you on your hands and knees on the divan."

Horace lowered his trousers to the backs of his knees and got in position while Lucas consulted the list. Horace didn't enjoy wallowing in dread the way some did, but he liked a little anticipation, so Lucas took his time before speaking.

"It says here you avoided speaking to Mr. Fetterly even though you owe him half a quid and had it on you. The Fetterlys are struggling to pay their own bills, if I'm informed correctly. Is this one of the days you went to the pub?"

"It is, Sir," Horace admitted with regret.

"I think you'll be more diligent about paying your debts after this, Horace." Lucas set his hand in the middle of the man's back so he would be able to feel Horace's reaction while he worked. "This will be fifteen minutes, Horace, and I won't go easy on you."

"Yes, Sir."

Lucas brought the paddle down on his left cheek in a loud *thunk.*

Horace choked out a pained noise. His back quivered beneath Lucas's palm.

Lucas peppered his ass until his hand began to sweat. By then, Horace was struggling to keep his head up.

Lucas gave him a brief break as he moved to the other side and put the paddle in his left hand. He'd practiced enough he had excellent control in both hands, and they'd arrived at a point where he was unleashing all his force. Horace's spine was squirming and writhing, his breath leaving him in sputtering gasps as Lucas delivered the final five minutes.

"Stay there, Horace," Lucas said as he put the paddle away and gave them both a moment to recompose. "We're going to try something a little different. I'm concerned about this cunt business." He set the list on the divan where Horace could see it. "I want you to understand how hurtful it would be to your precious Suzy if you were to take a word that you use when you're making love with her and throw it at her in anger. Take your drawers down. Then I want you to fold your arms and put your head on them."

"Like this, Sir?" He pushed his white drawers down until they were bunched atop his brown trousers around his bent knees, like a head of foam on stout. As Horace dipped his head down to the upholstery of the divan, his bare ass was pushed high in the air. He was a pale man. His hairy cheeks were bright red from the beating he'd already suffered.

"Are you embarrassed to present yourself like this, Horace?" Lucas moved so he stood behind him.

"Very much, Sir." He sounded miserable, but he didn't use any French.

"You should be."

Lucas gripped the braided handle of the tawse and ran the heavy leather tails through his loose grip, ensuring the edges were in good order so they wouldn't draw blood.

"You were thinking very uncharitable thoughts about a woman who revels in a word like 'cunt' when you fuck her. Do you know how precious that is? Not every wife welcomes her husband's attentions. You should cherish her."

"Yes, Sir. I do, Sir. I will, Sir."

"You won't forget again after this; I'll tell you that. You've got thirty lashes coming. Do you want to count them aloud?"

He was shaking. "Yes, Sir."

Good. Lucas liked that. If Horace needed a moment to catch his breath, he would hesitate. When he finally said the number, it would indicate he was ready for the next strike. These small, subtler communications were deeply important to Lucas, reassuring him that he was delivering exactly what was needed.

"I'm going to practice my backhand, so you'll have two right off the top, just a taste, so I can adjust my stance if necessary. Ready?"

"Yes, Sir."

Lucas swung the tawse in a swift crack against Horace's right cheek—

"One!"

Lucas tapped the leather on the back of his own shoulder and smoothly cracked the leather across Horace's left cheek.

"Two! Oh, fuck me, that stings." Horace whimpered.

"That wasn't even full force." Lucas examined where the strikes had landed, noting he'd only painted about half his cheek. Better to catch more of it. "Two more. Little harder."

"Three, four. *Fuck!*"

"You're starting to sound like you're complaining, Horace. If you don't like what's happening, you know how to stop it."

"Sorry, Sir. You're right. Start again from one."

"All right, lad. Here it comes."

Lucas took pride in his work, spacing the marks to cover as much area as possible, bringing Horace to the point of screaming out an agonized, "Twenty!" But his voice began to falter after that. By the time he got to thirty, he was barely audible.

"Well done, Horace." Lucas set the tawse on a side table so he would remember to clean and oil it later. "I'd like you to stand at the mantel for the caning. Take your shirt off so it's not in the way."

Horace was fighting back tears as he lifted his head and gave a self-conscious swipe of his sleeve to dry the puddle of drool and snot he'd left on the upholstery. He clumsily rose to his feet and took off his shirt but not his trousers. He liked the humiliation of shuffling around with his pants around his ankles, so Lucas usually had him do it at least once.

Lucas left the cane on the mantel where Horace could see it and fear it while he consulted the list.

"We've come to how you got to talking with your neighbor and lost track of your son. That is a very serious mistake, Horace."

"I know," he said heavily, voice echoing hollowly against the bricks in the fireplace. "I forgot Suzy asked me to keep my eye on him. He went back into the cottage, but he could have wandered into the road or down to the beach... It makes me sick to think of all that could have happened. I don't want you to spare me, Sir."

"I won't," Lucas promised. "And as I do this, I want you to think of all those terrible outcomes and the pain you would feel if any of them came about. You'll count again."

"Yes, Sir."

As he delivered the first twelve in a steady series, Horace's shoulders began to shake and he stopped counting. *Finally.*

This was the strange, difficult, yet exalting part of this exercise. It was the outcome Lucas always aimed for, not understanding why he liked to make a grown man cry, but there was something deeply satisfying in making Horace give up the last of his control and succumb.

Enormous pity rose in Lucas. A strange closeness at being entrusted to see Horace at his most defenseless.

"We're coming to the end, Horace. Do you need a minute?"

"No, Sir. Continue, please, Sir."

Lucas moved to the other side and started again, making Horace cry out his numbers in growing torment.

When they arrived at twelve, Lucas paused again. "The final twelve are the addition we added when you arrived. Would you rather save them for another time?"

"No. Now, please," he sobbed, head hanging and voice blubbering as he added, "Lieutenant."

"Very well. Lie down on the divan for them." Then he would be comfortable when it was over. "I'll make it quick."

"Thank you, Sir." Horace shuffled across and settled on his stomach, face buried in his folded arms. He cried with abandon as Lucas finished him off.

Lucas was sweating freely and swiped his sleeve over his forehead as he set aside the cane. He draped a light blanket over Horace's back, leaving his blistered ass exposed, since even that light weight would be too much at the moment. He squeezed his friend's shoulder.

"You took that well, Horace. I know exactly how remorseful you are for all of those things you did. You've been punished and should forgive yourself. I want you to lie here while I make the tea. I'm grateful to know you. You're a good friend and a good man. The ointment is here if you want it." He set the small tin beside his elbow. "We'll talk more in a few minutes."

Horace nodded, face still buried in his arms, shoulders still shaking with weeping.

"Thank you, Sir."

# CHAPTER THREE

Eleanor had had three things in mind when she'd proposed turning the dining room and front parlor into a tearoom. The most important had been to supplement Cornelius's income. He'd been a barrister but not in much demand. They had inherited this house from his parents, but it cost the earth to heat, and the taxes were prohibitive.

It had taken years to convince him this was a good idea. He'd insisted they take in boarders instead, but because Cornelius had been a pious, trying sort of man who loved to drone on and on, they had never been able to keep anyone long-term.

Eleanor had pointed out that they didn't have children, so a tearoom would fill her days and provide her female society. She had privately hoped to host meetings on women's suffrage, offer a small midday refuge for busy mothers, and perhaps employ a few widows who were in need of income themselves.

No sooner did she open the doors than Cornelius had taken over, reducing her to little more than a scullery maid while jabbering on at one table while ignoring another. Then he would complain that he'd been kept from the law office by her little "folly."

It had been a struggle to make ends meet, but when she finally began making a small profit, Cornelius had been diagnosed with consumption. His grand gesture at that point had been to hire Mr. Warden to run things so she could be at the beck and call of her husband.

Eleanor had wanted to resent Mr. Warden. Along with her other goals, she had thought opening the Holly Oak Tearoom would help her find a sense of independence and self-reliance. She had wound up relying on Mr. Warden, but from the moment she'd met him, she had appreciated his calm, commanding demeanor.

In the two years he had been in charge, he had increased the number of tables from five to eleven, purchasing extra teapots, cups, linens, and silver as necessary. By the end of last summer's high season, customers had been telling them that Holly Oak had been recommended by friends in London as *the* place to stop for refreshments while visiting Brighton.

Eleanor still wished to become self-sufficient, but she was second-guessing her desire to dismiss Mr. Warden—even though it had been a very strange week since he'd chastised her by sending her into the corner.

The memory of that accosted her at different times, making her embarrassed yet flushing her with heat. She was even more aware of him than ever, and, several times when she happened to glance at him, she found him looking at her.

It was disconcerting and strangely pleasurable. She began to wonder if a romance was blossoming between them.

Then she found the list.

It was a small sheet, folded into four. It was on the floor in the butler pantry where only she, Opal, and Mr. Warden ever stood. Opal had swept it before she left. Mr. Warden had just done his final round, checking all the windows and locking the front door before he put on his hat.

"Double-check Opal closed all the sugar bowls in the pantry," he said as he was leaving. "You don't want mice."

"Thank you, Lucas. I will. Have a nice evening."

"And you, Eleanor. Good night."

Eleanor opened the paper very absently, imagining it would be someone's shopping list, but no. That's not what it was at all.

*Visited the pub three times; strap, ten minutes*

The next line had a name blacked out.

*Saw Mr.– but avoided him despite the half quid I owe him in my pocket; paddle, fifteen minutes*

Another name had been blacked out, but he or she had been

called a very filthy word.

*Called – a cunt; tawse, thirty strokes*
*Talked to neighbor, allowed son to wander; cane, twenty-four*
There was a "+12" next to the last one, and her heart swooped. It was ridiculous to believe she knew that handwriting, but she saw that same neatly executed one and two all day on the chits Lucas Warden wrote for each table, summing up what they owed.

She quickly folded the paper and shoved it deep between her breasts before she locked the back door behind Lucas and hurried up to the room she had once shared with Cornelius.

There, in the light of the lowering sun, she sat by the window and reread the list again and again, trying to make sense of it. She turned the page this way and that, attempting to decipher the names that had been scratched out.

If this did belong to Lucas, how and why would he be in possession of such a thing? It couldn't be real. A strap across the hand was one thing, and she understood there'd been corporal punishment in the militia, but…

She closed her eyes, shivering as she thought of him saying, *You have accepted my correction. If something like this happens again, you'll call me Lieutenant or Sir.*

Weakness and guilt overcame her as her eyes went back to the words *strap* and *paddle* and *tawse* and *cane*. She read them again and again, searching for more repulsion inside her, but she only felt a macabre desire to know more. What would it feel like?

She stood to pull the shade, closed her door, and stood in the corner near the closet, then did something she hadn't done since she'd been young. She slapped her bottom through her skirts.

She barely felt it on either her hand or her backside.

Steeped in a sense she was behaving very sinfully, she began to undress. She had been taught very early that her body was not hers to explore or fondle or even be aware of beyond the very necessary acts of eating and voiding and covering what shouldn't be seen. Even when she and Cornelius had come together maritally, her mother had coached her she ought to stay beneath the covers and think of other things.

As Eleanor stood in her chemise and drawers, shivering even though the room was still warm from the day's sun, she felt callow and as confused as she'd been when her curves first began to burgeon. Back then, she'd been told to attract a man, a "good" one, but not in a fleshly way. She ought to be pious and quiet and sensible.

This body was a mystery to her, but as she ran her hands over thin muslin, the skin beneath tingled. Her breasts tightened. She pressed her palms over her nipples, embarrassed to see them stand up that way, then roamed over her hips and thighs and the buttons at her crotch. She felt a little as though she had to use the pot, but not really.

Her loins were heavy and filled with a tickling sensation she longed to rub, but her buttocks held a similar sensation, as if sensual tendrils were unfurling across these wide, round plains.

She rubbed all over the expanse of her backside, closing her eyes at how good it felt. She squeezed the ample flesh and picked it up, pushing her cheeks together, then letting them relax back into their natural state.

Her hands began to tap one then the other. She started slow, then harder. She thought about the belt and the paddle… Her hairbrush.

With her heart pounding and her netherlips feeling heavy, she picked up her hairbrush and turned her bottom to the mirror. She smacked it. It hurt enough she hesitated, but warmth spilled all through her bottom. She was deeply ashamed of what she was doing, but she did it again and experienced another thrill of pained elation.

She closed her eyes and imagined Lucas using his hand to clap her bottom. Perhaps he would bare her bottom so there was nothing between his palm and her skin. He would tell her sternly that she was being punished, and she knew he wouldn't stop until he had decided she was suitably remorseful.

Her arm was tired. She shifted the brush to the other hand and hit the other cheek, bracing herself by gripping the rung on the footboard of the bed. She bent a little deeper, going up on her toes as she found a spot on the bottom of her cheek that sent vibrations all the way up into her lower back.

This was the most immoral thing she'd ever done in her life. She wanted to stop. It hurt, but the sick knot in her stomach condensed as she continued, growing hotter and tighter and harder. It was alluring, pulling her toward something that sat out of her reach. Perhaps this intense yearning was her true punishment. She was frustrated and hurting, finding no true satisfaction in the act.

With a small cry to express how helpless and thwarted she felt, she threw the brush across the room. For the first time in her life, she wished Cornelius would come through that door and ask her to lie down for him. She had never enjoyed his rough thrusts. It had stung terribly in her most intimate flesh, but right now she would welcome it. It would scratch an infernal itch unlike anything she had ever experienced.

Feeling like a fool, she spared a thought to making herself some dinner, but she only wanted to lie down and sulk.

She fell asleep and dreamt fitfully of Lucas and a sore bottom and his erection invading her with fast, hard thrusts. In her dream, her abdomen contracted and she was bathed in the most glorious flush of well-being.

• • •

"You seem distracted today, Eleanor." Lucas was suddenly in front of her, taking the tray of dishes that she'd brought into the kitchen for Opal to wash. "These are clean. I gave them to you to put away. Opal and I can finish closing if you would like to sit down."

"Oh, goodness. Thank you, Lucas. I am distracted. Would you, um…" She'd been trying to find the courage all day and could only speak to the knot in his tie. "Would it be an imposition to ask you to stay a few minutes after Opal leaves? There's something I'd like to discuss privately."

"Of course."

Thirty minutes later, Opal waved goodbye. She might be mature beyond her years, but she was also young enough to dismiss any impropriety between a middle-aged bachelor lingering in the home of a widow, believing them aged beyond amorous intentions.

"I've been told there could be a position for me at the bank if that's what this is about." They moved into the dining room, and Lucas held a chair for her. "I'm meeting with the manager next Wednesday."

"Oh." A deep despondency settled on her. "When would you leave?" She settled in the chair before recalling last night's nonsense with the hairbrush and flinched as her bottom met the hard seat.

Lucas noticed. His brows went up, and something wild flared in his eyes. He sat, watching her closely.

Her cheeks began to sting with a flush of self-conscious embarrassment.

"I'll stay until you've staffed up for the summer. I looked at your entries in the ledger. Your figures were allocated correctly. You've been running at a profit even through winter, so you don't need me any longer."

She made a noncommittal noise and sipped her tea. "We can talk more about that once you have a firm plan in place for yourself. Please don't feel rushed."

"Thank you." He looked up from squeezing lemon into his tea. "What did you want to discuss, then?"

"I'm not sure how to bring it up." She set her hands on the pocket of her apron. "I'd like to show you something, and I want you to know that I'm making no accusations about it belonging to you." Her cheeks burned hotter. "It was left in the butler pantry, which leads to a concern that it was dropped by a customer who had no business being there."

"What is it?" His expression grew very inscrutable.

She set the folded paper on the table between them and tucked her hands back into her lap, not trusting herself to hold her cup steady if she picked up her hot tea.

He opened the page long enough to glance at it, then refolded it. His gaze came up and captured hers as easily as a cat snared a fish in its claws.

"You and I have formed a bond of trust, Eleanor, so I am confident that this conversation will remain between us?"

"Of course."

"This is mine."

Her whole being seemed to ring as though struck like a bell.

"Or rather, it was given to me."

She realized that he was still holding her gaze with magnetic force. She didn't know if she was blinking or breathing. A fluttery sensation in the base of her throat made speech impossible. She had known it was his, but now she *knew*.

"I was a disciplinarian in the army. Some still come to see me to alleviate guilt or remorse. Other reasons," he added in a more absent way as if it didn't matter.

"And you cane them?"

"If that's what they request, yes."

"*Request*," she scoffed, then sat back as she realized she was sassing a very dangerous man.

"Eleanor," he said very gently. "This is a conversation. We will say what needs to be said and will walk away with a broader view of the other, but that is the only consequence."

"I don't understand why anyone would *want* that," she blurted, resenting that his list had reawakened this yearning inside her. "Or want to do it. Are you a…" She was only vaguely aware of that notorious writer and whispered, "Sadist?"

"No. I've seen them, though. Headmasters who reveled in humiliating and beating a student. I take pride in creating order. Calm. As for why someone might wish for a whipping, there are many reasons. Cleansing of a conscience." He nodded at the list. "Masochistic pleasure. For some, it's the only time they allow themselves to cry. In my mind, it doesn't matter why a person wishes to have their bottom tanned. If I can provide it in a way that leaves them satisfied, why should I not?"

"Because it's dirty!"

"People bathe," he said drily.

"And there are *many* people who want you to do this?" She folded her arms defensively while a white-hot knife of culpability sat in her belly. There were others like her?

"I have met several through the years, yes. But I was uniquely positioned." His mouth curled at his small joke. "In the militia and later in the army. Most men took their thrashings however they were meted out. Occasionally there would be one who followed orders well but seemed to show up for discipline more often than most. He would step out of line when he was sure I would witness it, ensuring he was caught. Once I realized what they were up to, I would take them aside for a conversation like this one. We worked out arrangements from there."

The knot in her abdomen doubled and pulsed. "That's not what this conversation is."

He pursed his lips. "I'll remind you that I need to be able to trust you, Eleanor."

A harsh, stinging flush rose under her skin, pushing against her cheeks and the backs of her eyes, burning across her chest and making her breasts feel prickly. Her nipples stood up against the weight of her blouse.

"Honesty is the cornerstone of this sort of arrangement. If you are not truthful with me, then I can't give you what you need."

Her pulse pounded in her ears, drowning out her own voice.

"I don't need it," she asserted but knew her voice was thin. Her palms were sweating where she clutched her hands together. "I'm only curious. And that's *your* fault because you left this for me to find. Didn't you?" She was growing overheated with guilt and discomfort with confrontation. "Kindly don't school me on being honest, Mr. Warden. If you wanted this conversation for your own ends, you should have opened it yourself, not engineered it."

"Guilty," he agreed, nodding with thoughtful acknowledgment. "I didn't see it that way, and I should have. Would you like to chasten me?"

"What? Send you into the corner? Would you even go?"

"Yes. I rarely make mistakes, but I take my correction when I do. You may punish me properly if you like. There is a wooden spoon in the kitchen that would be suitable."

She widened her eyes, mind scrambling to think, *Which one?*

"No," she decided as her heart rolled about in her chest like a loose marble. "We have both been a little dishonest. We should both be more forthcoming moving forward."

"I would like that. And in that spirit, tell me what you used on yourself."

Such a rush of blood came into her face, she feared her head would burst. She wanted to refuse. Lie. But she whispered "Hairbrush" into her lap.

He didn't laugh. "I'm glad you took that step. It tells me that you're willing to make this real, not leave it as a romantic fantasy in your head."

All of last night's conflicted longings arrived in her loins. "I don't know if I am. That's the truth," she said, lifting her eyes so he could read her confusion.

He nodded. "Take a few days to consider all we've talked about. Write out any sort of transgressions that sit on your conscience. Consider the punishment they might deserve."

"I don't wish to be caned!"

"I would never use it if that's not something you feel you

need. There are many options, Eleanor." He spoke calmly and reasonably. Reassuringly. "But if you are unable to write it down, you are not ready to endure it. This will be a good exercise for you to determine if you really want it. If you do compose something and wish to show it to me, we will discuss this further. Otherwise, I'll consider this matter closed." He rose without having tasted his tea and tucked the folded list into the pocket of his waistcoat. "Good evening."

# CHAPTER FOUR

fter three days of tension in which Lucas tried to remain as
indifferent as possible, while alternately berating himself
for revealing his predilection and polishing his knob morning
and night to fantasies of her red ass, he decided the best course
of action was to submit his resignation.

This was the outcome he had dreaded. Regret and remorse
sat heavily on him that he had bared himself to her. He had taken
such heart from the fact that she'd been curious enough to pepper
her own backside—that titillating knowledge refused to leave his
mind—but ultimately, he'd made her uncomfortable. She saw
him differently and, he feared, saw herself differently as well.

That bothered him most of all. He would hate to cause her
self-doubt when she was finally growing confident in herself. He
blamed himself for the way she had withdrawn, so he did what
he had to, no matter how much it pained him.

"The bank has asked me to start as soon as possible," he
told Eleanor one afternoon. "You and Opal are well equipped
to manage things. I agree that Mrs. Fetterly would be a very
good fit."

"Is this because I haven't… I'm struggling with my list." She
glanced to be sure Opal was not in earshot.

"Oh?" He nearly fainted with relief, truly not expecting
that. A soar of hope shot through him, but he caught himself,
schooling himself to be patient, not clumsy and urgent despite
the excitement flooding his veins. Had he not wished he had
handled this differently? He must. "There's no hurry. I'm at your
disposal anytime," he assured her.

"Thank you," she said shyly, then made him wait until his
last day of employment.

He didn't mind. Truly. It was a painful torture of anticipation, but he reveled in it, believing the relief at the end would be worth it.

As they were closing up the tearoom on his final day, Eleanor timidly handed him a sealed note.

"Thank you." His mouth went dry at the magnitude of her offering it. Of the enormous trust she was placing in him.

She watched him tuck the letter into the inner pocket of his jacket with a look of anxious dread.

"I could come by tomorrow afternoon to talk about it. Just a conversation," he clarified firmly, ignoring the way his blood was racing in his veins. *Be calm*, he ordered himself.

"On a Sunday?"

Sacrilegious, perhaps, but she closed the tearoom on Sundays. She went to church in the morning, and most families dined at home after. The shops weren't open, so there was no foot traffic.

"I suppose if—if that's convenient," she decided with a jerky nod.

He made himself wait until he was home and sipping his tea to read her list.

It damned near broke his heart, brimming with resentments against a dead man, many that were not so uncharitable as she might believe, but she was determined to chastise herself for them.

*It is not his fault we didn't have children. I resisted his attentions because I found them objectionable. I have come to regret my reluctance as I face such a desolate future alone.*

A twisting ache sat in Lucas's heart as he walked from his cottage to her house midday on Sunday, slipping down the lane and using his key to go in the back door to the kitchen.

She appeared from the small sitting room, pale hand gripping the edge of the doorframe, eyes wide. "I made tea," she said, foregoing a proper greeting.

She had clearly worked herself into a state of anxiety. It made him treat her with utmost tenderness.

"Thank you." He waited until they were seated, then took out the letter. He left it on the table next to the teapot. "Some people like to burn it at the end of our session."

"Do you think me a terrible person?" she blurted.

"No. I think *you* think you are a terrible person. You judge yourself too harshly, Eleanor. May I?" He indicated the teapot.

She seemed too nervous to pour. She nodded, so he filled their cups.

"I have a small understanding of the frustration you felt during your marriage. I chose to join the army for similar reasons that would have pressed you to find a husband. It seemed the best and, frankly, only option for a decent future for myself. I came from a family of four boys. Only my baby brother survives. He's in America. My mother sewed in a factory; my father moved bales of cotton until he was crushed by a wall of them. There was nothing to inherit, and, aside from my ability to read and write, I had no means of supporting myself. The army fed and clothed me and provided me a small income. I learned to manage a storehouse and spent a number of years as the paymaster sergeant. I learned to write a proper report, to train and lead, but there were costs to all of that."

He reached to drop the lump of sugar into her cup that he always saw her take along with a small dollop of cream.

"I had little say in what happened to me while I served. Even a visit to the latrine might have been denied in certain circumstances. I was sent to inclement places and told to do things that were objectionable. I often felt I was smarter than the men who gave me orders. It was a maddening way to live and nearly impossible to leave. I was in Canada when my twelve years were up. I could have stayed there and started a life, but I got drunk and accepted another nine. That's why I no longer imbibe," he confided with a self-deprecating smile. "At least I have a pension."

"Then why do you need this employment?"

"I didn't say it was a good pension."

The faintest of smiles touched her lips, but her expression faded back to pensive.

"If you open that," he invited, "you'll see I made some notes next to your suggested punishments."

Her eyes went so wide he nearly fell into them. He wanted to cup her pale face and press his mouth to hers and whisper against her cheek that all would be well. He wanted to *hold* her.

But he only watched her reach for the letter, sleeve catching at the spoon balanced on her saucer so it rattled. She gave a nervous jolt and searched the linen tablecloth for a spill.

"Be calm, Eleanor. We're only talking. But you'll see that I've crossed out the hairbrush and the wooden spoon. I could use it for a few strokes if you want to know how it feels, but I don't think you're ready for that."

The page shook in her hands as she opened it. She was trying to chew and swallow her own lips. "This says... This says, 'Over the knee and *under* the skirt.'"

"Yes. I would start over the skirt but take you down to your bare bottom. All with my hand, which means I will share some of the pain." He was drunk at the thought. Positively euphoric, but he forced himself to tamp down on that. "Over the knee is not something I do often, but I think you would find the closeness reassuring. Most people hold back their cries until they can't bear it. I would encourage you to scream and call me names. I could pin you so you could fight, if that sounds appealing?"

Her mouth was hanging open, her breaths moving in uneven pants, but she was not braced as though she wanted to flee or fight him. No, there was a delightful softness easing across her shoulders that made his cock hurt, he grew so thick and hard.

"You see what I've written at the bottom? If you wish me to continue, you would say 'London.' If you need me to stop, you say, 'France.'"

"And you would?"

"Always," he vowed.

"W-when?"

"Later in the week? I'm busy Tuesday evening, but—"

"I can't wait that long!"

"No?" He was definitely going to pass out from exhilaration. "You wish me to take you to London right now?"

"I do." She swallowed. "I've been thinking about it since I gave you the letter. Sir."

That tiny little appellation nearly undid him.

"Very well." He took out his pocket watch and consulted the time. "I will give you fifteen minutes to go upstairs and prepare yourself. Use the pot, give yourself a wash, take off your shoes, and loosen your clothing so I will be able to lower it as necessary."

He could see his words impacting her like a pebble landing in water, rippling out in circles of growing understanding that this was really going to happen.

"Do you need a few minutes in the corner to think about it?"

"No."

"No, Sir," he corrected. "Now go."

He stayed where he was, determined to use this time to get control over himself.

●●●

Eleanor had bathed before he arrived, but she was so nervous, she washed again. Her middle felt full of writhing snakes, hissing and releasing hot venom that seeped through the rest of her body.

She had spent days composing her letter, not sure she would go through with this until the moment had come to hand him her list of confessions. Releasing it to his gloved fingers had been the hardest thing she had ever done but had given her the oddest sense of having lifted the burden off herself and allowing him to carry it.

He knew who she was, deep in her core, and would decide how she must repent.

Not that it was easy to wait for his punishment. Her bedroom was taken up by the bed and the dresser. There was little room to pace, and she had left the shade drawn, so she couldn't look out the window. She could only wring her hands and wonder if she was right in the head.

At the last second, she decided she was too hot with her gray jacket over her blouse and skirt. She removed it and hung it on the hook, swinging around when she heard his footsteps arrive on the creaky top stair.

She had left the door open, so she could see that he had removed his jacket and held her letter. He stopped in the doorway and glanced around at the sparse furnishings and slanted ceiling before turning the full force of his attention onto her.

"Remember that you can stop me anytime, even right now. London." He pointed at the floor of the bedroom, then the stairs. "France."

"London," she murmured, head swimming.

He nodded. "This will be a time of learning for both of us. That's why it's important for you to tell me everything you're feeling while this happens. When this is over, I want you to feel I've helped you, even though I've hurt you."

He sat on the edge of the bed and gave a small bounce. It was hard as a rock and didn't give at all. He looked to the footboard and said, "I don't want you to kick that." He shifted a few inches and looked both ways. "That should do it."

He shifted so the backs of his knees were right on the corner of the mattress. He pulled a pillow into his lap and adjusted his feet so they were set one in front of the other, then consulted the letter.

"As we get better at this, you'll know to arrange your confessions so the punishment builds in intensity with the transgression.

For now, I'll take them out of order because the first one I want to address is your shame in wanting this. Curiosity is not a sin, Eleanor. Nor is wanting a swat on the ass. Once your curiosity is satisfied, you may be quite cured of the fantasy, so I propose you lie down here and let me fulfill it. I'll give you a dozen over the skirt. You'll know immediately if you want to continue."

"You're not my husband," she noted as she edged toward him. "It feels immoral to have you here, on our bed, even for this."

"I am not your husband," he agreed ironically, guiding her with a light touch that was as respectful as a waltz partner's. "If I had been given the chance to correct Cornelius, he would not have sat down for a week, and he most certainly would have treated you better after."

Lucas was strong, easily catching and supporting her so she didn't feel the least bit awkward as she settled her stomach across the pillow. His hand stayed on her outside hip, and his forearm rested on her lower back, securing her in the position as he shifted, tilting her deeper so her inside hip was against his warm abdomen. Most of her upper torso was supported on the mattress, as were her legs.

He was right; she liked being held by him and almost forgot why she was here.

"You may keep yourself propped on your elbows for the moment. I want to be able to hear you clearly. Are we still off to London, Eleanor?"

"Yes."

He tapped her bottom. "Yes, *Sir*."

"Yes, Sir."

"There will be twelve." He barely gave her time to brace before the flat of his hand landed on her left cheek.

"Oh!" Despite the layers of skirt, it stung. Not terribly, but the second one also choked an "*Oh*" from her startled lips.

He paused briefly, then four more came in steady succession. Heat blossomed across her bottom. She shifted, but his arm firmed to hold her steady right before he gave her four more, these ones a little harder. The final two really stung.

"That *hurt*," she told him.

"It was supposed to." He rested his hand on the back of her thigh and asked, "Well? Curiosity satisfied?"

She pondered a moment, then said, "Not quite, Sir. I'd like to see more of London."

"Good." His fingers wriggled between his stomach and her waist as he took out his pocket watch. "I'm going to give you a solid two minutes as punishment for all those times you resented Cornelius for hiring me so you could tend to him while he was sick. This will be a little harder, so fold your arms beneath your head and make as much noise as you like. You can kick and shout 'stop' and say you hate me, but unless I hear 'France' I'll keep going. Understood?"

"Yes, Sir." She ducked her head into her hands, thinking it probably wouldn't be so bad, but— "Ouch!" she cried.

He was using a lot more force and doing it more quickly, getting in a lot of strokes in his two minutes. It really stung even through her skirt. He peppered all around, too, slapping spots that hadn't felt much of his attention yet.

"It really hurts, Lucas!"

"Sir," he corrected and found a new level of impact.

She squealed her frustration and wiggled, but his grip on her tightened and his spanking continued.

"It hurts. It really, really hurts," she cried, backside burning.

"Ten more seconds." His hand landed at least twenty more times, then stayed on her bum and rubbed her cheeks while she sniffed back tears.

She was tempted to say "France," but now that he'd stopped, she was thinking again that it hadn't been that bad. There was a purging sort of relief in getting through it that made her feel almost proud.

She heard the rustle of her letter, and her stomach plummeted.

This wasn't over.

"You resented your husband for being sick and therefore reliant on you. That's understandable, Eleanor, but he had no one else, and he did provide you this house and the tearoom that is now your living. I won't say he was a great husband, but he was not a cruel or neglectful one, was he?"

"No."

"I'm going to give you three minutes on your drawers." He started pulling up her skirts.

"Three?" she asked with outrage, stomach twisting as her legs were bared.

"Four?" he suggested.

"Three please, Sir." She clenched her eyes in dread.

"It will hurt significantly more than what you've endured so far, especially since your bum is getting nice and pink. I can see the blush through this thin cotton."

She wriggled in embarrassment, far too aware that he was seeing her in such an ignominious position. The fact that she found it sinfully pleasing to expose herself this way was even more mortifying.

"As I do this, I want you to consider how ungrateful you were for all that you have now. Ready for London?"

She braced herself, but he didn't start until she squeaked, "Yes."

His hand smacked down, and a small cry leaped from her lips.

"I wasn't this *bad*, Lucas," she cried, kicking her legs.

"Sir." Smack. "Did you love him?" Smack. "Did you honor him?" Smack. "Did you obey?"

"Ow, ow, ow." Her eyes were already wet, but now she began to properly cry, hating him for making her face her own failings. She had tolerated Cornelius. Her respect had been begrudging. She had done anything she could to get her own way without openly defying him. It had been years and years of her life that now felt wasted.

"Did you wish you had married someone else?" Smack, smack, smack.

He wasn't giving her any time between them, and she could only huddle and try to bear it. Her nose was running as bad as her eyes. Hard sobs were working their way up from where she was trying to keep them locked in her chest.

"Did you wish he would *die*, Eleanor?"

"Yes!" she screamed.

His hand landed hard, and she thought for a moment that was the end of it. She gulped, trying to catch her breath.

Then his fingers slid to fiddle to the left of her tailbone. She hadn't put on her combination underwear. She wore a petticoat over a chemise and drawers. He was searching out the button that would allow the back flap to open wider.

"Are we going all the way to London, Eleanor?"

She was shaking and disoriented. Cool air brushed her hot bottom as he widened the cotton to expose her from hip to hip, from tailbone to the place where her crack met the seam of her thighs.

Her teeth touched her bottom lip. The word "France" sat in her throat, but he reminded her gravely, "It's a terrible thing to wish anyone dead, Eleanor."

"I know," she moaned, lying limp over his lap, tears leaking from her eyes. "I was just so *frustrated*."

"This will be five minutes on your bare ass. You're going to think it's caught fire." In a move that seemed well practiced, he gave a small shift of his leg from beneath her thighs and gave her a hitch, and, before she realized what he'd done, her legs were trapped in the scissor of his.

She gasped and tried to come up on her elbows to look over her shoulder at him.

"Give me your hands so I can pin them behind your back."

"I'll be helpless!" she protested.

"Isn't that how you felt? You've come this far, so let's finish it." He caught one wrist and guided it behind her back, neatly dumping her onto her face on the mattress. "Five minutes and all the screaming you want. Once it's done, it's done. You'll never have to think of it again. Give me your other hand."

With a whimper, she did, strangely pleased that he understood so well how trapped she felt. He took her wrists in one cuffing hand, a finger folded between them, and pressed them into her lower back. She wriggled, testing his hold, and discovered he was actually very strong. She could hardly move at all.

"Leaving the station," was his only warning before his hand cracked down on her bare ass in a loud slap that exploded pain across her cheek.

"Oh, fuck!" She had never said that word in her life. She wriggled harder, using all the worst language she knew, but he had her firmly pinned.

"You fucking asshole. You *cunt*." Rage and hurt had her in its grip. She let it spew out of her. She put all her strength into trying to get away, but he kept spanking, tanning the hell out of her ass while she screamed, "You fucking cunt, I fucking hate you. *I hate you*."

She wasn't talking to Lucas, though. She was yelling into her marital bed the words she had wanted to say to the man who had shared it. The one who was in a grave and had never taken the time to understand her even a fraction of the way Lucas was doing by slapping his cupped hand so mercilessly against her ass.

"I hate you," she said again, this one on a broken sob, because her tears were growing stronger than her rage.

She quit struggling as her external pain melded with her inner pain, breaking some kind of barrier in her. She began to cry without restraint. She knew he was continuing to spank her, but she didn't care. In fact, she was glad for the way it seemed to push her sobs out, forcing her to release all the poison that had been festering within her.

Then the spanking stopped, and his grip on her wrists eased.

He rubbed between her shoulder blades and said, "There you go. You did it. Well done, Eleanor."

She was still sobbing, so she didn't hear him clearly, but his voice sounded winded and unsteady.

He somehow eased himself from beneath her and settled her on her side, the pillow tucked against her chest.

She was so boneless with exhaustion, she would have let him do anything to her.

"I want you to rest here like this while I go downstairs."

He was leaving? Such a terrible desolation engulfed her, she hugged the pillow and cried piteously into it.

"Shh." He stroked her hair. "I'll be back in a moment. I promise."

Had she spoken her thoughts aloud? How humiliating. Of course, she was lying here with her skirts around her waist, her drawers splayed, and her sorry ass to the wind. Her humiliation was complete.

She continued to weep as the stairs creaked beneath his retreat.

Soon, the step squeaked again. She lifted her face to see he had brought her tea.

"It's cold, but I'd like you to have a few sips. Come up on your elbow." He helped her, and she took a few gulps. "There you go. Lie down again. On your stomach."

He set the cup on the night table and took a small tin from his pocket.

"I'm going to put some of this ointment on you to soothe your skin. You did so well, Eleanor. I'm really proud of you." His weight tipped the mattress, and then three fingers began to move in slow circles over her tender, bruised behind, thoroughly touching every inch.

It felt nice for him to be so attentive, but it hurt enough to make her sniffle.

"I know," he murmured. "You'll be sore for a few days, but

the pain will remind you that you've been punished. There's no point in feeling guilty any longer."

"You didn't…" She clenched her eyes, wondering if maybe she was a masochist. "You didn't address the other."

"The part where you didn't encourage his attentions?" He sighed and let the weight of his hand sit in the middle of her back. "I'm sorry he was so inept, Eleanor. I would like the chance—someday; not today—to show you that things can be different on that front."

She turned her head so she could see him. He was staring at her bottom.

"You want to make love to me?"

He knelt at the side of the bed and brushed a strand of hair from where it was caught on her lashes. His expression was somber. "It's always been a wish of mine to find a woman who understood this side of my life. One who wants sex, but this, too. Will you think about that for me? Consider if you would let me spank you—not so hard as today, just enough to excite us, then fuck? I think that would be extremely satisfying for both of us."

"I can't doubt you. I feel as though I'm floating," she said with bemusement.

He smiled. "This is as intimate as lovemaking. Thank you for sharing this with me today." He leaned to place the tiniest of kisses on her temple before he pulled the far edge of the coverlet over her. "Stay here and rest. I'll clean the tea things and lock the door on my way out."

# CHAPTER FIVE

Lucas began his new job the next morning. He expected it would be a good fit for him, but he was not at his best when he arrived. He really had meant to only have a conversation with Eleanor, but the temptation to see how compatible they were had been too strong.

It had gone better than he could have imagined, but overnight, his elated mood had plummeted into a heavy concern that he'd demanded too much of her. Shown her too much of himself. Each of his arrangements was a little different, but *Eleanor* was different. His feelings for her were different. She was new to this, and they'd exorcised some very grim worries on her part.

He was tied up all week in his new job and thought about walking over on his lunch hour, but he didn't want to see her amid a crowd. He walked by twice on his way home but didn't see her. The shades were pulled, and, from the glimpse he had through the crack, she had someone new working with her, a woman in yellow.

He dropped a note with his key through the letter slot, inviting her to visit him after church at the cottage any Sunday if she wished to talk.

Two weeks went by, and he grew convinced she wanted nothing more to do with him. It was quietly devastating, turning him into the most morose employee at the bank. He thought about asking Horace to flog him for his own stupidity. He should have been satisfied with his life as it was but had pushed for more. Now he had lost even her friendship.

Then he looked up from shaking out his welcome mat and here she came, sailing up to him in a bright, sunny gown.

"It was you. I saw a woman in bright yellow working the

tearoom the other day and…" He was dazzled. "You look very fetching, Eleanor."

"Thank you, Lucas." Her smile nearly bowled him over. "I have decided that mourning is for the doves. I shall sing like a canary. Of course, my voice is more that of a crow, but…" She brushed that aside with a wave.

His eyes and throat were hot with pleasure, his cheeks hurting under a wide smile. "May I offer you tea?"

"Thank you."

For the next forty minutes, they caught up on tearoom gossip and he described his duties as a teller at the bank.

"I was concerned when I didn't hear from you," he admitted after a time and searched her expression for signs of rejection.

"I was trying to write you another list."

His heart lifted at that news. "But?" he prompted.

She traced the edge of her saucer with the seam in the fingertip of her lace glove. "May I be completely forthright?"

"I would be offended if you weren't."

"It feels paradoxical." She lifted a worried brow. "I wrote that I wish to have sex outside of marriage, which is immoral, but then you would spank me for wanting it before committing that sin with me. And even though I believe you would never lie to me, I struggle to believe I'm capable of enjoying lovemaking. How do I reconcile all of that?"

*This is what falling in love feels like*, Lucas realized. It genuinely felt like falling, as though the air was rushing past his ears while he plummeted and tried to grasp for purchase. He honestly didn't care that he might land on his face. He would leap all the same.

"You allow me to court you," he suggested.

• • •

"You want to?" Eleanor lowered her lashes. "I thought you merely wished to have a convenient widow friend."

"I wish to have *you*, Eleanor. In my life in all possible ways."

"Really? I'm not particularly interesting or special," she warned. She hadn't felt wanted in her first marriage, or even noticed more than a convenient piece of furniture.

"Really," he assured her. He stood and drew her to her feet before him, holding her hands lightly in his own. "You're very special. I insist that you believe me or there will be consequences."

She couldn't help that her eyes widened in titillation. She had been thinking nonstop about his promise since the afternoon he had alleviated her guilty conscience, made the most intriguing of promises, kissed her temple, and disappeared.

"This here..." He tilted her chin up with a crooked finger and brushed his thumb across her lips. "This is our beach here in Brighton. We will not be going anywhere else, not London or France, but I very much want to enjoy the day here."

He lowered his head, and she instinctively set a hand on his chest, but this was not a soggy-lipped smearing of kippers across her mouth. This was a smooth, hot press of tea and lemon. It was everything that Lucas was—commanding, confident, knowledgeable, and caring. He was in no hurry, and he read her as well today as he had when he'd spanked her. He drew back to let her catch her breath before returning with a little more passion.

Soon she had her arms twined around his neck, and his were folded behind the small of her back. His kisses were making her stand on her toes, wishing to increase the pressure. Nervous excitement had her thinking, *Maybe he's right.*

He eased back enough to circle the tip of his nose against hers. "We are not going to London today," he reminded. "But I'll show you my *un*sitting room if you'd like to see it. Talking only, but I want you to know exactly who I am."

He took her by the hand and showed her his various

implements and how he positioned different people on different furniture. She was gruesomely fascinated, stomach tangling up into that deliciously uncomfortable knot that sat as a needy weight in her belly.

"I regard these as tools, not toys," he told her as he relocked the cabinet. "But you could make a list of the ones that intrigue you." He stroked under her chin, into her throat, eyes narrowed in consideration. "And once I have *that* list in hand, I will write down what rewards might be yours if you allow me to use them."

"Sir!" She closed her hand on his sleeve, vision going white at the edges.

"And she scolds me with my own title." He looked delighted. "Shall we walk down to the beach?"

"And look for that place I refuse to name for fear you will quit on me?"

"It's not possible to see all the way across the channel. We're safe," he said with a lovely, tender look on his face.

They spent a very pleasant day wading in the water. By the end of it, she knew herself deeply in love with him, yet doubts in herself lingered. He said he wanted her in his life in all possible ways, but what if she couldn't live up to his expectations?

•••

Given their busy weeks—and some standing engagements Lucas had—it was a full month before they were able to arrange a private afternoon together.

By then, Eleanor had given him one list but had begun writing another. She was unsettled. Not blue and angry, but insecure and frustrated. Anxious.

"I think I might need the other kind," she told him dolefully when he slipped into her kitchen on a quiet Sunday afternoon. He had a small valise that sent her heart plummeting. "I'm feeling cross and wishing to yell at you." She held out the new list without looking at him.

He took it and said, "Let's sit down."

She did. Sullenly. And didn't look at him as she waited for him to read it.

"Eleanor, this is a mirror of the list we negotiated except you're saying you *don't* want the sex parts. It's not wrong to refuse sex. That's not something you should feel guilty about, so I refuse to punish you for it."

"But I do feel guilty."

"You shouldn't."

"You sound angry."

"I'm disappointed," he acknowledged, sitting a little straighter and finding a more neutral tone. "I was looking forward to this, but I accept that you're having second thoughts."

"I don't want to disappoint you! That's why I thought you should at least get...that."

"And then you would push me into the corner of your closet of resentment, and I would never get out. No, thank you, Eleanor. That's not how I want us to be. We are friends. We can do this if you genuinely feel a need for it." He flicked at the new list. "That other was a wish list that I thought excited us both. If it doesn't excite you, then it's not the right list. We tear it up and start again another day."

"I'm afraid," she blurted and sagged with relief at admitting it.

"Of me?" He sat back.

"Of not liking it. Of resenting you because you want sex and I don't. Then you'll stop liking me, and I'm in love with you, Lucas. I don't want to lose you."

"Tsk." He leaned to pick up her hands from her lap. "I love you, too. So there you go. We're stuck with each other no matter what."

She gave a pouty scowl at a joke that wasn't funny.

"You understand that London and France remain options no matter what we do? You like it when we kiss, don't you? And when I rub your bottom?"

She did like that. She liked when she could feel his erection against her stomach. That had always bothered her with Cornelius, making her feel pressured to let him push it inside her, but it was sweetly thrilling to know she aroused Lucas.

She chewed her lip. "Perhaps we could try a little, and if I don't like it, we quit?"

"We can quit anytime. I promise you."

"All right." She rose but faltered when he leaned to open his bag.

"Will you put this on for me?" He offered a petticoat in sumptuous, soft muslin. "Just this."

"Lucas." It was very good quality. "Where on earth did you find this?"

"When I went to London last week. I've been thinking about this a lot," he said ruefully.

She smiled, but his remark added to her sense of pressure.

Trying to overcome her misgivings, she went upstairs, changed, then hovered as ineffectually as she had the first time, worried for what would happen.

He used the water closet after her and came into the bedroom with his valise and a dampness around his hairline. He set the letter they'd passed back and forth onto the foot of the bed.

She hugged herself, but the first part was close to what they'd already done. She would lie across his lap, and he would "warm" her bottom and provide her "kisses and caresses" in return.

He sat down on the edge of the bed. "Are you ready?"

She hesitated. "What about the pillow?" He'd put it in his lap last time.

"This time I want you to feel how aroused I am."

She shot her arms straight at her sides, accusing, "You were aroused last time? The *whole* time?"

"Once it was there, it was there," he said drily. "I'm often aroused around you, Eleanor."

"But... You didn't do anything." Or try to make her do anything.

"That day was about something else. And I won't do anything today that you aren't ready and willing to try. Would you rather I put a pillow between us?"

It was going to be okay, she realized. Her qualms flowed away as though a cork had been pulled. Of course she was safe in Lucas's care. How silly of her to get so worked up.

She edged toward him, nibbling the corner of her lip. "Do you want to give me twelve real ones? For having doubts in you?"

"Your doubts are in yourself." He lightly snagged her hand and guided her closer, drawing her to lie across his lap. "After this, they'll be gone, I promise you."

It felt different this time, having the pressure of his hard thighs beneath her tense stomach. She wore only this one thin layer. The room was warm and so was his body, but she shivered. Her skin was covered in gooseflesh, and the raised pattern on the coverlet rubbed her nipples through the muslin as he pulled her more securely into the hot strength of his lap, then ran his hands over her as though checking for anything out of order.

He took care to tug and smooth the muslin, tucking it between her thighs, ensuring there were no wrinkles across her bottom, smoothing and smoothing it.

"How are you feeling?"

"That feels nice," she acknowledged of the loving way he was preparing her.

"We'll start with two minutes. I don't want you to count them. Pay attention to how it feels. Tell me if you want it harder or softer."

"Yes, Sir."

He squeezed her buttock. "Today, you call me Lucas."

"Yes, Lucas."

"Relax, then. Here it comes."

They started as love taps, but because there was only that

layer of fine cotton, she felt the heat and impact and soft sting. It warmed her all over, especially because he paused twice to smooth the muslin and give the backs of her thighs a reassuring squeeze.

"Still on our way to London, dearest?"

She rocked her hips with approval. "Yes, please."

"I'll give you two more minutes like this, then I'll lift your skirt and add more sting for three minutes. I want to hear how it's feeling for you. You don't have to use words unless you want to. Sighs and moans will do nicely."

"Okay."

"Okay, my darling, dearest Lucas," he corrected teasingly, then gave her a solid whack.

"Oof! Yes, my— *Ouch*. Darling!" She puffed out a breath as he gave her a fourth. "That's quite hard, dearest Lucas."

"I'll give you the same in a moment, and it will feel differently," he assured her as he rubbed and stroked with great familiarity over her hot buttocks. "Does this hurt the same way?" He gave her several more.

It *was* different. It stung, but each spank seemed to reverberate through her loins. A strange restlessness had her wriggling. Not to get away, but to ease…something. She made a noise, trying to express this tortured want.

He grunted in a way that sounded satisfied and kept up his spanking, stopping, stinging, and soothing. Each time he paused, she heard herself give a groan that emanated from her chest. As he spanked her, small whimpers left her, but she found herself concentrating on the way the impact caused her breasts to rub against the pattern in the coverlet. Her stomach tensed, and there was a distinct, intimate, growing heat between her thighs.

When he paused to lift the muslin to her lower back, she was both relieved and disappointed. He took his time, letting the trailing cotton tickle across her scorched bottom and aligning it across her tailbone in a way that seemed to please him.

"Such a pretty pink, darling. Open your legs a little—" He shifted her on his lap, touching the insides of her knees so she felt the runnels of cool air sweep up and touch cool fingers against her nether lips.

It was very intimate and exposing. She felt sinful allowing it, but there was also that wicked, carnal pulsing at doing something so indecent.

"Still looking forward to London, darling?"

"Yes, Lucas— *Fuck*."

"Three minutes, darling, unless I hear a different f-word." He paused after the first few, though, and rubbed all over her bottom. "So fucking pretty. Can you feel how hard I am?"

She could, but he opened his thighs a fraction and tilted her against him to increase the pressure of her hip against his hardness.

The movement did something. Suddenly, her mound was pressed to his thigh in a different way. When he began to spank her again, each clap seemed to travel directly to her sex and ring a point like a bell.

She groaned, unable to express her pleasure-pain any other way.

He hummed a noise of pleasure. "Like that?" He usually moved his spanks all around the landscape of her wide bottom, but he began to concentrate on the spot beneath each cheek, at the tops of her thighs.

The spanks were snapping on the air, the pain enough to make her eyes water, but there was also that elusive spear of pleasure that kept piercing into her sex. She bit her lip, moaning at the exquisite torment of it, certain she couldn't withstand much more but never wanting it to end.

"That's three minutes, darling. You're doing so well." His hand stroked the back of her thigh.

"London," she moaned. "Please, Lucas."

"Oh, love," he groaned. "I'll come in my trousers if we don't change things up. But I'm glad you like it." His hand slid up the back of her thigh and in. Long fingers reached to stroke her plump lips and the small aperture they protected. "Fuck, you're wet. *Eleanor.*"

He gathered her up and flipped her, setting her tender ass on his hard thighs as he found her mouth with his. They kissed with abrupt passion, and when he thrust his tongue between her lips, she moaned at the sensations that shot down her front and into that place.

She had only ever heard murmurs of this sort of libidinous hunger, one that had her clinging to him and suckling at his lips and behaving with even less dignity than when she'd been over his lap letting him spank her. She rubbed her breasts against his chest, hardly knowing what she was doing, only that she needed pressure there.

When he lifted his head, his nostrils were flared with strain, his breaths hissing.

"Can we try something? It's not on the list."

"What?" *Anything* was her next half-rational thought.

He tilted her onto her back on the bed, keeping her bottom near the edge. He lifted her petticoat to her waist and drew one of her knees up, then the other, tucking each of her hands behind them as he bent her legs. He braced a knee in the mattress next to her hip, took hold of one ankle, and pinned her knees up like that so she was fully exposed to him.

He caressed the backs of her thighs and the inner aspects of her buttocks. His tickling touch avoided her mound and lips, but he could still see everything. *Everything.* She bit her lip with embarrassment, maybe even a hint of shame that she would allow him to hold her like this and stare with such a lascivious expression, but there was something very freeing in having no choice in the matter. He had her at his mercy, and for some inexplicable reason, that made her inner flesh clench and throb with delight.

"I didn't think you'd get this wet, this quickly. I'm so glad this excites you as much as it does me. So glad, Eleanor." His thumb circled her small opening and rubbed the slippery fluids he found there along the sensitive tissues toward her bottom hole. "Can I spank you like this?"

He looked at her with such a light of lust and love and joy in his eyes she could only nod.

"Thank you," he breathed and firmed his hold on her to bring down his first clap.

He wasn't gentle and didn't tell her how much she would have to endure, but she didn't care. She groaned and gave herself up to the hurt and vulnerability and humiliation of being held in such a debasing position.

Then she nearly cried with joy when he paused to run his thick thumb between her compressed folds, working her erotic juices into her flesh, pinching her swollen lips, making her shake with desire. That's what this was. Shocking, encompassing, mindless desire.

"Does this hurt, darling?" His finger slid into her with slick ease, making her moan and clamp down on the intrusion.

She shook her head, moaning, "London."

"Your pussy is so sweet and tight. Will you take my cock? I won't come inside you, but I think you will. I want you to. I want you to know I will never fuck you unless you're this wet and aching for it."

His finger left her, and she was so bereft, she could only whimper, "Yes, please, Lucas."

He didn't undress, only opened his trousers and dropped them off his hips to the middle of his thighs.

His cock was fat and dark, engorged with arousal and leaking fluid of its own. He squeezed his shaft and ran his thumb over the bulbous head, anointing himself. Then, with a light touch, he urged her to relax her legs open, keeping her hands behind her knees as he traced his cock along her cleft, notched against her opening. He pressed.

She tensed, expecting pain.

"Hurt?" He eased back slightly.

She shook her head. It was only a little discomfort as he pressed again, and she concentrated on relaxing. The wide dome stretched her; then he was in. He leaned his weight forward as he forged to the depths of her sheath, broad and hard, until his balls were nestled in her spread crack.

It felt incredible. No pain, only a deeply satisfying fullness. The itchy, tickly need was still there, but this helped. A lot.

He leaned over her, arms straight as he braced his fists in the mattress beside her shoulders. His eyes were closed, his lips pulled back with tension.

"Fuck, you feel good." His eyes opened to slits. "Look how we fit together. Feel it." He nodded at her hand.

She removed her grip on her leg and lifted her head to watch as she ran her fingers down to where her flesh was stretched around the root of his. What a vulgar thing to do!

But she let herself explore that thick shaft buried in her, unconsciously making a V of her fingers so she could feel both sides of him.

He groaned and pulsed his hips.

Such waves of pleasure went through her, she let her head fall back, unable to hold it up.

"Keep doing it," he commanded.

She did, picking up her head and holding his glittering gaze as she rubbed. He began to move in longer, more deliberate strokes. When her leg quivered, he shifted his arms so he held her knees up and open.

That seemed to elongate her pussy, and suddenly the head of his cock was rubbing a place inside her that intensified all the sensations from her outer rubbing and gathered her up in a great wave.

"Lucas," she gasped.

"Let it happen, darling." He moved faster. Harder. "Squeeze me. Bear down on it."

Something did happen. A wall of resistance in her seemed to break. An outpouring of pleasure struck, and it was as if her pussy began to sob and weep in relief. Sharp contractions caused gushes of wetness. Cries rose from the very depths of her heart. Emotions were wrenched from her, but they were soaring, joyous, triumphant ones.

The waves of ecstasy seemed to hold on to her forever, keeping her in this euphoric state where nothing existed but the glide of his cock moving so powerfully inside her.

Eventually, he slowed. The rapturous waves receded to pleasant ripples. She blinked her eyes open, floating in a state of sheer bliss.

Lucas was still braced over her, his cock ever so hard inside her. She thought she might like him to stay there forever.

"Any time you feel I'm giving you more than you can stand, I want you to remember this moment. You nearly destroyed me, Eleanor," he said in a raspy voice. He eased out of her and used the edge of her petticoat to dry her soaked bottom and stomach. "That was fucking amazing. I love you more than you could possibly comprehend."

"You can finish inside me if you want to," she said shyly, eyeing his thick, glistening cock and discovering she would very much like to feel it inside her again.

"I would like to paint your pink ass with my come, if you don't mind. We'll save risking pregnancy for when we're married."

"Are we going to marry?" she asked, still in a dreamy state.

"I think we should, yes. I'm liable to kill any other man who sees you like this." He was undressing but paused to reach out and fondle her breast. He flicked his thumb across the nipple that stood against the cotton.

She couldn't help the throaty, sensual noise that left her.

"I thought you wanted to finish on me. Should I roll onto my stomach?"

"I'd rather work you up again with a few swats, then make you come with my tongue."

"Lucas!"

"If we're going to marry, you'd best know all my predilections, darling." He moved to his valise and withdrew the leather paddle she had written down as intriguing. "Would you like to hold your knees again? A taste for you, then a taste for me?"

A latent pulse hit the sweet spot at the top of her sex. Her belly rippled with the delicious sort of fear that she was growing to crave.

She brought her knees up to present herself in a very unladylike manner.

"Yes, please, my dearest, darling Lucas."

*The End*

# Make a Scene

*Make a Scene* will put on a show that you might find impossible to look away from, however the main character is a widow who just lost her spouse, and the story contains consensual public humiliation, classist opinions, and pressure to conceive, so readers who may be sensitive to these, please take note.

# CHAPTER ONE

*March 1876, London*

"Did you tread on my gown?" Viola Stanley, Duchess of Yeadonfell, whirled on the footman, Nelson.

He was taken aback and instantly reddened, standing to his full six-foot height, eyes widened in shock. He was dressed in his finest livery, wearing his powdered wig and new gloves and stockings. His wide shoulders and freshly shaved jaw made him even more handsome than footmen were expected to be.

Viola read his horror at being called out in public here on the stoop of her London townhouse, in front of the dowager and everyone else in the courtyard who were leaving for the same ball. His hands flexed in agitation, and his mouth worked as he tried to find his voice.

"No-no, your grace. Of course not. I would never." His usual composure was completely scattered. His confused gaze met hers, asking, *Why are you doing this here? Now?*

Then that light, that precious light of adoration in his eyes before he dropped his gaze, abashed at having looked his superior in the eye. His Adam's apple bobbed, and his brow pleated in suffering. He shifted his weight, no doubt growing aroused.

A delicious surge of power went through her—one that would carry her through this charade of an evening and into what would come after.

Viola straightened her arms into the full skirt of her pale mauve gown.

"You were walking behind me," she pointed out loudly. "You're supposed to be in front of me. Now you've stepped on my gown, and you're lying about it. I felt a tug, Nelson. *How* do you tolerate him?" she demanded of her mother-in-law.

"Viola," Harriet chided. "You walked out in front of him. He was trying to move around you."

"You defend him when you should be ending his employment? Inspect my hem," she ordered Nelson with a point at the damp cobblestones. "Is it muddied? Torn? This is my first outing in a *year*, and you've ruined it." She turned her face away, refusing to look at him as he bent to one knee and picked up the hem of her skirt.

She had exerted herself with this display of temper and had to concentrate to sip a breath. Her corset was so tight she was growing light-headed. At least Nelson was here to catch her if she fainted.

"It seems fine, ma'am," he said in a cowed voice.

"Seems? Or *is*?" She looked down her nose at him. Was she going too far? He was crimson and trembling, but the fact he stayed down on one knee suggested he was trying to hide a bulge.

"It is undamaged," he said, expression anguished, eyes damp.

She pulled her mauve hem free of his gloved hand, shaking it into place.

"How could I possibly believe you? Kenneth will accompany us this evening. You will spend your evening writing me a letter of apology. And one of resignation to the dowager." She nodded at Harriet.

This was a step beyond the station she had always occupied. Even Kenneth sucked in a shocked breath. Nelson looked as though he might vomit.

"Viola." Harriet took a firm tone. "Nelson is *my* footman. *I* will decide whether he accompanies me and whether he remains employed."

Not anymore.

Viola took the power that Nelson had granted her over the last year and condensed it within herself, letting it propel her voice as she turned on Harriet and spoke loudly enough for her words to echo ominously off the facades of the homes surrounding this courtyard.

"Perhaps you should consider how you will spend *your* evening." It was as casually cutthroat as Harriet had taught her to be. "And every evening in future."

Harriet's hand went to her jet broach.

*Yes. I am* your *superior now.*

Viola swept up her skirts and nodded at Kenneth to open the carriage door.

"Do *not* catch my gown when you close it," she warned Kenneth as he held out a gloved hand to help her up the step.

"No, ma'am," he murmured.

At the bottom of the stoop, Harriet was flapping her fan, as red-faced as Nelson.

"I'll speak to her," Harriet promised Nelson. "But the note of apology is a good idea."

"Yes, ma'am. I'll start it immediately." He sounded as though he was fighting tears.

He would be crushed at being left behind. He'd taken such care with his appearance and had sounded excited about being out with her.

There was a hot knot of emotion strangling Viola's throat. She wanted him with her, but she had chosen to give him this gift. Would he see it that way? Would he accept it?

She would have to wait to find out.

Harriet joined her. The carriage lurched as it got underway.

• • •

*One year ago*

Nelson hurried out to the carriage with an umbrella. Kenneth trotted alongside him and set the step before Nelson opened the door.

The young duchess—as they referred to her belowstairs to

differentiate her from the dowager—was genuinely young. A ball for her twenty-first birthday had been in the works until she had abruptly become a widow last week.

She was heavily veiled as she emerged. Her hand clasped Nelson's with surprising desperation as she stepped down.

He wished he could ask her, *Are you well?* But of course, she wasn't. The funeral had been yesterday. The dowager had not yet asked them to restart the clocks. They had all been stopped and set to the time of her son's death. The young widow shouldn't even be making a social call, especially on such a miserable March day, but the dowager had sent for her, and Queen Victoria herself wouldn't refuse that woman's summons.

The London butler, Peeves, waited at the open door and bowed his head as they entered. "Your grace, my sincerest condolences."

She barely acknowledged him beyond allowing him to take her wet cloak. She turned to the mirror as she picked up her veil and began to arrange it on the brim of her hat, but the mirror was still covered, preventing her husband's soul from being trapped in the glass. The sigh she released was one of utter desolation.

She must be deeply stricken with sorrow. Her face was pale and wan as was the fashion, but naturally, not the result of powder or cosmetics. Nelson again felt an urge to comfort her in some way.

"Her grace is in her parlor," Mr. Peeves said. "Please allow Nelson to show you through, ma'am." Peeves was still moving slowly after surgery on his foot.

She glanced at Nelson and faltered, staring at him as though seeing him for the first time, as though he were a ghost, even though he'd been part of the household for a decade and a half.

"Ma'am?" Was she feeling faint?

She shook off whatever had struck her and waved at him to show her through.

She had never really noticed him before, and now he was

uncomfortably aware of himself as he led the way. Was one of his stockings sagging? How was the back of his hair? Smooth? Why did his feet feel too big for his legs? He was a footman, for God's sake. All he had to do was walk, but he seemed to have forgotten how.

"Her Grace the Duchess of Yeadonfell," Nelson stated as he entered the parlor and held the door.

"Thank you, Nelson. Close the door and stay to serve our tea." The dowager nodded at the cart that had already been wheeled in. "Viola." The dowager didn't rise, not even for the wife of her dead son, killed abruptly in a horse-riding mishap. "How are you?"

"The same as yesterday." Viola arranged her crepe skirts as she sat, then removed her gloves and draped them across her lap.

"Of course. But women in our position do not have time for such triflings as grief. We have far greater concerns, don't we? I wish to know if you're well. Or rather, if you've ceased to be *un*well."

The strange question caused such a potent silence, Nelson glanced up. The teacup he held rattled in its saucer.

The noise drew the attention of the young duchess, who gave him an appalled look that made his chest tighten. Embarrassed heat began to crawl up his throat toward his cheeks. At the same time, an inexplicable excitement crept into his trousers, thickening his cock.

*Not now*, he silently begged his body, but he couldn't help it. He'd always found her appealing to look at with her nearly black hair and skin that held a warm, olive hue rather than the more common ivory. Her nose carried a handful of dark freckles, as though she'd been spattered with mud, and her eyes were big and round and clear as green glass.

What poor excuse for a poet was he? She would spit in his face if she knew he was comparing her to a muddy bottle of gargle solution.

At the thought of her discovering his thoughts and treating him with contempt for them, he reddened even more. She continued to watch him as he brought the filled cups and set them on the table between the two ladies. If he spilled a single drop, he would cry. His discomfiture was growing so acute, his throat was swelling shut. The backs of his eyes stung.

What if she noticed? What if she realized what was in his head? In his trousers? The duke had gone into the ground *yesterday*. She would be revolted by him.

The more he thought of her haranguing him for it, the more he wanted to step into the pantry and mercilessly pull on his turgid, unruly cock. His heart began to knock so hard in his chest, he thought both women must hear it. The silence was drawing out like a fine, sticky cobweb, wafting and drifting to a corner he couldn't reach.

When he added sugar to the dowager's cup, the plop was inordinately loud.

"Any strange appetites? Nausea?" the dowager prodded, picking up her cup to stir without so much as a clink of her spoon.

"Is that *really* why you brought me out on a day like today?" Color had finally arrived in the young duchess's cheeks as bright stains of anger.

"You've been married nearly three years," the dowager pointed out in a tone that scolded, as if the duchess was a slow-witted child and she was straining her patience to explain herself. "The title is about to go to the great-grandson of my late father-in-law's uncle. All of this will be gone. You and I will share the dowager's cottage unless Stanley's heir is on the way."

"I have an income," the young duchess said with quiet dignity, picking up her cup and saucer.

"Does that mean you are *not* expecting? Your settlement will not pay enough to keep that townhouse my son insisted on occupying. Your father's investments have not worked out as planned. Did you know that? He wrote last month, asking Stanley for funds. Do you think a new duke will support your family? He will have his own priorities. You and I and your family will fall hard and fast unless Stanley's heir arrives forthwith."

Another profound silence.

*Dear God.* Nelson was so uncomfortable at witnessing this, he sidled into position to the right of the tea cart and pretended he was one of the window drapes.

The young duchess stirred her tea with agitation. She sent him another aggrieved look for bearing witness to such a personal conversation.

Tapping her spoon onto her saucer, she said, "If I am enceinte, it's too soon to tell."

"It won't take long for the truth to come out. Let us make a plan if you *become* unwell."

That word again. It finally clicked in Nelson's head. Women had a spell of some kind that occurred on a mysterious timetable. Nelson didn't know much about it beyond the fact that if it ceased to happen, it indicated a baby could be on the way. No wonder the young duchess had been called for so urgently and was glaring holes in him for eavesdropping.

He swallowed and stared at the far wall, standing as still as he possibly could, willing himself invisible.

"What sort of plan would you suggest for that event?" the young duchess asked as though bored by the conversation. "There's nothing that could be done at this stage."

"I disagree. You only need a prompt visit from a suitably titled man who already has an heir but no wife. I've begun making a list."

Was that why she had dictated those names to him yesterday? Nelson had to work to keep his guilt off his face for helping her compile them. He'd even suggested a few once he'd seen the pattern. *Shit.*

"You want me to remarry? *Now?*" The young duchess was outraged.

"That wouldn't secure the title, would it? No. You'll have to seduce him—"

The duchess dropped her jaw in astonishment.

"Beg a few nights of comfort, then," the dowager amended with impatience. "Either way, things must be accomplished quickly so we can pass off his result as my son's. Don't look so aghast. You think this is the first time such a tactic has been employed? The man we choose will understand. He'll wait patiently until you are out of mourning to court you, knowing that upon your marriage, he will assume the role of father to his own son, who happens to be the infant Duke of Yeadonfell. He'll have influence over the estate, but we can address how that will be managed in the marriage contract. One way or another, all will be well."

"For *you*," the young duchess protested. "You're not the one expected to engage in congress with a stranger. I can't believe you would suggest it!"

"I have done my duty in ways you cannot imagine," the dowager said with a cutting bitterness that drew frost onto the windows. "That is what this title demands. You don't deserve to possess it if you don't understand that."

The young duchess sat straighter. The air became electrified.

Nelson held his breath, certain from the arch of her black brows that the younger woman meant to defy the older. It was as though two trains were bearing down on each other along the same track. Nelson feared for the smaller one; he really did.

*He* knew the dowager to be cold-blooded, but what she'd suggested was so calculating, so hard-hearted, he felt pity for the young duchess. *Fight back*, he willed her.

Her gaze flicked up to his, eyes now the darker green of a wild jungle. Her pupils had shrunk to pinpoints.

Something flickered across her expression. She dropped her attention to her teacup.

Nelson *felt* her retreat. He tasted her helplessness and

degradation before a woman who was more powerful. His heart turned over with anguish for her.

The dowager sensed her win and dropped her tone to something more conciliatory even as she pressed her point home.

"Women are created to become wives and mothers, Viola. That's all we can be. If motherhood is your future, is it not far better to be the mother of a duke?"

The only response was a flex of distress in the younger woman's neck.

"We'll remove to Ulverly House and stay there until this is sorted," the dowager decided.

The young duchess brought her head up. "I wired my parents. I said they should not come here as I wished to join them in New York."

"They will understand that a woman cannot travel at such a delicate time." The dowager punctuated with her it's-all-settled smile.

After a long moment, the young duchess seemed to lose any substance within her. Her shoulders sloped with despair. She set her untouched tea on the table. "I have a terrible headache. I wish to go home now."

"Nelson will accompany you. Ensure she's ready to travel by ten tomorrow morning," the dowager instructed him. "I'll send my carriage so we can travel together."

The young duchess paused in pulling on her gloves. "You don't trust me?"

"Of course, but contingency plans are always wise. As we've just established." The dowager looked at Nelson again. "You understand how important this is."

*Do not let her out of your sight*, she seemed to say.

"Yes, ma'am." Despite the bloodless war he had just witnessed, a thrill of excitement struck his chest. Equally, he was intimidated at the thought of being tasked with minding the duchess, especially when she made no effort to hide how insulted she was. She rose without another word and made impatiently for the door.

He hurried to open it for her.

She had every right to her antipathy. What an ordeal, being forced to answer the dowager's invasive questions and submit to her ruthless machinations, all in front of a servant. He was embarrassed for her and would have been utterly humiliated if he'd been in her skirt and shoes.

*Don't think of it*, he urged himself, but here came a squirming, wicked titillation as he imagined being the one ordered to appear in a gown and veil, prodded with uncomfortable questions, forced to share private details about himself, then told what degrading act he must submit to if he wished to keep the social standing he'd managed to attain.

His inappropriate, twisted desires tortured him at the best of times. They were exacerbated as the young duchess looked straight at him while Peeves helped her with her cloak, as though she had made up her mind to give him a piece of her mind and was only waiting for the opportunity.

*Oh God.* The wriggling excitement dug deeper into his groin, fattening his cock and tightening his arsehole with anxious tension as he held the umbrella for her out to the carriage.

The more his embarrassment intensified, the more his arousal grew. That embarrassed him further—and on it went. If there wasn't such a sharp wind, he would be straining the buttons of his breeches. As it was, his heart was pounding and his body going hot and cold with dread and anticipation. When he helped her into the carriage, he was blushing. He couldn't tell if she noticed, because she was hidden by the veil again. His stomach was completely in knots.

As he stepped onto the back of the carriage, he felt like a dog with its throat exposed, whimpering in expectation of death but still longing for approval.

# CHAPTER TWO

*W*omen are created to become wives and mothers. That's all we can be.

Viola had heard versions of that all her life. As often as she had been stuffed into gowns and adorned with ribbons, however, she had never once felt particularly womanly. It wasn't that she wished she'd been born a man or coveted the life men led, only that she felt very little affinity for the things other women seemed drawn to: fashion and society, children and homemaking.

Her mother had sworn she would feel differently once she was married, but that had been a coercion. As a duchess, Viola had been as ambivalent as ever. The lovemaking side of marriage hadn't been as unpleasant as she had feared. It turned out she had an appetite for that, but the balls and gossip and hairstyling? No, thank you.

*Once you have children…*her mother had further attempted to persuade, but Viola had quit falling for that refrain.

And yet, for the last week, she had deluded herself with the thought: *Now that I'm a widow…*

As it turned out, even *that* was a lie. She could *not* slip off to America and survive on her marriage settlement, escaping her viper of a mother-in-law once and for all.

Oh, it galled her to hear through *Harriet* that her father needed money. It was just like Stanley not to have told her himself. Her husband had been opinionated and condescending and boorish. It hadn't surprised Viola in the least that he'd broken his neck falling from a stallion he couldn't manage.

She wished she could blame him for the catastrophe she faced, but as Harriet had laid out their dire situation, the acrid taste of culpability had sat on the back of Viola's tongue. Wearing a preventative had been one of the few decisions she was able to make for herself, and she'd had to hide it from everyone, including her husband. She had believed she would have time later for carrying and birthing their required heir, but her time had run out.

Honestly, she had never felt more like a woman than she did in this moment, realizing she had so little choice in what would happen to her simply because she had no man in her life. Even an infant or *unborn* male possessed more power than she had as a grown woman. At least if there was the potential of an heir in her womb right now, all would be well.

What if she did manage to fall pregnant in the next month, though? There was no guarantee she would birth a son. *What then?* She would risk her life with a pregnancy to arrive in equally dire straits *and* have another mouth to feed.

If she did have a boy, she would be forced into a fresh marriage so she could spend the rest of her life under the thumb of yet another man. It was infuriating!

The carriage stopped, and a soaked Nelson opened the door. He held an umbrella for her, teeth chattering, but making no complaint.

*Mother's little pet*, Stanley had called Nelson behind his back one night last Christmas. Stanley had been deep into a bottle of port, and they'd left Ulverly House the next day to visit his friends from Oxford. *Neither has the first idea.*

Viola had forgotten all about that drunken confidence until today, when she'd glanced at Nelson as he invited her to follow him. She'd thought she'd seen the spirit of her dead husband. The truth had been there in the shape of his jaw and his chestnut brown hair. On a superficial level, he resembled Kenneth, the other footman who had been employed to match him in height and coloring. Anyone thinking they saw a familiarity in Nelson would jump to that likeness—if they noticed him at all. Why would they? He was a footman.

But as Harriet had delivered her boastful and rancorous *I have done my duty in ways you cannot imagine*, Viola had come very close to making a very scathing comment.

Nelson's earnest, ale-brown eyes had stopped her. He was older than her by at least four or five years, but he had an air of innocence about him. Sweetness, if such a thing was possible in a man.

"Ma'am?" Nelson blinked lashes that were wet with rain. Wind spat the drops sideways so they hit beneath the brim of his hat. "Are you unw— I mean..."

He was shivering in his soaked livery but flushed red, looking mortified at what he'd nearly said.

She found that streak of shyness in him endearing. It was as if he didn't realize he was virile and handsome and entitled to more. Not the title, she supposed, but much, much more than he'd been given. It leant a certain rightness to the wrongness of what she was contemplating.

"I presume if the dowager has pressed you upon me, you're at my disposal?" she asked as she climbed from the carriage.

"I—" He sounded as though he strangled on his tongue. "Yes, ma'am. Anything you need, please ask."

She held on to his wet glove, allowing him to protect her with the umbrella as they climbed the steps to the front door.

"I want you to find the duke's valet. Ask him to furnish you a bath and dry clothes. When you're presentable, meet me in my parlor."

• • •

Nelson wanted to believe the young duchess was concerned for his health, but he also wanted to retain his job and not fall asleep in a bath while she stowed away on a steamship.

He settled for a brisk wash with a pan of warm water and a hot cup of tea before he dressed in the plain wool trousers he'd been given, topping it with a white shirt and a blue pullover vest. His bow tie was soggy and starchless, but he felt underdressed without it, so he did what he could with it.

He hurried up the stairs and was relieved when he was shown into a dainty parlor that was clearly furnished for a lady's comfort. There were an armchair and footstool near the fire, a divan near the window, where the sun would fall on a fine afternoon, and a table and chairs for light meals.

She sat in the chair near the fire and looked surprised when he was shown in. "That was fast. Are you properly warm? Would you like to stand near the fire while we talk?"

"Thank you, ma'am." Since that seemed the most convenient angle for her, he moved into the spot she indicated.

"You've been with the family a long while; is that right?" she asked him.

"Almost since before I can remember." Truthfully, he didn't care to remember what had come before.

"And you've been a dedicated footman for the dowager for how long?"

"Since I was fourteen, I believe?" He resisted the urge to tug his earlobe or fidget in some other way. "It was gradual, ma'am. Carrying her parcels while she shopped, learning from my predecessor. That's how it started."

"I see. And you feel very loyal to her and the family."

Here it came. He squeezed his bare hands, wishing he'd been given gloves. He felt naked on many levels without his uniform. His sense of exposure started the infernal tickles of arousal in his pants. He tried to ignore them.

"The family has always been very good to me, ma'am. I know you're also family. I would never wish to seem divided about where my loyalties lie."

"But?" she prompted.

He shook his head, pleading, "No but. Only please don't ask me to choose where they *should* lie. Ma'am," he added belatedly. Had he overstepped? He felt more and more gauche by the second.

"I should think your loyalty lies with the dukedom." She chewed the corner of her mouth as though choosing her words very carefully. "If there was another duke on the way, that is where your allegiance would most lie. If my husband were still alive, or even the former duke, you would feel most obliged to him. You are bound by the bloodline, as it were. Would you say that's true?"

That sounded like a trick question, but he tentatively agreed. "I should think so, ma'am."

"What did you think of what you heard today? About the dowager's plan for me if I am not carrying the next duke?"

"I-I try not to listen, ma'am." He rubbed his damp palms on his thighs. As his uneasiness grew and he was reminded of how unbearable that meeting had been, his cock began to thicken. He dropped his gaze, hoping she wouldn't notice his growing arousal. He wound up staring at the way her breasts rose and fell beneath the black crepe she still wore.

That was inappropriate, too. Christ.

"What I might overhear, I would never repeat. Or judge, ma'am." *Please not now.* He folded his dangling hands over his crotch.

"I see." She didn't sound pleased. The ring of irritation in her voice made a shiver of hideously delicious anxiety trace its way down his spine and land as a weight in his belly. It increased the pressure in his pants.

*Bloody hell.* He dug his thumbnail against the inside of his wrist, hoping the pain would distract him.

"Perhaps I lack your good manners, Nelson, because I wish to tell you something I overheard that will change everything you think and feel about the family. You will judge them very harshly after."

He opened his mouth, wanting to beg her not to, but he was

instantly curious. Of course he was.

"First, I will tell you something about me that you may take to the dowager if your loyalty demands you must." She lifted her chin slightly. "I know I am not carrying the duke's child. I was unwell the day after he died. The duke and I had congress regularly, but I wore a preventative— I thought you don't judge what you hear?" she challenged sharply.

He wiped his hand over his face, erasing whatever shock had arisen there.

"I'm sorry, ma'am. It's only surprise." It had never occurred to him that a lady would do such a thing. Or tell him. It was as if he'd peeked up her skirt and seen it.

Now she was annoyed with him. Recognizing that made his nipples stand up, so sensitized he could feel the harsh cotton of his shirt as he shifted awkwardly, trying to regain a semblance of composure. Trying not to think of accidentally seeing her cunt. *Dear God.*

"Children have never appealed to me," she said crisply. "They seem messy and loud, and I'm told there is a lot of pain when one delivers. When I didn't conceive immediately after the wedding, I decided to put it off. I never dreamed my husband would die before I came around to the idea. Harriet was not wrong about the predicament we're in. I realize now I must find a man to father what I hope will be the next duke. I would like that man to be you."

"What? No. I couldn't." He was so taken aback, he stumbled into the fire screen, nearly knocking it over.

He caught himself on the mantel and hurried to right the screen, horrified by his clumsiness, deeply befuddled by her suggestion, but also affected. He wasn't even *good* at fucking a woman. He would disappoint her, and why did the idea of her taking him to task over that excite him nearly beyond bearing?

It took all his strength to face her again. He was tempted to pull the folded screen in front of him to hide what the slouch in his trousers didn't. He couldn't shove his hands in his pockets. It would be disrespectful to stand that way. He folded his hands over his telling bulge and hung his head, mortified.

"What do you know of your parents, Nelson?"

That surprised him into looking up.

"They died, ma'am. I'm an orphan. Farmers, I was told. I was placed with a wet nurse who fostered me until school age. Once I could read and write, I was given a position at Ulverly House."

He wasn't sure what he expected from her, but it wasn't pity. That's what he got, though. She canted her head and said "Tsk" in a way that judged him pitiful. Not in a good way. It stung. Deeply.

"As I said, the family has been very good to me," he said with dignity. "Coming from such a low birth, I could have wound up sweeping chimneys or begging on the street. Instead, I've become the dedicated footman to a dowager duchess. She values me very highly." He heard how boastful that sounded, and his cheeks were hot, but he had worked very hard to arrive where he was. He wouldn't allow his accomplishment to be dismissed.

"I know she does." The duchess was watching him closely, and her voice had quieted to a somber tone. "I said as much to the duke at Christmas. He then told me that you were the product of one of his father's many affairs. Sadly, your mother passed in the days after your birth, so the duke arranged for your care. I suppose the rest is more or less as you remember it. He brought you into his house once you were of an age, and the dowager developed a preference for you."

"But—" Nelson swallowed a hard lump from his throat. It only lodged as a sharp rock in his chest. His head was swimming as though it had fallen off and dropped in a river and was drifting far from his body. "That can't be true."

"It is." Her tone gentled some, but she remained matter-of-fact. "My husband said his father had made provisions that you be kept on staff your whole life and pensioned off in your later years."

"It's not true," Nelson insisted, hands closing into crushing fists. But he was remembering the old duke's occasional moments of interest in him and the recent duke's supercilious smirk. Nelson had thought Stanley treated him that way because he was older. *Better.*

It suddenly struck him how many times he'd been absently called "your grace" by a shopkeeper or other villager, if he happened to be out of his livery while on the street. But he had occasionally been gifted a worn cloak or out-of-fashion pair of trousers from his lordship, so he had put it down to wearing the man's clothes. It had been more than one or two coincidences, though. A dozen, at least.

An invisible band seemed to squeeze around his chest. Tears pressed behind his eyes and filled the back of his nose.

"I can't—" He choked on whatever he might have said, unable to find words or form them. He looked to the door, but he couldn't leave. He had an assignment to ready her for travel. Was this a trick to throw him off?

Through his gathering tears, he saw her looking sorry, not satisfied. She wasn't trying to hurt him, which made all of this worse.

What a laughable wretch he was, stumbling around, trying to earn the approval of his dead father's widow. Did the dowager suspect? Was this her way of getting back at the man who had scorned her? By keeping his son at her beck and call?

The pressure in his chest erupted in one uncontrollable sputter that he fought to contain behind his pressed lips. He didn't know if he could hold off the impending storm.

"Nelson, sit. Please. You're upset."

She rose and indicated the divan, but he shook his head violently. He couldn't. He was a footman. Dogs might be invited onto the furniture, but *he* didn't deserve that privilege.

Another heaving sob rose up to batter at his control, coming out as a helpless gasp, as though he was drowning.

"The footstool," she urged, tugging on his arm until he sank down to the rickety little seat.

It wobbled beneath him. His knees were practically at his ears. He braced his elbows on them and felt gangly and ridiculous. He tried to hide his face, but there was no stopping the tears that were welling to overflow his clenched eyes. Every memory of trying to please was hitting him along with the snickers from his *brother.*

In every way, Stanley had been Nelson's superior, but he'd been laughing at Nelson for something that wasn't his fault. For trying to be worthy of the opportunity he'd been given. He must have seemed so *ridiculous.*

"Oh, Nelson," the duchess murmured. Her warm, soft hand was trying to maneuver around the ones he was hiding behind. She brushed at the tears she found. "It was a cruel thing. You have a right to be angry."

"I'm humiliated," he sobbed, rubbing his sleeve beneath his running nose. "Usually I like it, but not like *this.*"

She cocked her head, puzzled. "What do you mean? You don't mean you enjoy being humiliated?"

"What?" Oh God. What had he said? He crossed his arms and buried his head on them. "Never mind. Send me away. I shouldn't burden you like this." He was sobbing, snotty as a child.

"You're perfectly fine here." Her hand stroked his hair, comforting him.

The sensation was so lovely, it was as if she was petting his heart. He sat very still, trying to stem his weeping while he willed her to continue that small kindness.

After some time, he calmed, and she brought her hands into her lap. Sighed.

He lifted his head, feeling adrift in a sea of emotions. His eyes were salted and sore, his throat still thick, his nose still clogged with emotion. He was liable to be battered by another wave any second, but in this instant, he was catching his breath.

Her expression was all compassion and apology. "I'm sorry I didn't tell you sooner. I haven't seen you since Christmas, and this last week…"

"You don't have to apologize, ma'am," he croaked.

A tiny smile came and went on her lips. "I think I do, given what I'm asking of you. Do you see why I want it to be you? And how it could work in both our favor? We needn't marry, but in exchange for doing this, I will ensure you're given what you're properly due as the son—and hopefully father—of a duke."

He shook his head, unable to take it in.

She took one of his hands to press it between her small, smooth ones.

"If I could give you more time to think on it, I would, but we must seize the day, as it were." Her mouth twisted with irony. "Take a little time," she allowed. "Have your evening meal. We'll talk again in an hour or two."

She rose. He stared up at her, taking too long to realize he was still sitting. He found his feet, thinking he must look like such a fool to her. He had *cried*. And let slip that he *liked*… Oh God.

Mortified to the point of speechlessness, he hurried from the room.

# CHAPTER THREE

W hat a sweet, darling man, Viola thought as she bathed and dressed in a nightgown and morning robe. Her husband had been a buffoon, constantly swollen with self-importance and lacking intelligence. She had genuinely feared a child of his would only perpetuate arrogant mediocrity.

She could love a child of Nelson's, though. His earnest expression and sensitive nature were appealing. She felt strangely protective of him after his display of emotion. The more she thought on it, the angrier she was on his behalf and the more she wanted to elevate him from where he'd been cast.

By ordering him into her bed? Not precisely, but it would be no chore to entertain him there. His physique was attractive, and he had that air of longing to please.

When he was shown into her parlor again, she smiled and set aside her book. Her maid was scandalized that she was meeting any man but her husband while wearing nightclothes, but Viola dismissed the woman with, "He's a footman, not the queen's consort. This is very time-sensitive, confidential business of the duke's. Close the door and do not interrupt us."

Nelson was still in his informal clothes. He looked deeply uncomfortable as they were left alone. Still suffering from what she'd revealed to him of his background?

"How are you feeling? Have you had time to consider things?" she asked gently.

"Not really." His hand started to go to the back of his head, but he forced it down to this side. "I don't know what to make of any of it."

"Understandable. And I want you to know that if you wish things to remain as they are with the dowager, I will not interfere in that, but I hope you're considering my offer. I will compensate you however you like."

"I…" His voice dwindled to a gurgle. He wiped his palms on his thighs. "Obviously, I think you're very…" He reddened. Footmen were not supposed to think anything of ladies.

A delighted glow came alive in her as she realized he found her attractive.

"It's flattering of you to think of me, ma'am, but I am certain to disappoint. And I'm still the product of—" Here he broke off and his expression flashed with real pain that said: *I'm humiliated.*

He had been degraded by his own family. Her instinct to shelter him warred with her determination to get herself pregnant without involving a man she would be forced to submit to later.

"Do you feel belittled by what I'm asking of you, Nelson? If my offer of compensation sounds—"

"No. I beg your pardon for interrupting, ma'am." He blushed harder. "I understand your need to have an heir, and, well, I do feel a loyalty to the family. There's a part of me that thinks if my blood has some blue in it, some of the duke's blood, I have an obligation to help you. But…" Uncertainty tortured his expression. His hands flexed in and out of fists before he folded them in front of his trousers.

A delightful realization struck her. "Are you aroused, Nelson?"

His eyes widened in horror. He looked as though he wished the house would collapse on itself, burying him in bricks and broken rafters.

"N— I don't wish to be," he said in a pained whisper.

How engaging he was with that reluctant desire of his.

"I'm confused." She folded her hands in her lap and inched to the edge of the chair's cushion as she studied him. "If you find me comely, what holds back? Is it that you don't wish to be used?"

His lashes fluttered, and his arms tightened into his body. His hand seemed to press against his bulge as though urging it to subside.

"No," he said on a voice that sounded strangled. "I don't mind that."

How curious. A subtle sensuality had been teasing her all evening as she considered what this night might entail. Seeing her effect on him sharpened her desires. She shifted on her seat, arching her back to press her weight into her loins, where arousal had begun to pool.

"Are you a virgin? Is that the issue?"

"Not really. There was a widow in the village I visited briefly, but I'm not very experienced." He was so anguished she could taste his discomfort.

"I wouldn't mock you for your performance, Nelson. I'll show you how to please me." Perhaps that would sweeten the pot.

He made a noise that was positively tortured, further piquing her sexual excitement. How novel to wield such power over someone!

"Nelson," she said firmly, testing her authority, "you haven't outright refused me, so I must insist that you tell me exactly why you are hesitating."

"I couldn't." His gaze met hers, pleading for leniency. "It's too embarrassing."

"How so? Is your..." She motioned to where his hands were crossed in front of him. "Crooked or malformed? Not up to the task in some way?"

"No." The heel of his hand was pushing into his cock, and he was biting his lip.

"Are you about to come?" she realized with shock. "For heaven's sake, don't waste it!"

●●●

"Please stop," Nelson begged and openly crushed his aching, about-to-burst cock through the rough wool of his trousers. He covered his eyes with his other hand, aghast at himself for behaving so improperly. "I won't. I swear I won't."

He was trying to convince himself he wouldn't, but he was fighting climax so ferociously he tasted blood on his lip. He was *so* close to creaming inside his borrowed trousers. He had definitely left damp stains on drawers that were likely soaking through to wool. Could she see it? He tried not to think of it, but it was so beguiling to imagine that horror.

"What is it you wish to stop? This conversation? You're saying you don't wish to bed me?" She sounded hurt.

"I do, but—" Oh *God*. This was the most exquisitely torturous moment of his life. She had brought him to this point so unwittingly, turning the knife with every invasive question that forced his chagrined answers.

She made an exasperated noise that found him wanting, pushing him right up to the edge of his self-control.

"I'll tell you," he groaned. "But please don't laugh. It's… I like it," he admitted with deep reluctance, but as he did, the greatest weight lifted off his chest. Shame licked at him like flames, but there was relief, too. "I like your scold," he explained, discovering a heady freedom in saying it aloud. "I like to feel…inadequate. When you said you would teach me…" He had to take a slow breath to control himself. "I *want* you to force me to reveal these things, even though I'm ashamed to feel this way. It makes me feel very helpless and pitiful but…excited."

"I see," she said in a tone of deep thought.

He didn't know what to make of that and was afraid to open his eyes.

After a moment, her cool voice said, "Put both your hands at your sides. Let me see the excitement you're hiding."

Dear, sweet Lord. He felt as though he bared his chest to a sword, but he did it.

"Look at me," she commanded.

He *couldn't*. Gritting his teeth, wanting to cringe and turn away, he opened his eyes and met her all-seeing gaze.

"This is what you meant when you said you normally like to be humiliated?"

It was a tremendous embarrassment to admit it but so blindingly thrilling to say, "Yes."

What must she think of him? Would she mock him for it? He wasn't sure he could take it if she did. This was the most vulnerable he'd ever felt in his life. He was nauseous at how far he'd allowed things to descend between them.

"But not all the time?" she asked as though trying to work out a riddle. "Do you grow aroused when the dowager scolds you?"

"No." Great heavens, no. "Only when a woman is young and pretty and..." His throat tightened. "*Better* than me."

"The dowager isn't better than you?"

"Oh, I shouldn't have implied that," he stammered with horror. "I—"

"Nelson, it's fine." Her small smile of amusement was agonizingly good at making him feel callow and bumbling. "Who, then? A maid? A lady in the street?"

"Yes," he admitted helplessly. "Sometimes I'll do something, stand in the way or cause some other inconvenience so a woman will notice me and tell me off."

"What do you do when that happens?"

"Don't make me say it." *Please, make me say it.* He looked down, wanting to cover what was obvious, but she'd told him to keep his hands at his sides. He had to endure her knowing how incapable he was of controlling himself. It made him clench his butt cheeks together, bracing for her scathing rebuke.

"If you're doing something bad, Nelson, you must own up to it," she insisted in a firm voice. "What do you do?"

He was going to fall in love with her. He knew it with the clarity that arrived on a cold, brilliant winter's morning, when all was crisp and sharp. His scalp and neck and shoulders were aprickle with defensiveness. His chest was tight, but there was something deeply gratifying in being forced to admit, "I stroke myself and think about it."

"Until you come?"

"Yes."

"That explains the time you allowed a carrot to fall off the platter onto the cloth beside my plate, doesn't it?" She sounded *very* annoyed.

"Yes," he groaned. He masturbated often to the memory of her reproachful look. She wouldn't remember that the drape of her sleeve had almost grazed his swollen cock, but he couldn't forget it.

Her vaguely disgusted "hmph" was like a pinch on the end of his cock, making him leak another stain of fluid.

"What else provokes you? Would it excite you if I were to, perhaps, insist you strip your clothing and stand there naked before me? So I can inspect you?"

His whole body went stiff. A burning need to run gripped him. At the same time, his feet rooted to the floor. His heartbeat pulsed in the tip of his cock, begging to be soothed while his balls grew so tight they ached.

"You wouldn't." He looked to the closed, unlocked door. "Would you?"

"Does that cause you distress? To think that you might be standing there without a stitch, cock hard, *submitting to my whims*, and anyone could walk in and discover us?"

Tears of anguished joy filled his eyes. He was back to quivering on the verge of climax.

"Or does it cause you pleasure?" she asked in a voice that had become husky and erotic.

He couldn't speak, only nod.

"Lock the doors. Remove your clothes. I don't care if anyone sees *you* naked, but I have more dignity."

He felt dizzy, as though he walked through a heavy mist, barely seeing his surroundings. Deep in the back of his mind, he understood that he was acquiescing, that they would at least attempt to make the heir she needed, but that was a far-off thought, pushed aside the way he was ignoring the betrayal he'd suffered.

In this moment, he was being handed his most secret and warped desire. He couldn't refuse.

He turned the key, then left his folded clothes on the seat of a chair at the table. When he was naked, he came around to stand near the fire before her. It was an act of courage. As a footman, he was meant to be handsome and had been told he was, but the path of her gaze across his shoulders and down his middle was a trickle of hot wax that stuck itself to his swollen, purple cock, making it throb in agony.

"Should I compare you to others I've seen?"

How many *had* she seen? From the odd time he'd seen other men, he'd determined that he was endowed well enough, but...

"Is it small?" His hand jerked, defensively wanting to cover himself even as he hoped she said he was a disappointment. The pit of his stomach was a nest of vipers, waiting on her judgment. *Please let it be harsh.*

"It will serve its purpose, I suppose," she said with a pithy arch of her brows. "Tell me more about your experience or lack thereof. Have you spent any time with your head between a woman's legs?"

His mind exploded at the thought. His mouth opened, searching for the air needed to form words.

"No," he managed to say, definitely certain he was falling in love. "You would have to tell me what to do. I'm sure I'd get it wrong."

"Ma'am," she reminded sternly, making him wince at his mistake. "I'm sure you will."

She waited a beat, watching him before she opened her robe to reveal her white nightgown trimmed in satin and lace. With little self-consciousness on her own part, she gathered the nightgown up around her waist, revealing her smooth legs.

She then arranged herself so she sat sideways on the edge of the chair's cushion, balanced on one hip. She drew her top knee up toward the arm, exposing her arse to him. Two round globes were presented with the plum of her pussy lips squeezed between her thighs, shadowed by fine hairs.

His knees almost gave out. He tried to swallow, but his tongue was in the way.

She picked up her book and said in a beleaguered tone, "Whenever you're ready."

His heart ought to be shriveling at this debasement. There wasn't much dignity in it for her, offering herself that way. Not unless he elevated her by worshipping what she offered. His mouth was already watering with the compulsion to do so.

He tried to shift the stool without fumbling it, but he couldn't seem to move with any degree of control. He dropped to his knees hard enough they rang with pain, but he barely felt it. His entire world had become what was before him. How to start?

He set a kiss on her cool, soft skin. He let his cheek rest against a warm round swell, smiling when he let his lips touch her again and felt a small shiver go through her. There was a scent here. Soap and rose water and an earthier, heavier fragrance that he understood originated in her sex. It was the nectar that drew bees.

His kissing, nuzzling lips found their way into the valley of her crack, forcing him to set his knuckles on the floor to brace himself as he slanted his head.

"Try licking?" she suggested with a bored flip of a page.

A moan of torture left his throat. He swept his tongue up and down her crack, over the pinched bud of her arsehole and down to the wiry hairs of her cunt. He discovered a tang there that exploded with flavor on his tongue, making his heart crash in his chest and his cock bounce where it hung from his crooked hunch.

He drilled his tongue into the hot, slick hole he found, nose pressed to her arsehole as he sought more of her juices, certain he could subsist on this alone.

"Eat more of my pussy." She hitched her knee higher and turned her back even more, ensuring her folds were fully accessible.

He switched to angle his head the other way, forehead pressed to the back of her thigh as he slithered his tongue along the plump, juicy petals of her cunt, using his lips to nip and nibble—

She jolted with surprise.

He paused.

"For God's sake, don't *stop*." She sounded infuriated, but she was trembling, breath labored.

She liked what he was doing.

He grasped one arm of the chair for balance and reapplied himself, seeking out the spot between her pinched folds that made her wriggle and breathe in jagged catches. Her book dropped from her hands. As he slurped and sucked, she gripped the back of the chair and arched her ass toward him, gasping, "There. *There*."

He set his hand on her thigh to keep her still and worked his tongue harder and faster on that spot, drilling into her slippery folds for the little nodule that caused tension to gather within her.

Suddenly, she released a soft cry. Her whole body convulsed, and her pussy seemed to soak his tongue with fluid.

He kept lapping at her. Lapping and lapping, cleaning her thighs and quim and along the crack of her ass while she panted and, eventually, sagged into the chair, sighing with gratification.

# CHAPTER FOUR

Viola had never climaxed so violently in her life. She was stunned. Utterly wrung out. But there was an empty ache inside her, too. That release had been incredible, but she wanted the stretch and the fullness and the friction. She wanted to *fuck*.

As Nelson sat back on his heels, chin wet and eyes glazed with stupefied lust, she shifted onto her tailbone and spread her legs.

He made a noise of bliss and started to lower his head to eat her again.

"No. Give me your cock."

"Are you sure?" He took his swollen cock in a squeezed fist.

"Yes."

He shuffled forward on his knees and watched closely as he poked at her. She helped, and in one thrust, he slid smoothly all the way to his root.

Oh, that felt good! He was more robust than his brother. So hard he was like iron. She squeezed him in welcome, enjoying the heat and solidness and the way he groaned as though tortured by the feel of her clenching around him.

"I don't think I can last." He gripped the arms of the chair.

"Don't disappoint me now, Nelson. Not when you've pleased me so well thus far." She caressed his jaw with her fingertip, finding his skin still damp from her juices. What a darling.

He made a helpless noise and began to thrust.

He *was* inexperienced. He made a face of concentration as he tried to find a rhythm, gritting his teeth as he fought to hold back his release. His hand hovered as though wanting to touch her breast before he grabbed the cushion beneath her hip instead.

Once he got the hang of it, he fucked her with steady power. His eyes were closed, his jaw clenched, his breath hissing with strain. She almost wanted to keep him in this state, but climax was creeping up on her, and they did have a higher purpose.

"Fuck me hard, Nelson. Fuck hard and fast and come inside me."

He leaped on her order, hips jerking and slapping erratically as he used a foot for leverage and caused the chair to scrape and shift. In a few powerful strokes, he drove her over the edge in a lovely rolling orgasm before he grabbed her hips and jammed his cock deep into her.

His arms bulged, his neck strained, and he threw back his head. He bared his teeth and groaned loudly while his cock pulsed and spurted and left a deep pool of heat within her.

...

He had no memory of sagging onto her, only became aware of her touch tickling the back of his shoulder. It hit him that he'd just fucked the young, bereaved duchess.

He jerked back onto his heels so quickly they both gave a squeak of discomfort as his cock pulled free of her pussy.

"What's wrong?" she asked with a dismayed blink.

"I—" *shouldn't have done that.* But she had wanted him to. *He* had wanted to.

Christ, he was confused.

"Did you not like it?" Her brow pleated in hurt.

Was she serious?

"Did *you*?" he asked.

"I did. Very much. Kiss me." She held up her arms. "Let me know you liked it, too."

He didn't know how to kiss. Not any more than he knew how to fuck, but he moved back between her legs and let her curl her arms and legs around him. The lace on her gown itched his chest, but her lips were soft and welcoming. She pulled on his lips the way he'd suckled on her pussy. Soon he was lost in tangled tongues and realized he was stroking her waist and thigh, thinking about putting his cock inside her again.

She noticed and tapped his half-hard cock. "Animal," she chided with a smile of approval. "Let's go to bed."

He followed her rather dumbly and, once there, didn't know what to do. He lay on his back beneath the blankets. She snuggled along his side, her head numbing his shoulder, her arm a soft weight across his waist.

"Are you angry with me?" she asked after a time.

"No. Why?"

"You're being very quiet. And I was rude to you, making you eat me like that."

He choked on a laugh. "I was in heaven."

"Were you?" She came up on her elbow and flashed him a smile that made sunshine explode within him. "I enjoy being eaten very much. There was a young curate with whom I used to trade favors, if you take my meaning. One of the reasons I married was to finally have proper sex and see if I liked it. I do." She nudged his side. "For someone who hasn't done much of either, you're very good at both. I can't wait to see how it feels as we get to know each other better."

His heart lurched. "You want to do this again?"

"Don't you?" Her face fell. "Was I too nasty? I thought you would tell me if I was being too hard on you." She frowned with concern. "I forgot that I'm a duchess and you're only— But Nelson, you *are* gentry."

In her mind, maybe, but it still didn't make sense to him.

"*Are* you angry with me? Please be honest." She splayed her hand on his chest.

"Not at you. I very much liked what you said and did." He dropped his arm over his eyes. A slicing pain went through him that was pure shame and guilt, no thrill whatsoever. "But I wish I wasn't like this."

"Do you know why you are?" she asked gently.

He shrugged, not wanting to talk about it, but when he lifted his arm, she was wearing a patient, compassionate expression that allowed him to open up a little.

"The woman I stayed with before coming to live at Ulverly House... She only had a single room and would take men in. She would tell me to sit outside the door while she entertained them. I could hear everything and..." He winced. "Sometimes I peeked through the door. It aroused me, but she would berate me if she caught me, and call me a nosy little prick. It was shameful of me to do it, so I try not to think of it." He turned his face away on the pillow. "I guess it's my punishment to react this way. When I get aroused at an inappropriate time or place, or a woman I find attractive is annoyed with me, I become overexcited. I hate myself for it, but I can't control it."

"May I tell you a secret?"

He brought his attention back to her.

"I liked that you let me order you that way. I have been buckling to my parents and my husband and the dowager for as long as I can remember. You made me feel powerful. Omnipotent." She wrinkled her nose at herself. "I thought, why can't I be this assertive when it counts? Thank you for showing me there can be delightful consequences to taking control."

"You're welcome?" he said ironically.

They shared a rueful smile.

She snuggled closer and let her head rest on his breastbone, arms hugged warmly on either side of his chest. He closed his eyes, savoring the soft swells of her breasts mashed to his ribcage.

"Will you do something for me, Nelson?"

"Of course, ma'am." He immediately cringed because it was so incongruous to call her that, especially when she said, "Will you put your arms around me?"

He did. It felt nice and set a pleasant warmth baking in his center.

"*Do* you want to do this again?" She sounded very hesitant

and fearful of rejection.

"If you do."

"It has to be what you want, too, Nelson." She lifted her head.

He couldn't lie, even though it was terrifying to admit, "I do."

"With or without the scolding?"

*Oh, Christ.* "With," he admitted, embarrassed by his desire.

She didn't mock him for it, only said solemnly, "If I cross a line, you *have* to tell me. I'll be very disappointed in you if you don't."

"You'd have to punish me," he prompted, lips going numb with excitement as he sank into the fantasy.

"I would," she agreed. "I'd have to..." Her gaze flickered around the firelit room. "I'd have to spank you with my hairbrush. On your *bare ass*." She looked at him, a question in her eyes as she left him an opportunity to protest.

"People might hear," he said, voice weakened by anguished delight. "I'd have to try not to cry out."

"They would still know afterward by your face. Your *tears*. You would probably have an erection just like this one." She closed her fist firmly around his hard cock, cutting off his breath as she squeezed him. "Because I won't let you fuck me if you've displeased me. You know that, don't you? I won't even let you stroke yourself to make it go away. You'll have to hold out until I'm no longer angry."

He opened his mouth. No words would emerge. She was not the least bit shy about roaming her touch down to cup his balls and fondle behind them, then sweeping her caress up to cup his knob, using her palm to polish it by working his fluid around and around.

"You would have a sore ass and a sore cock, and *everyone would know*."

"Please," he begged.

"Please, what? Do you want to eat me again?" She brought her wet palm up to his cheek and cupped his jaw, smearing his own musky essence on his face. "If you lick me now, you'll taste the seed you left inside me."

Good thing he was flat on his back. He nearly fainted.

"Make me," he whispered.

"Stay right where you are, then." She came up on her knees and reached for the headboard.

•••

Ulverly House wasn't nearly as suffocating as usual. The weather was typical lions and lambs of March, but Viola enjoyed quick tumbles with Nelson when the dowager rested in the afternoon. Nelson crept back to join Viola during the darkest hours of night.

Every chance she got, Viola sent him a look of impatience, rolling her eyes or huffing with exasperation at some imagined misstep he had made.

"Why are you constantly nitpicking Nelson?" the dowager asked at one point.

"Because he can do better," Viola said loftily, cutting him a glance and watching his cheeks darken at being spoken *of* rather than *to*.

Also, it kept the dowager from suspecting he was rogering Viola senseless.

"Are you sure you don't wish to tell her you know of your heritage?" she asked him on their fourth night. She was atop him, riding his hips with a lazy rise and fall of her own.

"I can't," he whispered. "She'll make me leave."

"I won't let her," Viola assured him.

It was dark, so she couldn't see his face, but his pulse of silence spoke volumes. He didn't think she had that much influence or power over the dowager.

His lack of faith hurt so much, she stopped moving altogether to absorb the pain. She wanted to believe she was pulling something over on the dowager by doing this with him, but the fact they were hiding their affair only proved she *was* weak. Otherwise, she would confront the woman outright.

"I like being a footman," Nelson whispered as though trying to reassure her—and maybe himself—that all was well. He ran his hands up her body to cup her breasts. "I like what you did to me at dinner."

She had called him out for missing a button from his jacket and forced him to say, *May I pour you more wine, your grace?*

"I thought you were going to cry."

"I did. In the pantry. Because you make me so happy." He sounded as though he was about to cry again.

He made her happy, too, but now there was this angst within her that she was letting him down. She grappled for confidence by grabbing his hands and pushing them to the mattress. She began to ride him with more purpose.

"You're going to come before I do, aren't you?" she mocked in a whisper, thrilling at the way he tensed in arousal. "Then I'll have to grind myself all over your face to get the satisfaction you fail to deliver. One day I'm going to tell all my friends that I fucked a footman whose incompetent cock popped like champagne. I would *rather* fuck a bottle of champ—"

"Oh, fuck," he gasped, arching his hips so hard under her that he lifted her knees off the bed and pushed her over the edge of control. Her abdomen contracted in a powerful orgasm that matched the pulsing of his cock within her.

"My heart is exploding," he panted as he bucked. "Oh, fuck. Oh, fuck."

As her waves of climax subsided, she melted upon him, drunk on a mix of sexual gratification and erotic influence. She would learn to use this power outside this bed. She would.

*Then* he would know he was safe with her.

• • •

Was there something filthy and degrading about how they were conducting themselves? Absolutely. Did he love it? So much.

Nelson was in such a fog of randy delight, he didn't process that they'd been here for three weeks until the dowager brought it up over the ladies' afternoon tea.

"My son has been gone one month. I assume, since you haven't told me any happy news, we should consult my list?"

Nelson's heart stopped.

"On the contrary," his lover said. "I was only waiting to be sure. It seems I am pregnant."

"Well, that *is* happy news! Is that not delightful, Nelson?" the dowager asked him.

"I— In every way, ma'am. Felicitations, your grace." He bowed his head, feeling hollow. Struck without warning. Kicked in the balls.

"Thank you, Nelson, but I prefer my tea hot. What are you waiting for? A woman in my condition ought to be pampered in every way."

"Of course." He narrowed all of his concentration onto pouring the tea and preparing each cup exactly as they each liked it, all the while fighting the bile that wanted to rise in the back of his throat. An anguished fire sat behind his heart.

How could she let him find out like this, by telling the dowager before informing him? It was beyond humiliating. It was degrading.

The young duchess picked up her cup, but he could feel her gaze on him. He heard a query in her "Thank you, Nelson."

He couldn't look at her. He was too hurt.

After a blistering moment of silence, the young duchess said, "I actually feel quite faint. Could you help me to my room, Nelson?"

"Allow me to call your maid, ma'am." He couldn't be alone with her right now. He hurried to the door and sent a message for the girl.

When Kenneth came in with the maid to support the duchess to her room, Nelson finally looked at her. Her green eyes were hot as the center of a flame, burning with betrayal.

He felt cruel in that moment. Small and hurt and petty, but he also thought, *Now you know how it feels.*

• • •

Nelson managed to evade her for over a week, but Viola was in the garden enjoying the early blooms and sunshine when he came to say, "The dowager invites you to join her for lunch, ma'am."

"I couldn't possibly," she said with her back molars glued together. "I might displease her footman."

"I'll tell her." He turned to go.

"Nelson," she hissed.

His back stiffened as though she'd lashed him. After a charged moment, he turned back to ask with exaggerated patience, "Yes, ma'am?"

"*Are* you displeased? About the baby?" She held her breath, anguished by the thought.

His face averted slightly, but he said, "No, of course not."

"Then why...?"

He flushed. Real pain flashed across his expression. "The way you did it. Telling her like that without telling me first."

Her heart sank. "I thought you would like it. That—"

"I didn't." He glanced toward the house. "I should go in before I'm questioned."

"Will you come later? When she's resting? Please?" She was reduced to begging. It undermined all the confidence she'd built over the last weeks. What was she, after all, but a vessel for a man's seed, controlled by the man who'd taken possession of her womb and heart? She had thought he would share her sense of triumph. Instead, he reviled her.

His stiff nod could have been agreement or merely that of a servant taking his leave. She had to wait until the afternoon, when she paced her parlor as she had done every day since offending him, hoping he would turn up.

When he quietly let himself in, she didn't know what to say. They both stood in thick silence for a long time.

"I misread you," she finally said. "I thought you would enjoy our private joke at her expense. I was wrong." *Obviously.* "I won't criticize you anymore—"

"It wasn't *that*, Viola." Her name seemed to burst out of him, and even though he looked hurt and furious, she was ridiculously pleased to hear it on his lips. "I thought you had some affection for me. Or at least some respect."

"I do." She hurried toward him. "I should have told you. I was still coming to terms with it myself. She caught me off guard. I didn't mean to hurt you."

"You did, though. I know I told you I wanted to be treated badly, but…" Tears were coming into his eyes, which made tears gather in hers. "But I want to be noticed, not erased. Not treated as if all those things we did, that I let you do to me, didn't matter. I gave you what you wanted. I gave you everything I *could*. My secrets. *Myself.* And you took it and threw it at her."

"Oh, Nelson." She wrapped her arms around him and rested her forehead to his thumping heart, hating herself for the pain she'd caused him.

He wriggled an arm free and swiped his sleeve across his eyes.

"But when I'm a sniveling wreck like this, I can see why you would think I'm nothing to regard or respect. I'm—"

"You're lovely, Nelson. You are." She squeezed him, trying to impress the words deep into him. "It was my mistake. I wanted to show you I could get the better of her so you would trust me to save us, but I failed. I was thinking of her and myself, not you, and I ruined what we had. Which breaks my heart."

"Save *us*?" He cupped her head and pressed his cheek to her hair. "I don't need you to save me, Viola. I have standing job offers elsewhere. I could take one tomorrow. I have stayed with the dowager because I wished to. More lately, I stayed for you, even though I was so angry the last few days, I told myself I *should* leave."

"Don't." She held tight to him. "Please, don't."

"I won't." He folded his arms around her. "I won't make any decisions until the baby is born. I am happy, by the way, even though it feels like the most impossible miracle. A gift. Now I'm going to cry again," he said with a sniff and a laugh at himself, scraping his palm over his cheek. "When will the baby come?"

"Christmas." She drew back, feeling very tender toward him as she used her thumb to help dry his tears. "Then we'll know if *you* saved *me*."

She was trying to make a joke of it, but they regarded each other somberly.

"What happens until then?" he asked.

"I'm not sure. I have to find a discreet way to ask the midwife if it's safe for me to have relations."

"You want to?" He brightened.

"Don't you?" She grasped his arm, fearful she was misunderstanding him again. "I won't put you on the spot or tease you or—"

"Viola." He squeezed her shoulders and looked to the ceiling. When he lowered his chin to look down at her, his gaze was full of contrition. "Why are you letting me use your given name? I've said it several times since I walked in here. It is beyond insolent."

"You're a very confusing man, Nelson."

"I know. I'm often confused myself."

"I told you that you had to tell me if I crossed a line. Remember?"

"I do. And I did," he pointed out drily.

"I suppose you did," she agreed with a wry smile. "So I cannot punish you."

"You could punish me a little," he said sullenly. "For sulking and not speaking to you right away about why I was angry."

"With my hairbrush? No." She narrowed her eyes. "Since your seed is no longer useful, you will leave it in your handkerchief. While I watch. Stand over there, closer to the window, where the light will allow me to see exactly what you are doing."

"Really?" His voice wavered with disbelief and dread and anticipation.

"Oh, yes," she insisted. "And I will pace here and listen while you confess all the filthiest things you have ever wanted to do to me."

"I couldn't. They're too depraved." But he sounded positively ridden with anguished lust. "I would offend a fine woman like you."

"I'm sure you already do. That's why I won't let you touch me. And if you don't start referring to me as 'ma'am' or 'your grace,' I will open my parlor door for anyone who walks by to see you with your cock in your hand."

"I think I love you." He hurried to move into position and unbuttoned his trousers. "Ma'am."

She loved him, too. But she saved telling him until after she had berated him into staining his handkerchief.

# CHAPTER FIVE

*March 1876, London*

Nelson felt a strange mixture of nausea and abandonment and acute arousal as the carriage pulled away without him.

He understood what Viola was doing, though. She had given him what he needed—her undivided, if angry, attention. Then she had turned it on the dowager in a ruthless, throwaway dismissal.

*Perhaps you should consider how you will spend your evening.*

As he walked back into the house, he understood that Viola was telling both of them that his attachment to the dowager was over.

He knew it was time to end it. He had hung on to his position so he could stay with Viola through her pregnancy, which had become fraught by the end. Thankfully, she had delivered a healthy son two days after Christmas, and all was well with the boy.

His given name was Stanley, which they had decided was for the best given their ruse, but Viola called her son by his second name, Robert, which was a name Nelson had suggested in one of their private moments. Even more often, she called the baby "my sweet boy" and gave every appearance of adoring him. In fact, she had defied the dowager and brought Robert with them to London, refusing to leave him at Ulverly while she met her social obligations of the season.

Nelson would like to think he had provided her the means to develop the strength and courage she was showing that old woman these days, but he had a feeling it was equally the instincts of a mama bear.

"I heard you got an earful and were left behind?" the nurse

said when he peeked in on the sleeping Robert.

Nelson flushed, stomach shriveling even as the tightness in his crotch pulled.

"Let me know if he's fussy. I'll walk him for you, if you like." He was as enamored with his son as Viola was but hurried to his room.

As he removed his wig and changed from his good livery to his day uniform, he found a stain where he'd knelt to inspect Viola's hem. He had wanted to kiss that ruffle of silk and the muddy slipper beneath. He wanted to crawl beneath her skirt and eat her forever. He loved her to death.

Because the same woman who had belittled him outside had quietly used the money her marriage contract granted her for birthing an heir to buy a small farm in Yorkshire, putting Nelson's name on the deed. It wasn't for helping her make their baby, but for him, because he was the son of a duke and she wanted him to have something even if no one else knew who he was.

He was tempted to lie on his bed and stroke himself to the memory of her bitching, *This is my first outing in a year, and you've ruined it.*

She couldn't care less about a damned ball, but she was determined to cement her place as *the* Duchess of Yeadonfell. It occurred to him that leaving him home was a stroke of genius on her part. The dowager was known to have him standing by like a trusty hound. Without him there, the dowager would be forced to admit that Viola's wishes had taken precedence over her own. If Viola were to begin appearing with Nelson at *her* side, it would be as if the baton had been unequivocally passed.

Now he really wanted to pound his cock, but he let his sexual frustration simmer. It would please her to know he had suffered in her absence. It made him shift around on his seat as he wrote, trying to find a comfortable position.

To Her Grace, the Dowager Duchess of Yeadonfell,
Madam,
    I wish to thank you for the opportunity to serve you
all these years. It has been my honor.
    As I anticipate that you will soon move into the dowager
cottage at Ulverly, I humbly beseech you to release me
from my position as your footman so I may continue to
serve in the young duke's household.

He tapped the end of the pen on his lips a moment as he
considered, but he decided to keep it short and sweet. He signed
it and started a fresh sheet.

To Her Grace, the Duchess of Yeadonfell
Madam,
    It is with the deepest humility that I beg your
forgiveness for treading on your gown this evening. I am
sick with guilt and shame over my clumsiness.

His cock was nearly bursting and began to leak as he let
himself sink back into that sense of exposure she had brought
on him.

You were right to call me out. I expect better from
myself, and you should as well.
    My position as first footman on the household staff
means everything to me. I couldn't bear to lose it. You
may recall asking me once where my allegiance resided.
Service to the duke is my highest honor and obligation. To
serve him is to serve you. I swear I will do anything
(he underlined it) to make up for my behavior and earn
your charitable opinion of me.
    With my deepest regards,
    Nelson Davis

The women came home early from the ball. The dowager wore a cross look, and her florid expression suggested she'd had one too many sherries.

"I do not accept this," she said hotly, throwing his letter into the fire.

"I do," the duchess said, calmly refolding the letter he'd written to her. "You may have Kenneth," she informed the dowager. "Nelson is mine. Although, your letter could have been more specific in how you will make up for your behavior," she informed Nelson. "I expect you will need a great deal of instruction on how to please me. Start by checking the fire in my parlor, then draw my bath."

"Right away, ma'am. Thank you." He bowed his head and tried not to reveal his smile of anticipation as he walked away.

*The End*

# Temptress with a Teapot

*Temptress with a Teapot* features a married woman, who is sexually intimate with a man other than her husband, and while this is consensual between all persons involved, readers who may be sensitive to this, please take note.

# CHAPTER ONE

*June 1878, Berlin*

"Not that one, love," Rainer Stormont murmured in his wife's ear as he noticed where her gaze had strayed. "He has a wife, a mistress, and a lot to lose if his uncle grows displeased with him."

Bernice kept her chin down and tilted only her lashes up as she sent him a glance that both scolded and entreated at once.

Denying her any man had the effect of catnip on a kitten, only encouraging her to go after him more. Normally, Rainer enjoyed that game.

"Someone else will come along," he promised.

Her mouth pouted briefly but quickly smoothed into a welcoming smile as the object of her interest approached.

"Rainer." Franco Petrucci reached out his hand in enthusiastic greeting. "It's been so long, I didn't immediately recognize you. Are you here with the delegates from London?"

"I'm on staff at the embassy as Under Secretary to Lord Russell." Rainer nodded across the ballroom to indicate the British Ambassador here in Berlin. As he released Franco's hand, he said, "Please meet my wife. Bernice, Franco Petrucci was one of my counterparts during my time as an attaché in Venice. Ten years ago? Eleven?" Rainer grimaced as he calculated the passage of time and self-consciously stroked his beard. At least he didn't yet have any of the salt that sprinkled Franco's black hair and mustache.

Even with his graying hair, Franco was still a handsome man, and, despite Rainer's warning that nothing could happen between the pair, Rainer felt the twitch of an inconvenient erection as he watched Franco's gaze skim over Bernice with masculine assessment. His old friend must be wondering how a prim-looking woman like her could appeal to a man who had taken to sex with such an insatiable and varied appetite as Rainer had.

Given the delicate nature of his work, Rainer appreciated that Bernice dressed modestly and adhered to social graces. He also loved the hell out of the fact she liked to fuck other men and relay every filthy detail to him.

He watched closely as Bernice offered her ungloved hand. "It's a pleasure to meet you, Signor Petrucci."

In her constant correspondence with her mother in London, fashion and rules of comportment were always discussed at length. Royalty at home were eschewing gloves and so, Bernice's mother decreed, must Bernice.

"The pleasure is mine." Franco bowed over her bare knuckles in a polite but perfunctory way. Not rude but faintly dismissive. He had decided that Rainer had married her for duty, not beauty.

On first glance, Bernice looked to be exactly the sort of woman that a man of a certain age was encouraged to marry because he was able to support a wife and she was well suited to the role.

Bernice had a way of demanding men notice her, though. It was subtle. Perhaps she allowed her touch to caress Franco's fingers as he released her hand. Perhaps it was the steady way she met the other man's aloof stare.

Whatever it was, it caused Franco a tiny moment of confused reassessment as he considered whether she was signaling an attraction. His glance flew to Rainer's, shadowed with guilt at having an impure thought about Rainer's wife.

Rainer kept an impassive expression on his face and switched his attention to his wife as though he hadn't noticed anything amiss, but that small exercise of knowledge and power over another man pooled a heavy tingle in his balls the way a swallow of brandy might emanate warmth through his belly.

*Not this one*, he reminded himself.

"Do you recall asking me if I'd ever ridden in a gondola, and I mentioned a friend with a tremendous singing voice?" he reminded Bernice. "Franco was my guide that evening."

"Oh, how lovely." Bernice's voice warmed a pleasant few degrees without gushing, exactly as her mother had taught her. "I've always found my husband's stories from his years abroad to be interesting and informative. I shall hope that while you're here, I might enjoy something of a repeat performance." She fixed Franco with her most artless look. "And more education on the unique practices in your homeland."

Rainer wanted to pinch her ass for her impertinence.

"It would be my honor." Franco's nonplussed expression asked Rainer how much of that long-ago evening Rainer had revealed. Surely, Rainer hadn't told his bride that he had lost his virginity to a friend of Franco's mistress while Franco piloted the long, narrow boat through the moonlit canal?

Rainer had not only told her but had also replayed the night with her more than once. He gave away nothing now, however, only asking Franco, "Your wife is well? Has she accompanied you?" He already knew that Franco had sent his mistress ahead so she would be in residence here when he arrived.

"Odetta is well and busy with our children. I'm here with my uncle." Franco nodded at the muttonchopped count who was speaking to Russell and Bismarck.

"The hope at the embassy is that the congress will arrive at a new treaty quickly," Rainer assured him with a banal smile. "You shouldn't be away from your family for long."

Franco sent him a dry look over Bernice's head. He would happily stay away for years if it meant he could spend his nights with the woman he preferred over the wife who despised him.

"You must allow us to extend our hospitality if you're at loose ends while you're here," Bernice insisted to Franco with her most earnest smile. "I won't have you missing the comforts of home."

The cheek of her tonight. Neither of them had taken to

spanking, but Rainer was thinking of suggesting another go once they were home.

Bernice's soft brown eyes were filled with subdued laughter as she set her fingertips on Rainer's arm, then pointed. "I see Emily looking for me. Will you excuse me, please?"

"Of course." Rainer could feel the waves of curiosity coming off Franco as the other man surreptitiously angled to watch Bernice depart, no doubt noticing her lack of bustle.

The natural form with only a little padding was also the latest fashion, according to Rainer's mother-in-law, along with a small train that swished saucily as Bernice sauntered away.

"Bernice has a close relationship with Lord Russell's wife," Rainer explained. "She supports her with hostess duties and such."

"Marriage to the right woman can be an excellent career move," Franco said without irony. "You met her in London?"

"Through Whitley, yes."

"Ah, good ol' Whitley. How is he?"

"Dead."

"My condolences."

"A great loss to British diplomacy," Rainer said with the circumspection that kept him employed in this field.

Truth was, he'd loathed the man. Whitley had been a family friend through Rainer's relations on his mother's side. The arrogant nob had been very tightfisted and patronizing, dragging Rainer across Europe as his errand boy for a decade, all the while doling out enough promises with his penurious wages to keep Rainer clinging to a vision of a bright future for himself. Franco had had a much better situation with his uncle, but for a young man with nothing more than a few years at Eton and the ability to pen an excellent report, Rainer had had to pin his hopes on Whitley.

It had paid off. Whitley had provided Rainer the experience to thrive in foreign affairs, and, when Whitley's health began to

fail, he had named Rainer his de facto heir—on the condition
that Rainer married a bride of Whitley's choosing, of course.
The old fart had excelled at negotiation, because he always got
something when he gave something up.

"Whitley was acquainted with Bernice's father," Rainer
offered, since it was benign enough information. "The Right
Honorable Sir Charles Kelvin. He's an MP, grandson of an earl.
Her mother has an aunt at court. We married four years ago,
spent a year at the offices in Madrid, and moved to Paris after
Whitley died. We arrived here eighteen months ago."

"Children?"

"Unblessed as yet." They actively took measures to put it off,
enjoying a freedom they would not get back once babies came
along.

"She seems a good fit for a man in our position," Franco
said politely, but he was still eyeing Rainer as though suspecting
there was more to their marriage than met the eye. His gaze
strayed back to Bernice as she finished up her chat with Emily
and glanced their way.

Bernice's expression was so alight with her particular inner
glow of adventure, Rainer's cock gave another threatening tug.

"Do you mind if I invite her to dance?" Franco asked, perhaps
similarly moved.

"By all means," Rainer said with a negligent shrug of permission, but he did mind, he discovered, and wasn't sure why.
Bernice understood the difference between games and irrevo-
cable actions that could jeopardize his career and their very
comfortable situation. When he said *Not that one*, she knew he
meant it and always respected his decision.

As for Franco, he was probably more interested in discovering
what Bernice saw in Rainer than any more prurient reason to
get her alone.

Rainer had had his own doubts about whether they would
be a good fit. After his father had died in Crimea, Rainer had

been raised by his extremely repressed mother. When she had caught him committing the solitary vice at nine, she had caned his hands black, screeching about the risk of blindness between accusing him of aberrance and corruption.

As it turned out, she was not entirely wrong. Rainer was deeply perverse. Ribald and salacious. All the lewd things because, once he had begun having sex, he'd had no use for rules except to avoid disease and accusations of treason. Children and animals were off the table, but everything else was worth considering if not sampling. His past lovers included adults of all ages, races, sexes, and proclivities.

Bernice had seemed as puritanical and sexless as his mother. While she had observed every minute detail of social manners, pouring his tea and placing a drop of milk into it, asking mundane questions about his preferences in theatre and music, he had been wondering if the small nest egg Whitley had promised him was worth the profound boredom he was liable to face with her.

Then, in the middle of her father's droning on about a political rival, Rainer had caught her gaze stroking over his chest and lap. When she realized he had taken note, her reaction had not been embarrassment. A faint flush had touched her cheeks, and her gaze had flitted away. The tip of her tongue had briefly appeared as she wet her bottom lip. Her posture had straightened, drawing his gaze to her breasts straining against the demure bodice of her gown.

It had been a small thing, but he'd taken himself in hand the minute he was home, imagining her tongue darting out to taste the dew that formed on the eye of his cock. He had milked himself dry every day until he saw her again.

Each time he met with her, she found a subtle and beguiling way to catch his notice and tempt him. When she had accidentally stood on the front of her skirt as she reached overhead for a book that she insisted on loaning him, she had somehow left him wondering if he'd really seen the shape of her mound beneath the taut layers of her skirt or only conjured that heated fantasy.

"How inelegant of me. Would you mind reaching that off the shelf?" She had waited until he stepped closer before removing herself from the space, making his entire body rigid with awareness of how near she'd been for those brief seconds.

For weeks, she had been deliriously maddening, never overt yet impossible to resist. Their first kiss had occurred behind a column at a theatre, when she had lifted on tiptoe to seal their mouths together, sucking on his lips as she drew away, pulling his cock to attention in one brief, lurid slurp.

"I wanted to know what that was like," she had whispered. "Don't tell Mother. She'll forbid me from seeing you again."

She'd walked one direction, and he'd gone another, exiting out the nearest door to a brisk wind that cooled his blood and allowed his erection to subside.

The day he proposed, he had walked with her in her parents' garden, compelled to say, "I'm thinking of speaking to your father, but I want to know first—are you a virgin?"

She had halted, startled. "Why would you imagine otherwise?"

"I'm not saying it matters." He had very ambiguous feelings about it. "I have some experience." Vast, actually. "It would be hypocritical of me to be upset if you also did."

He expected dismay, but her eyes had widened with intrigue. His fascination with her had intensified.

"If I'm honest," he had continued carefully, "there's a part of me that enjoys the idea that you would bring enough experience to our union to make an interesting bedroom companion." He had run his tongue over his teeth, aware that he was about to insult her. "On the other hand, if you have enough sophistication to seduce me, there is the possibility you have been seduced. I should like to know if I'm in danger of a disease or liable to be taking responsibility for another man's child."

Instead of a huff of affront or a protestation of innocence, she had asked with very believable and shy delight, "Am I seducing you?"

"You know you are."

"I'm trying," she allowed with a small, sultry smile. "It's nice to know it's working."

"You're really a virgin?"

At her nod, a deliciously wicked desire to drag her into sin with him overcame him. What sort of man wished to defile such an innocent?

Him. That's who.

"Prove it," he coaxed, thinking if she was this shameless and responsive now, how much more licentious would she become? He was dying to find out.

Her short, thick lashes blinked, bemused. "How?"

He glanced around, then chucked his chin at the spot where the garden wall had been abandoned mid-repair. "Go around there and lift your skirts. I will examine for myself."

It had been a dare—one meant to test the powers between them more than any genuine interest in her innocence or lack thereof.

She had reacted in the most stimulating way possible. He still masturbated to the memory. Her shoulders had softened as though her entire body had weakened with delight. As though he had given her the greatest gift she could imagine. She had flushed and shivered and asked breathlessly, "You want me to let you touch me between my legs?"

In other circumstances, he would have read her flush as a woman on the verge of climax. He'd nearly come in his trousers seeing her react that strongly.

"Yes." A rush of omnipotence had had him rooting his feet in the ground, trying to recapture his control as she walked away, moving around the wall and out of sight.

When he followed her, he found her gathering her skirts, casting an anxious frown around the quiet forest behind the garden. She stood out of the wind and out of sight of the house, exposing her frilled drawers and the overlapping slit that ran down their front.

His blood had filled his cock so fast, he had nearly fainted.

He'd braced an elbow on the wall, aware *he* was visible from the house, and extended his other hand.

The danger that they could be discovered at any second had added an extra layer of titillation to his stealing this caress. The primal beast in him had wanted to tear that fine cotton open so he could see her pussy. He'd made himself move slowly, not wanting to alarm her, but as he worked his fingers through the slit and felt the dampness on the edges of cotton and the silken hairs of her mound wet with her arousal, he'd had to swallow and lock his knees.

Slick moisture had coated his fingertips as he'd slithered his touch into the hot, slippery petals of her cunt. She had made a shaken noise of shocked pleasure as he spread that abundant lubrication around and sought the source. Her voice had squeaked and her lashes had fluttered and her fists had clenched harder on her gathered skirts.

Keeping an eye out for witnesses, he had worked his middle finger into her tight channel, feeling her inner muscles clamp nervously. Her breathing was shaken and uneven, her teeth set against her bottom lip.

"Am I hurting you?"

"No. But this is very bad of me. P-promise me you will never tell M—mmm. Ohh. I didn't know it would feel like this." She pushed her mound into his hand.

Her folds flowered open against his palm. She was awash in slippery juices that he longed to taste. He wanted them all over his lips and chin. His cock was ragingly hard. All he could think was that he wanted to shove her against that wall and fuck her with all his might.

Her inner muscles were convulsively squeezing his finger in

what he thought might be the first twitches of orgasm. Pink stole across her cheeks, and she shivered in delight.

He withdrew his finger, but when he tried to push two inside her, her thighs instinctively jolted, and she made a small noise of distress, glancing at him with concern.

He made himself stop and step back. He wiped his hand with his handkerchief, all of him trembling in arousal. In desire for her.

She had dropped her skirts and blinked her eyes, giving him a look of such dazzled, wanton need, he had made up his mind.

"A short engagement." He pinched the tip of his cock through his trousers. "I'm eager for our wedding night."

# CHAPTER TWO

——————✥ᴥ✥——————

Since only a quarter of the men had brought their wives, the dance floor was not crowded.

"You dance very well," Franco said politely.

"As do you," Bernice replied. It was true. He guided her with a delightfully confident hold.

She could feel his gaze sweeping over her face, and when he spun them to avoid another couple, he dragged her close for one breath. His firm arms and unfamiliar cologne made her swoon with feminine delight.

Or perhaps it was her husband's words. *Not that one.*

The sheer audacity of considering an affair against her husband's express wishes was enough to send dangerous flutters of arousal through her limbs, feeding what was already a deep attraction.

Bernice didn't fall in lust with every man she met. She liked the ones who dressed well, spoke with confidence, and carried an air of virility. Franco had all of that. He had a similar build to Rainer's, but he wasn't as tall and was a little more broad-shouldered. He was six or seven years older than Rainer's thirty-one and wore only a mustache, where Rainer wore his mustache with a beard that was scrupulously trimmed to a point. Franco combed his hair to the side, but it held a slight wave that accentuated his strong, elegant bone structure.

With his sensual bottom lip and his deeply set eyes, he possessed the quintessential look of an Italian seducer. Bernice was smitten.

She pretended to misstep so her body came up against the front of his again, breasts mashing to the hard wall of his chest. The evidence against her stomach suggested he was growing hard inside his black trousers.

A pulsing thrill shot deep into her loins.

His nostrils flared, and he gave her a shrewd look. "You're not entirely what you seem, are you, Mrs. Stormont?"

"I don't think I'm particularly special." Her mother had drilled into her that Bernice was mousy and unremarkable with her plump figure and plain, brown hair and ordinary face. There was no point trying to be a beauty, her mother had always insisted. Far better to be realistic and prove her worth with an uncompromising character.

In spite of her lack of outward allure, or perhaps because of it, Bernice delighted in gaining a man's attention, especially one who had a wife, a mistress, and a lot to lose. Watching temptation edge into his hard expression made her pussy throb with excitement.

"I think you're exceptional, and I have to wonder if your husband knows that," Franco murmured.

"If he doesn't, that would be his loss, wouldn't it?" Rainer always knew everything, but she adored this corner where lust intersected with risk, so she wallowed in it while she was here.

Bernice had barely grown the first buds of breasts when she had sat in a hayloft, listening to her eldest brother and his mates below, comparing notes. She hadn't fully understood what they were saying, but she had known by their hushed voices that her mother would be horrified that she was being exposed to such graphic conversation. Knowing she was committing a criminal act by eavesdropping had heightened her reaction to their boasts of fondling bare breasts and pinching nipples and fingering the nether lips of a young woman until she moaned with pleasure. A guilty sensation between her legs had made it nearly impossible to stay still and quiet so she wouldn't be discovered.

Curiosity had gotten the better of her once they left. She had lifted her skirts and begun to caress herself, discovering how ticklish and lovely it felt. Over time, she'd discovered her body was capable of intense pinnacles of pleasure, but her arousal was always most sharply provoked by the musty scent of straw and taboo thoughts of her brother's friends discovering her with her skirts up and being overcome with a desire to touch her themselves.

For the first year of her marriage, it had been enough that Rainer had been unable to keep his hands off her. Bernice had shared all of her most explicit imaginings with him, and soon he had begun to tease her with them. *That young man is picturing you without your gown. That earl is known to seduce other men's wives. Would you let him?*

By the time they moved to Paris, she had begun to openly flirt with men she desired—discreetly, and always within sight of her husband, since it was as much for his pleasure as her own. One day when she'd been alone, the man who owned the flower shop had pressed her into an alcove and said, "Your husband must not satisfy you if you are always inviting me to make love to you."

He had kissed her passionately, startling her.

Her guilt when she'd told Rainer had been heavily weighted to the fact she'd allowed the kiss to go on. She had enjoyed both the newness of the stranger's taste and caress and the utter sinfulness of being unfaithful.

*It won't happen again*, she had vowed.

Rainer had been remarkably unperturbed, which wasn't to say he wasn't affected. *If it does, use one of these.* He'd given her a skin and shown her how to apply it. Then they'd fucked for hours, the intensity of their orgasms leaving them breathless and stunned.

Bernice and the flower man had never found enough time or privacy for a full-fledged affair, but she had let him bury his nose in her tulips and had tasted the strength of his stem. Her first more definable infidelity had been with a married banker who had "assisted" her with her safety deposit box. Rainer still sometimes referred to her assignations as "a visit to the bank."

And he very occasionally greeted her desire to visit the bank with a refusal to lend.

*Not that one.*

He would have his reasons, and she would respect them. She loved him too much to jeopardize their marriage by ignoring his very broad but firm boundaries. However, she did enjoy window shopping even when she couldn't buy.

"I imagine you'll have many commitments with the congress and your uncle." She left the barest of pauses to acknowledge Franco's mistress. "I'll leave it to Rainer to arrange with you a suitable day to join us for tea."

"I would enjoy that, Mrs. Stormont." Franco gave her another look, as though he understood that more than their waltz was over but wasn't sure why. "Thank you for the dance." He led her back to Rainer.

●●●

"You were teasing Franco," Rainer accused when he arrived in her bedroom much later that evening. He wore only a morning robe, and there was already a tent in the front of it, denoting his arousal.

"Only a little." She sat at her dressing table and continued brushing out her hair, smoothing the bristles over her long tresses in slow, luxuriating strokes. It was midsummer, and the day's heat had been trapped inside the room by the drawn curtains. She wore only her muslin nightgown. "I don't understand why you're denying me. Is it not up to him whether to cheat on his mistress and wife, or risk his uncle's wrath? Why are you protecting him? Are there political implications you can't discuss with me?"

Rainer took the hairbrush but didn't respond.

Bernice let her hands fall into her lap while he gathered sections and painlessly picked out the tangles from the ends.

It created a quiet tension between them, his accusation, her question, the pair of them not speaking, as though her hair was of primary importance and must be attended to before any other discussion.

Rainer was a remote and introspective sort of man. She understood that was why he was valued so highly by the ambassador, but his guardedness came between them sometimes. It hurt her when it did. She felt it as a rejection, especially because they were usually very open with each other.

He caught her searching his expression in the mirror. His jaw tightened as he went back to brushing.

"When I met Franco, I was still Whitley's unpaid attaché. Essentially an indentured servant. Franco had the patronage of a titled man, a generous income, a wife, *and* a kept mistress. I had nothing—not even sexual experience."

"He's quite a bit older than you."

"Not that much, but he was infinitely worldly. He pitied me for my situation with Whitley and insisted on arranging my sexual initiation, as though he was doing me an act of charity. He enjoyed using his sophistication to make me feel inferior and ensured that *I* felt it. I still might have that sense if I didn't have you."

"Are you saying you would feel jealous if I had a dalliance with him?"

"I might, yes."

"Darling." She stole the brush and left it on the dressing table, then turned on her bench and clasped his hand as she looked up at him. "You know you're the only one I love. It feeds my vanity to be charmed and seduced, but my passions are inflamed by the act of teasing and beguiling a man, not the man himself." She knew there was something sinful in that, but Rainer had taught her not to feel shame for her desires, no matter how unconventional they may be.

"I know." He caressed her cheek. "And my debauched soul feeds on the knowledge you're as libidinous as I am. Nothing makes my cock harder than knowing you've just had someone else's in you." He drew her to her feet and clasped her hand against his chest, where his heart thumped steadily in his rib cage. His mouth thinned. "I like having the secret of our arrangement, though. If you had an affair with Franco, he would learn that I allow these dalliances, or he would think he had pulled the wool over my eyes. Either way, he would feel superior, whereas..." Rainer tucked his chin to look down at the fingers he was weaving between her own. "I could deny him discovering what a treasure you are and know that I have something he never will."

"Ah. Then I will not fuck him," Bernice decided, loving her husband more than ever in this moment of his revealing his vulnerability to her. She caught the point of his beard in the scissor of her two fingers and gave it a playful tug. "But I will flirt with him mercilessly so he will covet what you have."

His mouth twitched, and he flicked his gaze downward. "Your nipples are hard. Are you thinking of him now?"

"I'm reacting to your possessiveness. There are few things that make me wetter than being wanted. You know that."

He skimmed his thumbs along the base of her throat. His splayed fingers gathered her hair, then he let the weight of his hands sit in the tresses, forcing her to tilt her head up to his. His erection nudged her stomach.

"I saw the way he looked at you. He wants you." His face was hard, but his green eyes flashed with heat. "Have you been thinking about how he might fuck you if you gave him the chance?" Rainer's hand went down her front. He pushed the light cotton of her nightgown between her thighs, forcing the fabric against her hot mons with insistent pressure. "I think you have."

A thud of sensation rocked her. Her knees weakened, and she grasped at his arms for support. He worked his hand into the notch of her thighs until her breathing grew uneven and she shifted her legs apart.

He didn't accept the invitation. He dropped his hand away

and turned her so they could both see the damp stain in the mirror, the cotton translucent enough to reveal the shadow of her bush.

"Tell me what you would ask him to do to you, if he were here with you right now." He lightly tucked her hair behind her ear and dipped his head so she felt his breath with his whisper. "You only have tonight before I catch you and put a stop to it."

Her scalp tightened, and her breasts swelled so quickly, her nipples felt as though they would pop. She set her hands on the table before her, arching her back. "Lift my gown. Quickly. Fuck me before he comes home and catches us." She invited him with a come-hither glance over her shoulder.

"He's Italian, love. A man with experience and imagination." His knee shifted the small bench with a screech of wooden legs on wooden floor. It was no longer directly behind her. *He* was. He lifted her nightgown. "If I were him and only had you for a night, I would insist you display yourself like this."

He set her knee on the bench so her thighs were forced apart. The coolness of the room struck her damp flesh and swirled in a rush up the gape of her nightgown.

"Do you not want him to caress you?" He lifted her gown higher and stroked her thigh, then squeezed her bared buttock. "Kiss you? Tell me exactly what you want him to do."

"I want him to say I'm more enticing than his wife." Her breath fogged the mirror in front of her face as she leaned harder on her hands. "I want him to say he came to me because even his mistress is not so lewd and willing to do everything he wants. He can't stop thinking about me even though he knows it will destroy everything he holds dear."

"My wife is very pretty," Rainer said in a voice that seduced her. "But she hides it under starch and lace. She never lets me touch her the way I want to." He stroked her ass and thighs and pushed her gown up higher so he could feel her breasts fall into his palms. "Her tits are perfect for fucking, and I often dream of coming all over her throat."

He took her nipples in a firm pinch that held her still as he inched closer. His robe had fallen open, and the edges were tickling her legs. She could feel the heat and rough hairs of his thighs against the backs of hers. The heavy length of his cock left a wet kiss on her tailbone.

"She doesn't let me rest my cock in the crack of her ass purely for the stimulating sight of it."

"Does she let you fuck her in the ass?"

"No. And neither does my mistress. Are you telling me you let your husband do that to you?" Rainer's one hand smoothed over her belly. He deliberately avoided her pussy but ran his light touch around the edges of her bush and drew circles in the dampness that was sliding in runnels down the inside of her thigh. "What a degenerate you married, my dear, to ask that of you."

"I know, but he's mine," she gasped, scrambling among her pots and perfumes for the tin of ointment they used for that wicked practice. She set it where he could reach and arched invitingly. "I love him for all his filthy desires."

"Are you not going to ask your new lover to lick that cunt of yours? Because he can smell how aroused you are." Rainer leaned over her to suckle her earlobe, setting his teeth against it to hold her even more in his trap.

Her pussy clenched on itself, and all she could do was brace her splayed hand on the mirror and moan, "I don't need it."

"No, you don't," he agreed as he guided his cock down between her legs and rubbed his tip in the abundant nectar he found. When he probed at her soaked entrance, he slipped in without any effort.

He straightened and took hold of her hips as he pressed, filling her in one firm thrust that brought his hips flush to her ass. "Look," he commanded.

She dragged her eyes open to see her own carnal expression framed by her falling hair. Her pose was vulgar with her breasts exposed and swaying. Her husband stood behind her with his robe hanging off his shoulders. The light in his eyes was love and lust, power and humble gratification. Inside her, the broad shape of his cock pressed the walls of her cunt, filling her with anticipation of the friction to come.

"This pussy ruins men for all other women. That's why I never take lovers myself." His steely cock twitched inside her, making her mindless with arousal. "I only need you."

For a moment, her guilt at dallying with other men rose enough to penetrate her fog of desire. Then he set his hand on the dressing table and used his other to reach between her legs.

"Show him why he is destroying himself by fucking you. Come all over my fingers, my unbridled little wife." He played his touch over the swollen knot of nerves between her folds.

Her inner muscles clamped down on his thickness, and lightning went zinging through her lower back and thighs.

He kept toying and playing, pumping lightly until she had shivered and shuddered through two intense orgasms.

"So wanton. Now I'll take you up on that offer to fuck you in the ass." He reached for the tin, staying inside her as he scooped a generous gob of the rose-scented concoction and worked it against the tight rim of her arsehole.

She loved when he fingered her while fucking her. She loved the sensations, the pinch and ache that played against the softer pleasure of his cock sitting in her sated pussy. She grew freshly aroused and wetter still when he deepened the heavy intrusion in that dark place, working his finger in and out.

Her shivers of delicious depravity intensified when she felt the pulse of him inside her, telling her how much he enjoyed watching what he was doing.

Most of all, she loved this moment when he slid free of her pussy and prodded at that tighter hole with the wide crown of his cock head. He was always generous with the ointment, but the stretch always hurt a little. Just enough to make her groan in pleasure-pain as he filled her and steadily impaled her.

In his reflection, his nostrils were pinched, his cheeks flushed, his gaze still fixated on the way she was offering herself to be defiled in this way.

He lifted his gaze and met hers in the mirror. "I love that you're a greedy slattern who lets me fuck you any way I want. Play with your pussy. Show me how insatiable you really are."

As he began to pump, she braced a hand on the mirror and worked her fingers into the empty, hungry cavern of her cunt, loving the brush of his heavy balls against her knuckles, thrilling at the sheer dissoluteness in what they were doing.

Rainer gave her everything she needed, most especially the sort of carnal pleasures she craved. She shouldn't want or need other men, certainly not one he'd forbidden, but as the memory of Franco's avid stare drifted into her mind, her hand moved faster.

So did Rainer. The intensity of pleasure gathered in her loins. Sensations condensed to one powerful coil of anticipation that could only be borne so long. In a sudden rupture, she was released into acute waves of elation.

With a shout of gratification, Rainer clutched her shoulder and hip as he buried his cock deep in her ass and pulsed with his own fulfillment.

# CHAPTER THREE

Rainer was not invited into Bismarck's meetings at the Reich Chancellery. From what he was hearing, that was a lucky thing. It sounded like the chancellor was even more short-tempered than usual.

Solving the Eastern Question by redrawing borders through the Balkans was not the only work to be done with so many of Europe's great powers gathered in Berlin, however. Rainer was charged with seizing any chance to meet with ministers, ambassadors, and other surrogates to advance Britain's foreign interests.

It was not high-stakes work, but it allowed him to grow his influence and reinforce small alliances. He knew his own value and was confident that after a few more years as under-secretary, he would receive a promotional posting as a chargé d'affaires to some lesser country where he would finally have command of his own work.

Thankfully, Bernice was adventurous enough to embrace a life abroad and make the most of it. He did want to offer her a good life in every way, which was why he skimmed the unfamiliar faces passing him as he escorted a Turkish officer down to the Round Salon.

Not that Rainer had ever chosen his wife's lovers before. She took the men who appealed to her, and he only interfered if he thought there could be repercussions with his work. Otherwise, he viewed her liaisons as a husbandly indulgence the way another man might spoil his wife or mistress with jewelry or furs. He liked to give her what she wanted and see her glow with the pleasure of receiving it.

That was not quite how she looked when he spotted her in

the salon.

As a further enticement for delegates to visit the British embassy and thus be persuaded into private meetings with the likes of Rainer, Lady Russell was offering tea and cakes every afternoon. It was a time of day when the main congress broke so cigarettes could be smoked, tempers could cool, and a man could softly snore in a chair if he found one comfortable enough.

Bernice and other embassy wives were helping to serve and keep things civilized. The salon was becoming more popular by the day, and there were already several pockets of men gathered here to rehash the day's discussions.

Franco was among them, but his focus was on the delicate negotiation of a second helping of kuchen. He held a plate of crumbs, and Bernice was pursing her lips with deliberation over whether to refill it. Whatever Franco said to convince her made her lower her gaze demurely as she set the wedge of cake on the plate.

To anyone else, she was maintaining her modesty and a suitable distance, but Rainer recognized that small curl of pleasure at the corners of her lips. The stain of color across her cheekbones was not shyness or affront. It was the first sign of her roused desire. If Franco was watching her breasts, he might discern a hitch in her breath.

A confused mix of emotions struck Rainer as he witnessed her reacting to the other man. There was the same rush of stubborn possessiveness that had been torturing him since the night he had introduced them, but that was superficial. He trusted Bernice. No, the guilt of denying her was a sharper pang.

He felt small for having such a pale reason to refuse her as his sense of inferiority to Franco, especially when he was exactly as titillated by those signs in her as he was by any of her other encounters.

Rainer had not put any limits on his own sexual explorations when he'd been in the first throes of discovering his capacity for pleasure. He enjoyed reliving that newness through Bernice. And, even though he had never developed a partiality to lovemaking with men, he found it deeply stimulating to hear her describe how it felt for her to make love with them. When he saw her being overtaken by desire for cock, he *felt* it. And liked it.

Maybe therein lay his darkest fear, though. While Bernice always enjoyed her trysts, part of the appeal for him was the small secret they shared in her telling him about it. There was always a chuckle over a fumbled caress or another sign that her partner lacked the skill that Rainer possessed. It fed his ego, and he enjoyed that as much as anything else.

Franco was very experienced and adept, though. What if he gave Bernice more pleasure than Rainer ever had?

By the same token, if Franco could give her that, was it within Rainer's right to deny her?

*Fuck.* He didn't think he could. Fuckety fuck.

"Rainer," Bernice said as she spotted him. She smiled warmly, but as he came closer, he saw the shadows of compunction in her eyes. The entreaty.

She was reacting to Franco against her will and felt guilty for it.

That turned a knife in Rainer's belly. He recalled how deeply it stung to be blamed for something so natural and unstoppable.

He had to snatch for his composure when his instinct was to walk around the table, cup her cheeks, and kiss her with ferocious passion, until she was ready to let him fuck her on the floor in front of everyone, purely to show her that passion was a gift and she should never feel guilty for experiencing it.

Fuck, fuck, fuckety fuck.

Whether he condoned her screwing Franco or not, this dilemma had become a test of his principles, their arrangement, and the very foundation of their marriage.

●●●

Rainer wore his most inscrutable expression—the one that told her he had closed her out in some way.

Bernice hid her anguish with her most meaningless smile while she used a serviette for the extremely important work of removing three specks of cake crumb from the snow-white tablecloth.

"I was trying to inveigle my promised invitation to your home," Franco said. "Mrs. Stormont tells me she must check with you first. Since when is the wife not the queen of a man's social calendar?"

"I can't possibly guess Rainer's schedule," Bernice said, fighting to hide the guilt she felt in so much as talking about arranging a meeting with Franco, even an innocent one that was meant to include Rainer. "You have so many commitments with important people right now, I know," she said to her husband.

"Am I not one of them?" Franco said with a glare of mock insult at Rainer.

"I thought your evenings might be tied up with important people of your own," Rainer said with a blithe look.

Franco's mouth tightened at the small checkmate before he said, "I would make room for the engaging Mrs. Stormont." He turned his gaze of liquid admiration upon her.

Bernice couldn't help the blush that warmed her cheeks. He was being very elegant with his pursuit, making his interest clear without coming on too strong. *That blue is lovely on you*, he had said of her gown yesterday. He had laughed at one of her little asides and had insisted she sing a few bars of a song with him, proclaiming them a perfect harmony.

She was finding him so charming, she had rubbed herself to orgasm twice this morning after Rainer had left for work, imagining Franco taking her on the chancery desk at the Italian embassy.

But she couldn't let that happen. She couldn't bring herself to hurt Rainer.

The truth was, she would never be so understanding if he had affairs. If she were a better wife, she might suggest he visit Franco's mistress while she entertained Franco, but she would be devastated if he went through with it. She had discovered that even though she enjoyed being desired by other men, she *needed* to be the only woman Rainer desired.

It was very petty of her, but there it was.

"Bernice?"

"Yes?" She realized Rainer had been speaking to her. "I beg your pardon?"

"Dinner? Thursday?"

"Oh, yes. We have no other engagements."

"Excellent. Do you care to bring your uncle?" Rainer asked Franco. "Russell has been trying to pin him down for an agreement on common interests."

"Are you trying to ruin your wife's evening? No, I'll bring wine. If I could bring a gondola, I would, but I promise to sing if you ask." He winked at Bernice, instantly making her think of making love in the swaying bottom of a boat.

She looked down to hide the sensual curiosity that flooded through her, hearing Rainer say crisply, "Come to my office now, then. I'll give you some notes to provide to your uncle."

"He used to be fun, you know." Franco leaned toward her across the table. "At least I'm here to entertain you, since it seems *he* no longer remembers how."

She smiled weakly, unable to look at her husband as the men walked away.

●●●

"Are you angry with me? Should I have made an excuse?" Bernice asked later that evening, once they had caught their breath from torrid and wordless lovemaking.

"I'm the one who invited him." Rainer was staring at the

ceiling. He still wore the remote expression that had had her swallowing his cock the minute they were alone, trying to reach him.

She could feel this horrible distance between them, and it was making her anxious. She snuggled closer and stroked her thigh across his.

"I haven't been encouraging him."

"You don't have to. He can see how you react, same as I can." He gave her a wry look and played with her hair.

"I don't mean to," she said, withdrawing in distress.

He moved to cover her. "I know." He combed his fingers into her hair on either side of her face and nibbled at her jaw. "And the fact I've forbidden him makes the temptation in you all the stronger. *I know that.*"

"I don't mean to be like this." The corners of her mouth insisted on pulling down. It was hard to hold his eyes while the misery of struggle consumed her.

"Darling." His thumb caressed her cheek. "I love you exactly as you are."

She doubted it. She thought about Franco *all the time*.

"When I was young and fantasized about my brothers' friends, I loved that my mother would be horrified if she found out," she confided huskily. The rebellion of doing something illicit had lent a piquant guilt to her furtive friggings. "The same thing is happening with Franco. The more I tell myself you would disapprove, the more I think of doing it and not telling you. I don't want to lie to you. I don't want to lose your love."

She had to bite her bottom lip because it had begun to tremble.

"You wouldn't. I would be hurt if you lied to me," he acknowledged. "It would break me in half if you fell in love with someone else and left me."

"I wouldn't." She ran her hands over his naked shoulders.

He shifted, using his knee to spread her legs before he guided his fresh erection into her still-damp pussy. As he sank into her, his nostrils quivered.

She sighed, relaxing beneath him as she felt their emotional connection restoring itself.

"I remove my ban," he said in such a low, heavy voice, she wasn't sure she had heard him correctly. She paused in rubbing her calves against his buttocks.

"On Franco?" she asked.

"Yes."

"Why? Because you think it will make me want him less?"

"I can't control how you feel, love. That's what this conversation is about." He adjusted her beneath him so he was able to penetrate a fraction deeper.

She imagined the pulse of his cock was his heart and gripped him with her pussy muscles, holding tight to him.

"Is it a test?" Was he trying to see if he could trust her?

"It's an opportunity. Fuck him or don't. Tell me or don't. I will continue to love you no matter what you decide."

"Rainer." She cupped his bearded jaw, awed by the gift of a love that was so unconditional. "Do you... Would you want to share me with him?"

They had talked about that in the past, but she had always felt self-conscious at the idea of Rainer watching her make love with someone else. She didn't think she would be able to let herself go. Rainer had always thought he would become too controlling and that his being there would steal the excitement from her confessing about it later.

"Another time, perhaps." He nuzzled her cheek. "This would be for you. Make it happen however you want it."

"You really wouldn't mind?" She played with the shell of his ear. He was placing a lot of responsibility on her with this decision.

"Do you want me to mind a little bit?" He started to withdraw, then reached to the bedpost above her. He used his grip to add power as he surged back into her, muscles flexing under her hands as he did.

Her senses came alive in a searing rush. She arched and moaned with delight.

They had only made love a short while ago, but he was steely hard. She could feel the need in him as he fucked her with deliberate, powerful strokes, as though making her his.

She clung to him, digging her nails into his back and lifting her hips for the slam of his, streaking toward an intense orgasm with shocking speed.

When it arrived, he caged her in hard arms and loosed himself, driving fast and hard, pounding into her convulsing pussy, drawing cries of carnal joy from her throat.

With a sudden snarl, he pulled out and jabbed his wet cock against her belly, pooling hot come there as he replaced his cock with his hand and continued to fuck her with his fingers while they both groaned in the throes of gratification.

As his three fingers stilled inside her clinging lips and her thighs trembled and his tongue swept out to lick her throat, he said, "Don't let him come inside you. That would piss me off."

●●●

When Rainer had moved Bernice to Berlin, part of the inducement had been the use of a small, furnished apartment. It wasn't grand, but it was well located near the embassy and was more modern than most. They didn't have hot-water pipes like the ambassador's residence, but they had cold running water, a proper water closet, and a coal-fired, cast-iron parlor stove that warmed the front room nicely once the sun faded for the day.

They also had two maids and a very good cook. With their help, Bernice had the menu decided and the table set before she dressed for company.

"You look lovely," Rainer said as she appeared. He smoothed a frill on her shoulder that insisted on kinking the wrong way.

"Thank you. So do you." He looked very smart in his evening suit with his hair and beard freshly trimmed.

He searched her gaze.

*I haven't decided*, she wanted to sob.

Thankfully, she didn't have to. Not tonight. She was looking forward to seeing Franco away from the public eye, but also with Rainer's steady presence here to distract the man. She would be able to observe her potential quarry and consider whether he was worth what it might cost her with regards to her husband.

"Signor Petrucci has arrived," the maid announced, entering the parlor with a curtsy, Franco behind her. "And a note, sir." She offered it to Rainer, then took the hat Franco handed to her and disappeared.

"Good evening," Bernice greeted Franco. "Welcome to our home."

"I'm pleased to be here."

They both looked to Rainer, who looked up from the card he was reading.

"This is inconvenient. I've been called back to the embassy."

"Now?" Bernice asked with shock and a small zing of dangerous thrill. It happened occasionally, but she had a feeling Rainer had arranged it.

"Some emergency?" Franco asked with a frown of genuine concern. "Anything I ought to know about?"

"Only ruffled feathers that need smoothing. I won't be more than an hour. Please stay and keep Bernice company until I return. She put a lot of thought into the evening. I wouldn't want to deny either of you the enjoyment of it. All right, darling?" Rainer brushed his lips against her cheek, hovering an extra second so she might say no, she would rather he stay.

The awareness was in her that she ought to say exactly that, but temptation locked her throat. It still felt as though her taking Franco as a lover would make her husband feel as though an affair was more important to her than he was, but Rainer straightened and gave her one final look. There was no hint of anger or disappointment, only a warm light of acceptance.

She could have cried and wanted to squeeze him in gratitude.

But he was gone.

She had a decision to make.

# CHAPTER FOUR

"That's unfortunate," Franco said with a facetious smirk. "Now he can't corner me into a discussion on tariffs and excise."

"Instead, I'll force you to debate Italian opera over German."

"There is no debate. *Obviously*," he said pithily.

She bit back her smile, slowly turning so she continued to face him as he prowled their small parlor. Franco held out a hand to feel the heat off the stove, took in a simple painting of a snow-covered landscape, then paused to examine a bottle of schnapps next to the brandy on the sideboard.

"Please, help yourself."

"Not yet." He smelled the red and white peonies in the vase on the writing desk.

She didn't understand why she grew so aroused during moments like this that were as uncomfortable and dangerous as they were ripe with possibility, but as the clock ticked loudly in the silence, her awareness of opportunity heightened. She had been yearning and fighting and longing for this. Now her stomach rolled with uncertainty, but she still had this breathless and undeniable craving for him to come near. To notice and touch her. To douse anticipation with relief.

"To be honest, I've been hoping for a private conversation with you." Franco's circumnavigation had arrived back at the door to the parlor. He gently closed it, leaving his hand flat upon it.

Her heart began to thud. Her blood hit the undersurface of her cheeks with a sting.

"About Rainer?" she asked faintly, playing obtuse because she was still uncertain she wanted to take this to its next steps.

"About you." He came toward where she stood with her bottom against the back of the mahogany and velvet sofa behind her. "And me. If that is a conversation you might like to have."

She tried to swallow and felt the tendons in her throat flexing. She was quivering on the razor's edge between apprehension and anticipation.

"I realize that is a very forward thing for a man to say to a woman who has perhaps only flirted with certain ideas."

She could only stare at his black bow tie. He stood very close.

"But you have flirted, Mrs. Stormont," he said with a faint smile. "Which is why I thought this conversation would be welcome. Rainer would never need to know."

She dropped her gaze farther, to the buttons on his waistcoat.

"And what of the woman who is staying above a boutique on Kurfürstendamm? Would she know?"

He drew back a fraction. "You *are* well informed, aren't you?"

"It seemed prudent to become informed, if I was intent on certain ideas." She lifted her gaze to meet his. Her stomach swooped at the boldness of making that admission.

"Intent," he repeated. The lusty satisfaction in his slow smile stoked the fire building inside her. "Then you likely know that my paramour is already annoyed that she must share me with my wife. I think we are better off keeping this our little secret."

He gave her earring a playful nudge so it swayed on her lobe.

Bernice knew what he was doing. He wanted to see if she would move away or accept the growing intimacy of his touch. She allowed it because she had decided to test him in her own way.

"I wouldn't know how to have such a conversation," she lied, glancing to the side. "Or why you would want a conversation like that with me. I'm very ordinary."

"Is that why you dress so demurely? You don't realize how exceptional you are? I assure you, a figure like yours can carry off something more eye-catching and should. You're a woman of beauty, confidence, and intelligence. Allow others to see it."

"I've always heard Italian men were very charming."

"All true, cara."

She drank up his compliments and flattery but dropped her gaze as though too bashful to meet his.

A heavy bulge sat against his trousers. Wanton desire swirled through her.

Franco allowed the backs of his fingers to graze the edge of her jaw. His tickling fingertip found the hollow beneath her ear before he trailed his touch under her chin, coaxing her to tilt her mouth and eyes up to his.

"Let me show you what you've been missing." He dipped his head so his lips were close enough to send a tingling spark jumping between them.

She set a light touch on his chest, more for the pleasure of feeling his hard breastbone. "Did you lock the door?"

He moved across to turn the key, then met her in front of the sofa.

Bernice discovered she enjoyed playing the nervous virgin, tangling her fingers before her so he had to take her hands apart himself before he could draw her closer.

"I don't intend to force myself on you. I thought you were intrigued?"

"I am. But it's very wrong, isn't it?"

"No one will ever know. I promise you." He drew her a little closer and touched his mouth to the corner of hers.

This was always a favorite part of hers, when she discovered how a man kissed. Whether his lips were smooth or full or soft or commanding. Franco's were warm and damp and skilled enough to steal across hers, drawing her into a deep kiss before she realized how easily she'd been captured.

It was thrilling, and she cupped his head as he slanted his mouth for a firmer fit, then slowly plunged his tongue between her lips. The relentless stimulation had her pussy growing wetter and wetter. She didn't realize that she had released a muted moan, or that his hand was massaging her breast, until she pressed into his palm and moaned again.

She drew back to catch her breath.

"Oh, cara, you are a delight." He drew her into another potent kiss, and his hands rubbed through her skirt, trying to find her hips and thighs beneath the padding across her bottom.

His erection was pressing insistently against her stomach. She covered it through his trousers, rubbing him before she remembered she was supposed to be shocked by all of this.

"Can I see it?" she asked, biting her lip.

"You may suck it if you want to." He opened his trousers and withdrew his dark, straining erection with its slight arc and thick vein and weeping tip.

He was a beautiful specimen. She didn't have to pretend awe as she explored his cock with light fingertips, then a roll of her thumb that spread the thick fluid across his head.

"I don't know if we should be doing this," she whispered, glancing at the clock. It had only been a quarter hour since Rainer had left.

"We have a little time. Open your gown." He began to unbutton the front of it himself, grunting as he thrust his cock into the tight, slippery fist she made for him. "That's good. Keep your hand just like that. Ah, fuck. And— Oh."

Her corset, a gift from her husband, was one of the finest silk. It had a pretty floral pattern and quilting on either side of the looped buttons down the front. The laces at the back could be tightened when she needed it, but this front closure allowed her to put it on herself and—when a man was in a hurry to access her breasts—to do so with the flick of a few loops of cord.

"Your tits are magnificent." Franco pulled aside the neckline of her cotton camisole so he could lift one breast free and wrap his hot mouth over her turgid nipple.

It felt incredible enough she tightened her hand on his cock and made him groan as he pushed with more power into her fist.

This was exactly the sort of encounter she relished. The clock was ticking, there were servants beyond the door who forced them to keep their moans muted, Franco was touching her as though he couldn't get enough of her, and the dark iniquity of it all combined into a potent excitement. If someone were to discover her right now, her embarrassment would be profound, but the danger of skirting all of that, of defying what was expected of her, brought all of her senses alive. Her muscles were tensed, her breathing uneven, her need to hurry and reach her pinnacle urgent.

But when Franco pressed her to the sofa and tried to lift her skirts, she balked.

"What's wrong?" he asked softly, going to his knees on the floor before her.

"I don't want you to come inside me."

He swore and ran his hands over his jacket. "I didn't bring a skin. I didn't expect... No matter. Next time. I'll eat you. You'll like it. You'll see."

She loved a good licking, so she let him lift her skirts and spread the slit of her drawers.

"Oh, cara," he said with approval as he gazed on her soaked curls. "We'll do it this way so you can move however it feels best for you." He rolled onto his ass in front of the sofa and tilted his head back against the seat. "Don't be shy. Kneel behind my shoulders and hold on to the back of the sofa."

Was it her birthday? The only place better than a cock for sitting on was a face.

She gathered up her skirts and shifted so she was straddled over his uptilted chin. As she grasped the back of the sofa and let her weight settle, she felt his tongue lick across her spread folds, exploring all the little crevices, poking into her entrance and sweeping up to toy with her knot.

As Franco burrowed his arm under her skirts so he could cup and squeeze her ass, encouraging her to rub herself harder on his lips and tongue, she began to rock her hips.

Oh, it felt good to grind on him. His mustache prickled and tickled and teased, and his tongue fucked into her. The utter filthiness and lack of inhibition made her arousal climb sharp and fast. She looked at the clock, calculating, "We only have a quarter hour. Rainer might be coming."

She let the urgency sink into her. Hurry or he would catch them. She had to hurry, had to come.

Franco slid two fingers into his mouth, then up into her pussy, fucking her with them as he sucked loudly on her sweet spot.

A sharp contraction seized her abdomen, then a need to bear down struck her. She had only ever come like this for Rainer, but as an intense wave arrived, she was frozen by the sharp pleasure of it. She could do nothing but hold still and let the contractions take her, biting back her cries of release.

Franco made a strangled noise of shock but kept thrusting his fingers into her and suckled at her until she was leaning on her folded arms, legs too weak to lift herself off his face.

And why would she want to when his tongue continued to lap at her cunt?

# CHAPTER FIVE

R ainer came back to the oddest tension between his wife and his old friend. He honestly couldn't tell if they had fucked or not.

On the one hand, Bernice had a softness to her that suggested she'd enjoyed some loving attention, but Franco was distracted, no longer attempting to charm. He left as soon as politely possible, declining an after-dinner schnapps or coffee.

Rainer went to his wife's bedchamber the moment he had undressed and washed for bed. Her maid was still brushing out her hair, but Bernice dismissed the young woman and let Rainer take the brush.

"Would you like to tell me what transpired?" he asked.

"It was odd. But nice," she hurried to assure him. "He's not a better lover than you. He's quite good, and I think if I didn't have you, I would have found him very skilled and diverting. Having said that, he's a little too... Hmm. I understand now what you mean about his acting as though he is doing a favor."

"He wanted you to believe your taking his cock was a privilege?" Rainer moved his hand to her shoulder and concentrated on not allowing it to clench there, but his protective instincts were well riled.

"That seemed his attitude, but we didn't fuck. I didn't have a skin, and neither did he. So I sat on his face."

"Did you." Unsure if he was pleased or dismayed, Rainer went back to brushing out her hair. "Lucky Franco."

"I came all over him." She bit her lip ruefully. "*All* over him."

"Lucky Franco," he repeated with a smirk. "Did you suck him off?"

"That's the odd part. He behaved as though he had all the

experience and control, but I guess he was frigging himself while I was on his face. He was so excited when I came, he popped himself all over the inside of his jacket. He was put out by that, but he also said he has never made a woman spurt before, only heard about it. He was ever so smug at making me come that way."

"Such a kind chap, doing good works for all the needy women, hmm?"

"Exactly." She rolled her eyes. "I gave him one of your handkerchiefs from the writing desk. I doubt we'll see it again."

He shrugged that off.

"And then I said…" She cringed her shoulders up. "I wasn't meaning to be unkind, but I was honestly surprised that he'd never made a woman come like that before. I said, 'Rainer makes me gush all the time.'"

He dropped his hands to his sides, scolding, "Bernice."

"Well, it's true. Then he went to the water closet to clean himself up, and I tidied myself. We had a drink, and I waited for him to ask if I wanted to see him again for a proper fuck, and he didn't invite me, so I don't suppose that will happen."

"Are you disappointed?"

"No." She chewed the corner of her mouth a moment. "Are you sorry you let it happen?"

"No." He went back to brushing. "But I'm glad it won't happen again."

"I know. It's too… It's not fun when I'm worried that you'll be hurt. As soon as it was over, I missed you." She reached up to cover his hand.

He moved to pick her up and sat down on the bench so she was in his lap, facing the mirror with him. He rested his chin on her shoulder as he looked at their reflection.

"I missed you, too. Usually I'm excited for you, but this time I was worried. It felt different."

She nodded. "Maybe I'll take a break from taking lovers."

"That's up to you." He folded his arms around her. "Or stick to men I don't know. See how you feel."

"I do love you," she told him with soft fervency. "I love that you love me, even though I'm like this."

"I love you for the same reason," he said matter-of-factly and tenderly kissed her cheek. "Would you like to sit on *my* face?"

"I would." She wriggled an acknowledgment of the fact that their sexy talk, difficult as it had been, had still aroused him. "Would you like to come down my throat first?"

"I very much would."

Smiling her most beguiling smile, she slid to her knees and parted his robe.

# EPILOGUE

*Four months later...*

"I t's a filthy, wet day out there," Rainer said as he entered the apartment. His trousers were speckled and his collar damp despite the fact he had worn his overcoat and left an umbrella in the tin by the door. "You were smart to stay home today, love."

She smiled at their maid, who took his coat to hang it behind the stove in the kitchen.

"I actually ran out to visit the bank this morning," she confessed with a small lilt of nervous excitement.

"Did you?" Rainer's brows went up. "Shall we talk about that in the parlor?"

They moved into the room where the maid had already started a cozy fire. While Bernice closed the door and turned the lock, Rainer poured two measures of brandy.

"It was more accurately the insurance office." She accepted the glass he offered and sipped. The alcohol sent a burn down her throat and into her veins, but she was already tingling with a different intoxication.

"The one who left a card for me the other day? You said you weren't sure."

She hadn't been. After Franco, she hadn't felt a need for the attentions of other men, but this particular young man had struck her fancy. He was shy and portly, learning the insurance trade from his uncle. He'd been very nervous as he went door-to-door, persuading the ladies of the house to encourage their husbands to purchase fire and accident insurance.

Bernice had invited him into the parlor, where the maid had come in and out with tea service. While she politely listened to his spiel, Bernice had done those small things that always titillated a man. She had ensured her skirt was pulled tight to one thigh, had provided a generous view down her décolletage, and had brushed a hair from his knee.

By the time he'd left, he'd been bright red and stammering, holding his hat before the front of his trousers and clearly smitten.

She had ridden Rainer's cock for ages that evening, collapsing, exhausted, and certain she wouldn't think of the young man again.

"I happened to see him on the next street over when I was informing Mrs. Heller that you had received a new posting and we would depart for the island of Malta soon. He was so endearing, continuing his efforts to drum up business despite his bashfulness. I realized I wouldn't rest until my curiosity was satisfied," she told her husband. "Do you mind?"

"I am only wishing I'd made an effort to meet the man so I could have a picture in my head. Otherwise I am nothing but intrigued," Rainer assured her. "Tell me everything. Where did you tryst with him?"

"In his office." She gave a small grimace of culpability. "He thought I was there as a client, so he introduced me to his uncle. That man was a crusty old gentleman with a bible on his desk and no time for a woman thinking she could speak on her husband's behalf. He was in the next room when I made my advances. We had to be very quiet."

"Bernice," Rainer chided indulgently. "You have completely ruined that poor young man, haven't you?"

"He was looking at me with such infatuation, Rainer. I could see he was aroused and didn't know how to disguise it. I would like to think I gave him a good start in the art of lovemaking, since he was a *virgin*."

"Oh, my love." Rainer chuckled softly. "Was it nice for you at all?"

"It was." She had very much enjoyed the whole thing. "He was at war with himself at first, certain he would be smote for his lustful thoughts, but he couldn't help himself. His yearning for me got the better of him. I made sure of it." It had been highly titillating to tease and provoke him.

"How?" Rainer set his hips against the back of the sofa, and his hand moved the front of his trousers, where he caressed his erection through the wool. "What did you say?"

"First I told him I needed to be assured his was an agency that could be trusted, that anything we said or did behind the closed door would be held in complete confidence. He promised it would; then, I asked him if he had ever been the plaything of a married woman and whether he would like to be."

"Clearly the answer was 'yes.'"

"After he got over the shock, he was very eager and very embarrassed of his lack of knowledge. Fortunately, he was also open to instruction, which is good, because his first kisses were sloppy. We rectified that. He nearly came in his trousers when I stuck my tongue in his mouth."

Rainer grunted a sexy noise. "I want your tongue in my mouth right now, but I want the rest of this story. Did you undress? Had he ever seen a naked woman?"

"I unbuttoned my gown and said he could touch me through my chemise. He *loved* my titties. I think he would have kissed and suckled at my nipples all day if I had not put a skin on him and shown him where to put his cock."

"Did he not eat you?" His gaze was fixed on her beneath heavy eyelids.

"Oh, yes. I told him to get onto his knees and learn how a woman is made. I lifted my skirts and spread my pussy lips. I said, 'Suck on your finger and get it wet, then push it inside.' I showed him there was another more delightful nipple he could turn his tongue loose upon." She pressed her gown to her mound, fingers spread as if she held her lips opened, and pointed to the source of her sweetest sensations. "It was lovely, but he kept stopping to ask if he was doing it right."

Rainer gave a soft chuckle, but his breathing was jagged with arousal—which was why she was being so graphic in her descriptions. "Did he make you come?"

"A little one. He was astonished when I gasped and stroked his hair. He didn't know women could reach such a peak from lovemaking. It seemed to light a determination in him, especially when I said I might come again if he fucked me well. We did it on his desk. He was clumsy at first, looking over his shoulder. I thought he might be too nervous to finish, but once he had his hands and lips on my titties again, he settled in and enjoyed it. So did I. His cock was not terribly big but very hard. He held out longer than I expected for a first time. He wanted to make me come again, and I did. I told him I was proud of him after, for ensuring I got mine."

"Oh, Bernice." Rainer shook his head. "Is he hopelessly in love with you now?"

"A little." She wrinkled her nose. "He was weepy when I kissed him goodbye. He said he loved me and wanted to see me again. I reminded him I was already married and leaving for Malta. I assured him he would find himself a suitably lustful woman so long as he was willing to be attentive to her pleasures."

"Isn't that the truth." Rainer straightened and took her glass, setting it aside with his own. Then he pivoted her so her hips were against the back of the sofa. "Is your pussy still soft and swollen from his cock? Is your greedy little cunt hungry for dessert?"

"Always."

He locked his mouth to hers as he lifted her skirts and gave it to her.

*The End*

# That Tickles

*That Tickles* is a story that will transport you across the world and leave you smiling, however it does contain brief instances of misgendering and workplace bullying, so readers who may be sensitive to these, please take note.

# CHAPTER ONE

---

*April 1874, Auckland, New Zealand*

After three months of losing his guts nearly every day, Darby O'Sullivan knew exactly what he looked like as he shakily disembarked in Auckland—a woman. He'd whacked his overgrown hair as short as he could and tied a band around his chest, but he had a small, whiskerless chin, and with his stomach so hollow, the difference between his waist and the width of his hips was exaggerated.

So much for leaving the past behind. That was almost as demoralizing as the muscle he'd lost. He felt weak as a kitten when he shouldered his duffel bag of worldly belongings to make his way through the entry gate.

"Twenty-four?" he was asked with a skeptical look as his papers were reviewed.

"I look young; I know." This body of his was determined to ensure he'd never be taken seriously.

Fortunately, a family with a screaming baby was behind him. His entry was quickly finalized so they could be moved along as well.

Darby stepped out to sunshine that lifted his spirits.

"Domestic help over here," a woman called out to him. "We can give you a room in our dormitory."

"I'm a bricklayer." That earned him a few looks, since he sounded as young as he looked. He ignored them and joined the crowd at the job board.

All the postings under "Tradesmen" instructed men to appear first thing at different sites if they wanted work. He memorized names and directions, then moved to another board advertising rooms to let. A widow operated one with a price he could afford.

He'd sold what he couldn't bring with him, but it hadn't amounted to much.

As he started up the road into the city proper, he bought a meat pie from a girl with a basket of them. He wanted to buy the whole basket, but he still felt drunk and dizzy from the ship. His legs were unsteady, and he expected the ground to come up and meet each step.

It was a fine day for relearning to walk, though. The sky was a bright blue, the sun warm, the breeze fresh. He had to remind himself it was autumn, even though it was the second of April. It felt like a pleasant summer's day.

Auckland was more of a bustling center than the rural farmlands, grass huts, and unfriendly natives he'd been led to expect. Everyone he saw wore clothing made of cotton and wool, much like his own, regardless of skin color or tattoos on their chins. A few women were wrapped in shawls, but even those were plaid.

As he glanced for a street name, his attention went farther down a road, where timber buildings were being pulled apart and replaced by more permanent stone structures. He noted the unmistakable worksite of a brick foundation. A handful of men were moving in and around it, one carrying a hod.

Darby made for it the way a hound went after a squirrel.

As he came even with it, he saw what looked likely to become a hotel and pub with a cellar. Or it could be the fancy home of a man who'd made his riches in the South Island's gold rush and was planning to invest in railroads.

"Lookin' for a husband, luv?" someone called out.

"Are you?" Darby drawled, not the least intimidated by shit that came out of men's mouths. After his mother had died, it was all Darby had known. "Who's in charge here?"

The one who'd spoken to him gave Darby's yellowed shirt and patched dungarees a puzzled second look. He called out, "Gavin!" and chucked his chin.

Darby looked across to a tall, husky fellow with russet hair and a thick beard. He was burly and masculine without even trying, thirty or so, and cussing out another man in a good-natured Scottish burr. When he heard his name, he glanced across.

"Aye?"

"I'm looking for work, sir," Darby said.

"There's a pub on Queen's always needs a hand. Might have something at the hotel farther up."

"Stonework, sir. I'm a journeyman bricklayer." Or would be if his father had seen fit to qualify him. Darby ought to be a master stonemason, given his skill and experience, but his father had died before he'd been persuaded to call the company O'Sullivan and *Son*.

Gavin snorted. "You're fifteen? Sixteen?"

"Twenty-four, sir. I worked under my father since I could lift a trowel."

"Looks like that's all you could lift," the prick who'd proposed said under his breath.

The men who'd stopped working to eyeball him gave a rippled chuckle. Darby ignored him.

"Put me to work for an hour," Darby offered to Gavin. "If you're happy with the result, I'll come back tomorrow."

"Let me see your hands," Gavin said.

Darby moved forward to show his lack of calluses. "I've been on a ship for three months. Just walked off. Haven't even found a place to sleep yet."

"I'll give you a place to sleep," the clown offered.

"Is it the bottom of a river?" Darby asked in a friendly tone over his shoulder. "Because that's where I'm thinking of making *your* bed."

That got a few chokes of laughter from their audience and a lazy "Get fucked" from the asshole.

When Darby brought his attention back to Gavin, he saw

a hint of approval in the older man's eyes, enough to warm something in him that he usually ignored. Darby kept an arm's length between himself and sexual attraction. Things got very complicated very quickly. This wasn't that, though. Or at least, that's not all it was. Darby understood that Gavin wasn't about to hire someone who got into pissing contests with his crew. A foreman wouldn't want to hold anyone's hand, either. Darby had just demonstrated he could take care of himself, hopefully reassuring Gavin he wouldn't have to worry about him.

"One hour," Gavin agreed. "You can pick up on the wall there between those two footings."

"Thank you, sir."

"Call me Gavin."

"Good to meet you, Gavin. I'm Darby." He held out his hand.

"I'll learn your name if I decide to keep you on. Get to it. Time's ticking."

Darby nodded and walked down to where he'd be working. He dug into his bag for his tools and, as each one came to hand, began to feel a little more at home.

•••

"She's a girl. Isn't she?"

"I heard 'bricklayer,'" Gavin said, brushing off the baffled comment of a man he'd hired two months ago. He would love to fire the prat. He was more muscle than brains, but such men had their uses when it came to stonework.

Men slight as dandelion fluff were less useful, but Gavin had to respect Darby's confidence and initiative, looking for work before he looked for a bed.

Also, Gavin had a soft spot for slender, pretty men. He was inclined to at least keep Darby around until the end of the day and see if they had anything else in common.

"Get back to work," he told the rest of his crew but stayed

where he was, watching how particular Darby was about his tools and where they were placed. He wobbled under the weight of the hod, but Gavin remembered how soft he'd been after his own journey from Scotland a decade ago, so he held back his sarcasm.

Once he got properly started, it was clear Darby knew exactly what he was doing. He was a leftie, but his trowel and level were in constant motion and moved around as though part of his body. He used exactly enough mortar, rarely slopping it and picking up any small gobs that happened to fall. His courses were level and even. As the wall came up, he bent to clean his edges, always knowing where his tools were without looking. He kept up a steady pace that almost seemed to put him in a trance, brick after brick landing in place with precision. All the while, he was ducking and keeping himself out of the way, aware of the work going on around him.

Gavin set the muscle-brained twit to providing Darby bricks and got back to work himself.

Darby said an absent "Ta" a few times but didn't chatter or stop working until Gavin walked over and said, "Finish that tomorrow, Darby. We're stopping for today."

Darby straightened to his middling height and pushed his hand into his lower back, blowing out a breath. "What was that? Two hours?"

"Two and a half."

He grimaced at his work. "Lost my speed as well as my strength. Felt good to be back at it, though. Thanks." He held out a hand to shake. His knuckle was freshly scuffed and still bleeding. He made a noise of dismay and swiped his hand on the seat of his trousers, then offered it again.

Gavin shook that soft hand, liking the strong grip he got in return.

"Comin' to the pub, Gav?"

"No, I'll look after our wee lad here. You have *one*, then get your arses home to bed. Anyone comes to work drunk or hungover tomorrow, I'll clobber ya *then* fire ya."

•••

Darby disliked when people pointed out how short or skinny he was, but at least Gavin had called him a lad. Considering the fact Gavin had to be at least six feet tall and had arms bigger around than Darby's body, Darby supposed he was "wee" by comparison.

Darby was intrigued by Gavin and appreciated his offer but made himself say, "You don't have to look after me. I was making my way to a house owned by Widow Grayson."

"It's a few doors down from mine. I'll walk you. If she doesn't have anything, we'll find something at my house. Either way, I'll buy you dinner and a beer for your work today."

Did Gavin hold his gaze a heartbeat longer than necessary? Darby tried to ignore the swoop in his stomach and nodded. He bent to clean his tools, telling his pulse to settle down as he put everything back in his bag.

Gavin seemed equally fussy about ending his day on a tidy note. He set boards to keep passersby from falling in the hole and ensured everything was stowed and covered before he paid a man who apparently patrolled the area at night for thieves.

"Your father taught you well," Gavin commented as they began walking.

Gavin took up much of the walkway and seemed to tower over Darby. That should have annoyed him. He hated men who used their size to intimidate, but that's not how this was. Gavin wasn't trying to take his bag, either. They were two men walking. Equals. It was comfortable, and Darby liked him for it.

"Da was trying to keep me busy and out of the way. Ma died when I was six. After losing her and two other babies, he couldn't bear to put me in an orphanage or leave me with a minder, so I went to work with him. When someone from the mechanics institute offered to teach him to read, we learned together. Same with our mathematics."

"He's gone now?"

Darby nodded, throat growing a lump that barely allowed his soft, "Aye."

Gavin made a gruff noise of pity. "I see it hurts, but it's good you mourn him. Mine was a prick. I left Scotland to get away from him. Whether he's dead or not, he's dead to me, and I'm not sorry about it."

That made Darby want to give him a pat of compassion, not that Gavin seemed to need it, but it did sound like a sad way to feel about one's father.

"What led you here?" Gavin asked.

"I saw an ad for free passage. One of Da's workmates was willing to write me a reference as a tradesman, so I got on in steerage. Fuck me, I thought that ship was trying to kill me."

Gavin flashed a grin that showed a missing tooth at the back. "It's bad, isn't it?"

"They were rationing the fresh water by the end. I had a wash in salt water this morning, but these are my 'clean' clothes and haven't been laundered since I left. I can't wait for a proper scrub."

"You need it. You're ripe," Gavin confirmed with a wry smirk.

"Shit." A sting of embarrassment hit his cheeks.

"You're all right." He nudged Darby with his elbow, nearly knocking him over.

"That's sea legs and starvation," Darby said as he staggered. "I'll toughen up. I swear."

"You'd better." They were both grinning as they arrived at a house and Gavin nodded at the front door. "That's the Grayson house. I'm the one with a blue door down the end."

Darby nodded and climbed the steps to knock. Mrs. Grayson came to the porch. She agreed to let a room to Darby once Gavin identified himself and told Darby the wage he would be making.

"We'll have steady work until the weather puts a stop to it," Gavin assured them both. "You'll have a little extra saved up by then, unless you drink it."

Darby wasn't a heavy drinker. His rent included breakfast and dinner. A full bath, laundered clothes, and a meat pie for midday were extra, but knowing he had work tomorrow, Darby was willing to pay for all of those as a small treat for surviving his journey.

"Can I take you up on dinner later in the week?" Darby asked Gavin. "I'll clean up and have an early start so I'm fresh tomorrow."

"Aye," Gavin said with a nod, but Darby thought there was some disappointment in his expression.

It caused a small wobble inside Darby that had nothing to do with his recent deprivations. He liked Gavin and wanted to know him better, but friendships were often as knotty as sexual interest for him. He didn't want to screw up the employment he needed by letting things get too personal too quickly.

"What time do I turn up tomorrow?"

"Work starts at seven sharp."

"I'll be there before then. Good night."

# CHAPTER TWO

Through the next weeks, Gavin overheard a few speculative remarks about Darby, but he only had one response.

"He works harder and complains less than you do. Get on with it."

Indeed, Darby only complained when he let himself down, bitching as he strained under a full hod of bricks. "This shouldn't be this hard for me."

What he lacked in strength, he made up in speed, staying level, and working clean. When it came to heckling, he took a three strikes approach, ignoring the first couple of remarks before throwing out a retort. He never got too cutting or pissy and was always funny enough to get a chuckle from those who heard it, which earned the crew's grudging respect.

Gavin was glad. Darby's work was too good to let him go, but he didn't hire troublemakers. Within a few weeks, Gavin was leaving Darby in charge while he went to quote new jobs. By then, they were busy enough he had some new hires in the mix. Gavin came back in time to hear Darby down in the hole, having it out with one of them.

"Mate, you're not square," Darby said to a tall, lanky fellow called Nick. "You'll have to start again."

"Who the fuck are you to tell me what to do? I don't *have* to do anything."

Gavin's instinct was to get down there and protect Darby. With steady work and meals, he was filling out across the shoulders and was well-liked by most of the crew, but he was still a smaller sort and treated like a kid half the time. Even so, Gavin couldn't leave him to run the men if he wasn't able to. Gavin made himself hang back but moved so he could keep an eye on what happened.

"I'm the foreman when Gavin's not here, but you're right," Darby said. "I can't make you fix it. I'll fix it myself if you want to leave."

"You can't fire me." The prick got right up on Darby, hands closing into fists. He stood close enough the rest of the lads put down their tools.

One called out, "Oy. Fighting will get you fired."

Darby didn't back down. "I'm not fighting. Or firing you. I'm saying we've all had to clean our bricks and start again. If you want this job, that's what you'll do. If you don't want to do that, move along, because if you keep at it, you're making more work for me later. But I'll tell you what. If you change it and I'm wrong, I'm the one Gavin will fire."

Darby turned to walk away, which was a bold fucking move. He watched the faces of the other men. He would know if Nick made a move, and Darby's hand was so tight on his trowel, Gavin had no doubt it would have gone between a pair of Nick's ribs swift and deep if it came to it. Gavin held his breath.

Nick scowled at Darby's back, then looked to the three courses he'd laid.

"Maybe it's your square, mate," someone said. "Try mine."

"He didn't even measure it. How the fuck would he know if it's square or not?"

"Darby's been around. He knows his shit. And he's right; there's no shame in starting over. That's why we're here, isn't it?" It was an ironic reference to the fact they'd all come from afar.

As the tension seeped away and the man grudgingly knelt, Gavin moved down to where Darby was working and asked, "All well here?"

"Coming along, but the timber delivery was late. That's why the scaffold isn't ready for the south wall yet."

"I'll see what I can do to make up that lost time." Gavin nodded and dropped a hand on Darby's shoulder in a clap of appreciation as he left.

By the time their next payday rolled around, the job was ahead of schedule, which put all the lads in jaunty spirits. They headed to the pub, where Darby had his usual one beer before rising to leave.

The crew protested, but Darby said, "I promised to paint my landlady's back porch tomorrow."

"Is that what they're calling it these days?" someone chirped.

"She promised me a week's worth of midday meat pies in exchange. Make of that what you will." Darby grinned at the laughter he'd provoked as he gathered his things.

Gavin rose to leave with him and was also called out.

"You think I don't have back porches to paint? You rabble will enjoy your night more without the bosses here, anyway." He sent a look toward the prat who'd given Darby a hard time earlier in the week, silently conveying, *Yeah, I said "boss*es*."* The pair seemed to have mended things, so he didn't make any more of it than that.

Darby noted the distinction and waited until they were outside to say, "You heard about that?"

"I listened to it. I thought it was worth letting all of them know I would back you if it came to it."

Darby acknowledged that with a grunted, "Thanks."

"I suppose that sets a line between you and the rest of the lads," Gavin said, taking note of Darby's cool response.

"I do that myself," Darby said with a twist of his mouth. "Otherwise, I'd stay in the pub with them. I don't enjoy the company of drunks. You always leave, too," Darby noted with a glance upward.

Gavin nodded. "I don't mind a beer or two, but they start to remind me of my old man. Do you like snapper? There's a place I know batters it and fries it with chipped potatoes. We could take it to mine."

Darby sent him a look that wasn't exactly wary, but he

definitely sniffed an ulterior motive. Which Gavin had. They were forming a comfortable working friendship, one strong enough Gavin would trust him to get any job done well, but he wanted to know Darby better on a personal level.

He wanted to know if Darby also wanted that.

Darby nodded agreement, and they soon picked up their paper-wrapped meal and took it to Gavin's home.

"You didn't tell me you were a member of the royal family," Darby said of Gavin's top-floor suite of rooms. He had a small dining and sitting area, a bedroom through a pair of doors, and a wee balcony beneath a gabled roof. "You even have your own throne." Darby peeked in on the WC.

"Don't tell the lads, but I own the house." Gavin wasn't sure why he confided that. He usually kept his business to himself, same as Darby seemed to. "I should say, the bank owns it. Luella and I rent rooms to pay it off. She runs it day to day. Cleans up after me."

"You're married?" Darby asked with what looked like tremendous shock and a hint of poorly disguised disappointment.

"No. Hell, no," Gavin said with a dry chuckle. "Luella lost her husband and let me buy in so it's not so much on her. We get on well enough, but I'm not the marrying type." Make of *that* what you will, he told Darby with a straight-on look.

"Me neither," Darby said, briefly holding Gavin's gaze in a way that gave Gavin's cock a tug before Darby looked down with a small frown.

They both sat to eat. For a few minutes, there was only a crinkle of paper and the crunch of batter as they tucked in.

As the silence thickened, Darby begrudgingly said, "Go ahead and ask, then."

"What?" Gavin knew exactly what he was talking about, but he only said, "Whether you like the fish? I can tell you like it, or you wouldn't be eating as though you'd never seen food before."

"Still trying to put my weight back on. But did you really

invite me here to eat fish?" Darby's brows lifted. "Not for a private conversation?"

"I'm not going to ask you anything I wouldn't ask any of the lads," Gavin said gruffly. He did have questions, but: "You want me to know something more than where you're from or how old you are, you'll tell me."

They ate in silence another few minutes before Darby said, "I do like the fish. Thank you."

"I am dying to know if you're Protestant or Catholic, though," Gavin said, holding a straight face.

"Fuck you." Darby slid his boot to knock it against Gavin's beneath the table.

He broke and chuckled. "Sensitive topic, is it?"

"A little of each, if you must know. Da was Catholic. Left Ireland at sixteen, got on as an apprentice in Yorkshire. Married Ma when he got his journeyman papers. She was Protestant. I was never much of either 'til I was in the belly of that ship. Then I prayed to God every day for Him to kill me."

Gavin snorted and rose to fetch his bottle of whiskey, pouring a little into a pair of glasses that he brought to the table. He was realizing if he wanted Darby to open up, he'd have to do the same.

"Ask me why I'm not the marrying type," he prompted as he sat again and pushed a glass across.

"You want me to know something, you'll tell me," Darby said with a quirk of his lip.

Darby's mouth was intriguing in itself, with an upper lip that jutted out a little and a bottom lip that was not quite as wide, so it gave off a thoughtful quality—which Darby seemed to be, always choosing his words carefully and never acting on impulse.

Gavin was spending a little too much time thinking about that expressive mouth along with the rest of this young man when it was late and dark.

"You're a little prick sometimes, you know that?" Gavin said good-naturedly. "If you're not going to make it easy on me, I'll talk plain. I get the sense you have things you keep to yourself. So do I. That gets heavy to carry, even for a big man like me." He took a gulp of his whiskey, cutting through the grease lingering on his tongue. "I'm not interested in a wife because I'm not interested in women. When I share that bed—" He nodded through the pair of doors. "It's with a man. Not as often as I'd like, either." He hitched his chair around so he could kick out his feet.

"I see." Darby was finishing his last bites. He chewed and swallowed. "Is that why you've brought me here? To invite me there? Because I haven't shared a bed with anyone. Ever."

"Really?" That took Gavin aback. "You're a good-looking lad. Clean up well. Thought some girl would have given up a kiss by now."

"I didn't say I hadn't kissed anyone," he retorted. "Girls and boys, as it happens." He crumpled up his paper and took a sip of whiskey. His brows came together in a way that suggested conflicted thoughts, then he admitted in a low voice, "I prefer men, too."

"I didn't mean to pry, but I thought we might have that in common."

Darby's brows scrunched even lower as he muttered, "There's plenty we don't."

That's what Gavin suspected as well, but: "You'll tell me if you want to."

"Does it make a difference to my work?" Darby asked impatiently.

"What? Fuck, no. You've seen what I've got working for me. I'm not letting you go unless you drink, fight, or steal. So don't do any of those things," he ordered gruffly.

Darby let out a half laugh and turned his own chair, relaxing back into it. His thumb moved restlessly on the side of his glass.

The air between them had shifted, no longer heavy with what wasn't being said, but now thick with, *What now?*

"Da loved me with his whole heart, but he didn't know what to make of me. He blamed himself. Thought because he'd raised me around men and taught me a trade that it turned me away from what I looked like I was born to be. As I grew older, he kept trying to marry me off to his journeymen. Two of them proposed, one before he died and one after. I liked them both, but they wanted me to settle into running a household and give them children. Fuck, Gavin, can you imagine how you'd feel if someone flat out told you to put on a gown and cook for a man and squirt out a baby?"

Gavin might have had more trouble understanding Darby's struggle if he wasn't predisposed to walk a different path himself.

"Sure be easier if we fell in with the way we were told to behave, wouldn't it?"

Darby made a grumbled noise and sipped his whiskey, then allowed, "It does lighten the load to talk about it. It really doesn't bother you?" He sent him a sideways look.

"What's to be bothered by?" He was glad to have a friend he could speak with openly.

"I don't know. You're the one who pointed at the bed a few minutes ago and said you like to share it with *men*. I thought you were hinting at something."

"It's crossed my mind we might spend some time there." More like the thought had moved in and wouldn't leave. "Would you want that?"

"Depends what you expect to happen there, doesn't it?"

Darby was throwing down words like bricks, keeping a wall firmly between them.

Gavin heard his defensiveness and had an urge to chuckle at how ironic it was that Darby was worried about rejection. Gavin was the one with the bigger secret, but the more he'd thought about getting naked with Darby, the more he wanted to confide in him.

It was risky, and he shifted uncomfortably, wondering what

Darby would think of him.

"You want the truth; I'll tell you. Usually, if I share a bed, I like getting fucked up the bum." He fucking loved that, in fact.

"Well, I can't help you, can I?" Darby said sharply, jaw clenching.

"I didn't say that to hurt you. I said 'usually.'"

"I'm not hurt."

"Fuck you, you're not. We're being honest, so I told you what I usually do." He was handling this badly, putting his own bricks between them. He hadn't expected to be so fucking nervous. His palms were sweating, for Christ's sake.

"Nice chat, then. Thanks for dinner. I'll go." Darby slugged back the last of his whiskey and rose.

"Christ, Darby. You want me to wait until we're in that bed to tell you something like that?"

"Do you want me to tell you how many men have taken for granted that I would *get* into a bed with them?" He leaned on the table. "Fuck *you*, Gavin. It's never going to happen."

•••

"Sit down. I didn't tell you what else I like." Gavin rose, and Darby's heart soared into his throat.

This was already an uncomfortable confrontation that had gone too far, but as quickly as alarm stung his veins over the hardened expression on Gavin's face, Gavin walked away into the bedroom.

"You know what *I* like?" Darby said to his back. "Exercising my choice to leave a room if I don't want to be in it." It came off as petulant when he had a clear path to the door and Gavin was all the way over there, kneeling down on the far side of his bed, retrieving something from beneath it.

Darby's hands were in fists, his chest still tight over their hard words, but Gavin was no threat. He set a long, flat box on the edge of his bed, opened it, and held up a feather duster.

"I'm not cleaning your fucking house, Gavin." What the fuck was wrong with this man?

"I heard you, ya prat. You're a man, not a woman. I'm telling you this is what I like. To be…" His voice faded out like a fizzling candle. "Tickled."

Of all the words that could have come out of Gavin's mouth in that moment, Darby had not expected that one. Ever.

"Tickled," he repeated to be sure he'd heard it correctly.

Gavin reached into the box and started throwing out paintbrushes and strips of fur, something that looked like a riding crop with a ball of duck down on its end, beads on a string, and a bouquet of colorful ribbons sagging from a wooden handle.

Darby couldn't make sense of it. There was still a voice in the back of his head telling him it was time to leave, but he was rooted to the floor by surprise. "Are you being serious?"

"Don't be a prick about it." Gavin stood to his full height, still in the bedroom on the far side of the bed, arms folded, chin set into a belligerent angle. "You think I can tell anyone about this?" He waved at the various implements. "It's hard enough to say I want a man in my bed."

Darby bit the inside of his cheek and nodded slowly while his mind raced. "You're right. I was being a prick." He was stunned to the bottoms of his feet, though. He'd never heard even a whisper that this was something anyone liked.

"Maybe you can't fuck me bum," Gavin said in a low, deep voice. "But I thought maybe you'd be willing to try this?"

# CHAPTER THREE

⚋⚋⚋⚋⚋⚋⚋⚋⚋⚋⚋

Any lingering wariness in Darby had turned firmly to compassion and curiosity.

He moved into the bedroom and had an urge to pick up and examine the fan-shaped paintbrush. It looked like the quality an artist might use, with bristles made of mink or some other fine animal hair, but he was damned possessive of his work tools, so he gave Gavin's items the same respect. He kept his hands to himself while he simply looked.

"I'm a little confused," Darby said carefully. "This isn't like, I don't know, a warm bath that feels nice. It's something you like… in bed? Like kissing and…" Darby hadn't done much more than that, so he didn't know what else to say.

"Yes." Gavin gave a defensive nod. "I like this as much as…" He looked to the ceiling as though calculating. "Maybe more than getting fucked in the bum. It's hard to say because I can't fuck myself and I've never done this"—he waved at the items—"with anyone else." He rubbed his palm on his thigh and nodded at the bed. "But if I think about someone doing this to me, I get really fucking horny."

*Like me?* Darby's heart lurched. Sensations he usually ignored settled warmly in his pelvis. "How, um, how did you realize you liked this?"

"Dunno. I always have," Gavin said with a self-conscious shrug. "I can remember rubbing fur on my stiffy when I was real young. Later, when I wore a kilt and the wind was just right and the wool tickled my bare legs, I would come. That happened before I was old enough to have any jism. Got a surprise when *that* started to happen." He pushed his hair off his forehead and reached for a long feather. "Have you seen an emu yet? This is one of their tail feathers."

As he held it, the long, narrow feather danced lightly on the air. He motioned for Darby to come around and offer his hand.

Darby did, and the soft vanes in the feather stroked in a barely there touch over the back of his hand and between his fingers. He turned his hand over, and Gavin slithered it across his palm, then made a circle around his wrist.

"Doesn't that feel nice?"

It was like a kitten looking for a pat. It made Darby feel soft inside but gave him a tickle on his skin that he wanted to rub away.

"Fuck, I'm getting hard just touching you with it." Gavin swallowed and set the feather aside.

"You're getting hard tickling *me*?"

"Don't be like that," he grumbled.

"I'm not laughing at you, Gavin." Darby looked up into his friend's face. "I'm surprised; that's all. I've spent a lot of time thinking about what it means to be a man, and, like you said, it'd be easier if we fit into what we've been taught. This doesn't fit what I believed ten minutes ago, but that doesn't make it wrong."

"Yeah, I had certain ideas about what it means to be a man, too."

They shared a look that was wry but painfully unguarded.

"I..." Darby looked down at the implements so he didn't have to face the weight of expectation in Gavin's gaze. "This is easily something I can accept." It was kind of a thrill to be able to offer Gavin something he couldn't get from anyone else. It was deeply flattering that he'd confided such a secret. "But I am as virginal as a bride on her wedding night. You should know I won't ask you to fuck me. Ever. Not in the front hole, anyway. That's kind of the reason I'm still a virgin. I don't know what I want in bed." Or out of it, for that matter. Darby was working on being Darby, not trying to fit into anyone else's expectations of who he was supposed to be.

Gavin nodded. "That's fair. Figuring out what you like is

usually a matter of trying a few things, though. You could, for instance, kiss me. See if that's something you'd like to do more of."

Darby looked up at him, liking that Gavin was so direct, but also bemused by the hint of shyness that had come into his expression.

"Yeah, I could," Darby said facetiously. "But you're all the way up there."

Gavin brushed aside his tickling tools and sat on the edge of his bed. "Better?"

He looked surprisingly boyish and earnest, him with his bushy beard and thick brows and warm brown eyes.

It was a strange moment for Darby. He was used to men coming on to him and trying to "be the man." Most of the time, they were trying to prove they could turn Darby into what they thought Darby ought to be. It was so objectionable, whatever attraction Darby might have felt usually died a quick death.

Everything was different with Gavin. He not only accepted him as he was but was offering to let him take charge. It was exciting, if intimidating in a different way. What the fuck did he know about making things good for another man?

Darby wasn't a coward, though. He would settle for being workmates with Gavin, but he wanted more with him. They were on their way to a deep friendship, and this, well, it was something Darby hadn't really imagined he could have with Gavin. If he could, however, he wanted to try.

Darby stepped into the space between Gavin's legs and did something he'd been dying to do. He curled his fists into the man's beard and held Gavin's face steady as he pressed his mouth to Gavin's warm lips.

Gavin's breath held the faint scent of whiskey. His whiskers brushed Darby's chin and upper lip, tickling, which was so Gavin, it made Darby smile.

Then Gavin let his mouth go soft and parted his lips. A rush of excitement had Darby rubbing his mouth across Gavin's, deepening the kiss in a way that was pure instinct and made him hungry in a very earthy way.

For a few moments, this was all Darby knew: the warmth radiating off Gavin's bulk, his wiry whiskers against his palms, the brush of his tongue meeting his own. A low moan sat in Darby's throat, blocking his breath, but Darby didn't care. This was everything he needed in life, right here.

When Gavin's wide hand came to his hip, Darby paused, but Gavin only rubbed his thigh, then gave his ass a light squeeze. The embers of arousal in the pit of Darby's belly sparked into a higher flame. He groaned openly into Gavin's mouth and gave him more tongue, enjoying the different textures and the way the other man sucked on him.

They drew each other even closer, Darby with his arms around Gavin's shoulders, Gavin with his thick arms catching above and below Darby's ass.

The kiss went on a long time, filling Darby with more and more heat. More and more languid desire until Gavin roamed his big hand to Darby's ass again, fondling and squeezing.

Darby lifted his head, gasping for breath.

"No?" Gavin moved his hand to Darby's hip.

"Yes. I like it."

"Me, too." Gavin smirked as he moved both his hands to Darby's ass and greedily clenched his fingers into his crack. "I would fuck this ass if you wanted me to."

"Good to know," Darby said, ridiculously happy despite how daunting that sounded.

Being this close with another person had always felt awkward and tentative. Darby's lack of experience meant he didn't know how to communicate what he wanted, but for once, this was easy and natural. Playful.

"Can I?" Darby drew back enough to reach for the nearest object, the fan-shaped paintbrush. He showed it to Gavin in a silent request for permission to use it on him.

He half expected Gavin to refuse or at least show some hesitancy. This desire of his seemed deeply personal, but Gavin's eyes lit with excitement. His shoulders went soft, and his breathing changed.

"Yes," he breathed as though he was being offered water on the hottest summer's day.

His reaction was so profound, a small rush of power went through Darby. How could such a tiny thing topple such a big man?

He very lightly touched the bristles between Gavin's brows. As he painted the edges of one bushy brow, Gavin's eyes fluttered closed in what looked like utter bliss. When Darby trailed it across Gavin's closed eyes, Gavin released a strangled noise.

*How intriguing.* Darby traced the bristles down the side of his nose, watching Gavin's nostrils flare, then around the edges of his beard and across his lips and onto his throat.

As Gavin lifted his chin and his Adam's apple bobbled, Darby captured his mouth in another hard kiss while lightly playing those bristles into the collar of Gavin's shirt and up the side of his neck to the spot beneath his ear.

Gavin released another garbled noise and clenched his fist in the seat of Darby's trousers. He was shaking.

"You really like this." Darby lifted his head in wonder, watching as he brought the tickling touch to Gavin's ear and traced all the whorls.

Gavin's arms banded around him. He clung so hard, Darby could barely breathe.

A strange, exciting tension curled in Darby's abdomen. He wanted to laugh, this was so fun, but it was sexy as hell at the same time. A dampness arrived between his legs that usually annoyed him, but this time he liked it.

"Do you want to take your shirt off?" Darby asked.

"Fuck, yes," Gavin groaned. He barely opened a couple of buttons before he yanked the whole thing over his head and threw it away without looking where it landed.

He was muscled and meaty, with thick red-brown hair across his pale chest and down his stomach to his navel. His arms were as big as Darby's thighs.

Darby squeezed and stroked his hand down to the bend of Gavin's elbow and back up to where his neck met his shoulder. When he moved in and kissed him, Gavin smelled of sweat and the breeze they'd been in today while they worked. He smelled like Darby's new home.

Darby couldn't help making their kiss a deep, hard one. Something possessive was rising in him—something that wanted all of this man to himself.

Their kiss grew so involved, Darby didn't realize he'd dropped the paintbrush until he felt naked skin under both his splayed palms as he roamed his touch across Gavin's back.

"Do you want me to use the brush or...?" Darby was kind of dazed.

Gavin looked the way he felt. His wet lips were parted. A flush sat on his cheeks, and his eyes were clouded with lust. "Do whatever you want. This feels so fucking good." He massaged down Darby's hips to his thighs and back to his waist.

Before he picked up anything else, Darby wondered, "Do you like the kind of tickle that's—?" He slid his hand to Gavin's ribs and dug his fingers in.

"Fuck, no!" Gavin quickly brushed his hand away, barking a startled laugh. "No. I mean, it makes me laugh. Do it some other time when we're horsing around, and I'll give it back in spades, but you're killing the mood."

"Oh." A smile lingered on Darby's lips as he reached for the colorful ribbons bound to the wooden handle. "Where did you get this?"

"Made it. Luella was throwing those scraps away," Gavin said sheepishly.

"And you like to run it across your skin? Fast or slow?"

"Slow," Gavin said, drawing out the word and see-sawing his shoulders as Darby played the silken tails of ribbons from one side to the other, trailing the ribbons across the back of his neck. His breathing hitched, and his nipples stood out like shards of pinkish-brown stone.

"Lie back. Do you want to open your trousers?"

"So bad." Gavin eased onto his back and opened his buttons, sliding his hand in and pulling out a generously built, fully hard cock. He gave it a few hard pulls with his fist. "I could come right now."

If he ever thought that monster was getting up this small, tight ass, he was dreaming, but Darby thought he would enjoy sucking it.

Gavin's expression changed as he looked into Darby's expression. He tentatively offered, "Do you want to get undressed? Show me what you like? We could come together, or...?"

"This is fine. I'm enjoying it. Put your hands up over your head."

"Oh, fuck." Gavin swallowed and did, mouth opening to release a helpless sound as Darby very lightly skimmed the ribbons across his chest.

Darby made sure to graze each of Gavin's nipples and let the ribbons slither down his ribs and into his armpits. Gavin's whole body arched, and his cock twitched. He was soon leaking a puddle of fluid onto his stomach, biting his lip, rocking his hips back and forth while he trembled with arousal.

"Can you come like this?" Darby asked softly.

"I think I might," Gavin said with an anguished look on his face. "Kiss me."

Darby was braced on a hand over him but slid down beside him and propped himself on an elbow. He shifted closer so he could drop his thigh over Gavin's. He leaned down to lick into Gavin's mouth as he played the ribbons over Gavin's throbbing cock.

Gavin groaned in torture and closed one arm around Darby, holding him close as he kissed him back with eager passion.

"Oh, fuck, lad," he moaned as his whole body grew taut.

"You're close? What if I…" Darby let the ribbons fall away and ever so lightly traced his fingertips over Gavin's hairy balls and around the tangle of hair, across his upper thighs and against his tense stomach.

As he gently, gently tickled Gavin's cock, starting at the base and working toward the tip, Gavin made a noise of deep torment. He clamped both arms around Darby's shoulders, dragging him half atop him to suck on Darby's lips as he came in strong spurts across his own naked chest.

●●●

"I barely touched you," Darby teased as Gavin returned from washing up.

If Gavin had had a fantasy beyond being tickled into orgasm by someone he liked, it might be this: Darby sprawled amid his toys. He was playing the puff of duck down against his cheek and chin and wore a glow of arousal along with a smug curve on his lips.

"You fucking destroyed me, you bastard." Gavin dropped onto the bed behind him and pulled Darby into the curve of his body, wanting to somehow drag him all the way inside himself, where he could keep him forever.

As he kissed his neck and Darby ground his ass into his satisfied cock, Gavin let his hand trail down to Darby's crotch out of reflex.

Darby stiffened. Gavin immediately brought his hand back to Darby's hip.

"That was really incredible," he said gruffly. "I only want you to feel as good as I do right now."

"I know. And thank you, but—" Darby sighed with a

frustration that was more than sexual, but he relaxed into him again.

Gavin cradled him, glad for this small show of trust even if Darby wasn't ready for more. Still, Gavin offered, "I could tickle you. See if you like it?"

"Take off my shirt? I have tits, Gavin." Darby sounded annoyed.

"So do I." Gavin was no lean, wispy thing like Darby. He had muscle but also bumps and rolls. "Hey." He nudged his knee behind Darby's. "Tell me what you like to do when you play with yourself. What's *your* tickle stick?"

Darby huffed a laugh and said, "My tickle stick is a little bump, but I like to think about getting it sucked. I rub it until nothing else matters."

"I'll suck you off right now if you want me to."

"No." Darby shifted restlessly, maybe a little excited by the thought. "But thank you."

Gavin grunted and settled his head on his bent arm, pulling Darby in closer. "Are you worried I wouldn't get it right? I am, too. But I don't want you to leave here thinking I'm a selfish prick who gets his and goes to sleep. I want you to want to come back and do this again." He gave Darby a playful pinch in the stomach.

Darby eyed him over his shoulder, somber again. "I will. This feels good, but... We're too different. Physically."

Were they, though? Gavin could feel the tension in Darby and knew most of it was unsatisfied desire.

"You could show me your ass," he realized. "I could play the feather over it. Or just let me rub and play with it. I'm dying to, you know."

"Really?" Darby's tone changed to one of consideration.

"Hell, yeah. But be warned. I've spent a lot of time sneaking peeks at it. I might have to take a bite of it."

"Idiot," Darby grumbled, hesitated, double-checked with another look over his shoulder at him, then shifted so he could open his belt.

Gavin had just come his brains out, but he was titillated as hell when Darby got his trousers loose enough to lower them down his thighs and show his pale, firm ass. Darby rolled onto his stomach and pillowed his head on his arms, then turned his face to gaze warily at Gavin.

"See, that's tempting enough to sit in a bakery window." Gavin brushed Darby's shirt up to the middle of his back so he could rub his hairy face all over Darby's buns, shoving his nose in his crack and tickling him with his whiskers, making Darby wiggle and laugh. "You like it?"

"Your beard feels good," Darby said, sounding as though he was smiling.

"How about my teeth?" Gavin scraped a mock bite against Darby's cheek, making Darby wiggle.

"Yeah, I like that, too."

"Let's see what else you like." He reached across Darby to gather some of his toys closer. He set his string of beads, all about the size of his fingernail, in a line along Darby's crack. "I'm going to leave that there because I like the look of it. You mind?"

"No." Darby's ass flexed, and the beads slid a little deeper into the valley. "It's like I can feel your eyes on me. That's kind of…" He shifted again, working his hand beneath him and into his trousers.

"Oh." Gavin felt a little tug in the flesh between his thighs as he realized what Darby was doing. "Are you going to rub your cock, Darby?"

"Do you mind?"

"Not in the least." He was kind of touched that Darby was willing to be that flagrant in front of him. "I'm gonna have to grab my own again, this is getting so interesting. All right, then. What do you think of the feather?"

He drew patterns on Darby's ass, swirling the downy vanes along the bottoms of his cheeks and the backs of his thighs.

Darby made a noise and started to move, swore.

"Stop?"

"No. It's maddening, but I kind of like it, and I like knowing it's you doing it. Do you like doing it?"

"Fuck, yes. I like watching you wiggle. I'm going to be thinking about this for the rest of my life." He kissed Darby's ass again before he returned to tickling it. "Is it making you horny?"

"More like when I try to get away—" Darby's breath hitched. "It makes me rub myself... Oh, fuck this feels good," Darby groaned.

Gavin chuckled and leaned down for another lick of his smooth ass. He blew across the damp patch and ran the feather to the back of Darby's thighs and up to his lower back, and he watched Darby pump his hips in uneven jerks.

The more he slowed the tickle, the more Darby seemed to grind himself harder into his hand. His moans were muffled by the bedding, but Gavin could see him tensing up with readiness.

He replaced the feather with his beard and whispered, "I wish you'd let me put my finger up your ass, Darby."

He was so caught up in the sight of Darby pumping his hips, Gavin practically felt Darby's release when it struck. Darby thrust his hips into the mattress and groaned hard. His pleasure was so visceral and powerful, Gavin damned near cried with happiness at hearing it. At being part of it.

Gavin scooped Darby closer while he was still shaking and panting, rolling him so they were face to face. They kissed deep and rough and sexy, then slowing to lazy and tender.

Gavin was naked and Darby still half-dressed. His shirt was up, exposing his stomach down to the top of his pubic bone. His trousers were loose and his ass still hanging out. Gavin palmed it, pretty much unable to keep his hands off those delicious cheeks.

Eventually Darby blinked his eyes open and said, "That was unexpected. Thank you."

"Anytime." Gavin let a wicked grin pull at his mouth. "I mean that."

# CHAPTER FOUR

D arby was thinking this move to New Zealand was the best thing he ever could have done. He had steady, well-paid work and enjoyed friendships on the jobsite and in his rooming house. After three months of lifting bricks, his body was back to what felt more natural. In fact, he felt more like the man he'd always wanted to be, now that he wasn't surrounded by people who had known him through childhood. A few of his mates teased him about finding a wife, but there were enough bachelors among them that it was easy to brush that off.

Darby also had Gavin. At work he was Darby's employer, but he treated him like an equal. He often asked him to consult as they approached a new job or section and regularly left Darby in charge of a crew. And even though Gavin was a master stonemason himself, he wasn't afraid to back off from a tricky bit of work to say, "I'd rather it was done right the first time. You do it."

Away from work, they were equals in a different way. They fucked around with tickle toys, kissing and touching and doing whatever else felt good. They kept it light because neither of them was the marrying type and they were sharing enough in physical ways that they didn't need to spill their guts or hearts.

At least, that's how Darby felt. He wouldn't have opened up as much as he had with Gavin if he didn't trust him. Gavin had shown him his own soft side. They were good.

Then, in the space of a week, shit fell apart. The weather turned to rain, so Gavin sent all the men home for the rest of July. He no sooner did that than one of the sites had a slough of earth knock out part of a wall that hadn't fully cured.

Darby worked alongside Gavin to fix it, but they were soaked to the skin after.

"Come around after you change. We'll go to the pub," Gavin suggested.

"Not tonight." Darby hadn't been over to Gavin's for a few days, and he saw the question come into Gavin's eyes but dodged making any explanations. "I'll talk to you tomorrow," he assured him.

Gavin nodded, then surprised him an hour later, turning up downstairs.

Not wanting to air his business in the common room, Darby brought Gavin up to his room. It wasn't anywhere near as fine as Gavin's living space. There was nowhere for Gavin to sit, only a bed and a small bureau. Darby liked that the room was cheap enough he was able to put away for these rainy days when he wouldn't have income, but his spare accommodation was yet another reminder that he and Gavin were actually very different.

"You avoiding me, Darby?" Gavin asked with his typical no-nonsense demeanor. "We haven't seen each other outside work in days."

"I'm on the rag," Darby confided with a dismayed twist of his lips.

Gavin gave a laugh, then quickly sobered when Darby didn't join in.

"Shit. You're serious." Gavin's expression grew concerned. "Are you all right?"

"Fine," Darby said flatly. He had known a man once who had lost the ability to walk after a factory accident. Darby had resolved to be grateful for his working legs and not to be angry over what was between them, but: "I'd rather stay in is all."

"We can pick something up, eat at mine."

They could eat here, too, but Darby didn't suggest it. He felt very misunderstood in that moment and shrugged Gavin off. "I'd rather have a quiet night alone."

"All right." Gavin nodded.

Darby could see the frustration in him. Gavin could tell

something wasn't right, but Darby didn't feel like explaining himself.

After a moment when Gavin seemed to be making up his mind, Gavin said, "I'll be in and out the next few days, but come by if you want to talk."

"I will." Darby nodded and saw him out, aware he was being a bit of a prick, but he also had a sawing pain in his middle and a glum awareness that it was his da's birthday tomorrow. He was homesick as hell.

His gloominess passed once the day and the rain did. By then, Darby was feeling like an ass for pushing Gavin away. He cleaned himself up and walked down to Gavin's, hoping to smooth over their rough patch.

Luella smiled as Darby knocked at the back and entered the kitchen. "Gavin's mate dropped by with beer again. I think they're still up there."

Again? A small twist of jealousy went through Darby. He straightened his face and went up the stairs, but the door to Gavin's room opened as Darby reached the landing.

A handsome man of thirty or so came out, still laughing at whatever Gavin had just said. He had dark brown hair and tanned skin, bright white teeth and a bushy mustache. He paused in buttoning his coat when he saw Darby.

"Darby?" His one quirked brow said, *I don't know what I expected, but you're not it.*

Such a pit of snakes came alive in Darby's guts, he nearly hissed and struck.

Gavin pulled his door wider, face blanked with surprise. "You're here."

Gavin exchanged a glance with his guest that suggested culpability. Maybe they'd been fucking; maybe they hadn't. Far more of a betrayal was the fact that Gavin had been talking about him. That was such a knife to Darby's self-esteem, he turned around and went straight back down the stairs.

• • •

"Darby. Mate," Gavin called.

Gavin had never believed looks could kill, but the glower Darby had just sent him had nearly stopped his heart. Gavin brushed past Terrance and clomped after Darby.

Fucker was fast. He was out the back door and halfway down the lane before Gavin caught his arm and stopped him. Gavin was sharply aware they were performing for all the nosiest of his neighbors.

"Come on." He dropped his hand and jerked his head toward the house. "You're not even going to talk to me?"

"What's to talk about? Have fun."

"Have fun doing what? Hmm?" Gavin set his hands onto his hips so he wouldn't grab Darby and march him where he wanted him. "What do you think I've been doing?"

"Whatever it was, that's your fucking business, Gavin. But he knew my name." Darby pointed at himself, and his voice thinned to almost nothing. "Whatever you told him about me is no one's business but mine."

"Fuck," Gavin muttered and swiped his hand over his hair. "That's not how it was," he grumbled, but it was a little like that. Not really, but enough that he felt a pinch of guilt and deserved that hot look of anger from Darby. "Will you let me explain? He brought me something I want to show you."

"Not interested."

"No?" Gavin's temper lit. "Fuck you, then. The only reason I was talking about you was because you've been on my mind all day every day, but could you so much as show your face for a cup of tea? No. You're not the only one whose feelings are hurt, you little prick."

He had to go or he would say something even worse. He started tromping back, walking straight through the puddles that were lingering after the rain.

As he went through his front gate, Darby caught it before Gavin could slam it closed. They glared at each other.

"I didn't think you'd care that I wasn't around. You said you had things to do."

"Well, I'm not going to pine up in the attic like a fairy princess, am I?" He waited until Darby came through, then closed the gate and flicked the latch.

Darby followed him up. Thankfully, Terrance had found his own way out. This was uncomfortable enough without making awkward introductions.

Gavin closed his door and moved straight over to pour them each a neat whiskey.

"Who was he?" Darby asked, staying on his feet.

"Terry and I were friendly some years ago." Gavin set the glasses on the table.

"Friendly like you and I are friendly?"

"Yes and no." Had Terry's cock been in his ass? Yes. But: "We don't suit. Terry is a get-rich bloke always looking for the next thing and therefore always broke. He left for America three years ago, and that was for the best because it let us end on good terms. He's just arrived back and came by fishing for a place to stay. I had to tell him I was a one-man man these days. He asked if that man had a name, so I told him."

"Hmph." Sounding marginally mollified, Darby sank into the chair, but he frowned into his whiskey. "You could have let him fuck you if you wanted to."

"Oh, aye. I can see how well that would have gone over." Gavin dropped into his own chair. "I won't say it didn't cross my mind, either. But nice as a quick fuck sounded, I knew it would hurt you. Terrance isn't who I want, anyway. I like what you and I have."

"I do, too." Darby sank lower into his chair. His brows were so disgruntled they were pretty much one wrinkled line. "But I feel bad that I can't do that to you."

"I know you do. You've said it more than once." Gavin grappled a minute, trying to recover his patience while wondering if he was liable to make things worse between them. "I think you feel worse about that than I do. I wish you'd tell me more about how it is for you, you know."

Darby let out a hacked-off sigh. Gavin reached across to give his wrist a tap.

"You don't have to. You've never once asked me to talk about my father, but you've left enough openings I know I could. I'm glad you don't ask me to wade into that muck, but that's why I left you alone this last week. I thought that's what you wanted. I was surprised the other day because I hadn't thought about the fact that— Fuck, Darby." He was still reeling from it. "I could get you pregnant."

"No. You couldn't. Because I don't want that. *Ever.*" Darby turned his head to level a stark look at him.

"Me, neither," Gavin assured him. "I already have ten kids tracking mortar all over my jobsite."

"You'd better not be counting me in that," Darby grumbled into his glass.

"Nine and a half," Gavin corrected.

"Fuck you," Darby said, but he was sounding less angry.

Gavin smirked and topped up their drinks.

"Look, mate. I imagine I'd be pissed if I was bleeding and didn't want to be, but you don't have to hide that from me. It doesn't change my view of you."

"It wasn't about that. I mean, yes, I put you off because of that, but I was missing my da." Darby spoke into his glass. "I didn't want you to see me cry."

"Ah, ya dumb shit." He gave Darby's arm a light nudge. "No shame in those tears. You nearly made me cry shutting me out. Come here." He gave Darby's sleeve a tug.

"I did not." But he came around and let Gavin pull him into his lap.

"Did," Gavin insisted. "I've been sitting here wondering if I pissed you off because I did something or *should* have done something, and I didn't know what it was. Either way, I just wanted to see you. Then you showed up and threw a fucking dagger into my heart."

Darby combed his fingers into Gavin's beard and cradled his face the way Gavin liked him to, looking on him like Gavin was something worth looking at. It made his heart unsteady in his chest but warmed him through.

"I was jealous," Darby admitted grudgingly. "Soon as Luella said you'd had a mate come around a few times. I knew I shouldn't be. We haven't made any promises, but it hurt to think you'd moved on." He swallowed. "I didn't want you to see me cry about that, either."

"I'm not going anywhere, ya git." Gavin's voice was gruff with the emotions rising in him. They kissed, and Gavin dragged him in closer, glad to have him back where he belonged. Fuck, he felt nice, all wiry muscle and firm ass rubbing close to his cock.

Darby relaxed into him but drew back enough to ask, "What did you tell him about me?"

"That you're a better stonemason than I am."

"You have a better head for business."

"Mmm. I said that, too."

"What?" Darby drew back. "That you have a better head for business?"

"That you're loyal as fuck and it's nice to know I've earned it from you. I said I've been thinking you and I could turn this into a partnership. Partly that was to get his nose out of my business, but it's true. I have been thinking that."

"We can talk about it, but I don't mind working under you. I'm not afraid to tell you when you're wrong."

"I've noticed. That's why I think we could work well as partners. Plus, you're even more of a skinflint than I am. You're willing to live like a gold miner in the bush."

"You inspired me. I want my own house one day." Darby's gaze gleamed with admiration, filling Gavin with a bubble of something like laughter. Pure happiness, maybe.

"What I didn't tell him was that I think you should come live here and buy out Luella. She's talking about going to live with her sister. We can come back to that, though." Gavin's heart lurched as Darby dropped his gaze. He gave Darby's thigh a squeeze. "I've never met anyone I wanted to spend all my time with the way I do with you, you know. I'm not going to fuck around with other men, because you're the one I want. I hope it's the same for you?"

Gavin's heart was in his throat. He felt even more bare-assed than he had the day he'd shown Darby his tickle toys.

"I do," Darby said quietly. "I really do. But I worry I'm not going to be enough for you."

"In what way?" He'd opened up his whole life to Darby. He wouldn't have done that if he didn't think Darby should be part of all of that.

"You know what way."

"All right, lad." Gavin winked one eye closed. "I don't know how you'll react, but let me show you what Terrance brought me."

●●●

Darby didn't know what to expect, but Gavin set him on his feet and went across to pull out his box of toys. He withdrew what looked like a cheap, paper-bound magazine.

"Terrance got himself all the way to New York, over to London and all manner of places on the continent. He persuaded every manner of business to give him money for advertising in his catalogue and charged me three shillings for this." Gavin shook the thin booklet. "But he might finally be onto something. It's full of things men of our persuasion might enjoy and things women use on women. There's even an electric vibrating mechanism with various attachments." Gavin waved to invite Darby onto the bed.

Darby came across, and they settled on their stomachs, the catalogue before them.

"I've heard of dildos," Darby said as he noted a cobbler advertising the making of custom leather ones. "I didn't know where to get one." New York, apparently, but there were glass ones made in Italy and rubber ones that could be ordered from London. "This one has a harness," he noted with excitement, taking the booklet out of Gavin's hands so he could look more closely at the illustration. "I could fuck you with that."

"See? I hoped you'd find this interesting. You want me to suck your cock while you read this?"

Darby eyed him. They'd done that a few times, but Darby still had some self-consciousness about it. "You really want to?"

"I've been horny for days, reading that thing cover to cover. You first, then me."

"Deal." Darby rolled onto his back and lifted his hips to help Gavin pull his pants off.

# CHAPTER FIVE

"Well, who the fuck are you?" Gavin asked as Darby emerged from the water closet, naked but for the harness and the band he liked to wear around his chest.

"I'm the man who's going to fuck you in the ass if you want to get naked and get on that bed." Darby weighed the rubber dildo in his palm.

He'd been wearing a harness with a small leather bulge for weeks and liked the way it made him feel. Gavin had noted it made him walk differently and stand taller. This was a new harness and a bigger dildo, one Gavin assured him he could take. It had arrived yesterday and had taken some fiddling the get everything positioned so it felt right, but Darby was horny as hell now.

Gavin stood and gave himself an adjustment before he began to unbutton his shirt. "Did you put that little plug up your ass?"

"I did. That's why I'm so ready to get inside you. I nearly came walking out here." It was a stern little pinch that made him think of Gavin shoving his finger up his ass when he sucked him off, something he often did, which Darby loved.

"You look really fucking sexy like that."

"Yeah? You want a kiss? Come and get one." Darby was feeling all kinds of cocky.

Gavin dropped his clothes on the way and let Darby pull his head down so he could kiss him hard. Gavin grunted as he sucked on Darby's tongue, and his wide hands roamed across Darby's hips and thighs.

"You're really going to do this?" Gavin sounded drunk with lust.

"You want me to?"

"What do you think?" Gavin looked down at his straining cock where fluid was collecting in its eye.

Darby resisted the urge to taste him and said, "Get one of your toys. I want to make sure this is really good for you."

"You mean you want to kill me?" Gavin grabbed his cock and squeezed it. "Fuck, Darby."

His face was flushed with excitement, though. He got into his box and brought out a stick with a bobble of frayed yarn on the end.

It took them a few minutes to find the position that would work best because Gavin was so much bigger than Darby. He finally settled on his back and tucked his hands behind his knees to draw them up.

Darby greased his dildo and Gavin's exposed arse, then shifted to press the head of the dildo against his hole. As he pressed, Gavin's face contorted.

"Hurt?" he asked.

"A little, but I like it." Gavin's breath was ragged with arousal.

Darby gave a few test thrusts, pleased with the way the dildo glided in and out of Gavin while also stimulating him. There was the press of the dildo's base against his flesh as he thrust in and the pull of the harness around his hips when he withdrew, shifting the plug in his ass. Darby almost forgot the tickle stick, he was so caught up in the sensations of fucking.

When he did trail the yarn over Gavin's chest and down his stomach to the back of his thigh, Gavin shook and swore.

Darby gave a few more thrusts, grazing the soft yarn down his own stomach and against Gavin's balls, teasing both of them. Darby didn't get as worked up as Gavin from tickling, but he liked it. Watching Gavin lose his control was always a thrill, too.

As the tendons in Gavin's neck stood out and his teeth bared, Darby began to move with more purpose. His own arousal intensified. He had to drop the stick and hug Gavin's thigh, leaning in to get the pressure where he wanted it.

Gavin was swearing in sweet agony and gave his cock two pulls, then he was coming, his entire body bucking beneath Darby's quickening thrusts. Darby pushed the dildo deep into him and ground his hips, getting off on all of it, the excitement, the power, the rock of the plug in his ass, the feel of Gavin shivering under him. His whole body clenched, and the release honestly felt as though it transmitted straight down that rubber cock into Gavin's ass.

He was drained after, collapsing on him, shaking with exertion and gratification.

After they caught their breath, they pulled apart. Darby set the harness on the floor and Gavin dried himself with one of the handkerchiefs he kept on the night table for exactly that.

They rolled back together, and Gavin practically smothered Darby, he hugged him so hard and kissed him so deeply.

"Good?" Darby asked as he gasped for air.

"Damn good work for a virgin. You like it?"

"Ass." Darby dug his fingers against Gavin's ribs.

Gavin jerked and let him go, laughing, then gave Darby a taste of his own medicine.

They chuckled and rolled around a minute, wrestling and teasing before they settled down with sighs of contentment.

"Hey, Gav? There's something you should know," Darby said.

"What's that?"

"I think I love you." Darby had expected to feel more naked after that admission, but it felt good to say it.

"I love you, too. Been wanting to say it awhile," Gavin said.

Darby came up on an elbow and leaned to kiss Gavin, long and slow, allowing all the softness inside him to flow out.

Then he asked, "Want to get dressed and go to the pub?"

"I could have a beer."

"I'll go to my room, get cleaned up." Darby slept across the hall now. Or rather, that's where he pretended he slept. He spent most nights in here, where he slept between doing other things with Gavin.

When he got downstairs, Gavin was chatting with Patricia. Luella had gone to Wellington. Patricia cleaned the rooms and looked after their boarders.

"We could go by that site on Queens on our way," Gavin suggested. "I want your thoughts before I finalize their quote."

"We'll probably eat at the pub," Darby told Patricia. "Don't worry about us for tea."

"Have a nice evening, chaps."

They did.

*The End*

# The Rubber Match

*The Rubber Match* is a fun little tale of two men who love to have balloons at their private parties, however modern "looners" will want to know that these men are "poppers." If you prefer your balloons to remain intact, this may not be the story for you. Readers who may be sensitive to this, please take note.

# CHAPTER ONE

*January 1878, Manaus, Brazil (spelled Manaos at the time)*

Joaquim Pinheiros experienced both homesickness and a sense of homecoming when he left the steamship in Manaos. The smell was different, and the Portuguese voices around him were laced with accents and words he didn't comprehend, but monsoon-like rain fell in sheets. The humidity beneath the downpour and the jungled shore was enough like Canacona to give him a pang near his heart.

Maybe it was simple relief at no longer freezing to death in the damp winter of Lisbon.

*Ah, Joki, you're too Indian, not enough Portuguese,* his uncle had teased, then bought him a smart velvet jacket for Christmas.

Joki had packed the jacket into his trunk once he neared the equator and had dug up his lighter one this morning. He pulled it over his bone-colored linen trousers and matching waistcoat, light cotton shirt, and blue silk tie. His cousin in São Paolo had gifted him an umbrella, which Joki opened after leaving instructions with the purser that he would return for his luggage as soon as he found a room.

What he wouldn't give for the leather sandals he wore at home when it was like this. His shoes would be caked in mud before he reached the town square.

Was there a town square? He was given to understand every luxury imaginable was being shipped to Manaos, but like the bicolor water he'd seen as the ship had moved into Rio Negro, this seemed to be a place of contrasts.

Joki had thought his cousin was teasing him when he'd said he would see two rivers running side by side in the same channel, one half of the water creamed coffee, the other dark tea. It had been true, but here it was all black water in the canals.

Someone called from a canoe, asking if he wished to be carried anywhere. Joki declined, uncertain where he was going. When he'd asked his cousin for a map, he'd been met with another laugh. "The land changes every season with the floods."

That was likely why many of these buildings close to shore were only haphazard thatched huts. Perhaps they were washed away by the time the rain let up. He made for the stone cathedral perched on higher ground. It was an instant familiarity to see the bell tower and tall arched windows. His grandmother had worried he would lose his soul, traveling so far from home, but he didn't feel so far away, after all.

The babble of a covered market drew him as much to step out of the rain as to ask for directions. Someone offered him turtle stew; another hawked dried fish. He perused the crates of unfamiliar nuts and fruits, spices and medicine. There was every type of wooden handcraft from spoons to stools, bolts of cotton in arrays of colors, and goods from perfumes to jewelry and clocks.

Women with babies and baskets wove between jabbering men smoking cigars as they struck deals with a handshake. Some wore European clothing with hats and a jacket; most were in some half-dressed version of it. Others were bare foot and wore only a loincloth.

A man caught Joki's eye or, rather, piqued his sexual interest. He had a mature air of thirty or more, definitely older than Joki's twenty-four. His skin was olive beneath his tan, his hair a light brown and cut evenly in a line across his brow. His face was clean-shaven and rugged, giving away little as he dickered with the stall owner.

He wore trousers cut off below the knee and sandals of some unfamiliar material. Rubber? His loose shirt was open at the throat, revealing a necklace of teeth and claws that Joki had no doubt the man had harvested himself. The man's chest was broad and muscled, his stomach and hips flat, his thighs straining the dun color of his pants, all radiating strength and confidence.

Joki swallowed and made himself look away while he tried to ignore the sensation of a vine unfurling in his middle and a more visceral sensation of his cock reaching and lifting.

His preference for men was another reason his grandmother feared for his soul. His uncle was more circumspect, wishing to keep their lands in the family and profitable but willing to be strategic about how that was accomplished.

Joki risked another glance and saw the man exchange a dull, brownish ball the size of a mango for... Were those pale, wrinkled skins *balloons*?

His heart joggled in his chest.

Joki had bought a few in Lisbon that looked like that. He'd pretended they were for his cousin's children, not putting together that he was coming into the rainforest where the material to make balloons was sourced. They really *did* have everything in Manaos, he thought with a private, exhilarated grin.

He watched the man push the balloons into the bag slung over his shoulder, but when Joki lifted his gaze, he discovered the other man had spotted him. He glared a silent, unmistakable, *What the fuck are you staring at?*

That hard look and the fact the man's hand probably smelled like the rubber he'd handled made Joki's cock stand up so hard and fast that his balls hurt.

He had two choices—slink away in guilt, or acknowledge that he'd been staring.

Since he wanted to purchase some balloons himself, he held his folded umbrella in front of his tented trousers and walked straight up to the stranger.

"I wonder if you could direct me to the home of Dom Miguel de Souza?"

The man flicked his gaze down to the muddy cuffs of Joki's linen trousers, hooked on the dripping umbrella, then brought his attention back to Joki's thick brows and trimmed beard.

Joki had spoken in Portuguese but was judged "foreign." He felt it and was annoyed by it even though it was true.

No, he realized just as quickly. This was bitter disappointment at being rebuffed when, for a soaring moment, he'd thought he'd found someone like him. Maybe more like him than anyone could be.

Which was an impossible fantasy that shouldn't have entered his head. His throat constricted, and he shifted his feet as the man continued to glower at him.

Did he not speak Portuguese?

"Senhor, I can tell you where to inquire," the stall owner began, lifting a hand to point.

"My brother-in-law delivers to the casa grandes. He'll know." The object of Joki's lust slapped a soggy hat on his head. It was the same sand-brown color as his pants. The moment he walked into the rain, water drained off the brim in a steady stream down his back.

Joki quickly popped his umbrella open and tried to catch up to the man's long stride. "Would you like—" He tried to hold the umbrella over the other man, but he was taller and didn't seem to care.

"Why did you ask if I know him? Do you think I work for him? I don't. I work for myself."

Joki almost said, *Who?* But his mind caught up. Miguel de Souza, the rubber baron his uncle had told him to meet.

"Are you an aviador? A seringueiro?" If things didn't work out with de Souza, Joki might need one of each.

"Among other things."

"A man of mystery."

Another dark glower came his way.

*I'm not flirting*, Joki wanted to say, but his cheeks stung. He *was* flirting. At least, he was trying to. Failing miserably.

"I'm Joaquim Pinheiros. From Portuguese India, via Lisbon. Call me Joki." He tried to offer his free hand.

His guide cut across in front of him and went into a shop.

Joki came up short, then followed, shaking out his umbrella before he left it on the stoop and entered a cluttered storehouse of dry goods. The sharp scent of spices was layered over a pungent scent Joki recognized as roasting coffee beans.

A child in a loin cloth was squealing, "Tio Andre!"

*Andre.* Joki tucked that away to whisper in his sleep.

Andre picked up the boy and spoke with him in a local language that Joki only followed because the boy tried to peer into Andre's bag.

When he reached in, Joki expected Andre to offer the balloons and experienced a pang that only children were supposed to enjoy them.

Instead, Andre gave the boy a bamboo flute and received a hug in exchange.

The boy ran off, tooting it, while the storekeeper drawled a sarcastic, "Obrigado."

"He's looking for Miguel de Souza." Andre thumbed toward Joki.

"Not taking deliveries this week. Family is away." The storekeeper lifted a negligent shoulder.

"Ah. Unfortunate." Joki had been hoping de Souza would offer accommodation. "Could you recommend where I might let a room until they return? Nothing too expensive." He had to save his funds for the seedlings he hoped to buy.

The storekeeper grimaced. "It's rainy season." He glanced at Andre. "Do you want to give him your room and stay at the house with us?"

Andre's mouth curled with dismay, but to Joki's surprise he asked, "How long are you staying?"

Joki licked his lips and could have sworn Andre noticed, which made Joki's voice falter.

"I-I'm not sure. A few weeks? It will depend on how long it takes me to conduct my business. How big is your room? Could we share it?" *I will suck your cock every single night if you ask me to.*

Andre nodded curtly. "It's upstairs. I'll show you."

• • •

Andre Ruiz wasn't sure what to make of this Joki.

Manaos was overrun by every kind of man these days—investors, escaped slaves and their hunters, migrants from the drought, and immigrants from all corners who set up bakeries and ironworks and tailoring shops. Most new arrivals wore looks of wary shock. Many whimpered about the sticky heat or the rain or whatever snake had curled up on the stoop they could not sit upon.

Joki was clearly an outsider with his accented Portuguese. His clothes spoke of money, as did his connection to one of the wealthiest barons in Manaos, but he amiably followed Andre up the narrow stairs into very crude accommodation.

The simple, one-room sleeper had been occupied by Andre's sister and her husband until they'd built a proper home nearby, where his brother-in-law's mother could live with them and help mind the babies—which was why Andre was not anxious to sleep there. Children rose early, and women asked single men a lot of questions about their plans for the future.

But his sister was expecting again and could use the extra income. Andre paid for the use of this room in favors and security and whatever he hunted or foraged. He could still do that if he shared it with Joki, he rationalized. It would provide a win-win for all.

Especially if Joki was the sort of man he thought he was.

"It's primitive," he warned as he opened the door and showed Joki in, expecting a cringe. There was a sink with a drain but no tap. The cupboards and dishes were well-used, the floor stained, and the walls unpainted. The only light came through the single window. There was a small table, two chairs, and his bed was a hammock hung from the two posts that held up the roof. The roof needed replacing as soon as the rain let up.

"Stove and water closet are downstairs." He went across to tap his toe against the bucket collecting the roof leak. "Running water is here."

"Ha." Joki had a wide smile with sharp corners that showed all his teeth. It was engaging, especially when his eyes lit up with the thrill of adventure. "Do you have another hammock?"

"Doesn't take long to make one."

"Perfect. If you'll have me, I'll stay." Joki's infectious grin was the same one he had offered Andre in the middle of a private moment at the market.

Andre's heart had stopped when he'd looked up to realize his purchase had been noted. It had caused the same flash of threat he experienced when he came face-to-face with a jaguar or other animal that could eat him.

Then he'd realized Joki was *interested*. Andre still wasn't sure if he was embarrassed or pleased by the sparks of heat that were coming to life in his crotch. He tended to keep his fucking away from Manaos, since his sister had to live here and the church took a grim view of men who liked men.

Andre leaned his shoulder on the thick post, taking a more deliberate look at his new roommate. Joki was smaller in stature than Andre but not delicate. Wiry and agile-looking. His black hair held a charming curl on the ends, and his face darkened as he withstood Andre's unabashed perusal. His thick cock was resting against the front of his trousers, and this time he was making little effort to hide it.

Andre's cock twitched in response.

"Don't you want to know what it will cost you?" he asked.

Joki squeezed the back of his neck and flushed even more. "I guess I should have asked."

Andre gave him a figure he thought was fair.

"I can afford that." Joki nodded, but an air of expectancy filled the room. "Are you...comfortable with this arrangement?"

"Sharing my nights with another man? Yes." Andre looked straight into his soul. "I'm very comfortable with that."

Joki's breath left him. He licked his lips so they were shiny as they formed a silent, "Fuck."

A spear of sexual need struck behind his balls. Andre let his crooked grin pull at the side of his mouth. "Need help with your luggage?"

# CHAPTER TWO

J oki detoured back into the market on their way to the dock. He purchased a pair of sandals from the rubber stall, "And six balloons." He was aware of Andre staring holes through him as he did.

"For my young cousins in São Paolo," Joki said, meeting Andre's gaze without flinching. *Ask me what they're really for. I dare you.*

It was dangerous to tease this man. Andre had the sort of dominant personality that told Joki he would be fucked and fucked hard when it happened, but his knees were weak with anticipation of it.

He was equally titillated by the feel of the rubber skin moving against the powder inside it as he rolled an empty balloon sack between his finger and thumb. Apparently, he was going to spend all day hard as a stone pestle, aroused by every single thing around him.

"How are these made?" Joki asked the stall owner as he finished his purchase. Until Lisbon, he'd only seen the balloons he had to assemble himself, gluing two sheets of rubber together. These were all one piece with a rolled lip for inflating. Their pear shape and uniformity made them much more beguiling than the ones he was used to.

"Trade secret." The man tapped the side of his nose and eyed Andre. "I have to protect my business."

"Fair enough." Joki negotiated a price for a gross and promised to pick them up in a few days, getting another look from Andre as they carried on to the dock.

"How many cousins do you have?"

Joki snorted and asked, "Do *you* know how they're made?"

"Dipped on a form," Andre said begrudgingly. "He won't tell me what's added to keep the rubber supple, though."

Supple. *Yesss.* Joki nearly groaned aloud, thinking how much he enjoyed that give and resistance when he fondled an inflated balloon. His throat grew hot thinking of it. The balloons he'd just bought were burning a hole in his pocket, keeping the heat baking in his groin.

He swallowed and glanced up self-consciously, afraid his predilections were written all over his face.

Andre was watching him and glanced away, profile unreadable, but rather than a hitch of fear that his arousal had been observed, Joki's sense of anticipation intensified.

They retrieved his things and started back to the storehouse.

"It's not very heavy," Andre remarked of the trunk they carried between them. "What's that for?" He nodded at the Wardian case in Joki's free hand.

Rainwater streamed off the house-shaped box made from framed glass. There was a tray in the bottom deep enough to hold dirt and small root balls.

"My uncle wishes for us to try a rubber plantation at home."

"Good luck. They die on plantations," Andre said flatly. "It's been tried, and they catch disease when they're planted too close together. Plus, you need a lot more than that will hold to tap any quantity."

"We'll start small, see if we can get them to take. My uncle is an avid reader of scientific papers and market projections. We share ownership of the land, and he financed this trip to retrieve what he has arranged for me to buy, so…"

"Understood."

"Would you be in trouble for associating with me if that's my purpose?"

"Only if it works."

Joki snorted, liking Andre's dry sense of humor.

They dropped his belongings in their room, both soaked to

the skin from their walk.

Andre said, "Dry off. I'll ask my sister if she'll make the hammock for you. If not, I'll get the rope and we'll make it up before we find something to eat."

"Thank you." Joki removed his soaked jacket and hung it on the hook near the door, checking that the door latched closed behind Andre.

Dare he risk it? He took out one of the balloons and touched it to his lips.

•••

Andre's sister, Ines, had just arrived to pick up her son. She promised to have the hammock ready by bedtime, allowing Andre to go straight back up the stairs.

He didn't bother knocking. It was his room.

Joki had stripped off his wet things and hung them on the hooks. He sat on the floor, back against the wall, wearing only knee-length cotton drawers tied low across his hips. He had one knee bent up, hiding his lap.

He was four or five breaths into blowing up a balloon. He pinched the neck and removed it from his mouth, flushed beneath the brown of his complexion.

"I wanted to see how big they get," he said, guilty tension sitting across his cheekbones.

"So, see." Andre closed the door and leaned on it, crossing his arms over his chest. He had thought they would wait until dark, when his brother-in-law was no longer downstairs and possibly able to hear them, but here they were.

And he really wanted to know if Joki was as titillated by balloons as he was.

After a brief pause, Joki cupped the bottom of the growing sphere and brought the neck to his lips. He set a kiss there. His cheeks rounded, his chest swelled, then he released his breath into it. The balloon grew.

Andre bit his lip.

He didn't know why this got him so hard. His first sexual encounter had been with his cheek pressed to a balloon, so that probably had something to do with it. The smell and tackiness of a freshly inflated balloon was enough to make him horny any day. He'd found a bubble of dried caucho on a tree once, soon after he'd been given his own trail of trees. He'd cooked it solid and played with it for two days before it burst. At times, he'd set it against his lips and tongued it, imagining it was the tip of a cock, driving himself wild with his imaginings. He still did the same thing with balloons, jacking so hard his come shot clear across the tapping shack.

Sometimes he got to fuck actual men, and that was fantastic, but the one time he'd suggested playing with a balloon while they played with each other, he'd been firmly shut down. His partner's reaction had told Andre that sex between men wasn't as unnatural as the church wanted them to believe, but sex with balloons was definitely a step beyond.

He'd been embarrassed and discreet about it ever since.

But as Joki's chest swelled again, preparing to exhale into the balloon, Andre knew he'd met his match. Joki was holding his gaze in a blatantly sexual way, as though his mouth was pulling on Andre's cock rather than blowing into the balloon.

Andre thought he might come just watching him, but he wanted more.

"That's enough," Andre said, voice rasped with arousal. "Let me see."

Joki held up the balloon. It was a translucent yellowish silver, the imperfections in the rubber's thickness giving its skin a subtle swirling pattern. Joki's unsteady hand caused it to bob ever so slightly.

"And." Andre jerked his chin to indicate Joki's knee. Joki straightened his leg and revealed the way he was tenting his light cotton drawers. His brown chest was thick with hair that ran all the way to his stomach where his navel was creased by his slouched seat against the wall. There was a damp stain where his cock was leaking with excitement.

He was a fucking fantasy come true.

Andre came across and took the melon-sized balloon. As he tied it off, he asked gruffly, "Let me watch?"

Joki's eyelids fluttered in reaction. He opened his drawstring and pushed the waistband down to reveal a very hard cock of admirable proportions, dark and thick with an ample nest of hair coating his balls. He spread his legs as he lifted and cupped his balls, squeezing the base of his cock in the ring of his finger and thumb. A pearl of white appeared on his dark, bulbous tip.

As Joki began to run his loose fist up and down his shaft, Andre dug his fingers into the swollen shape of the balloon, testing how much pressure it could bear.

Joki dragged his heavy-lidded gaze up to his. "Don't pop it. Not yet."

"I won't." Andre opened his own trousers and worked one-handed to free his aching cock from his own drawers.

Joki groaned and crushed the purple head of his cock.

"Shh," Andre chided. "He'll hear you downstairs." He cradled the base of his cock in one hand and balanced the balloon on its length.

The diameter of the balloon was a little wider than his cock was long, but Joki looked up at him with adoration as he came onto his knees and pressed his forehead into the balloon, tongue searching.

The first flick of Joki's tongue across the taut point on the underside of Andre's tip was whip sharp, searing Andre's whole body in a hot-cold shiver of exquisite pleasure. His cock hardened even more. It swelled and *reached* for Joki's tongue.

As the balloon compressed dangerously against his belly, Andre distantly wondered how he had thought this was a good idea, but it was so erotic, he let it continue.

Joki leaned in, one hand clenching the back of Andre's thigh for balance. His lips worked to capture and encircle the head of his cock, prevented by the balloon from taking more than the tip. He suckled and pulled, hot and wet, while his tongue continued to swirl and dig into his hole.

*Fuck, fuck, fuck.* Andre wanted to growl and roar. His balls were nearly inside out they were gathered up so tight. He wanted to pump his hips and drive himself down Joki's throat, but the balloon was already compressed dangerously. It cushioned the small bounce of his hips while threatening to burst if he became too aggressive. The rubber caught a few of his pubic hairs, pulling painfully, but that only heightened his excitement as Joki tilted his head, eager to suck in more of his cock. As much as he could get.

Joki was making noises deep in his chest, a hum that Andre longed to feel if he could only get himself far enough into Joki's throat. Joki shifted, dropping his drawers and splaying his knees as he jerked himself. He had the whole of Andre's cockhead in his tight lips and was sucking so hard, he was threatening to pluck the tip right off. Andre felt the tingle starting in his lower back.

"I'm going to come," Andre rasped as he stroked Joki's tense neck and felt his shoulder shaking with how fast he was pounding himself.

When Joki's breath began to hiss and his shoulders only went stiff and still, Andre quit holding back. He gritted his teeth to lock his voice in his chest and gripped Joki's shoulder. His come erupted, burning a path from his balls up his shaft to shoot deep into Joki's mouth.

Which was when Joki grabbed Andre's ass in two hands and shoved his mouth so far onto Andre's pulsing, throbbing cock, the balloon burst between them with a loud bang.

# CHAPTER THREE

"*Fuck!* Are you hurt?" Andre jerked back, pulling his cock free of Joki's suctioning lips, dragging a long thread of come with it. He rubbed his belly beneath the fall of his shirt. "That stung *me*."

"Andre?" a male voice called from the bottom of the stairs.

Andre sent the door such a wild look of horror and astonishment, Joki couldn't help his burst of unfettered laughter.

Andre tried to put his cock away as he crossed to the door. He paused to give a disgusted look at his hand, which was covered in come and had fragments of torn rubber in it.

That was even more comical. When he shouted at the closed door without opening it, yelling, "I dropped something. It's fine," Joki lost it altogether.

He fell onto his back on the floor, laughing so hard he clutched his belly, nearly crying.

Andre came to stand over him, looking every bit as thunderous and imposing as he had the first moment Joki had seen him.

But he'd just come in Joki's mouth while a balloon burst between them. That was riotously funny and filled Joki with giddy gratification.

"Idiot," Andre muttered, but he crouched to catch at Joki's chin, forcing his face to turn this way and that. "Did it cut you?"

"No." He absently touched his cheekbone where a burning sensation lingered. "Stung, but I closed my eyes." He was struggling to catch enough breath to speak, and he sighed with indulgence as Andre released him. He sagged bonelessly onto the floor and threw his arm over his head. "That was the most exciting thing I've ever done. Thank you."

"I thought I'd been shot," Andre muttered as he straightened and walked away.

Joki dissolved into fresh belly laughs. "You did not."

"I did not," Andre agreed, mouth curled in a dry smirk as he came back with a cloth that he swept across the smear on Joki's hip and the floor. "Thank *you*. It was exciting." He rinsed the cloth in the bucket and hung it over the edge of the sink to dry. He came back with a bottle of clear alcohol. "Cachaça?"

Joki had tried the fermented sugarcane juice at his cousin's. He sat up to sip the potent liquor straight from the bottle and handed it back. He was close enough to his trunk he was able to retrieve clean drawers without rising. He changed, then shifted so he was next to where Andre had lowered to sit with his back to the wall. Andre took a pull off the bottle, then handed it to Joki again.

"You're sure you're not hurt?" He touched two fingertips to the spot Joki would wear like a brand of honor if it had cut him and scarred, but it was only a tiny welt. "I didn't expect you to do that, or I would have moved it out of the way."

"I was trying to make it pop. I'm glad it did." He took another smug sip. "I've never met anyone else who liked balloons. A man, I mean. Who likes all the same things I do." He met his gaze to underscore what he meant.

"Me, either." Andre still looked a little disturbed by what they'd done.

Joki wanted to kiss him but only leaned enough to nudge him playfully with his shoulder before sitting straight again.

"I was wrestling with another boy over a balloon once," Andre said. "He pinned me beneath him. I had my arms around it." He ducked his head as he demonstrated how he'd hugged the balloon. "You know what it's like when you're young. Everything makes you hard, and I already knew I preferred boys. I was so aroused when it happened, I could never see a balloon again without going stiff at the sight of it."

"I can't remember not getting hard from them." Joki let his

head fall back on the wall. "I was very young when my uncle rubbed one into my belly. We were both laughing, but as you say, it took nothing to cause an erection, and I was in ecstasy. A few years later, I was given a kit to make my own, and the smell and the feel of it... I couldn't keep my hands off my cock. Gave myself my first orgasm that day."

"And today was your second?" Andre handed him the bottle.

"Mmm, yes." Joki chuckled, then sipped, but didn't take much because he was growing drunk enough that he set the bottle aside and shifted without thinking, forcing Andre to straighten his legs so Joki could straddle his thighs. He braced his arm on the wall next to Andre's head and leaned in to kiss along the other man's jaw, dabbling his tongue against his ear.

Andre's breath caught.

"Do you still like to be mounted?" Joki whispered.

"Not as much as I like to mount." Andre's hands cupped Joki's ass and squeezed, then dragged him deeper into his lap.

Joki melted onto him, pressing his mouth over Andre's.

Andre rubbed his back and kissed him with the sort of dominant self-assurance Joki had instinctually known the man possessed. His tongue swept in, and his hands squeezed Joki's muscles the way he'd groped the balloon, testing the resilience.

Andre broke their kiss. "But once I'm inside this ass, I don't want my brother-in-law shouting up the stairs. So, get dressed, pretty boy. I'll buy you a meal and some cocoa butter."

●●●

They spent a few hours moving in and out of the rain. Andre helped Joki get his bearings in the flooded, crooked streets by using the igarapé, the river that cut through the city, as a focal point. They stopped and listened to music while drinking cachaça watered down with lime juice before Andre got the direction to the de Souza home and took Joki past it so a servant could confirm that yes, the family were in Rio and were expected back in a week or so.

They found a free table on the covered veranda of a hotel, where Andre ordered two plates of grilled ox fish with beans, rice, and manioc.

"Ox? I don't eat beef," Joki said.

"It swims in the river."

Joki was skeptical but agreed to try it.

"Tell me more about why you're here," Andre prompted.

"My uncle is aware of the problems the British had in getting tree seeds to sprout. The long journey seemed to rot them. He thought if I took seedlings to India, I might have better luck. Through his connections in Lisbon, he arranged for Miguel de Souza to start them. I'll transport them home in the box you saw. I have a second case in the bottom of my trunk."

"In the jungle, they like to have space. It will be several years before you can tap, you know. Eight or ten maybe."

"I'll write to you when they're ready. Ask you to come and show me how it's done."

Andre snorted, never once having considered leaving the jungle, but he was curious enough to ask, "What's it like where you live?"

"Not unlike this. Sometimes. We have monsoons for a few months, then it's sunny and hot, but we're close enough to the sea that we have a little breeze. We have monkeys." He nodded at the one that reached out of the dark to steal a morsel from another patron's plate. "The birds sound different, but we have crocodiles and snakes and all the insects and fevers my relatives in Lisbon warned might kill me here."

"Jaguars?"

"Tigers." Joki showed his teeth. "I have a skin from the one I shot because it was patrolling our village, taking livestock and stalking children. It's longer than my arms." Joki stretched them out.

For some bloodthirsty reason, Andre was aroused by Joki taking out such a dangerous predator. He badly wanted to lean across and kiss his arrogantly pursed lips. He sipped his drink instead.

"You own land?"

Joki nodded. "Several hundred acres. We grow mango and cashew, coffee, cardamom. Some of it is salt fields. Some pineapple. The rice hasn't been doing well. That's why my uncle wants to try rubber. You?"

"I have a license for a seringal of nine estradas. Two thousand trees or so. My father worked it with a few other families when he was alive. Taught me. My mother and sister were there to farm and forage while we tapped and smoked, so we never relied on aviators for our supplies. It's more of a struggle as a single man, but the aviators take advantage. That's how families wind up indentured."

"And when it's like this and you can't tap?"

"I hunt with my mother's relatives. She was Mura. She's gone, too. Yellow fever. But there's a market for nearly anything if you're willing to go into the jungle and drag it out. I fetch what's available, and that keeps me solvent and able to supply myself when I go back in to tap." He shrugged, not beholden to an uncle or anyone else. It was the way he liked it.

"I lost my parents, too. My grandmother raised me, and my uncle came and went. He's my father's brother, so he owns half the land, but his wife doesn't like India. That's why I had to go to Lisbon to see him. Oh, shit. I should have told you." Joki blinked. "It's still so new, I genuinely forgot," he said with a choked laugh but an earnest look of apology.

"What?"

"I'm married."

Andre sat back, more surprised by the fact he was annoyed than actually surprised. He'd fucked married men before. He hid his preference himself, so he didn't judge those who were pressured to marry despite having other desires.

Even so, he was struck by an unusual possessiveness that didn't make sense given he'd met Joki mere hours ago. His new lover was only here for a short time, so he really shouldn't get attached.

"You're angry I didn't tell you before we..." He didn't finish.

"No." Not at Joki. At himself for reacting so strongly to something that shouldn't be affecting him at all.

"My uncle has a namorada." Joki poked at his food with his fork. "Shortly after I arrived in Lisbon, she learned she was carrying his child. My uncle has always suspected my inclination, so he asked me to marry her. He has no children with his wife. I'm his heir. This way his child can inherit through me." He shrugged.

"Is she an opportunist?"

"My wife?" Joki smirked at saying the word. "No more than anyone else. She's closer to your age than mine and will stay in Lisbon with her mother until the baby is born. He'll bring them out next year."

"Hmph." Andre leaned forward to take up eating his own meal again. "Does that bother you? Being pushed into marrying and taking on the responsibility of his child?"

"No. I like children. It was bothering me that I wasn't likely to have any."

Andre hadn't given much thought to it. His sister and her children were enough family that he felt no deep voids or needs for his own.

"It does bother me a little now," Joki said with a frown of reflection. His eyes looked as dark as the river, the candlelight glowing as a single tiny spark there. "If I didn't have obligations at home and to them, I might have lingered here."

His tone of regret at their limited time squeezed the air in Andre's lungs. He tended to face what was before him and not look too far into the future. Men came and went, and he never formed more than a convivial regard, but Joki was different.

Special. Joki already knew something about him no one else did.

And that made their short-lived time together something not to be squandered.

"Are you finished eating?" Andre asked. "Because I'm ready to go."

# CHAPTER FOUR

Andre looped his arm around Joki's waist from behind as they entered the room above the storehouse. He dragged Joki back into his bigger body with a crash. His hot mouth opened on the tendon where Joki's neck met his shoulder. His cock was already hard and prodding Joki's ass.

Joki's knees nearly gave out.

"Longest fucking goodnight of my life." Andre's muffled words referred to the five-minute conversation they'd had with Andre's brother-in-law moments ago. He'd been locking up as they returned.

Joki chuckled, then strangled on pleasure as Andre made sucking noises against the side of his neck, likely pulling marks that his dark skin may or may not hide. Andre's teeth closed on his earlobe.

"Want me to fuck you?" Andre ran his hand across Joki's chest, flicking his thumb across Joki's hardened nipples, back and forth.

Joki let the bundled hammock they'd picked up on their way home slither out of his weakened arms. "Oh, yes."

Andre's hand went down Joki's front to squeeze his hard cock through his trousers. "You really do. Get undressed."

Andre moved to light the lantern on the table, setting his bag on a chair before he pawed through it. He came up with the jar of cocoa butter they'd bought along with a handful of balloons.

"You know oil makes them pop?"

"Yeah." Joki had made that mistake before.

They both stripped off their wet clothes and hung them. Joki stepped into Andre's big frame, shivering with pleasure as their cool, damp skin adhered and their hard cocks brushed. They kissed, hot and deep. Andre's ass was firm and round against his palming hands, his tongue quick to battle with his own.

"Quit distracting me. I've got plans for you. Come here." He moved Joki closer to the sink and fetched a balloon. He came back and went to his knees in front of Joki, admiring Joki's cock, fondling him and getting familiar, thumb riding in the crease down one side of his balls, fist stroking and giving a nice squeeze.

When he leaned forward to roll his lips and tongue over him, licking down his shaft and blowing on his balls, Joki groaned and planted his feet wider.

"No. Keep them closer." He tapped his ankle so there was only the width of his hand between Joki's knees. He very tenderly nestled the empty balloon sack between Joki's thighs.

"Oh, *fuck*." Joki squeezed the end of his cock. He was going to come. *Right now.*

Andre chuckled. "Stay still. Don't come."

If it burst and stung his balls...

Joki moaned with helpless joy, and Andre hadn't even started yet. What the hell was wrong with him that he was just as excited to watch Andre's mouth purse and feel his cheek brush the top of his thigh when he set his lips against the opening of the balloon as he had been when Andre had licked him?

Andre blew. The balloon became solid between his thighs. With each hissing breath, the pressure increased, filling up the space toward his balls. Joki started to shake. It was a balloon, for fuck's sake, but he barely had the strength to stand still. His legs were so shaky, only the tacky dampness of his skin kept the thing lodged there.

The thin wall of rubber pressed upward to touch his balls, pushing into them with dangerous warning.

"It's going to break." *He* was. His hand had been clenched over his cock, trying to ease the ache, but he began to jerk himself.

"Don't. Not yet." Andre brushed his hand off his cock. His knuckles brushed Joki's bobbing erection as he tied off the balloon. "Can you turn? Put your hands on the back of the sink."

It was a tiny maneuver, one that shifted the balloon so it rubbed and pulled the hairs on his balls and inner thighs. As Joki bent to reach the far edge of the sink, Andre straightened to stand behind him.

"That's something to see." He roamed his touch over the back of Joki's thighs, his ass, and the balloon, making the tiniest reverberations go through the inflated skin into Joki's balls.

Joki could hear his own ragged breaths filling the room, declaring his excitement.

"If you move too much, you're either going to lose the balloon or the butter will drip and pop it, so stay nice and still. Hear me?" Andre gave his ass a playful pat.

"You're a fucking monster." At this rate, he was liable to fall in love with him.

Andre chuckled and fetched the butter. He took out a generous gob and adhered it to Joki's lower back. Then he took a smaller portion that he rubbed between his hands to melt it. He began massaging it into Joki's ass, teasing him with the tip of his finger but making him wait for penetration. He gave him lots of time to enjoy the sensation of the balloon compressing and expanding between his thighs as he was fondled and greased.

"How often do you get fucked?" Andre's finger finally probed, making Joki tremble.

"Not often enough. Never like this." He could hardly speak.

Andre paused to take more butter. He pushed his finger in deep, pulled it out, worked in two. "I hope you like it slippery. I do. Yeah, it's already running onto the balloon."

"Then fuck me already."

"Soon." Andre kept fingering him, deliberately tapping a place inside Joki that was making his cock weep a string of fluid onto the floor.

"I think I'm going to come. Or cry. Or something," Joki warned, so aroused he felt drunk on it.

Andre's hands left him, and Joki glanced back to see Andre was coating his cock in butter, and that was a sight all in itself, watching his fist work over that thick muscle and leave it gleaming and sleek.

"Ready?"

"Fuck, yes."

Andre stepped behind him and leaned in, cock searching for his arsehole.

"When that thing bursts, we're both going to feel it. Aren't we?"

"Good. You deserve it." Joki's voice garbled into a groan as the thick head of Andre's cock pressed with determination, forcing his way in, wide and slippery and hot. The deep ache intensified as his hips came flush with Joki's ass.

Joki's stomach rippled in tense reaction. The balloon shifted and strained, pushing higher against his thighs and balls as Andre's weight pressed on it from behind.

"I really am going to come," Joki gasped. *And cry.* He was so overcome with excitement and arousal and apprehension that the balloon would burst, his eyes were damp and his throat felt scorched and thick. He held himself very still, shaking with the effort to do so.

"Can you wait for me?" Andre reached around to squeeze his cock in a grip that bordered on pain. "You want me to fuck you soft or hard?"

"Hard." He was dying. "If it pops, keep going."

Andre's teeth scraped against his shoulder again. "I think I might have to keep you, Joki. You're too perfect."

He withdrew and thrust back in with undeniable power.

The balloon relaxed and swelled between his thighs while the rest of Joki shuddered under the impact. His cock quivered so hard he thought it would split in two.

As Andre pulled back and slapped back into him, the sensations rippled up to Joki's scalp and down to the soles of his feet.

"Yes?"

"*Yes.*" But oh fuck oh fuck, he was going to rip this sink off the wall. "Bust me in half."

Andre's hands bit into his hips, and he started thrusting hard and fast, stomach and thighs slapping into his skin, plumping the balloon while striking his cock against the bell inside him that rang pleasure through Joki in loud peals.

As he sped up and their flesh slapped louder, their sweat mingled with the butter. Slippery trickles ran into the space between their thighs so they were messy and greasy and groaning loudly at how good it was.

The balloon was going to pop. Joki knew it. The skin would be thinning by now. It was going to happen; he knew it. Any second. *Oh, fuck.* He was trying to hold on, trying to keep it between his thighs, squeezing to hold it in place—

The explosion happened with a bang that sent a lacerating pain across his balls, snapping his control. His come left him as though shot from a cannon, making his stomach ache with the force of it. It burned deliciously as it pumped out in throbbing spurts while Andre shouted and thrust deep, holding tight to him while filling his ass with his own searing load.

•••

Andre had never had the sort of companion who was not only amusing and willing to hop into a canoe for a soggy trip into the jungle to hunt tapir, but also eager to fuck while playing the most delightfully filthy games with balloons.

They didn't always use them. It was nice to lazily suck each other off before starting their day or stroke each other against a tree under a dripping canopy of green.

It was also amusing to lie in a hammock with a balloon between them, kissing and playing with each other's cock, feeling the balloon shift and breathe with their own increasing pants and tension, seeing if they could keep it from popping before they did.

One night, Andre blew up enough balloons to fill Joki's hammock, then had him lay on his back across them. Andre had stood beside it, drew Joki's ankles to his shoulders, and hooked his fingers in the strings of the hammock to fuck him in a long, endless sway.

"It feels like I'm on a cloud," Joki had said dreamily.

He'd made a memorable picture splayed out like that, blissful in his debauchery. The air had been laden with the smell of rubber and their mingled scent, the rain a soothing patter. Andre really did want to keep him forever.

It wasn't meant to be, however. On their tenth day of what Joki was jokingly calling his honeymoon, they received a message that the de Souza family had returned.

"I'll help you carry the cases over," Andre offered.

"I was only going to talk to him to see what he has, but come along if you want."

He did want. Andre was growing protective of a man who didn't need it. Joki was young but also resourceful and self-assured, undaunted by the challenges of life here.

Barons, however, were notoriously willing to exploit whomever they could if there was a chance of improving profits on sugar, coffee, rubber, or whatever else was viable. Like many coming into Manaos, even the wealthy were fleeing the drought in the east. Many of the cotton and cattle barons had brought their laborers here and were snapping up great tracts of untouched jungle. They pushed farmers and slaves onto tapping trails as quickly as they could cut them, then held them hostage with overseers and a supply boat that overcharged for meat and rice while underpaying for the rubber they collected.

Miguel de Souza proved himself to be exactly that. He mentioned striking a deal in Rio to bring in more labor by May and quickly assessed Andre as a knowledgeable local.

"I need an aviador. I can make it worth your while," de Souza offered.

"I have my own seringal."

"And soon you will, too, hmm?" He smiled at Joki as he invited them through his villa of marble floors, past a piano and a harp, through a door of mahogany "crafted in Italy," and out to a long shed built against a stable.

It didn't escape Andre's notice that Joki was not particularly impressed by the wealth that confronted them. He and de Souza seemed to have a comfortable affinity. Whereas de Souza had been quick to offer Andre employment, he treated Joki as an equal, mentioning trade opportunities and offering introductions with various go-betweens.

"Here we are. My botanist had such success I told him to keep at it. Whatever you don't take, someone else will." He let them into a shed where two long lines of tables were topped with flat wooden trays holding a few inches of dirt. From each one, a half dozen seedlings sprouted, all healthy and forming their third and fourth groups of leaves.

"I'm going to need that second case," Joki said facetiously to Andre.

"You're going to need a lot of fresh water." Andre walked down the aisle between the plants, considering their height and how best to keep them alive for weeks on the sea. Andre couldn't give Joki advantageous introductions, but he could help him succeed in the mission that had brought him here.

Behind him, Miguel was saying he would take a down payment and allow Joki's uncle to forward the balance if Joki took more seedlings than originally negotiated.

"Leave this with me for a few days while I discuss arrangements with the shipping company," Joki requested and shook the man's hand.

As they made their way down to the steamship office, Joki was quiet.

Andre was trying not to dwell on the fact that his lover was preparing to leave him. Rather, he threw himself into those arrangements to help reconcile himself to the reality of it.

"Are you worried how much the ships will charge for storing or using fresh water? I have an idea. Rather than use the glass case, cover the trays with slatted wooden tops—something to let in a little light. They don't need much. They're used to being on the jungle floor. Make it strong enough you can stack them and tall enough to fit water-filled balloons under the lid. They won't disturb the seedlings too much. They might even stabilize them. You can prick one every few days to let the water dribble down. You may not even have to open the lids to do it."

Joki frowned up at him. "Is that what *you're* thinking about? How quickly to get me on my way?" He made an impatient noise and brushed his hand through the air. "I can visit the dock by myself. You don't have to escort me everywhere like I'm a child."

"No? You're acting like one." Joki really was a part of de Souza's world. *Prick.*

Joki's ridiculously long eyelashes were catching rainwater. He blinked fast over an angry glare and walked away.

# CHAPTER FIVE

I t was a brilliant idea, damn him. Joki was still hurt that Andre
didn't seem to care that he would leave soon, but he had to
be grateful for Andre's excellent suggestion on how to transport
the seedlings.

From the moment the message had come that de Souza was
back, Joki's heart had been growing heavier. It had stung when
Andre seemed to effectively hand him his coat. Did the things
they'd done together, to each other, not matter to him at all?

In the past, Joki had had the occasional one-time tryst, but
he'd only had two real lovers before, one of them a fumbling
crush who had rightly leaped on a chance to study at Oxford
and left abruptly. The other had been a cook on a ship who had
romanced and seduced Joki the first week of every month for a
year before disappearing without a word.

He had learned it was best to keep his emotions from
becoming too involved, but he and Andre shared more than a
desire for men. They liked *balloons*. Joki had never revealed that
to anyone. It forged a stronger than usual connection between
him and Andre.

They had different lives, he knew, but they had a similar
sensibility and outlook. Andre tended to be more serious and
direct and stubborn, but he had a tender, thoughtful side. That's
why he was trying to find a practical solution to Joki's very real
problem. Joki realized it was actually a very caring gesture that
Andre was trying to help him succeed.

*Damn it.*

The shipping company promised to reserve Joki their largest
stateroom—one with several windows. They gave him the ap-
proximate dimensions so he could plan how many crates would fit.

When he picked up his balloon order at the market, he was told where to source cheap lumber and the labor to build the crates. He stopped at the mill and was assured that with so many hands waiting around Manaos for the rain to let up, his wooden boxes could be made within two or three days and the cost would not be prohibitive.

With no excuses left to stay out, he went back to the storehouse, half expecting his things to be sitting in the rain on the stoop. They weren't.

Andre was home. He wore only his drawers as had become their habit when they were relaxing here. He sat sideways in the chair with his back to the wall, his arms on the chair back and the table, the bottle of cachaça in his hand.

"I was being an asshole," Joki admitted and threw an offering of loose balloons onto the table before stripping his wet clothes. "I like it here. It pisses me off that I have to leave."

"You like being *here*?" Andre used the neck of his bottle to indicate their rough accommodation. "What sort of house do you live in at home? One like de Souza's?" He narrowed his eyes with suspicion.

"Not *that* grand." But grand enough. "When my grandmother was a child, her family was very big. Additions were made." Then his uncle's wife had tried to bring it up to her aristocratic standards when she'd lived there, adding a number of new, luxury touches.

"You have several hundred acres, you told me. Your uncle owns a house in Lisbon and paid for your journey to see him there and come here and go home. What could you possibly like about being *here*, Joki?"

"Now *you're* being an asshole." He stripped out of wet drawers and hung them before shaking out the ones he'd rinsed this morning and hung to dry. They were still damp, which usually made them a blessed coolness as he pulled them on, but he left them on the hook and came across to take the bottle.

Andre gave it up easily. He hadn't had much from it. He was morose, not drunk.

Maybe Joki should take some comfort from that. He took a pull of the bottle, then gave it back.

"I like being with you." He nudged his foot against Andre's outstretched and crossed ankles. "Is that so hard to believe? Is this"—he motioned between them and flicked at the balloons—"so common in your life that you don't wish we could prolong it?"

"No one gets a long, happy life, especially if you're a man like we are."

"Fuck. Whoever made you believe that? Even if you don't, isn't that all the more reason to hang on to happy times when you can?" Joki picked up the cocoa butter and straightened his sheet in the bottom of his hammock before rolling into it. "Come here."

Andre seemed to debate a moment before he rose and shot the bolt he'd installed on the door the day after Joki had moved in. As he arrived at the side of the hammock, he dropped his drawers.

"No balloons?" Joki asked.

"No. Just you. Roll that way."

Joki turned away, and Andre joined him with the ease of a life spent climbing in and out of such contraptions. The hammock swayed as they rearranged themselves into a half spoon with Joki half on his back beneath Andre as he loomed over him. Andre's cock was hardening against Joki's hip.

They kissed and Andre ran his hands all over him, reminding, "Shh," when Joki let a moan slip free.

"I can't help it," Joki whispered, cupping his face. "You make me feel so good."

Especially when he was like this. Most times they fell on each other like animals, and Joki *loved* it when they were both at their limit, fucking rough and hard. That was glorious, and the ensuing aches and pains later were a delightful reminder of their passion.

This, though, was more than passion. When Andre touched him like this, thorough and tender and hungry, Joki felt wanted in a way that made his throat hot. He felt *loved*.

When they were both greased and shaking, Joki rolled away and Andre spooned him to slip inside him. He reached over Joki's head to tangle his fingers in the rope. His toes curled on mesh near Joki's ankle, and Andre used his leverage to pull himself deep and tight into Joki's ass. The ropes creaked, and they swayed.

"You're giving me a thing for fucking in hammocks," Andre whispered against his ear. "You know that, don't you?"

"Not a thing for Indian men?"

"No one will ever compare to you. Fuck, you feel good." He surged inside him again, hairy chest rubbing his back, thighs hard and slippery where they were woven with his own.

*What could you possibly like about being* here, *Joki?*

How did he even need to ask?

●●●

They didn't argue again, but Andre had lost his ability to laugh easily or even say much of anything at all.

He'd been angry with Joki that day they'd parted in the rain. Then he had come back to the crude room that he *charged* Joki to sleep in despite the fact they were fucking.

Andre wasn't poor, but he didn't have much—a little rainy-day money and the right to work his ass off collecting caucho for half the year. He'd been so embarrassed by the time Joki came home, it had been hard to look at him.

Joki didn't hold his mood or his lesser circumstances against him. He always seemed willing to offer more than Andre would think to ask for, and it made Andre want to do more for him.

Instead of talking about any of that, he applied himself to helping Joki take measurements and calculate how many cases he would need. They checked with the balloon maker and learned the powder inside the balloons was a type of soapstone, unlikely to harm the seedlings. When it came to fastening the balloons inside the lid, Joki came up with the idea of using a sheet of rubber pre-pricked with pinholes to keep the balloons in place. It would also catch the water if a balloon happened to burst.

By the time he was readying for departure, he had forty cases ready, each equipped with enough water for three weeks. The ship was liable to take six weeks to reach Goa.

"Even if you lose half of them, you'll still have enough for a good-sized estrada."

He expected Joki to make a facetious remark like, "When I'm your age." He didn't. He set his hand on Andre's shoulder. "I'll ask you one more time. Will you come with me?"

Andre was surprised how much it hurt to shake his head yet again. "No. This is my home. My life."

It was true, but when Joki nodded and left his head hanging a moment, as though absorbing a blow, Andre felt like a bastard for denying him anything he wanted.

"I'll send for you when they're ready to tap." Joki picked up his head. He was trying to smile, but his eyes were shiny with tears.

"If they stay alive that long, my honor would demand that I come." They both knew he was joking. He wouldn't expect Joki to wait a decade for him. This was goodbye, because it had to be.

But it hurt like hell.

•••

Andre thought he would die of loneliness after Joki left. In fact, he had gone into the jungle, and the first letter only caught up to him because his brother-in-law sent him supplies.

Andre,

I arrived home safely. I lost seventy-eight seedlings on the journey and six unloading from the ship. Can't blame the porter. It was me and my unsteady sea legs.

Best wishes to your family,

Joki

• • •

Some weeks later, another:

Andre,

This week I planted fifty seedlings in different conditions, all well protected by heavy foliage. I'm waiting to see what we lose to foraging animals. The rest are thriving in the front parlor.

I imagine you're in the jungle and won't receive this for many weeks. I'll write again anyway so you'll have an update when you return to Manaos.

Yours sincerely,

Joki

• • •

Andre,

We lost fewer to wildlife than I expected. I planted the rest because monsoon season is upon us. I thought the seedlings would feel at home and hopefully root well.

Can you believe I walk my "estradas" every day in the pouring rain so I can check on each one? I think of you as I do, imagining you doing the same.

I hope you are well.

Joki

•••

*Andre,*

*The fine weather has arrived and so has my family. Forgive me, but I think my daughter, Calisto, is the most precious thing I've ever seen or held. If there were more room on this card I would write only of her.*

*I've asked that she stay here with me when my wife visits Lisbon, which she intends to do soon. I take Calisto with me when I check the trees, which all grow well. I tell her about Manaos so I may indulge myself with recollections of my time there.*

*Your sentimental correspondent,*
*Joki*

•••

"He has a daughter," Andre's sister said after Andre set aside the card, proving that she read his mail when it arrived.

"Apparently." Joki seemed very happy. Good for him.

"But it doesn't sound like his wife..." She trailed off as she adjusted the fussy baby in the sling she wore.

"What?" he prompted, even though he was certain he didn't want to hear it.

"It doesn't sound as though his marriage is a happy one."

"I don't think it's unhappy." He thought of Joki's practical attitude on the matter. "It's not a close marriage, the way yours is. That's all."

"Regardless, I have to wonder if you're really going to wait until his trees are ready to tap before you go?" She lifted her brows.

Andre might have been discreet about his private activities, but she knew him too well to be fooled completely. He lined up the edge of the card with the edge of the table, pretending his cheeks were not glowing with culpability.

"I've considered going now that the rains are on us again." The days alone in the jungle had been excruciating enough. The thought of spending endless soggy months in Manaos, without Joki, was intolerable.

"It would be easy enough to find someone to oversee your seringal if you decided to stay through next season. You could arrange it before you go."

"I was under the impression you liked having me around," he said drily.

"Not when you can hardly muster a smile for me or my children. I haven't seen you laugh once since Joki left, but you smile when you read his cards. If he makes you happy, you should go to him."

"It's expensive." But he'd already looked into shoveling coal to pay his way. That way he could hold on to enough cash for a return ticket. "I *would* miss you if I was that far away, you know."

"As you should," she said with a pointed look. "But I don't want you to miss this." She waved at the baby and the house. "Not if there's a way you could have something like it."

"I don't think I will ever mourn the fact I'll never have a baby chewing on my teat, but that's a very sweet sentiment." He rose and kissed her hair. "Thank you. I'll think about it."

That was a falsehood. He had already decided.

# EPILOGUE

*Six years later...*

"No!" Joki grabbed Andre's arm, stopping him from chopping into the tree with an axe.

"Joki." Andre lowered his arm. "It won't hurt the tree. I swear it. I will only check this one tree. If it dies, it's only one. You still have a hundred more." Plus the ones they'd been growing from cuttings for the last four years.

The rubber trees were taking to India as well as Andre had, which was to say they were thriving.

"I've worked so hard to get them this far," Joki said with a grimace of apology at the tree. "I feel bad chopping into it. Ungrateful."

Andre shook his head at him. "Here." He reached into his pocket and pulled out a balloon. "I was saving it for after, as a celebration. You hold on to it and think about how many of those we can make if these trees are ready to bleed caucho."

"That is a pleasant thought." Joki pulled at the balloon in a well-practiced stretch before starting to bring the neck to his mouth. He paused as he noticed Andre watching him. "What? Go ahead." He nodded at the tree.

"I can't now, can I? All I can see is you and that fucking balloon." All this time had passed, and watching Joki blow up a balloon still hardened his cock.

"Oh?" Joki ran the tip of his tongue around the hole of the balloon. "This distracts you, does it?"

"You know it fucking does." Andre threw the axe into the trunk and tackled his lover. His partner. The love of his life. They worked alongside each other every day, bickered over how to raise their three children, and pretended Joki was the boss when they both knew that when they were like this, Andre was definitely the one who took control.

He soon had Joki bent over a log, the balloon swollen and trapped between Joki's trembling thighs, both of them shaking with excitement as they fucked, both of them releasing lusty, gratified groans when the balloon burst at the same moment they did.

They came back to the trail still fixing their clothes, half drunk on cock and erotic satisfaction and their love for each other.

They found a crooked stream of white gold leaking down the trunk of the rubber tree.

*The End*

# ENTANGLED
## BRINGS THE
*Heat*

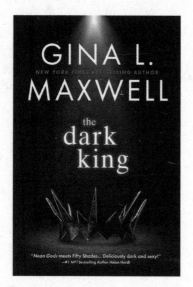

## THE DARK KING

*NY Times* bestselling author Gina L. Maxwell is back with the first in the Deviant Kings series set in a modern world but with a dark, erotic fantasy twist perfect for fans of *Neon Gods*.

## FOLLOW ME DARKLY

One chance encounter is all it took for Skye to find herself in the middle of a Cinderella story... but self-made billionaire Braden Black is no Prince Charming, and his dark desires are far from his only secret.

## WHITE LIES

Nick is only playing the role of a stranger to find out if Faith is the one who hurt his family. Soon the truth will be revealed. And where the white lies end—obsession begins.

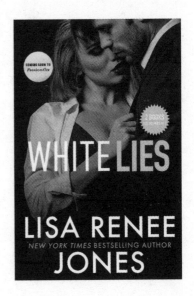

# ENTANGLED
## BRINGS THE
*Heart*

## CONFESSIONS IN B-FLAT

*Essence* bestselling author Donna Hill brings us an emotional love story set against the powerful backdrop of the civil rights movement that gripped a nation—a story as timely as it is timeless...

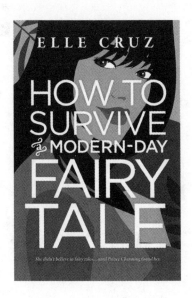

## HOW TO SURVIVE A MODERN-DAY FAIRY TALE

Bookworm Claire may wish she had a fairy godmother, but in the twenty-first century she knows the only way to get her happily ever after is by letting her heart be her guide...

## THE THINGS WE LEAVE UNFINISHED

Told in alternating timelines, *The Things We Leave Unfinished* examines the risks we take for love, the scars too deep to heal, and the endings we can't bring ourselves to see coming.

AMARA

an imprint of Entangled Publishing LLC